BOB HAMPTON OF
PLACER

RANDALL PARRISH

1st WORLD
LIBRARY
Literary Society

Bob Hampton of Placer

Randall Parrish

© 1st World Library, 2007
PO Box 2211
Fairfield, IA 52556
www.1stworldlibrary.com
First Edition

LCCN: 2007927864

Softcover ISBN: 978-1-4218-4569-2
Hardcover ISBN: 978-1-4218-4485-5
eBook ISBN: 978-1-4218-4653-8

Purchase *"Bob Hampton of Placer"*
as a traditional bound book at:
www.1stWorldLibrary.com/purchase.asp?ISBN=978-1-4218-4569-2

1st World Library is a literary, educational organization
dedicated to:

- Creating a free internet library of downloadable ebooks

- Hosting writing competitions and offering book publishing
scholarships.

Interested in more 1st World Library books? contact:
literacy@1stworldlibrary.com
Check us out at: www.1stworldlibrary.com

1ˢᵗ World Library Literary Society

Giving Back to the World

"If you want to work on the core problem, it's early school literacy."

- James Barksdale, former CEO of Netscape

"No skill is more crucial to the future of a child, or to a democratic and prosperous society, than literacy."

- Los Angeles Times

"Literacy... means far more than learning how to read and write... The aim is to transmit... knowledge and promote social participation."

- UNESCO

"Literacy is not a luxury, it is a right and a responsibility. If our world is to meet the challenges of the twenty-first century we must harness the energy and creativity of all our citizens."

- President Bill Clinton

"Parents should be encouraged to read to their children, and teachers should be equipped with all available techniques for teaching literacy, so the varying needs and capacities of individual kids can be taken into account."

- Hugh Mackay

CONTENTS

PART III — ON THE LITTLE BIG HORN

PART I

FROM OUT THE CANYON

CHAPTER I

HAMPTON, OF PLACER

It was not an uncommon tragedy of the West. If slightest chronicle of it survive, it must be discovered among the musty and nearly forgotten records of the Eighteenth Regiment of Infantry, yet it is extremely probable that even there the details were never written down. Sufficient if, following certain names on that long regimental roll, there should be duly entered those cabalistic symbols signifying to the initiated, "Killed in action." After all, that tells the story. In those old-time Indian days of continuous foray and skirmish such brief returns, concise and unheroic, were commonplace enough.

Yet the tale is worth telling now, when such days are past and gone. There were sixteen of them when, like so many hunted rabbits, they were first securely trapped among the frowning rocks, and forced relentlessly backward from off the narrow trail until the precipitous canyon walls finally halted their disorganized flight, and from sheer necessity compelled a rally in hopeless battle. Sixteen,—ten infantry-men from old Fort Bethune, under command of Syd. Wyman, a gray-headed sergeant of thirty years' continuous service in the regulars, two cow-punchers from the "X L" ranch, a stranger who had joined them uninvited at the ford over the Bear Water, together with old Gillis the post-trader, and his silent chit of a girl.

Sixteen—but that was three days before, and in the meanwhile not a few of those speeding Sioux bullets had found softer billet than the limestone rocks. Six of the soldiers, four already dead, two dying, lay outstretched in ghastly silence where they fell. "Red" Watt, of the "X L," would no more ride the range across the sun-kissed prairie, while the stern old sergeant, still grim of jaw but growing dim of eye, bore his right arm in a rudely improvised sling made from a cartridge-belt, and crept about sorely racked with pain, dragging a shattered limb behind him. Then the taciturn Gillis gave sudden utterance to a sobbing cry, and a burst of red spurted across his white beard as he reeled backward, knocking the girl prostrate when he fell. Eight remained, one helpless, one a mere lass of fifteen. It was the morning of the third day.

The beginning of the affair had burst upon them so suddenly that no two in that stricken company would have told the same tale. None among them had anticipated trouble; there were no rumors of Indian war along the border, while every recognized hostile within the territory had been duly reported as north of the Bear Water; not the vaguest complaint had drifted into military headquarters for a month or more. In all the fancied security of unquestioned peace these chance travellers had slowly toiled along the steep trail leading toward the foothills, beneath the hot rays of the afternoon sun, their thoughts afar, their steps lagging and careless. Gillis and the girl, as well as the two cattle-herders, were on horseback; the remainder soberly trudged forward on foot, with guns slung to their shoulders. Wyman was somewhat in advance, walking beside the stranger, the latter a man of uncertain age, smoothly shaven, quietly dressed in garments bespeaking an Eastern tailor, a bit grizzled of hair along the temples, and possessing a pair of cool gray eyes. He had introduced himself by the name of Hampton, but had volunteered no further information, nor was it customary in that country to question impertinently. The others of the little party straggled along as best suited themselves, all semblance to the ordinary discipline of the service having been abandoned.

Hampton, through the medium of easy conversation, early discovered in the sergeant an intelligent mind, possessing some knowledge of literature. They had been discussing books with rare enthusiasm, and the former had drawn from the concealment of an inner pocket a diminutive copy of "The Merchant of Venice," from which he was reading aloud a disputed passage, when the faint trail they followed suddenly dipped into the yawning mouth of a black canyon. It was a narrow, gloomy, contracted gorge, a mere gash between those towering hills shadowing its depths on either hand. A swift mountain stream, noisy and clear as crystal, dashed from rock to rock close beside the more northern wall, while the ill-defined pathway, strewn with bowlders and guarded by underbrush, clung to the opposite side, where low scrub trees partially obscured the view.

All was silent as death when they entered. Not so much as the flap of a wing or the stir of a leaf roused suspicion, yet they had barely advanced a short hundred paces when those apparently bare rocks in front flamed red, the narrow defile echoed to wild screeches and became instantly crowded with weird, leaping figures. It was like a plunge from heaven into hell. Blaine and Endicott sank at the first fire; Watt, his face picturing startled surprise, reeled from his saddle, clutching at the air, his horse dashing madly forward and dragging him, head downward, among the sharp rocks; while Wyman's stricken arm dripped blood. Indeed, under that sudden shock, he fell, and was barely rescued by the prompt action of the man beside him. Dropping the opened book, and firing madly to left and right with a revolver which appeared to spring into his hand as by magic, the latter coolly dragged the fainting soldier across the more exposed space, until the two found partial security among a mass of loosened rocks littering the base of the precipice. The others who survived that first scorching discharge also raced toward this same shelter, impelled thereto by the unerring instinct of border fighting, and flinging themselves flat behind protecting bowlders, began responding to the hot fire rained upon them.

Scattered and hurried as these first volleys were, they proved sufficient to check the howling demons in the open. It has never been Indian nature to face unprotected the aim of the white men, and those dark figures, which only a moment before thronged the narrow gorge, leaping crazily in the riot of apparent victory, suddenly melted from sight, slinking down into leafy coverts beside the stream or into holes among the rocks, like so many vanishing prairie-dogs. The fierce yelpings died faintly away in distant echoes, while the hideous roar of conflict diminished to the occasional sharp crackling of single rifles. Now and then a sinewy brown arm might incautiously project across the gleaming surface of a rock, or a mop of coarse black hair appear above the edge of a gully, either incident resulting in a quick interchange of fire. That was all; yet the experienced frontiersmen knew that eyes as keen as those of any wild animal of the jungle were watching murderously their slightest movement.

Wyman, now reclining in agony against the base of the overhanging cliff, directed the movements of his little command calmly and with sober military judgment. Little by little, under protection of the rifles of the three civilians, the uninjured infantrymen crept cautiously about, rolling loosened bowlders forward into position, until they finally succeeded in thus erecting a rude barricade between them and the enemy. The wounded who could be reached were laboriously drawn back within this improvised shelter, and when the black shadows of the night finally shut down, all remaining alive were once more clustered together, the injured lying moaning and ghastly beneath the overhanging shelf of rock, and the girl, who possessed all the patient stoicism of frontier training, resting in silence, her widely opened eyes on those far-off stars peeping above the brink of the chasm, her head pillowed on old Gillis's knee.

Few details of those long hours of waiting ever came forth from that black canyon of death. Many of the men sorely wounded, all wearied, powder-stained, faint with hunger, and parched with thirst, they simply fought out to the bitter ending their desperate struggle against despair. The towering, overhanging wall at their back assured protection from above, but upon the opposite cliff summit, and easily within rifle range, the cunning foe early discovered lodgment, and from that safe vantage-point poured down a merciless fire, causing each man to crouch lower behind his protecting bowlder. No motion could be ventured without its checking bullet, yet hour after hour the besieged held their ground, and with ever-ready rifles left more than one reckless brave dead among the rocks. The longed-for night came dark and early at the bottom of that narrow cleft, while hardly so much as a faint star twinkled in the little slit of sky overhead. The cunning besiegers crept closer through the enshrouding gloom, and taunted their entrapped victims with savage cries and threats of coming torture, but no warrior among them proved sufficiently bold to rush in and slay. Why should they? Easier, safer far, to rest secure behind their shelters, and wait in patience until the little band had fired its last shot. Now they skulked timorously, but then they might walk upright and glut their fiendish lust for blood.

Twice during that long night volunteers sought vainly to pierce those lines of savage watchers. A long wailing cry of agony from out the thick darkness told the fate of their first messenger, while Casey, of the "X L," crept slowly, painfully back, with an Indian bullet embedded deep in his shoulder. Just before the coming of dawn, Hampton, without uttering a word, calmly turned up the collar of his tightly buttoned coat, so as better to conceal the white collar he wore, gripped his revolver between his teeth, and crept like some wriggling snake among the black rocks and through the dense underbrush in search after water. By some miracle of divine mercy he was permitted to pass unscathed, and came crawling back, a dozen hastily filled canteens dangling across his shoulders. It was like nectar to those parched, feverish throats; but of food barely a mouthful apiece remained in the haversacks.

The second day dragged onward, its hours bringing no change for the better, no relief, no slightest ray of hope. The hot sun scorched them pitilessly, and two of the wounded died delirious. From dawn to dark there came no slackening of the savage watchfulness which held the survivors helpless behind their coverts. The merest uplifting of a head, the slightest movement of a hand, was sufficient to demonstrate how sharp were those savage eyes. No white man in the short half-circle dared to waste a single shot now; all realized that their stock of ammunition was becoming fearfully scant, yet those scheming devils continually baited them to draw their fire.

Another long black night followed, during which, for an hour or so in turn, the weary defenders slept, tossing uneasily, and disturbed by fearful dreams. Then gray and solemn, amid the lingering shadows of darkness, dawned the third dread day of unequal conflict. All understood that it was destined to be their last on this earth unless help came. It seemed utterly hopeless to protract the struggle, yet they held on grimly, patiently, half-delirious from hunger and thirst, gazing into each other's haggard faces, almost without recognition, every man at his post. Then it was that old Gillis received his death-wound, and the solemn, fateful whisper ran from lip to lip along the scattered line that only five cartridges remained.

For two days Wyman had scarcely stirred from where he lay bolstered against the rock. Sometimes he became delirious from fever, uttering incoherent phrases, or swearing in pitiful weakness. Again he would partially arouse to his old sense of soldierly duty, and assume intelligent command. Now he twisted painfully about upon his side, and, with clouded eyes, sought to discern what man was lying next him. The face was hidden so that all he could clearly distinguish was the fact that this man was not clothed as a soldier.

"Is that you, Hampton?" he questioned, his voice barely audible.

The person thus addressed, who was lying flat upon his back, gazing silently upward at the rocky front of the cliff, turned cautiously over upon his elbow before venturing reply.

"Yes; what is it, sergeant? It looks to be a beauty of a morning way up yonder."

There was a hearty, cheery ring to his clear voice which left the pain-racked old soldier envious.

"My God!" he growled savagely. "'T is likely to be the last any of us will ever see. Wasn't it you I heard whistling just now? One might imagine this was to be a wedding, rather than a funeral."

"And why not, Wyman? Didn't you know they employed

music at both functions nowadays? Besides, it is not every man who is permitted to assist at his own obsequies—the very uniqueness of such a situation rather appeals to my sense of humor. Pretty tune, that one I was whistling, don't you think? Picked it up on 'The Pike' in Cincinnati fifteen years ago. Sorry I don't recall the words, or I'd sing them for you."

The sergeant, his teeth clinched tightly to repress the pain racking him, stifled his resentment with an evident effort. "You may be less light-hearted when you learn that the last of our ammunition is already in the guns," he remarked, stiffly.

"I suspected as much." And the speaker lifted himself on one elbow to peer down the line of recumbent figures. "To be perfectly frank with you, sergeant, the stuff has held out considerably longer than I believed it would, judging from the way those'dough boys' of yours kept popping at every shadow in front of them. It's a marvel to me, the mutton-heads they take into the army. Oh, now, you needn't scowl at me like that, Wyman; I've worn the blue, and seen some service where a fellow needed to be a man to sport the uniform. Besides, I'm not indifferent, old chap, and just so long as there remained any work worth attending to in this skirmishing affair, I did it, didn't I? But I tell you, man, there is mighty little good trying to buck against Fate, and when Luck once finally lets go of a victim, he's bound to drop straight to the bottom before he stops. That's the sum and substance of all my philosophy, old fellow, consequently I never kick simply because things happen to go wrong. What's the use? They'll go wrong just the same. Then again, my life has never been so sweet as to cause any excessive grief over the prospect of losing it. Possibly I might prefer to pass out from this world in some other manner, but that's merely a matter of individual taste, and just now there doesn't seem to be very much choice left me. Consequently, upheld by my acquired philosophy, and encouraged by the rectitude of my past conduct, I'm merely holding back one shot for myself, as a sort of grand finale to this fandango, and another for that little girl out yonder."

These words were uttered slowly, the least touch of a lazy drawl apparent in the low voice, yet there was an earnest simplicity pervading the speech which somehow gave it impressiveness. The man meant exactly what he said, beyond the possibility of a doubt. The old soldier, accustomed to every form of border eccentricity, gazed at him with disapproval.

"Either you're the coolest devil I've met during thirty years of soldiering," he commented, doubtfully, "or else the craziest. Who are you, anyhow? I half believe you might be Bob Hampton, of Placer."

The other smiled grimly. "You have the name tolerably correct, old fellow; likewise that delightful spot so lately honored by my residence. In brief, you have succeeded in calling the turn perfectly, so far as your limited information extends. In strict confidence I propose now to impart to you what has hitherto remained a profound secret. Upon special request of a number of influential citizens of Placer, including the city marshal and other officials, expressed in mass-meeting, I have decided upon deserting that sagebrush metropolis to its just fate, and plan to add the influence of my presence to the future development of Glencaid. I learn that the climate there is more salubrious, more conducive to long living, the citizens of Placer being peculiarly excitable and careless with their fire-arms."

The sergeant had been listening with open mouth. "The hell you say!" he finally ejaculated.

"The undented truth, every word of it. No wonder you are shocked. A fine state of affairs, isn't it, when a plain-spoken, pleasant-mannered gentleman, such as I surely am,—a university graduate, by all the gods, the nephew of a United States Senator, and acknowledged to be the greatest exponent of scientific poker in this territory,—should be obliged to hastily change his chosen place of abode because of the threat of an ignorant and depraved mob. Ever have a rope dangled in front of your eyes, sergeant, and a gun-barrel biting into your cheek at the same time? Accept my word for it, the experience is trying on the nerves. Ran a perfectly square game too, and those ducks knew it; but there's no true sporting spirit left in this territory any more. However, spilled milk is never worth sobbing over, and Fate always contrives to play the final hand in any game, and stocks the cards to win. Quite probably you are familiar with Bobbie Burns, sergeant, and will recall easily these words, 'The best-laid schemes o' mice and men gang aft agley'? Well, instead of proceeding, as originally intended, to the delightful environs of Glencaid, for a sort of a Summer vacation, I have, on the impulse of the moment, decided upon crossing the Styx. Our somewhat impulsive red friends out yonder are kindly preparing to assist me in making a successful passage, and the citizens of Glencaid, when they learn the sorrowful news of my translation, ought to come nobly forward with some suitable memorial to my virtues. If, by any miracle of chance, you should pull through, Wyman, I would hold it a friendly act if you suggest the matter. A neat monument, for instance, might suitably voice their grief; it would cost them far less than I should in the flesh, and would prove highly gratifying to me, as well as those mourners left behind in Placer."

"A breath of good honest prayer would serve better than all your fun," groaned the sergeant, soberly.

The gray eyes resting thoughtfully on the old soldier's haggard face became instantly grave and earnest.

"Sincerely I wish I might aid you with one," the man admitted, "but I fear, old fellow, any prayer coming from my lips would never ascend very far. However, I might try the comfort of a hymn, and you will remember this one, which, no doubt, you have helped to sing back in God's country."

There was a moment's hushed pause, during which a rifle cracked sharply out in the ravine; then the reckless fellow, his head partially supported against the protecting bowlder, lifted up a full, rich barytone in rendition of that hymn of Christian faith—

"Nearer, my God, to Thee!
Nearer to Thee!
E'en though it be a cross
That raiseth me,
Still all my song shall be,
Nearer, my God, to Thee!
Nearer to Thee."

Glazed and wearied eyes glanced cautiously toward the singer around the edges of protecting rocks; fingers loosened their grasp upon the rifle barrels; smoke-begrimed cheeks became moist; while lips, a moment before profaned by oaths, grew silent and trembling. Out in front a revengeful brave sent his bullet swirling just above the singer's head, the sharp fragments of rock dislodged falling in a shower upon his upturned face; but the fearless rascal sang serenely on to the end, without a quaver.

"Mistake it for a death song likely," he remarked dryly, while the last clear, lingering note, reechoed by the cliff, died reluctantly away in softened cadence. "Beautiful old song, sergeant, and I trust hearing it again has done you good. Sang it once in a church way back in New England. But what is the trouble? Did you call me for some special reason?"

"Yes," came the almost gruff response; for Wyman, the fever stealing back upon him, felt half ashamed of his unshed tears. "That is, provided you retain sufficient sense to listen. Old Gillis was shot over an hour ago, yonder behind that big bowlder, and his girl sits there still holding his head in her lap. She'll get hit also unless somebody pulls her out of there, and she's doing no good to Gillis—he's dead."

Hampton's clear-cut, expressive face became graver, all trace of recklessness gone from it. He lifted his head cautiously, peering over his rock cover toward where he remembered earlier in the fight Gillis had sought refuge.

CHAPTER II

OLD GILLIS'S GIRL

Excepting for a vague knowledge that Gillis had had a girl with him, together with the half-formed determination that if worse came to worst she must never be permitted to fall alive into the hands of the lustful Sioux, Mr. Hampton had scarcely so much as noted her presence. Of late years he had not felt greatly interested in the sex, and his inclination, since uniting his shattered fortunes with this little company, had been to avoid coming into personal contact with this particular specimen. Practically, therefore, he now observed her for the first time. Previously she had passed within range of his vision simply as the merest shadow; now she began to appeal faintly to him as a personality, uninteresting enough, of course, yet a living human being, whom it had oddly become his manifest duty to succor and protect. The never wholly eradicated instincts of one born and bred a gentleman, although heavily overlaid by the habits acquired in many a rough year passed along the border, brought vividly before him the requirements of the situation. Undoubtedly death was destined to be the early portion of them all; nevertheless she deserved every opportunity for life that remained, and with the ending of hope—well, there are worse fates upon the frontier than the unexpected plunge of a bullet through a benumbed brain.

Guided by the unerring instinct of an old Indian fighter, Gillis, during that first mad retreat, had discovered temporary shelter behind one of the largest bowlders. It was a trifle in advance of those later rolled into position by the soldiers, but was of a size and shape which should have afforded ample protection for two, and doubtless would have done so had it not been for the firing from the cliff opposite. Even then it was a deflected bullet, glancing from off the polished surface of the rock, which found lodgment in the sturdy old fighter's brain. The girl had caught him as he fell, had wasted all her treasured store of water in a vain effort to cleanse the blood from his features, and now sat there, pillowing his head upon her knee, although the old man was stone dead with the first touch of the ball. That had occurred fully an hour before, but she continued in the same posture, a grave, pathetic figure, her face sobered and careworn beyond her years, her eyes dry and staring, one brown hand grasping unconsciously the old man's useless rifle. She would scarcely have been esteemed attractive even under much happier circumstances and assisted by dress, yet there was something in the independent poise of her head, the steady fixedness of her posture, which served to interest Hampton as he now watched her curiously.

"Fighting blood," he muttered admiringly to himself. "Might fail to develop into very much of a society belle, but likely to prove valuable out here."

She was rather a slender slip of a thing, a trifle too tall for her years, perhaps, yet with no lack of development apparent in the slim, rounded figure. Her coarse home-made dress of dark calico fitted her sadly, while her rumpled hair, from which the broad-brimmed hat had fallen, possessed a reddish copper tinge where it was touched by the sun. Mr. Hampton's survey did not increase his desire for more intimate acquaintanceship, yet he recognized anew her undoubted claim upon him.

"Suppose I might just as well drop out that way as any other," he reflected, thoughtfully. "It's all in the game."

Lying flat upon his stomach, both arms extended, he slowly forced himself beyond his bowlder into the open. There was no great distance to be traversed, and a considerable portion of the way was somewhat protected by low bushes. Hampton took few chances of those spying eyes above, never uplifting his head the smallest fraction of an inch, but reaching forward with blindly groping hands, caught hold upon any projecting root or stone which enabled him to drag his body an inch farther. Twice they fired directly down at him from the opposite summit, and once a fleck of sharp rock, chipped by a glancing bullet, embedded itself in his cheek, dyeing the whole side of his face crimson. But not once did he pause or glance aside; nor did the girl look up from the imploring face of her dead. As he crept silently in, sheltering himself next to the body of the dead man, she perceived his presence for the first time, and shrank back as if in dread.

"What are you doing? Why—why did you come here?" she questioned, a falter in her voice; and he noticed that her eyes were dark and large, yielding a marked impress of beauty to her face.

"I was unwilling to leave you here alone," he answered, quietly, "and hope to discover some means for getting you safely back beside the others."

"But I didn't want you," and there was a look of positive dislike in her widely opened eyes.

"Didn't want me?" He echoed these unexpected words in a tone of complete surprise. "Surely you could not desire to be left here alone? Why didn't you want me?"

"Because I know who you are!" Her voice seemed to catch in her throat. "He told me. You're the man who shot Jim Eberly."

Mr. Hampton was never of a pronounced emotional nature, nor was he a person easily disconcerted, yet he flushed at the sound of these impulsive words, and the confident smile deserted his lips. For a moment they sat thus, the dead body lying between, and looked at each other. When the man finally broke the constrained silence a deeper intonation had crept into his voice.

"My girl," he said gravely, and not without a suspicion of pleading, "this is no place for me to attempt any defence of a shooting affray in a gambling-house, although I might plead with some justice that Eberly enjoyed the honor of shooting first. I was not aware of your personal feeling in the matter, or I might have permitted some one else to come here in my stead. Now it is too late. I have never spoken to you before, and do so at this time merely from a sincere desire to be of some assistance."

There was that in his manner of grave courtesy which served to steady the girl. Probably never before in all her rough frontier experience had she been addressed thus formally. Her closely compressed lips twitched nervously, but her questioning eyes remained unlowered.

"You may stay," she asserted, soberly. "Only don't touch me."

No one could ever realize how much those words hurt him. He had been disciplined in far too severe a school ever to permit his face to index the feelings of his heart, yet the unconcealed shrinking of this uncouth child from slightest personal contact with him cut through his acquired reserve as perhaps nothing else could ever have done. Not until he had completely conquered his first unwise impulse to retort angrily, did he venture again to speak.

"I hope to aid you in getting back beside the others, where you will be less exposed."

"Will you take him?"

"He is dead," Hampton said, soberly, "and I can do nothing to aid him. But there remains a chance for you to escape."

"Then I won't go," she declared, positively.

Hampton's gray eyes looked for a long moment fixedly into her darker ones, while the two took mental stock of each other. He realized the utter futility of any further argument, while she felt instinctively the cool, dominating strength of the man. Neither was composed of that poor fibre which bends.

"Very well, my young lady," he said, easily, stretching himself out more comfortably in the rock shadow. "Then I will remain here with you; it makes small odds."

Excepting for one hasty, puzzled glance, she did not deign to look again toward him, and the man rested motionless upon his back, staring up at the sky. Finally, curiosity over-mastered the actor in him, and he turned partially upon one side, so as to bring her profile within his range of vision. The untamed, rebellious nature of the girl had touched a responsive chord; unseeking any such result she had directly appealed to his better judgment, and enabled him to perceive her from an entirely fresh view-point. Her clearly expressed disdain, her sturdy independence both of word and action, coupled with her frankly voiced dislike, awoke within him an earnest desire to stand higher in her regard. Her dark, glowing eyes were lowered upon the white face of the dead man, yet Hampton noted how clear, in spite of sun-tan, were those tints of health upon the rounded cheek, and how soft and glossy shone her wealth of rumpled hair. Even the tinge of color, so distasteful in the full glare of the sun, appeared to have darkened under the shadow, its shade framing the downcast face into a pensive fairness. Then he observed how dry and parched her lips were.

"Take a drink of this," he insisted heartily, holding out toward her as he spoke his partially filled canteen.

She started at the unexpected sound of his voice, yet uplifted the welcome water to her mouth, while Hampton, observing it all closely, could but remark the delicate shapeliness other hand.

"If that old fellow was her father," he reflected soberly, "I should like to have seen her mother."

"Thank you," she said simply, handing back the canteen, but without lifting her eyes again to his face. "I was so thirsty." Her low tone, endeavoring to be polite enough, contained no note of encouragement.

"Was Gillis your father?" the man questioned, determined to make her recognize his presence.

"I suppose so; I don't know."

"You don't know? Am I to understand you are actually uncertain whether this man was your father or not?"

"That is about what I said, wasn't it? Not that it is any of your business, so far as I know, Mr. Bob Hampton, but I answered you all right. He brought me up, and I called him 'dad' about as far back as I can remember, but I don't reckon as he ever told me he was my father. So you can understand just what you please."

"His name was Gillis, wasn't it?"

The girl nodded wearily.

"Post-trader at Fort Bethune?"

Again the rumpled head silently acquiesced.

"What is your name?"

"He always called me 'kid,'" she admitted unwillingly, "but I reckon if you have any further occasion for addressing me, you'd better say, 'Miss Gillis.'"

Hampton laughed lightly, his reckless humor instantly restored by her perverse manner.

"Heaven preserve me!" he exclaimed good naturedly, "but you are certainly laying it on thick, young lady! However, I believe we might become good friends if we ever have sufficient luck to get out from this hole alive. Darn if I don't sort of cotton to you, little girl—you've got some sand."

For a brief space her truthful, angry eyes rested scornfully upon his face, her lips parted as though trembling with a sharp retort. Then she deliberately turned her back upon him without uttering a word.

For what may have been the first and only occasion in Mr.

Hampton's audacious career, he realized his utter helplessness. This mere slip of a red-headed girl, this little nameless waif of the frontier, condemned him so completely, and without waste of words, as to leave him weaponless. Not that he greatly cared; oh, no! still, it was an entirely new experience; the arrow went deeper than he would have willingly admitted. Men of middle age, gray hairs already commencing to shade their temples, are not apt to enjoy being openly despised by young women, not even by ordinary freckle-faced girls, clad in coarse short frocks. Yet he could think of no fitting retort worth the speaking, and consequently he simply lay back, seeking to treat this disagreeable creature with that silent contempt which is the last resort of the vanquished.

He was little inclined to admit, even to himself, that he had been fairly hit, yet the truth remained that this girl was beginning to interest him oddly. He admired her sturdy independence, her audacity of speech, her unqualified frankness. Mr. Hampton was a thoroughgoing sport, and no quality was quite so apt to appeal to him as dead gameness. He glanced surreptitiously aside at her once more, but there was no sign of relenting in the averted face. He rested lower against the rock, his face upturned toward the sky, and thought. He was becoming vaguely aware that something entirely new, and rather unwelcome, had crept into his life during that last fateful half-hour. It could not be analyzed, nor even expressed definitely in words, but he comprehended this much—he would really enjoy rescuing this girl, and he should like to live long enough to discover into what sort of woman she would develop.

It was no spirit of bravado that gave rise to his reckless speech of an hour previous. It was simply a spontaneous outpouring of his real nature, an unpremeditated expression of that supreme carelessness with which he regarded the future, the small value he set on life. He truly felt as utterly indifferent toward fate as his words signified. Deeply conscious of a life long ago irretrievably wrecked, every-thing behind a chaos, everything before worthless,—for years he had been actually seeking death; a hundred times he had gladly marked its apparent approach, a smile of welcome upon his lips. Yet it had never quite succeeded in reaching him, and nothing had been gained beyond a reputation for cool, reckless daring, which he did not in the least covet. But now, miracle of all miracles, just as the end seemed actually attained, seemed beyond any possibility of being turned aside, he began to experience a desire to live—he wanted to save this girl.

His keenly observant eyes, trained by the exigencies of his trade to take note of small things, and rendered eager by this newly awakened ambition, scanned the cliff towering above them. He perceived the extreme irregularity of its front, and numerous peculiarities of formation which had escaped him hitherto. Suddenly his puzzled face brightened to the birth of an idea. By heavens! it might be done! Surely it might be done! Inch by inch he traced the obscure passage, seeking to impress each faint detail upon his memory—that narrow ledge within easy reach of an upstretched arm, the sharp outcropping of rock-edges here and there, the deep gash as though some giant axe had cleaved the stone, those sturdy cedars growing straight out over the chasm like the bowsprits of ships, while all along the way, irregular and ragged, varied rifts not entirely unlike the steps of a crazy staircase.

The very conception of such an exploit caused his flesh to creep. But he was not of that class of men who fall back dazed before the face of danger. Again and again, led by an impulse he was unable to resist, he studied that precipitous rock, every nerve tingling to the newborn hope. God helping them, even so desperate a deed might be accomplished, although it would test the foot and nerve of a Swiss mountaineer. He glanced again uneasily toward his companion, and saw the same motionless figure, the same sober face turned deliberately away. Hampton did not smile, but his square jaw set, and he clinched his hands. He had no fear that she might fall him, but for the first time in all his life he questioned his own courage.

CHAPTER III

BETWEEN LIFE AND DEATH

The remainder of that day, as well as much of the gloomy night following, composed a silent, lingering horror. The fierce pangs of hunger no longer gnawed, but a dull apathy now held the helpless defenders. One of the wounded died, a mere lad, sobbing pitifully for his mother; an infantryman, peering forth from his covert, had been shot in the face, and his scream echoed among the rocks in multiplied accents of agony; while Wyman lay tossing and moaning, mercifully unconscious. The others rested in their places, scarcely venturing to stir a limb, their roving, wolfish eyes the only visible evidence of remaining life, every hope vanished, yet each man clinging to his assigned post of duty in desperation. There was but little firing—the defenders nursing their slender stock, the savages biding their time. When night shut down the latter became bolder, and taunted cruelly those destined to become so soon their hapless victims. Twice the maddened men fired recklessly at those dancing devils, and one pitched forward, emitting a howl of pain that caused his comrades to cower once again behind their covers. One and all these frontiersmen recognized the inevitable—before dawn the end must come. No useless words were spoken; the men merely clinched their teeth and waited.

Hampton crept closer in beside the girl while the shadows deepened, and ventured to touch her hand. Perhaps the severe strain of their situation, the intense loneliness of that Indian-haunted twilight, had somewhat softened her resentment, for she made no effort now to repulse him.

"Kid," he said at last, "are you game for a try at getting out of this?"

She appeared to hesitate over her answer, and he could feel her tumultuous breathing. Some portion of her aversion had vanished. His face was certainly not an unpleasant one to look upon, and there were others other sex who had discovered in it a covering for a multitude of sins. Hampton smiled slightly while he waited; he possessed some knowledge of the nature feminine.

"Come, Kid," he ventured finally, yet with new assurance vibrating in his low voice; "this is surely a poor time and place for any indulgence in tantrums, and you've got more sense. I'm going to try to climb up the face of that cliff yonder,—it's the only possible way out from here,—and I propose to take you along with me."

She snatched her hand roughly away, yet remained facing him. "Who gave you any right to decide what I should do?"

The man clasped his fingers tightly about her slender arm, advancing his face until he could look squarely into hers. She read in the lines of that determined countenance an inflexible resolve which overmastered her.

"The right given by Almighty God to protect any one of your sex in peril," he replied. "Before dawn those savage fiends will be upon us. We are utterly helpless. There remains only one possible path for escape, and I believe I have discovered it. Now, my girl, you either climb those rocks with me, or I shall kill you where you are. It is that, or the Sioux torture. I have two shots left in this gun,—one for you, the other for myself. The time has come for deciding which of these alternatives you prefer."

The gleam of a star glittered along the steel of his revolver, and she realized that he meant what he threatened.

"If I select your bullet rather than the rocks, what then?"

"You will get it, but in that case you will die like a fool."

"You have believed me to be one, all this afternoon."

"Possibly," he admitted; "your words and actions certainly justified some such conclusion, but the opportunity has arrived for causing me to revise that suspicion."

"I don't care to have you, revise it, Mr. Bob Hampton. If I go, I shall hate you just the same."

Hampton's teeth clicked like those of an angry dog. "Hate and be damned," he exclaimed roughly. "All I care about now is to drag you out of here alive."

His unaffected sincerity impressed her more than any amount of pleading. She was long accustomed to straight talk; it always meant business, and her untutored nature instantly responded with a throb of confidence.

"Well, if you put it that way," she said, "I'll go."

For one breathless moment neither stirred. Then a single wild yell rang sharply forth from the rocks in their front, and a rifle barked savagely, its red flame cleaving the darkness with tongue of fire. An instant and the impenetrable gloom again surrounded them.

"Come on, then," he whispered, his fingers grasping her sleeve.

She shook off the restraining touch of his hand as if it were contamination, and sank down upon her knees beside the inert body. He could barely perceive the dim outlines of her bowed figure, yet never moved, his breath perceptibly quickening, while he watched and waited. Without word or moan she bent yet lower, and pressed her lips upon the cold, white face. The man caught no more than the faintest echo of a murmured "Good-bye, old dad; I wish I could take you with me." Then she stood stiffly upright, facing him. "I'm ready now," she announced calmly. "You can go on ahead."

They crept among low shrubs and around the bowlders, carefully guarding every slightest movement lest some rustle of disturbed foliage, or sound of loosened stone, might draw the fire of those keen watchers. Nor dared they ignore the close proximity of their own little company, who, amid such darkness, might naturally suspect them for approaching savages. Every inch of their progress was attained through tedious groping, yet the distance to be traversed was short, and Hampton soon found himself pressing against the uprising precipice. Passing his fingers along the front, he finally found that narrow ledge which he had previously located with such patient care, and reaching back, drew the girl silently upon her feet beside him. Against that background of dark cliff they might venture to stand erect, the faint glimmer of reflected light barely sufficient to reveal to each the shadowy outline of the other.

"Don't move an inch from this spot," he whispered. "It wouldn't be a square deal, Kid, to leave those poor fellows to their death without even telling them there's a chance to get out."

She attempted no reply, as he glided noiselessly away, but her face, could he have seen it, was not devoid of expression. This was an act of generosity and deliberate courage of the very kind most apt to appeal to her nature, and within her secret heart there was rapidly developing a respect for this man, who with such calm assurance won his own way. He was strong, forceful, brave,—Homeric virtues of real worth in that hard life which she knew best. All this swept across her mind in a flash of revelation while she stood alone, her eyes endeavoring vainly to peer into the gloom. Then, suddenly, that black curtain was rent by jagged spurts of red and yellow flame. Dazed for an instant, her heart throbbing wildly to the sharp reports of the rifles, she shrank cowering back, her fascinated gaze fixed on those imp-like figures leaping forward from rock to rock. Almost with the flash and sound Hampton sprang hastily back and gathered her in his arms.

"Catch hold, Kid, anywhere; only go up, and quick!"

As he thus lifted her she felt the irregularities of rock beneath her clutching fingers, and scrambled instinctively forward along the narrow shelf, and then, reaching higher, her groping hands clasped the roots of a projecting cedar. She retained no longer any memory for Hampton; her brain was completely terrorized. Inch by inch, foot by foot, clinging to a fragment of rock here, grasping a slippery branch there, occasionally helped by encountering a deeper gash in the face of the precipice, her movements concealed by the scattered cedars, she toiled feverishly up, led by instinct, like any wild animal desperately driven by fear, and only partially conscious of the real dread of her terrible position. The first time she became aware that Hampton was closely following was when her feet slipped along a naked root, and she would have plunged headlong into unknown depths had she not come into sudden contact with his supporting shoulder. Faint and dizzy, and trembling like the leaf of an aspen, she crept forward onto a somewhat wider ledge of thin rock, and lay there quivering painfully from head to foot. A moment of suspense, and he was outstretched beside her, resting at full length along the very outer edge, his hand closing tightly over her own.

"Remain perfectly quiet," he whispered, panting heavily. "We can be no safer anywhere else."

She could distinguish the rapid pounding of his heart as well as her own, mingled with the sharp intake of their heavy breathing, but these sounds were soon overcome by that of the tumult below. Shots and yells, the dull crash of blows, the shouts of men engaged in a death grapple, the sharp crackling of innumerable rifles, the inarticulate moans of pain, the piercing scream of sudden torture, were borne upward to them from out the blackness. They did not venture to lift their heads from off the hard rock; the girl sobbed silently, her slender form trembling; the fingers of the man closed more tightly about her hand. All at once the hideous uproar ceased with a final yelping of triumph, seemingly reechoed the entire length of the chasm, in the midst of which one single voice pleaded pitifully,—only to die away in a shriek. The two agonized fugitives lay listening, their ears strained to catch the slightest sound from below. The faint radiance of a single star glimmered along the bald front of the cliff, but Hampton, peering cautiously across the edge, could distinguish nothing. His ears could discern evidences of movement, and he heard guttural voices calling at a distance, but to the vision all was black. The distance those faint sounds appeared away made his head reel, and he shrank cowering back against the girl's body, closing his eyes and sinking his head upon his arm.

These uncertain sounds ceased, the strained ears of the fugitives heard the crashing of bodies through the thick shrubbery, and then even this noise died away in the distance. Yet neither ventured to stir or speak. It may be that the girl slept fitfully, worn out by long vigil and intense strain; but the man proved less fortunate, his eyes staring out continually into the black void, his thoughts upon other days long vanished but now brought back in all their bitterness by the mere proximity of this helpless waif who had fallen into his care. His features were drawn and haggard when the first gray dawn found ghastly reflection along the opposite rock summit, and with blurred eyes he watched the faint tinge of returning light steal downward into the canyon. At last it swept aside those lower clinging mists, as though some invisible hand had drawn back the night curtains, and he peered over the edge of his narrow resting-place, gazing directly down upon the scene of massacre. With a quick gasp of unspeakable horror he shrank so sharply back as to cause the suddenly awakened girl to start and glance into his face.

"What is it?" she questioned, with quick catching of breath, reading that which she could not clearly interpret in his shocked expression.

"Nothing of consequence," and he faintly endeavored to smile. "I suppose I must have been dreaming also, and most unpleasantly. No; please do not look down; it would only cause your head to reel, and our upward climb is not yet completed. Do you feel strong enough now to make another attempt to reach the top?"

His quiet spirit of assured dominance seemed to command her obedience. With a slight shudder she glanced doubtfully up the seemingly inaccessible height.

"Can we?" she questioned helplessly.

"We can, simply because we must," and his white teeth shut together firmly. "There is no possibility of retracing our steps downward, but with the help of this daylight we surely ought to be able to discover some path leading up."

He rose cautiously to his feet, pressing her more closely against the face of the cliff, thus holding her in comparative safety while preventing her from glancing back into the dizzy chasm. The most difficult portion of their journey was apparently just before them, consisting of a series of narrow ledges, so widely separated and irregular as to require each to assist the other while passing from point to point. Beyond these a slender cleft, bordered by gnarled roots of low bushes, promised a somewhat easier and securer passage toward the summit. Hampton's face became deathly white as they began the perilous climb, but his hand remained steady, his foot sure, while the girl moved forward as if remaining unconscious of the presence of danger, apparently swayed by his dominant will to do whatsoever he bade her. More than once they tottered on the very brink, held to safety merely by desperate clutchings at rock or shrub, yet never once did the man loosen his guarding grasp of his companion. Pressed tightly against the smooth rock, feeling for every crevice, every slightest irregularity of surface, making use of creeping tendril or dead branch, daring death along every inch of the way, these two creepers at last attained the opening to the little gulley, and sank down, faint and trembling, their hands bleeding, their clothing sadly torn by the sharp ledges across which they had pulled their bodies by the sheer strength of extended arms. Hampton panted heavily from exertion, yet the old light of cool, resourceful daring had crept back into the gray eyes, while the stern lines about his lips assumed pleasanter curves. The girl glanced furtively at him, the long lashes shadowing the expression of her lowered eyes. In spite of deep prejudice she felt impelled to like this man; he accomplished things, and he didn't talk.

It was nothing more serious than a hard and toilsome climb after that, a continuous struggle testing every muscle, straining every sinew, causing both to sink down again and again, panting and exhausted, no longer stimulated by imminent peril. The narrow cleft they followed led somewhat away from the exposed front of the precipice, yet arose steep and jagged before them, a slender gash through the solid rock, up which they were often compelled to force their passage; again it became clogged with masses of debris, dead branches, and dislodged fragments of stone, across which they were obliged to struggle desperately, while once they completely halted before a sheer smoothness of rock wall that appeared impassable. It was bridged finally by a cedar trunk, which Hampton wrenched from out its rocky foothold, and the two crept cautiously forward, to emerge where the sunlight rested golden at the summit. They sank face downward in the short grass, barely conscious that they had finally won their desperate passage.

Slowly Hampton succeeded in uplifting his tired body and his reeling head, until he could sit partially upright and gaze unsteadily about. The girl yet remained motionless at his feet, her thick hair, a mass of red gold in the sunshine, completely concealing her face, her slender figure quivering to sobs of utter exhaustion. Before them stretched the barren plain, brown, desolate, drear, offering in all its wide expanse no hopeful promise of rescue, no slightest suggestion even of water, excepting a fringe of irregular trees, barely discernible against the horizon. That lorn, deserted waste, shimmering beneath the sun-rays, the heat waves already becoming manifest above the rock-strewn surface, presented a most depressing spectacle. With hand partially shading his aching eyes from the blinding glare, the man studied its every exposed feature, his face hardening again into lines of stern determination. The girl stirred from her position, flinging back her heavy hair with one hand, and looking up into his face with eyes that read at once his disappointment.

"Have—have you any water left?" she asked at last, her lips parched and burning as if from fever.

He shook the canteen dangling forgotten at his side. "There may be a few drops," he said, handing it to her, although scarcely removing his fixed gaze from off that dreary plain. "We shall be obliged to make those trees yonder; there ought to be water there in plenty, and possibly we may strike a trail."

She staggered to her feet, gripping his shoulder, and swaying a little from weakness, then, holding aside her hair, gazed long in the direction he pointed.

"I fairly shake from hunger," she exclaimed, almost angrily, "and am terribly tired and sore, but I reckon I can make it if I've got to."

There was nothing more said between them. Like two automatons, they started off across the parched grass, the heat waves rising and falling as they stumbled forward. Neither realized until then how thoroughly that hard climb up the rocks, the strain of continued peril, and the long abstinence from food had sapped their strength, yet to remain where they were meant certain death; all hope found its centre amid those distant beckoning trees. Mechanically the girl gathered back her straying tresses, and tied them with a rag torn from her frayed skirt. Hampton noted silently how heavy and sunken her eyes were; he felt a dull pity, yet could not sufficiently arouse himself from the lethargy of exhaustion to speak. His body seemed a leaden weight, his brain a dull, inert mass; nothing was left him but an unreasoning purpose, the iron will to press on across that desolate plain, which already reeled and writhed before his aching eyes.

No one can explain later how such deeds are ever accomplished; how the tortured soul controls physical weakness, and compels strained sinews to perform the miracle of action when all ambition has died. Hampton surely must have both seen and known, for he kept his direction, yet never afterwards did he regain any clear memory of it. Twice she fell heavily, and the last time she lay motionless, her face pressed against the short grass blades. He stood looking down upon her, his head reeling beneath the hot rays of the sun, barely conscious of what had occurred, yet never becoming totally dead to his duty. Painfully he stooped, lifted the limp, slender figure against his shoulder, and went straggling forward, as uncertain in steps as a blind man, all about him stretching the dull, dead desolation of the plain. Again and again he sank down, pillowing his eyes from the pitiless sun glare; only to stagger upright once more, ever bending lower and lower beneath his unconscious burden.

CHAPTER IV

ON THE NAKED PLAIN

It was two hundred and eighteen miles, as the crow flies, between old Fort Bethune and the rock ford crossing the Bear Water, every foot of that dreary, treeless distance Indian-haunted, the favorite skulking-place and hunting-ground of the restless Sioux. Winter and summer this wide expanse had to be suspiciously patrolled by numerous military scouting parties, anxious to learn more regarding the uncertain whereabouts of wandering bands and the purposes of malecontents, or else drawn hither and thither by continually shifting rumors of hostile raids upon the camps of cattlemen. All this involved rough, difficult service, with small meed of honor attached, while never had soldiers before found trickier foemen to contend against, or fighters more worthy of their steel.

One such company, composed of a dozen mounted infantrymen, accompanied by three Cree trailers, rode slowly and wearily across the brown exposed uplands down into the longer, greener grass of the wide valley bottom, until they emerged upon a barely perceptible trail which wound away in snake-like twistings, toward those high, barren hills whose blue masses were darkly silhouetted against the western sky. Upon every side of them extended the treeless wilderness, the desolate loneliness of bare, brown prairie, undulating just enough to be baffling to the eyes, yet so dull, barren, grim, silent, and colorless as to drive men mad. The shimmering heat rose and fell in great pulsating waves, although no slightest breeze came to stir the stagnant air, while thick clouds of white dust, impregnated with poisonous alkali, rose from out the grass roots, stirred by the horses' feet, to powder the passers-by from head to foot. The animals moved steadily forward, reluctant and weary, their heads drooping dejectedly, their distended nostrils red and quivering, the oily perspiration streaking their dusted sides. The tired men, half blinded by the glare, lolled heavily in their deep cavalry saddles, with encrusted eyes staring moodily ahead.

Riding alone, and slightly in advance of the main body, his mount a rangy, broad-chested roan, streaked with alkali dust, the drooping head telling plainly of wearied muscles, was the officer in command. He was a pleasant-faced, stalwart young fellow, with the trim figure of a trained athlete, possessing a square chin smoothly shaven, his intelligent blue eyes half concealed beneath his hat brim, which had been drawn low to shade them from the glare, one hand pressing upon his saddle holster as he leaned over to rest. No insignia of rank served to distinguish him from those equally dusty fellows plodding gloomily behind, but a broad stripe of yellow running down the seams of his trousers, together with his high boots, bespoke the cavalry service, while the front of his battered campaign hat bore the decorations of two crossed sabres, with a gilded "7" prominent between. His attire was completed by a coarse blue shirt, unbuttoned at the throat, about which had been loosely knotted a darker colored silk handkerchief, and across the back of the saddle was fastened a uniform jacket, the single shoulder-strap revealed presenting the plain yellow of a second lieutenant.

Attaining to the summit of a slight knoll, whence a

somewhat wider vista lay outspread, he partially turned his face toward the men straggling along in the rear, while his hand swept across the dreary scene.

"If that line of trees over yonder indicates the course of the Bear Water, Carson," he questioned quietly, "where are we expected to hit the trail leading down to the ford?"

The sergeant, thus addressed, a little stocky fellow wearing a closely clipped gray moustache, spurred his exhausted horse into a brief trot, and drew up short by the officer's side, his heavy eyes scanning the vague distance, even while his right hand was uplifted in perfunctory salute.

"There's no trail I know about along this bank, sir," he replied respectfully, "but the big cottonwood with the dead branch forking out at the top is the ford guide."

They rode down in moody silence into the next depression, and began wearily climbing the long hill opposite, apparently the last before coming directly down the banks of the stream. As his barely moving horse topped the uneven summit, the lieutenant suddenly drew in his rein, and uttering an exclamation of surprise, bent forward, staring intently down in his immediate front. For a single instant he appeared to doubt the evidence of his own eyes; then he swung hastily from out the saddle, all weariness forgotten.

"My God!" he cried, sharply, his eyes suspiciously sweeping the bare slope. "There are two bodies lying here—white people!"

They lay all doubled up in the coarse grass, exactly as they had fallen, the man resting face downward, the slender figure of the girl clasped vice-like in his arms, with her tightly closed eyes upturned toward the glaring sun. Their strange, strained, unnatural posture, the rigidity of their limbs, the ghastly pallor of the exposed young face accentuated by dark, dishevelled hair, all alike seemed to indicate death. Never once questioning but that he was confronting the closing scene of a grewsome tragedy, the thoroughly aroused lieutenant dropped upon his knees beside them, his eyes already moist with sympathy, his anxious fingers feeling for a possible heart-beat. A moment of hushed, breathless suspense followed, and then he began flinging terse, eager commands across his shoulder to where his men were clustered.

"Here! Carson, Perry, Ronk, lay hold quick, and break this fellow's clasp," he cried, briefly. "The girl retains a spark of life yet, but the man's arms fairly crush her."

With all the rigidity of actual death those clutching hands held their tenacious grip, but the aroused soldiers wrenched the interlaced fingers apart with every tenderness possible in such emergency, shocked at noting the expression of intense agony stamped upon the man's face when thus exposed to view. The whole terrible story was engraven there—how he had toiled, agonized, suffered, before finally yielding to the inevitable and plunging forward in unconsciousness, written as legibly as though by a pen. Every pang of mental torture had left plainest imprint across that haggard countenance. He appeared old, pitiable, a wreck. Carson, who in his long service had witnessed much of death and suffering, bent tenderly above him, seeking for some faint evidence of lingering life. His fingers felt for no wound, for to his experienced eyes the sad tale was already sufficiently clear— hunger, exposure, the horrible heart-breaking strain of hopeless endeavor, had caused this ending, this unspeakable tragedy of the barren waterless plain. He had witnessed it all before, and hoped now for little. The anxious lieutenant, bareheaded under the hot sun-glare, strode hastily across from beside the unconscious but breathing girl, and stood gazing doubtfully down upon them.

"Any life, sergeant?" he demanded, his voice rendered husky by sympathy.

"He doesn't seem entirely gone, sir," and Carson glanced up into the officer's face, his own eyes filled with feeling. "I can distinguish just a wee bit of breathing, but it's so weak the pulse hardly stirs."

"What do you make of it?"

"Starving at the bottom, sir. The only thing I see now is to get them down to water and food."

The young officer glanced swiftly about him across that dreary picture of sun-burnt, desolate prairie stretching in every direction, his eyes pausing slightly as they surveyed the tops of the distant cottonwoods.

"Sling blankets between your horses," he commanded, decisively. "Move quickly, lads, and we may save one of these lives yet."

He led in the preparation himself, his cheeks flushed, his movements prompt, decisive. As if by some magic discipline the rude, effective litters were rapidly made ready, and the two seemingly lifeless bodies gently lifted from off the ground and deposited carefully within. Down the long, brown slope they advanced slowly, a soldier grasping the rein and walking at each horse's head, the supporting blankets, securely fastened about the saddle pommels, swaying gently to the measured tread of the trained animals. The lieutenant directed every movement, while Carson rode ahead, picking out the safest route through the short grass.

Beneath the protecting shadows of the first group of cotton-woods, almost on the banks of the muddy Bear Water, the little party let down their senseless burdens, and began once more their seemingly hopeless efforts at resuscitation. A fire was hastily kindled from dried and broken branches, and broth was made, which was forced through teeth that had to be pried open. Water was used unsparingly, the soldiers working with feverish eagerness, inspired by the constant admonitions of their officer, as well as their own curiosity to learn the facts hidden behind this tragedy.

It was the dark eyes of the girl which opened first, instantly closing again as the glaring light swept into them. Then slowly, and with wonderment, she gazed up into those strange, rough faces surrounding her, pausing in her first survey to rest her glance on the sympathetic countenance of the young lieutenant, who held her half reclining upon his arm.

"Here," he exclaimed, kindly, interpreting her glance as one of fear, "you are all right and perfectly safe now, with friends to care for you. Peters, bring another cup of that broth. Now, miss, just take a sup or two of this, and your strength will come back in a jiffy. What was the trouble? Starving?"

She did exactly as he bade her, every movement mechanical, her eyes fastened upon his face.

"I—I reckon that was partly it," she responded at last, her voice faint and husky. Then her glance wandered away, and finally rested upon another little kneeling group a few yards farther down stream. A look of fresh intelligence swept into her face.

"Is that him?" she questioned, tremblingly. "Is—is he dead?"

"He wasn't when we first got here, but mighty near gone, I'm afraid. I've been working over you ever since."

She shook herself free and sat weakly up, her lips tight compressed, her eyes apparently blind to all save that motionless body she could barely distinguish. "Let me tell you, that fellow's a man, just the same; the gamest, nerviest man I ever saw. I reckon he got hit, too, though he never said nothing about it. That's his style."

The deeply interested lieutenant removed his watchful eyes from off his charge just long enough to glance inquiringly across his shoulder. "Has the man any signs of a wound, sergeant?" he asked, loudly.

"A mighty ugly slug in the shoulder, sir; has bled scandalous, but I guess it's the very luck that's goin' to save him; seems now to be comin' out all right."

The officer's brows knitted savagely. "It begins to look as if this might be some of our business. What happened? Indians?"

"Yes."

"How far away?"

"I don't know. They caught us in a canyon somewhere out yonder, maybe three or four days ago; there was a lot killed, some of them soldiers. My dad was shot, and then that night he—he got me out up the rocks, and he—he was carrying me in his arms when I—I fainted, I saw there was blood on his shirt, and it was dripping down on the grass as he walked. That's about all I know."

"Who is the man? What's his name?"

The girl looked squarely into the lieutenant's eyes, and, for some reason which she could never clearly explain even to herself, lied calmly. "I don't know; I never asked."

Sergeant Carson rose stiffly from his knees beside the extended figure and strode heavily across toward where they were sitting, lifting his hand in soldierly salute, his heels clicking as he brought them sharply together in military precision.

"The fellow is getting his eyes open, sir," he reported, "and is breathing more regular. Purty weak yit, but he'll come round in time." He stared curiously down at the girl now sitting up unsupported, while a sudden look of surprised recognition swept across his face.

"Great guns!" he exclaimed, eagerly, "but I know you. You're old man Gillis's gal from Bethune, ain't ye?"

The quickly uplifted dark eyes seemed to lighten the ghastly pallor of her face, and her lips trembled. "Yes," she acknowledged simply, "but he's dead."

The lieutenant laid his ungloved hand softly on her shoulder, his blue eyes moist with aroused feeling.

"Never mind, little girl," he said, with boyish sympathy. "I knew Gillis, and, now the sergeant has spoken, I remember you quite well. Thought all the time your face was familiar, but couldn't quite decide where I had seen you before. So poor old Gillis has gone, and you are left all alone in the world! Well, he was an old soldier, could not have hoped to live much longer anyway, and would rather go fighting at the end. We'll take you back with us to Bethune, and the ladies of the garrison will look after you."

The recumbent figure lying a few yards away half lifted itself upon one elbow, and Hampton's face, white and haggard, stared uncertainly across the open space. For an instant his gaze dwelt upon the crossed sabres shielding the gilded "7" on the front of the lieutenant's scouting hat, then settled upon the face of the girl. With one hand pressed against the grass he pushed himself slowly up until he sat fronting them, his teeth clinched tight, his gray eyes gleaming feverishly in their sunken sockets.

"I'll be damned if you will!" he said, hoarsely. "She's my girl now."

CHAPTER V

A NEW PROPOSITION

To one in the least inclined toward fastidiousness, the Miners' Home at Glencaid would scarcely appeal as a desirable place for long-continued residence. But such a one would have had small choice in the matter, as it chanced to be the only hotel there. The Miners' Home was unquestionably unique as regards architectural details, having been constructed by sections, in accordance with the rapid development of the camp, and enjoyed the further distinction—there being only two others equally stylish in town—of being built of sawn plank, although, greatly to the regret of its unfortunate occupants, lack of seasoning had resulted in wide cracks in both walls and stairway. These were numerous, and occasionally proved perilous pitfalls to unwary travellers through the ill-lighted hall, while strict privacy within the chambers was long ago a mere reminiscence. However, these deficiencies were to be discovered only after entering. Without, the Miners' Home put up a good front,—which along the border is considered the chief matter of importance,—and was in reality the most pretentious structure gracing the single cluttered street of Glencaid. Indeed, it was pointed at with much civic pride by those citizens never compelled to exist within its yawning walls, and, with its ornament of a wide commodious porch, appeared even palatial in comparison with the log stable upon its left flank, or the dingy tent whose worm-eaten canvas flapped dejectedly upon the right. Directly across the street, its front a perfect blaze of glass, stood invitingly the Occidental saloon; but the Widow Guffy, who operated the Miners' Home with a strong hand, possessed an antipathy to strong liquor, which successfully kept all suspicion of intoxicating drink absent from those sacredly guarded precincts, except as her transient guests imported it internally, in the latter case she naturally remained quiescent, unless the offender became unduly boisterous. On such rare occasions Mrs. Guffy had always proved equal to the emergency, possessing Irish facility with either tongue or club.

Mr. Hampton during the course of his somewhat erratic career had previously passed several eventful weeks in Glencaid. He was neither unknown nor unappreciated at the Miners' Home, and having on previous occasions established his reputation as a spender, experienced little difficulty now in procuring promptly the very best accommodation which the house afforded. That this arrangement was accomplished somewhat to the present discomfort of two vociferous Eastern tourists did not greatly interfere with his pleasurable interest in the situation.

"Send those two fellows in here to argue it out," he said, languidly, after listening disgustedly to their loud lamentations in the hallway, and addressing his remarks to Mrs. Guffy, who had glanced into the room to be again assured regarding his comfort, and to express her deep regret over the unseemly racket. "The girl has fallen asleep, and I'm getting tired of hearing so much noise."

"No, be hivings, an' ye don't do nuthin' of thet sort, Bob," returned the widow, good-naturedly, busying herself with a dust-rag. "This is me own house, an' Oi've tended ter the loikes of them sort er fellers afore. There'll be no more bother this toime. Besides, it's a paceful house Oi'm runnin', an' Oi know ye'r way of sittling them things. It's too strenurous ye are, Misther Hampton. And what did ye do wid the young lady, Oi make bould to ask?"

Hampton carelessly waved his hand toward the rear room, the door of which stood ajar, and blew a thick cloud of smoke into the air, his eyes continuing to gaze dreamily through the open window toward the distant hills.

"Who's running the game over at the Occidental?" he asked, professionally.

"Red Slavin, bad cess to him!" and her eyes regarded her questioner with renewed anxiety. "But sure now, Bob, ye mustn't think of playin' yit awhoile. Yer narves are in no fit shape, an' won't be fer a wake yit."

He made no direct reply, and she hung about, flapping the dust-rag uneasily.

"An' what did ye mane ter be doin' wid the young gyurl?" she questioned at last, in womanly curiosity.

Hampton wheeled about on the hard chair, and regarded her quizzingly. "Mrs. Guffy," he said, slowly, "you've been a mother to me, and it would certainly be unkind not to give you a straight tip. Do? Why, take care of her, of course. What else would you expect of one possessing my kindly disposition and well-known motives of philanthropy? Can it be that I have resided with you, off and on, for ten years past without your ever realizing the fond yearnings of my heart? Mrs. Guffy, I shall make her the heiress to my millions; I shall marry her off to some Eastern nabob, and thus attain to that high position in society I am so well fitted to adorn—sure, and what else were you expecting, Mrs. Guffy?"

"A loikely story," with a sniff of disbelief. "They tell me she's old Gillis's daughter over to Bethune."

"They tell you, do they?" a sudden gleam of anger darkening his gray eyes. "Who tell you?"

"Sure, Bob, an' thet's nuthin' ter git mad about, so fur as I kin see. The story is in iverybody's mouth. It wus thim sojers what brought ye in thet tould most ov it, but the lieutenant,—Brant of the Seventh Cavalry, no less,—who took dinner here afore he wint back after the dead bodies, give me her name."

"Brant of the Seventh?" He faced her fairly now, his face again haggard and gray, all the slight gleam of fun gone out of it. "Was that the lad's name?"

"Sure, and didn't ye know him?"

"No; I noticed the '7' on his hat, of course, but never asked any questions, for his face was strange. I didn't know. The name, when you just spoke it, struck me rather queer. I—I used to know a Brant in the Seventh, but he was much older; it was not this man."

She answered something, lingering for a moment at the door, but he made no response, and she passed out silently, leaving him staring moodily through the open window, his eyes appearing glazed and sightless.

Glencaid, like most mining towns of its class, was dull and dead enough during the hours of daylight. It was not until after darkness fell that it awoke from its somnolence, when the scattered miners came swarming down from out the surrounding hills and turned into a noisy, restless playground the single narrow, irregular street. Then it suddenly became a mad commixture of Babel and hell. At this hour nothing living moved within range of the watcher's vision except a vagrant dog; the heat haze hung along the near-by slopes, while a little spiral of dust rose lazily from the deserted road. But Hampton had no eyes for this dreary prospect; with contracted brows he was viewing again that which he had confidently believed to have been buried long ago. Finally, he stepped quickly across the little room, and, standing quietly within the open doorway, looked long at the young girl upon the bed. She lay in sound, motionless sleep, one hand beneath her cheek, her heavy hair, scarcely revealing its auburn hue in the gloom of the interior, flowing in wild disorder across the crushed pillow. He stepped to the single window and drew down the green shade, gazed at her again, a new look of tenderness softening his stern face, then went softly out and closed the door.

An hour later he was still sitting on the hard chair by the window, a cigar between his teeth, thinking. The lowering sun was pouring a perfect flood of gold across the rag carpet, but he remained utterly unconscious as to aught save the gloomy trend of his own awakened memories. Some one rapped upon the outer door.

"Come in," he exclaimed, carelessly, and barely glancing up. "Well, what is it this time, Mrs. Guffy?"

The landlady had never before seen this usually happy guest in his present mood, and she watched him curiously.

"A man wants ter see ye," she announced, shortly, her hand on the knob.

"Oh, I'm in no shape for play to-night; go back and tell him so."

"Sure, an' it's aisy 'nough ter see thet wid half an eye. But this un isn't thet koind of a man, an' he's so moighty perlite about it Oi jist cudn't sind the loikes of him away. It's 'Missus Guffy, me dear madam, wud ye be koind enough to convey me complimints to Misther Robert Hampton, and requist him to grant me a few minutes of his toime on an important matter?' Sure, an' what do ye think of thet?"

"Huh! one of those fellows who had these rooms?" and Hampton rose to his feet with animation.

The landlady lowered her voice to an almost inaudible whisper.

"It's the Reverend Howard Wynkoop," she announced, impressively, dwelling upon the name. "The Reverend Howard Wynkoop, the Prasbytarian Missionary—wouldn't thet cork ye?"

It evidently did, for Mr. Hampton stared at her for fully a minute in an amazement too profound for fit expression in words. Then he swallowed something in his throat.

"Show the gentleman up," he said, shortly, and sat down to wait.

The Rev. Howard Wynkoop was neither giant nor dwarf, but the very fortunate possessor of a countenance which at once awakened confidence in his character. He entered the room quietly, rather dreading this interview with one of Mr. Hampton's well-known proclivities, yet in this case feeling abundantly fortified in the righteousness of his cause. His brown eyes met the inquisitive gray ones frankly, and

Hampton waved him silently toward a vacant chair.

"Our lines of labor in this vineyard being so entirely opposite," the latter said, coldly, but with intended politeness, "the honor of your unexpected call quite overwhelms me. I shall have to trouble you to speak somewhat softly in explanation of your present mission, so as not to disturb a young girl who chances to be sleeping in the room beyond."

Wynkoop cleared his throat uneasily, his naturally pale cheeks flushed.

"It was principally upon her account I ventured to call," he explained in sudden confidence. "Might I see her?"

Hampton's watchful eyes swept the others face suspiciously, and his hands clinched.

"Relative?" he asked gravely.

The preacher shook his head.

"Friend of the family, perhaps?"

"No, Mr. Hampton. My purpose in coming here is perfectly proper, yet the request was not advanced as a right, but merely as a special privilege."

A moment Hampton hesitated; then he arose and quietly crossed the room, holding open the door. Without a word being spoken the minister followed, and stood beside him. For several minutes the eyes of both men rested upon the girl's sleeping form and upturned face. Then Wynkoop drew silently back, and Hampton closed the door noiselessly.

"Well," he said, inquiringly, "what does all this mean?"

The minister hesitated as if doubtful how best to explain the nature of his rather embarrassing mission, his gaze upon the strong face of the man fronting him so sternly.

"Let us sit down again," he said at last, "and I will try to make my purpose sufficiently clear. I am not here to mince words, nor do I believe you to be the kind of a man who would respect me if I did. I may say something that will not sound pleasant, but in the cause of my Master I cannot hesitate. You are an older man than I, Mr. Hampton; your experience in life has doubtless been much broader than mine, and it may even be that in point of education you are likewise my superior. Nevertheless, as the only minister of the Gospel residing in this community it is beyond question my plain duty to speak a few words to you in behalf of this young lady, and her probable future. I trust not to be offensive, yet cannot shirk the requirements of my sacred office."

The speaker paused, somewhat disconcerted perhaps by the hardening of the lines in Hampton's face.

"Go on," commanded Hampton, tersely, "only let the preacher part slide, and say just what you have to say as man to man."

Wynkoop stiffened perceptibly in his chair, his face paling somewhat, but his eyes unwavering. Realizing the reckless nature before him, he was one whom opposition merely inspired.

"I prefer to do so," he continued, more calmly. "It will render my unpleasant task much easier, and yield us both a more direct road for travel. I have been laboring on this field for nearly three years. When I first came here you were pointed out to me as a most dangerous man, and ever since then I have constantly been regaled by the stories of your exploits. I have known you merely through such unfriendly reports, and came here strongly prejudiced against you as a representative of every evil I war against. We have never met before, because there seemed to be nothing in common between us; because I had been led to suppose you to be an entirely different man from what I now believe you are."

Hampton stirred uneasily in his chair.

"Shall I paint in exceedingly plain words the picture given me of you?"

There was no response, but the speaker moistened his lips and proceeded firmly. "It was that of a professional gambler, utterly devoid of mercy toward his victims; a reckless fighter, who shot to kill upon the least provocation; a man without moral character, and from whom any good action was impossible. That was what was said about you. Is the tale true?"

Hampton laughed unpleasantly, his eyes grown hard and ugly.

"I presume it must be," he admitted, with a quick side glance toward the closed door, "for the girl out yonder thought about the same. A most excellent reputation to establish with only ten years of strict attendance to business."

Wynkoop's grave face expressed his disapproval.

"Well, in my present judgment that report was not altogether true," he went on clearly and with greater confidence. "I did suppose you exactly that sort of a man when I first came into this room. I have not believed so, however, for a single moment since. Nevertheless, the naked truth is certainly bad enough, without any necessity for our resorting to romance. You may deceive others by an assumption of recklessness, but I feel convinced your true nature is not evil. It has been warped through some cause which is none of my business. Let us deal alone with facts. You are a gambler, a professional gambler, with all that that implies; your life is, of necessity, passed among the most vicious and degrading elements of mining camps, and you do not hesitate even to take human life when in your judgment it seems necessary to preserve your own. Under this veneer of lawlessness you may, indeed, possess a warm heart, Mr. Hampton; you may be a good fellow, but you are certainly not a model character, even according to the liberal code of the border."

"Extremely kind of you to enter my rooms uninvited, and furnish me with this list of moral deficiencies," acknowledged the other with affected carelessness. "But thus far you have failed to tell me anything strikingly new. Am I to understand you have some particular object in this exchange of amenities?"

"Most assuredly. It is to ask if such a person as you practically confess yourself to be—homeless, associating only with the most despicable and vicious characters, and leading so uncertain and disreputable a life—can be fit to assume charge of a girl, almost a woman, and mould her future?"

For a long, breathless moment Hampton stared incredulously at his questioner, crushing his cigar between his teeth. Twice he started to speak, but literally choked back the bitter words burning his lips, while an uncontrollable admiration for the other's boldness began to overcome his first fierce anger.

"By God!" he exclaimed at last, rising to his feet and pointing toward the door. "I have shot men for less. Go, before I forget your cloth. You little impudent fool! See here—I saved that girl from death, or worse; I plucked her from the very mouth of hell; I like her; she's got sand; so far as I know there is not a single soul for her to turn to for help in all this wide world. And you, you miserable, snivelling hypocrite, you little creeping Presbyterian parson, you want me to shake her! What sort of a wild beast do you suppose I am?"

Wynkoop had taken one hasty step backward, impelled to it by the fierce anger blazing from those stern gray eyes. But now he paused, and, for the only time on record, discovered the conventional language of polite society inadequate to express his needs.

"I think," he said, scarcely realizing his own words, "you are a damned fool."

Into Hampton's eyes there leaped a light upon which other men had looked before they died,—the strange mad gleam one sometimes sees in fighting animals, or amid the fierce charges of war. His hand swept instinctively backward, closing upon the butt of a revolver beneath his coat, and for one second he who had dared such utterance looked on death. Then the hard lines about the man's mouth softened, the fingers clutching the weapon relaxed, and Hampton laid one opened hand upon the minister's shrinking shoulder.

"Sit down," he said, his voice unsteady from so sudden a reaction. "Perhaps—perhaps I don't exactly understand."

For a full minute they sat thus looking at each other through the fast dimming light, like two prize-fighters meeting for the first time within the ring, and taking mental stock before beginning their physical argument. Hampton, with a touch of his old audacity of manner, was first to break the silence.

"So you think I am a damned fool. Well, we are in pretty fair accord as to that fact, although no one before has ever ventured to state it quite so clearly in my presence. Perhaps you will kindly explain?"

The preacher wet his dry lips with his tongue, forgetting himself when his thoughts began to crystallize into expression.

"I regret having spoken as I did," he began. "Such language is not my custom. I was irritated because of your haste in rejecting my advances before hearing the proposition I came to submit. I certainly respect your evident desire to be of assistance to this young woman, nor have I the slightest intention of interfering between you. Your act in preserving her life was a truly noble one, and your loyalty to her interests since is worthy of all Christian praise. But I believe I have a right to ask, what do you intend for the future? Keep her with you? Drag her about from camp to camp? Educate her among the contaminating poison of gambling-holes and dance-halls? Is her home hereafter to be the saloon and the rough frontier hotel? her ideal of manhood the quarrelsome gambler, and of womanhood a painted harlot? Mr. Hampton, you are evidently a man of education, of early refinement; you have known better things; and I have come to you seeking merely to aid you in deciding this helpless young woman's destiny. I thought, I prayed, you would be at once interested in that purpose, and would comprehend the reasonableness of my position."

Hampton sat silent, gazing out of the window, his eyes apparently on the lights now becoming dimly visible in the saloon opposite. For a considerable time he made no move, and the other straightened back in his chair watching him.

"Well!" he ventured at last, "what is your proposition?" The question was quietly asked, but a slight tremor in the low voice told of repressed feeling.

"That, for the present at least, you confide this girl into the care of some worthy woman."

"Have you any such in mind?"

"I have already discussed the matter briefly with Mrs. Herndon, wife of the superintendent of the Golden Rule mines. She is a refined Christian lady, beyond doubt the most proper person to assume such a charge in this camp. There is very little in such a place as this to interest a woman of her capabilities, and I believe she would be delighted to have such an opportunity for doing good. She has no children of her own."

Hampton flung his sodden cigar butt out of the window. "I'll talk it over to-morrow with—with Miss Gillis," he said, somewhat gruffly. "It may be this means a good deal more to me than you suppose, parson, but I'm bound to acknowledge there is considerable hard sense in what you have just said, and I'll talk it over with the girl."

Wynkoop held out his hand cordially, and the firm grasp of the other closed over his fingers.

"I don't exactly know why I didn't kick you downstairs," the latter commented, as though still in wonder at himself. "Never remember being quite so considerate before, but I reckon you must have come at me in about the right way."

If Wynkoop answered, his words were indistinguishable, but Hampton remained standing in the open door watching the missionary go down the narrow stairs.

"Nervy little devil," he acknowledged slowly to himself. "And maybe, after all, that would be the best thing for the Kid."

CHAPTER VI

"TO BE OR NOT TO BE"

They were seated rather close together upon the steep hillside, gazing silently down upon squalid Glencaid. At such considerable distance all the dull shabbiness of the mining town had disappeared, and it seemed almost ideal, viewed against the natural background of brown rocks and green trees. All about them was the clear, invigorating air of the uplands, through which the eyes might trace for miles the range of irregular rocky hills, while just above, seemingly almost within touch of the extended hand, drooped the blue circling sky, unflecked by cloud. Everywhere was loneliness, no sound telling of the labor of man reached them, and the few scattered buildings far below resembling mere dollhouses.

They had conversed only upon the constantly changing beauty of the scene, or of incidents connected with their upward climb, while moving slowly along the trail through the fresh morning sunshine. Now they sat in silence, the young girl, with cheeks flushed and dreamy eyes aglow, gazing far off along the valley, the man watching her curiously, and wondering how best to approach his task. For the first time he began to realize the truth, which had been partially borne in upon him the previous evening by

Wynkoop, that this was no mere child with whom he dealt, but a young girl upon the verge of womanhood. Such knowledge began to reveal much that came before him as new, changing the entire nature of their present relationship, as well as the scope of his own plain duty. It was his wont to look things squarely in the face, and unpleasant and unwelcome as was the task now confronting him, during the long night hours he had settled it once for all—the preacher's words were just.

Observing her now, sitting thus in total unconsciousness of his scrutiny, Hampton made no attempt to analyze the depth of his interest for this waif who had come drifting into his life. He did not in the least comprehend why she should have touched his heart with generous impulses, nor did he greatly care. The fact was far the more important, and that fact he no longer questioned. He had been a lonely, unhappy, discontented man for many a long year, shunned by his own sex, who feared him, never long seeking the society of the other, and retaining little real respect for himself. Under such conditions a reaction was not unnatural, and, short as the time had been since their first meeting, this odd, straightforward chit of a girl had found an abiding-place in his heart, had furnished him a distinct motive in life before unknown.

Even to his somewhat prejudiced eyes she was not an attractive creature, for she possessed no clear conception of how to render apparent those few feminine charms she possessed. Negligence and total unconsciousness of self, coupled with lack of womanly companionship and guidance, had left her altogether in the rough. He marked now the coarse ragged shoes, the cheap patched skirt, the tousled auburn hair, the sunburnt cheeks with a suggestion of freckles plainly visible beneath the eyes, and some of the fastidiousness of earlier days caused him to shrug his shoulders. Yet underneath the tan there was the glow of

perfect young health; the eyes were frank, brave, unflin-
ching; while the rounded chin held a world of character in its
firm contour. Somehow the sight of this brought back to him
that abiding faith in her "dead gameness" which had first
awakened his admiration. "She's got it in her," he thought,
silently, "and, by thunder! I'm here to help her get it out."

"Kid," he ventured at last, turning over a broken fragment of
rock between his restless fingers, but without lifting his eyes,
"you were talking while we came up the trail about how we'd
do this and that after a while. You don't suppose I'm going to
have any useless girl like you hanging around on to me, do
you?"

She glanced quickly about at him, as though such unexpected expressions startled her from a pleasant reverie.
"Why, I—I thought that was the way you planned it
yesterday," she exclaimed, doubtfully.

"Oh, yesterday! Well, you see, yesterday I was sort of
dreaming; to-day I am wide awake, and I've about decided,
Kid, that for your own good, and my comfort, I've got to
shake you."

A sudden gleam of fierce resentment leaped into the dark
eyes, the unrestrained glow of a passion which had never
known control. "Oh, you have, have you, Mister Bob
Hampton? You have about decided! Well, why don't you
altogether decide? I don't think I'm down on my knees
begging you for mercy. Good Lord! I reckon I can get along
all right without you—I did before. Just what happened to
give you such a change of heart?"

"I made the sudden discovery," he said, affecting a laziness
he was very far from feeling, "that you were too near being a
young woman to go traipsing around the country with me,

living at shacks, and having no company but gambling sharks, and that class of cattle."

"Oh, did you? What else?"

"Only that our tempers don't exactly seem to jibe, and the two of us can't be bosses in the same ranch."

She looked at him contemptuously, swinging her body farther around on the rock, and sitting stiffly, the color on her cheeks deepening through the sunburn. "Now see here, Mister Bob Hampton, you're a fraud, and you know it! Didn't I understand exactly who you was, and what was your business? Didn't I know you was a gambler, and a 'bad man'? Didn't I tell you plain enough out yonder,"—and her voice faltered slightly,—"just what I thought about you? Good Lord! I haven't been begging to stick with you, have I? I just didn't know which way to turn, or who to turn to, after dad was killed, and you sorter hung on to me, and I let it go the way I supposed you wanted it. But I'm not particularly stuck on your style, let me tell you, and I reckon there's plenty of ways for me to get along. Only first, I propose to understand what your little game is. You don't throw down your hand like that without some reason."

Hampton sat up, spurred into instant admiration by such independence of spirit. "You grow rather good-looking, Kid, when you get hot, but you go at things half-cocked, and you've got to get over it. That's the whole trouble—you've never been trained, and I wouldn't make much of a trainer for a high-strung filly like you. Ever remember your mother?"

"Mighty little; reckon she must have died when I was about five years old. That's her picture."

Hampton took in his hand the old-fashioned locket she held out toward him, the long chain still clasped about her throat, and pried open the stiff catch with his knife blade. She bent down to fasten her loosened shoe, and when her eyes were uplifted again his gaze was riveted upon the face in the picture.

"Mighty pretty, wasn't she?" she asked with a sudden girlish interest, bending forward to look, regardless of his strained attitude. "And she was prettier than that even, the way I remember her best, with her hair all hanging down, coming to tuck me into bed at night. Someway that's how I always seem to see her."

The man drew a deep breath, and snapped shut the locket, yet still retained it in his hand. "Is—is she dead?" he questioned, and his voice trembled in spite of steel nerves.

"Yes, in St. Louis; dad took me there with him two years ago, and I saw her grave."

"Dad? Do you mean old Gillis?"

She nodded, beginning dimly to wonder why he should speak so fiercely and stare at her in that odd way. He seemed to choke twice before he could ask the next question.

"Did he—old Gillis, I mean—claim to be your father, or her husband?"

"No, I don't reckon he ever did, but he gave me that picture, and told me she was my mother. I always lived with him, and called him dad. I reckon he liked it, and he was mighty good to me. We were at Randolph a long time, and since then he's been post-trader at Bethune. That's all I know about it, for dad never talked very much, and he used to get mad when I asked him questions."

Hampton dropped the locket from his grasp, and arose to his feet. For several minutes he stood with his back turned toward her, apparently gazing down the valley, his jaw set, his dimmed eyes seeing nothing. Slowly the color came creeping back into his face, and his hands unclinched. Then he wheeled about, and looked down upon her, completely restored to his old nature.

"Then it seems that it is just you and I, Kid, who have got to settle this little affair," he announced, firmly. "I'll have my say about it, and then you can uncork your feelings. I rather imagine I haven't very much legal right in the premises, but I've got a sort of moral grip on you by reason of having pulled you out alive from that canyon yonder, and I propose to play this game to the limit. You say your mother is dead, and the man who raised you is dead, and, so far as either of us know, there isn't a soul anywhere on earth who possesses any claim over you, or any desire to have. Then, naturally, the whole jack-pot is up to me, provided I've got the cards. Now, Kid, waving your prejudice aside, I ain't just exactly the best man in this world to bring up a girl like you and make a lady out of her. I thought yesterday that maybe we might manage to hitch along together for a while, but I've got a different think coming to-day. There's no use disfiguring the truth. I'm a gambler, something of a fighter on the side, and folks don't say anything too pleasant about my peaceful disposition around these settlements; I haven't any home, and mighty few friends, and the few I have got are nothing to boast about. I reckon there's a cause for it all. So, considering everything, I'm about the poorest proposition ever was heard of to start a young ladies' seminary. The Lord knows old Gillis was bad enough, but I'm a damned sight worse. Now, some woman has got to take you in hand, and I reckon I've found the right one."

"Goin' to get married, Bob?"

"Not this year; it's hardly become so serious as that, but I'm going to find you a good home here, and I'm going to put up plenty of stuff, so that they'll take care of you all right and proper."

The dark eyes never wavered as they looked steadily into the gray ones, but the chin quivered slightly.

"I reckon I'd rather try it alone," she announced stubbornly. "Maybe I might have stood it with you, Bob Hampton, but a woman is the limit."

Hampton in other and happier days had made something of a study of the feminine nature, and he realized now the utter impracticability of any attempt at driving.

"I expect it will go rather hard at first, Kid," he admitted craftily, "but I think you might try it a while just to sort of please me."

"Who—who is she?" doubtfully.

"Mrs. Herndon, wife of the superintendent of the 'Golden Rule' mine"; and he waved his hand toward the distant houses. "They tell me she's a mighty fine woman."

"Oh, they do? Then somebody's been stirring you up about me, have they? I thought that was about the way of it. Somebody wants to reform me, I reckon. Well, maybe I won't be reformed. Who was it, Bob?"

"The Presbyterian Missionary," he confessed reluctantly, "a nervy little chap named Wynkoop; he came in to see me last night while you were asleep." He faced her open scorn unshrinkingly, his mind fully decided, and clinging to one thought with all the tenacity of his nature.

"A preacher!" her voice vibrant with derision, "a preacher! Well, of all things, Bob Hampton! You led around by the nose in that way! Did he want you to bring me to Sunday school? A preacher! And I suppose the fellow expects to turn me over to one of his flock for religious instruction. He'll have you studying theology inside of a year. A preacher! Oh, Lord, and you agreed! Well, I won't go; so there!"

"As I understand the affair," Hampton continued, as she paused for breath, "it was Lieutenant Brant who suggested the idea of his coming to me. Brant knew Gillis, and remembered you, and realizing your unpleasant situation, thought such an arrangement would be for your benefit."

"Brant!" she burst forth in renewed anger; "he did, did he! The putty-faced dandy! I used to see him at Bethune, and you can bet he never bothered his head about me then. No, and he didn't even know me out yonder, until after the sergeant spoke up. What business has that fellow got planning what I shall do?"

Hampton made no attempt to answer. It was better to let her indignation die out naturally, and so he asked a question. "What is this Brant doing at Bethune? There is no cavalry stationed there."

She glanced up quickly, interested by the sudden change in his voice. "I heard dad say he was kept there on some special detail. His regiment is stationed at Fort Lincoln, somewhere farther north. He used to come down and talk with dad evenings, because daddy saw service in the Seventh when it was first organized after the war."

"Did you—did you ever hear either of them say anything about Major Alfred Brant? He must have been this lad's father."

"No, I never heard much they said. Did you know him?"

"The father, yes, but that was years ago. Come, Kid, all this is only ancient history, and just as well forgotten. Now, you are a sensible girl, when your temper don't get away with you, and I am simply going to leave this matter to your better judgment. Will you go to Mrs. Herndon's, and find out how you like it? You needn't stop there an hour if she isn't good to you, but you ought not to want to remain with me, and grow up like a rough boy."

"You—you really want me to go, don't you?"

"Yes, I want you to go. It's a chance for you, Kid, and there isn't a bit of a show in the kind of a life I lead. I never have been in love with it myself, and only took to it in the first place because the devil happened to drive me that way. The Lord knows I don't want to lead any one else through such a muck. So it is a try?"

The look of defiance faded slowly out of her face as she stood gravely regarding him. The man was in deadly earnest, and she felt the quiet insistence of his manner. He really desired it to be decided in this way, and somehow his will had become her law, although such a suspicion had never once entered her mind.

"You bet, if you put it that way," she consented, simply, "but I reckon that Mrs. Herndon is likely to wish I hadn't."

Together, yet scarcely exchanging another word, the two retraced their steps slowly down the steep trail leading toward the little town in the valley, walking unconsciously the pathway of fate, the way of all the world.

Randall Parrish

CHAPTER VII

"I'VE COME HERE TO LIVE"

Widely as these two companions differed in temperament and experience, it would be impossible to decide which felt the greater uneasiness at the prospect immediately before them. The girl openly rebellious, the man extremely doubtful, with reluctant steps they approached that tall, homely yellow house—outwardly the most pretentious in Glencaid—which stood well up in the valley, where the main road diverged into numerous winding trails leading toward the various mines among the foothills.

They were so completely opposite, these two, that more than one chance passer-by glanced curiously toward them as they picked their way onward through the red dust. Hampton, slender yet firmly knit, his movements quick like those of a watchful tiger, his shoulders set square, his body held erect as though trained to the profession of arms, his gray eyes marking every movement about him with a suspicion born of continual exposure to peril, his features finely chiselled, with threads of gray hair beginning to show conspicuously about the temples. One would glance twice at him anywhere, for in chin, mouth, and eyes were plainly pictured the signs of strength, evidences that he had fought stern battles, and was no craven. For good or evil he might be trusted to act instantly, and, if need arose, to the very death. His attire of fashionably cut black cloth, and his immaculate linen, while neat and unobtrusive, yet appeared extremely unusual in that careless land of clay-baked overalls and dingy woollens. Beside him, in vivid contrast, the girl trudged in her heavy shoes and bedraggled skirts, her sullen eyes fastened doggedly on the road, her hair showing ragged and disreputable in the brilliant sunshine. Hampton himself could not remain altogether indifferent to the contrast.

"You look a little rough, Kid, for a society call," he said. "If there was any shebang in this mud-hole of a town that kept any women's things on sale fit to look at, I'd be tempted to fix you up a bit."

"Well, I'm glad of it," she responded, grimly. "I hope I look so blame tough that woman won't say a civil word to us. You can bet I ain't going to strain myself to please the likes of her."

"You certainly exhibit no symptoms of doing so," he admitted, frankly. "But you might, at least, have washed your face and fixed your hair."

She flashed one angry glance at him, stopping in the middle of the road, her head flung back as though ready for battle. Then, as if by some swift magic of emotion, her expression changed. "And so you're ashamed of me, are you?" she asked, her voice sharp but unsteady. "Ashamed to be seen walking with me? Darn it! I know you are! But I tell you, Mr. Bob Hampton, you won't be the next time. And what's more, you just don't need to traipse along another step with me now. I don't want you. I reckon I ain't very much afraid of tackling this Presbyterian woman all alone."

She swung off fiercely, and the man chuckled softly as he

followed, watchfully, through the circling, red dust cloud created by her hasty feet. The truth is, Mr. Hampton possessed troubles and scruples of his own in connection with this contemplated call. He had never met the lady; indeed, he could recall very few of her sex, combining respectability and refinement, whom he had met during the past ten years. But he retained some memory of the husband as having been associated with a strenuous poker game at Placer, in which he also held a prominent place, and it would seem scarcely possible that the wife did not know whose bullet had turned her for some weeks into a sick-nurse. For Herndon he had not even a second thought, but the possible ordeal of a woman's tongue was another matter. A cordial reception could hardly be anticipated, and Hampton mentally braced himself for the worst.

There were some other things, also, but these he brushed aside for the present. He was not the sort of man to wear his heart upon his sleeve, and all his life long he had fought out his more serious battles in loneliness and silence. Now he had work to accomplish in the open; he was going to stay with the Kid—after that, *quien sabe*? So he smiled somewhat soberly, swore softly to himself, and strode on. He had never yet thrown down his cards merely because luck had taken a bad turn.

It was a cheerless-looking house, painted a garish yellow, having staring windows, and devoid of a front porch, or slightest attempt at shade to render its uncomely front less unattractive. Hampton could scarcely refrain from forming a mental picture of the woman who would most naturally preside within so unpolished an abode—an angular, hard-featured, vinegar-tempered creature, firm settled in her prejudices and narrowed by her creed. Had the matter been left at that moment to his own decision, this glimpse of the house would have turned them both back, but the girl unhesitatingly pressed forward and turned defiantly in through the gateless opening. He followed in silence along the narrow foot-path bordered by weeds, and stood back while she stepped boldly up on the rude stone slab and rapped sharply against the warped and sagging door. A moment they stood thus waiting with no response from within. Once she glanced suspiciously around at him, only to wheel back instantly and once more apply her knuckles to the wood. Before he had conjured up something worth saying the door was partially opened, and a rounded dumpling of a woman, having rosy cheeks, her hair iron-gray, her blue eyes half smiling in uncertain welcome, looked out upon them questioningly.

"I've come to live here," announced the girl, sullenly. "That is, if I like it."

The woman continued to gaze at her, as if tempted to laugh outright; then the pleasant blue eyes hardened as their vision swept beyond toward Hampton.

"It is extremely kind of you, I'm sure," she said at last. "Why is it I am to be thus honored?"

The girl backed partially off the doorstep, her hair flapping in the wind, her cheeks flushed.

"Oh, you needn't put on so much style about it," she blurted out. "You're Mrs. Herndon, ain't you? Well, then, this is the place where I was sent; but I reckon you ain't no more particular about it than I am. There's others."

"Who sent you to me?" and Mrs. Herndon came forth into the sunshine.

"The preacher."

"Oh, Mr. Wynkoop; then you must be the homeless girl whom Lieutenant Brant brought in the other day. Why did you not say so at first? You may come in, my child."

There was a sympathetic tenderness apparent now in the tones of her voice, which the girl was swift to perceive and respond to, yet she held back, her independence unshaken. With the quick intuition of a woman, Mrs. Herndon bent down, placing one hand on the defiant shoulder.

"I did not understand, at first, my dear," she said, soothingly, "or I should never have spoken as I did. Some very strange callers come here. But you are truly welcome. I had a daughter once; she must have been nearly your age when God took her. Won't you come in?"

While thus speaking she never once glanced toward the man standing in silence beyond, yet as the two passed through the doorway together he followed, unasked. Once within the plainly furnished room, and with her arm about the girl's waist, the lines about her mouth hardened. "I do not recall extending my invitation to you," she said, coldly.

He remained standing, hat in hand, his face shadowed, his eyes picturing deep perplexity.

"For the intrusion I offer my apology," he replied, humbly; "but you see I—I feel responsible for this young woman. She—sort of fell to my care when none of her own people were left to look after her. I only came to show her the way, and to say that I stand ready to pay you well to see to her a bit, and show her how to get hold of the right things."

"Indeed!" and Mrs. Herndon's voice was not altogether pleasant. "I understood she was entirely alone and friendless. Are you that man who brought her out of the canyon?"

Hampton bowed as though half ashamed of acknowledging the act.

"Oh! then I know who you are," she continued, unhesitatingly. "You are a gambler and a bar-room rough. I won't touch a penny of your money. I told Mr. Wynkoop that I shouldn't, but that I would endeavor to do my Christian duty by this poor girl. He was to bring her here himself, and keep you away."

The man smiled slightly, not in the least disconcerted by her plain speech. The cutting words merely served to put him on his mettle. "Probably we departed from the hotel somewhat earlier than the minister anticipated," he explained, quietly, his old ease of manner returning in face of such open opposition. "I greatly regret your evident prejudice, madam, and can only say that I have more confidence in you than you appear to have in me. I shall certainly discover some means by which I may do my part in shaping this girl's future, but in the meanwhile will relieve you of my undesired presence."

He stepped without into the glare of the sunlight, feeling utterly careless as to the woman who had affronted him, yet somewhat hurt on seeing that the girl had not once lifted her downcast eyes to his face. Yet he had scarcely taken three steps toward the road before she was beside him, her hand upon his sleeve.

"I won't stay!" she exclaimed, fiercely, "I won't, Bob Hampton. I'd rather go with you than be good."

His sensitive face flushed with delight, but he looked gravely down into her indignant eyes. "Oh, yes, you will, Kid," and his hand touched her roughened hair caressingly. "She's a good, kind woman, all right, and I don't blame her for not liking my style."

"Do—do you really want me to stick it out here, Bob?"

It was no small struggle for him to say so, for he was beginning to comprehend just what this separation meant. She was more to him than he had ever supposed, more to him than she had been even an hour before; and now he understood clearly that from this moment they must ever run farther apart—her life tending upward, his down. Yet there was but one decision possible. A life which is lonely and dissatisfied, a wasted life, never fully realizes how lonely, dissatisfied, and wasted it is until some new life, beautiful in young hope and possibility, comes into contact with it. For a single instant Hampton toyed with the temptation confronting him, this opportunity of brightening his own miserable future by means of her degradation. Then he answered, his voice grown almost harsh. "This is your best chance, little girl, and I want you to stay and fight it out."

Their eyes met, each dimly realizing, although in a totally different way, that here was a moment of important decision. Mrs. Herndon darkened the doorway, and stood looking out.

"Well, Mr. Bob Hampton," she questioned, plainly, "what is this going to be?"

He glanced toward her, slightly lifting his hat, and promptly releasing the girl's clinging hand.

"Miss Gillis consents to remain," he announced shortly, and, denying himself so much as another glance at his companion, strode down the narrow path to the road. A moment the girl's eyes followed him through the dust cloud, a single tear stealing down her cheek. Only a short week ago she had utterly despised this man, now he had become truly more to her than any one else in the wide, wide world. She did not in the least comprehend the mystery; indeed, it was no mystery, merely the simple trust of a child naturally responding to the first unselfish love given it. Perhaps Mrs. Herndon dimly understood, for she came forth quietly, and led the girl, now sobbing bitterly, within the cool shadows of the house.

CHAPTER VIII

A LAST REVOLT

It proved a restless day, and a sufficiently unpleasant one, for Mr. Hampton. For a number of years he had been diligently training himself in the school of cynicism, endeavoring to persuade himself that he did not in the least care what others thought, nor how his own career ended; impelling himself to constant recklessness in life and thought. He had thus successfully built up a wall between the present and that past which long haunted his lonely moments, and had finally decided that it was hermetically sealed. Yet now, this odd chit of a girl, this waif whom he had plucked from the jaws of death, had overturned this carefully constructed barrier as if it had been originally built of mere cardboard, and he was compelled again to see himself, loathe himself, just as he had in those past years.

Everything had been changed by her sudden entrance into his life, everything except those unfortunate conditions which still bound him helpless. He looked upon the world no longer through his cool, gray eyes, but out of her darker ones, and the prospect appeared gloomy enough. He thought it all over again and again, dwelling in reawakened memory upon details long hidden within the secret recesses of his brain, yet so little came from this searching survey that the result left him no plan for the future. He had wandered too far away from home; the path leading back was long ago overgrown with weeds, and could not now be retraced. One thing he grasped clearly,—the girl should be given her chance; nothing in his life must ever again soil her or lower her ideals. Mrs. Herndon was right, and he realized it; neither his presence nor his money were fit to influence her future. He swore between his clinched teeth, his face grown haggard. The sun's rays bridged the slowly darkening valley with cords of red gold, and the man pulled himself to his feet by gripping the root of a tree. He realized that he had been sitting there for hours, and that he was hungry.

Down beneath, amid the fast awakening noise and bustle of early evening, the long discipline of the gambler reasserted itself—he got back his nerve. It was Bob Hampton, cool, resourceful, sarcastic of speech, quick of temper, who greeted the loungers about the hotel, and who sat, with his back to the wall, in the little dining-room, watchful of all others present. And it was Bob Hampton who strolled carelessly out upon the darkened porch an hour later, leaving a roar of laughter behind him, and an enemy as well. Little he cared for that, however, in his present mood, and he stood there, amid the black shadows, looking contemptuously down upon the stream of coatless humanity trooping past on pleasure bent, the blue smoke circling his head, his gray eyes glowing half angrily. Suddenly he leaned forward, clutching the rail in quick surprise.

"Kid," he exclaimed, harshly, "what does this mean? What are you doing alone here?"

She stopped instantly and glanced up, her face flushing in the light streaming forth from the open door of the Occidental.

"I reckon I'm alone here because I want to be," she returned, defiantly. "I ain't no slave. How do you get up there?"

He extended his hand, and drew her up beside him into the shaded corner. "Well," he said, "tell me the truth."

"I've quit, that's all, Bob. I just couldn't stand for reform any longer, and so I've come back here to you."

The man drew a deep breath. "Didn't you like Mrs. Herndon?"

"Oh, she's all right enough, so far as that goes. 'T ain't that; only I just didn't like some things she said and did."

"Kid," and Hampton straightened up, his voice growing stern. "I've got to know the straight of this. You say you like Mrs. Herndon well enough, but not some other things. What were they?"

The girl hesitated, drawing back a little from him until the light from the saloon fell directly across her face. "Well," she declared, slowly, "you see it had to be either her or—or you, Bob, and I'd rather it would be you."

"You mean she said you would have to cut me out entirely if you stayed there with her?"

She nodded, her eyes filled with entreaty. "Yes, that was about it. I wasn't ever to have anything more to do with you, not even to speak to you if we met—and after you'd saved my life, too."

"Never mind about that little affair, Kid," and Hampton rested his hand gently on her shoulder. "That was all in the day's work, and hardly counts for much anyhow. Was that all she said?"

"She called you a low-down gambler, a gun-fighter, a—a miserable bar-room thug, a—a murderer. She—she said that if I ever dared to speak to you again, Bob Hampton; that I could leave her house. I just couldn't stand for that, so I came away."

Hampton never stirred, his teeth set deep into his cigar, his hands clinched about the railing. "The fool!" he muttered half aloud, then caught his breath quickly. "Now see here, Kid," and he turned her about so that he might look down into her eyes, "I'm mighty glad you like me well enough to put up a kick, but if all this is true about me, why shouldn't she say it? Do you believe that sort of a fellow would prove a very good kind to look after a young lady?"

"I ain't a young lady!"

"No; well, you're going to be if I have my way, and I don't believe the sort of a gent described would be very apt to help you much in getting there."

"You ain't all that."

"Well, perhaps not. Like an amateur artist, madam may have laid the colors on a little thick. But I am no winged angel, Kid, nor exactly a model for you to copy after. I reckon you better stick to the woman, and cut me."

She did not answer, yet he read an unchanged purpose in her eyes, and his own decision strengthened. Some instinct led him to do the right thing; he drew forth the locket from beneath the folds of her dress, holding it open to the light. He noticed now a name engraven on the gold case, and bent lower to decipher it.

"Was her name Naida? It is an uncommon word."

"Yes."

"And yours also?"

"Yes."

Their eyes met, and those of both had perceptibly softened.

"Naida," his lips dwelt upon the peculiar name as though he loved the sound. "I want you to listen to me, child. I sincerely wish I might keep you here with me, but I can't. You are more to me than you dream, but it would not be right for me thus deliberately to sacrifice your whole future to my pleasure. I possess nothing to offer you,—no home, no friends, no reputation. Practically I am an outlaw, existing by my wits, disreputable in the eyes of those who are worthy to live in the world. She, who was your mother, would never wish you to remain with me. She would say I did right in giving you up into the care of a good woman. Naida, look on that face in the locket, your mother's face. It is sweet, pure, beautiful, the face of a good, true woman. Living or dead, it must be the prayer of those lips that you become a good woman also. She should lead you, not I, for I am unworthy. For her sake, and in her name, I ask you to go back to Mrs. Herndon."

He could perceive the gathering tears in her eyes, and his hand closed tightly about her own. It was not one soul alone that struggled.

"You will go?"

"O Bob, I wish you wasn't a gambler!"

A moment he remained silent. "But unfortunately I am," he admitted, soberly, "and it is best for you to go back.

Won't you?"

Her gaze was fastened upon the open locket, the fair face pictured there smiling up at her as though in pleading also.

"You truly think she would wish it?"

"I know she would."

The girl gave utterance to a quick, startled breath, as if the vision frightened her. "Then I will go," she said, her voice a mere whisper, "I will go."

He led her down the steps, out into the jostling crowd below, as if she had been some fairy princess. Men occasionally spoke to him, but seemingly he heard nothing, pressing his way through the mass of moving figures in utter unconsciousness of their presence. Her locket hung dangling, and he slipped it back into its place and drew her slender form yet closer against his own, as they stepped forth into the black, deserted road. Once, in the last faint ray of light which gleamed from the windows of the Miners' Retreat, she glanced up shyly into his face. It was white and hard set, and she did not venture to break the silence. Half-way up the gloomy ravine they met a man and woman coming along the narrow path. Hampton drew her aside out of their way, then spoke coldly.

"Mrs. Herndon, were you seeking your lost charge? I have her here."

The two passing figures halted, peering through the darkness.

"Who are you?" It was the gruff voice of the man.

Hampton stepped out directly in his path. "Herndon," he said, calmly, "you and I have clashed once before, and the less you have to say to-night the better. I am in no mood for trifling, and this happens to be your wife's affair."

"Madam," and he lifted his hat, holding it in his hand, "I am bringing back the runaway, and she has now pledged herself to remain with you."

"I was not seeking her," she returned, icily. "I have no desire to cultivate the particular friends of Mr. Hampton."

"So I have understood, and consequently relinquish here and now all claims upon Miss Gillis. She has informed me of your flattering opinion regarding me, and I have indorsed it as being mainly true to life. Miss Gillis has been sufficiently shocked at thus discovering my real character, and now returns in penitence to be reared according to the admonitions of the Presbyterian faith. Do I state this fairly, Naida?"

"I have come back," she faltered, fingering the chain at her throat, "I have come back."

"Without Bob Hampton?"

The girl glanced uneasily toward him, but he stood motionless in the gloom.

"Yes—I—I suppose I must."

Hampton rested his hand softly upon her shoulder, his fingers trembling, although his voice remained coldly deliberate.

"I trust this is entirely satisfactory, Mrs. Herndon," he said.

"I can assure you I know absolutely nothing regarding her purpose of coming to me tonight. I realize quite clearly my own deficiencies, and pledge myself hereafter not to interfere with you in any way. You accept the trust, I believe?"

She gave utterance to a deep sigh of resignation. "It comes to me clearly as a Christian duty," she acknowledged, doubtfully, "and I suppose I must take up my cross; but—"

"But you have doubts," he interrupted. "Well, I have none, for I have greater faith in the girl, and—perhaps in God. Good-night, Naida."

He bowed above the hand the girl gave him in the darkness, and ever after she believed he bent lower, and pressed his lips upon it. The next moment the black night had closed him out, and she stood there, half frightened at she knew not what, on the threshold of her new life.

CHAPTER IX

AT THE OCCIDENTAL

Hampton slowly picked his way back through the darkness down the silent road, his only guide those dim yellow lights flickering in the distance. He walked soberly, his head bent slightly forward, absorbed in thought. Suddenly he paused, and swore savagely, his disgust at the situation bursting all bounds; yet when he arrived opposite the beam of light streaming invitingly forth from the windows of the first saloon, he was whistling softly, his head held erect, his cool eyes filled with reckless daring.

It was Saturday night, and the mining town was already alive. The one long, irregular street was jammed with constantly moving figures, the numerous saloons ablaze, the pianos sounding noisily, the shuffling of feet in the crowded dance-halls incessant. Fakers were everywhere industriously hawking their useless wares and entertaining the loitering crowds, while the roar of voices was continuous. Cowboys from the wide plains, miners from the hidden gulches, ragged, hopeful prospectors from the more distant mountains, teamsters, and half-naked Indians, commingled in the restless throng, passing and repassing from door to door, careless in dress, rough in manner, boisterous in language. Here and there amid this heterogeneous population of toilers and adventurers, would appear those attired in the more conventional garb of the East,—capitalists hunting new investments, or chance travellers seeking to discover a new thrill amid this strange life of the frontier. Everywhere, brazen and noisy, flitted women, bold of eye, painted of cheek, gaudy of raiment, making mock of their sacred womanhood. Riot reigned unchecked, while the quiet, sleepy town of the afternoon blossomed under the flickering lights into a saturnalia of unlicensed pleasure, wherein the wages of sin were death.

Hampton scarcely noted this marvellous change; to him it was no uncommon spectacle. He pushed his way through the noisy throng with eyes ever watchful for the faces. His every motion was that of a man who had fully decided upon his course. Through the widely opened doors of the Occidental streams of blue and red shirted men were constantly flowing in and out; a band played strenuously on the wide balcony overhead, while beside the entrance a loud-voiced "barker" proclaimed the many attractions within. Hampton swung up the broad wooden steps and entered the bar-room, which was crowded by jostling figures, the ever-moving mass as yet good-natured, for the night was young. At the lower end of the long, sloppy bar he stopped for a moment to nod to the fellow behind.

"Anything going on to-night worth while, Jim?" he questioned, quietly.

"Rather stiff game, they tell me, just started in the back room," was the genial reply. "Two Eastern suckers, with Red Slavin sitting in."

The gambler passed on, pushing rather unceremoniously through the throng of perspiring humanity. He appeared out of place amid the rough element jostling him, and more than one glanced at him curiously, a few swearing as he elbowed them aside. Scarcely noticing this, he drew a cigar from his pocket, and stuck it unlighted between his teeth. The large front room upstairs was ablaze with lights, every game in full operation and surrounded by crowds of devotees. Tobacco smoke in clouds circled to the low ceiling, and many of the players were noisy and profane, while the various calls of faro, roulette, keno, and high-ball added to the confusion and to the din of shuffling feet and excited exclamations. Hampton glanced about superciliously, shrugging his shoulders in open contempt—all this was far too coarse, too small, to awaken his interest. He observed the various faces at the tables—a habit one naturally forms who has desperate enemies in plenty—and then walked directly toward the rear of the room. A thick, dingy red curtain hung there; he held back its heavy folds and stepped within the smaller apartment beyond.

Three men sat at the single table, cards in hand, and Hampton involuntarily whistled softly behind his teeth at the first glimpse of the money openly displayed before them. This was apparently not so bad for a starter, and his waning interest revived. A red-bearded giant, sitting so as to face the doorway, glanced up quickly at his entrance, his coarse mouth instantly taking on the semblance of a smile.

"Ah, Bob," he exclaimed, with an evident effort at cordiality; "been wondering if you wouldn't show up before the night was over. You're the very fellow to make this a four-handed affair, provided you carry sufficient stuff."

Hampton came easily forward into the full glow of the swinging oil lamp, his manner coolly deliberate, his face expressionless. "I feel no desire to intrude," he explained, quietly, watching the uplifted faces. "I believe I have never before met these gentlemen."

Slavin laughed, his great white fingers drumming the table.

"It is an acquaintance easily made," he said, "provided one can afford to trot in their class, for it is money that talks at this table to-night. Mr. Hampton, permit me to present Judge Hawes, of Denver, and Mr. Edgar Willis, president of the T. P. & R. I have no idea what they are doing in this hell-hole of a town, but they are dead-game sports, and I have been trying my best to amuse them while they're here."

Hampton bowed, instantly recognizing the names.

"Glad to assist," he murmured, sinking into a vacant chair. "What limit?"

"We have had no occasion to discuss that matter as yet," volunteered Hawes, sneeringly. "However, if you have scruples we might settle upon something within reason."

Hampton ran the undealt pack carelessly through his fingers, his lips smiling pleasantly. "Oh, never mind, if it chances to go above my pile I'll drop out. Meanwhile, I hardly believe there is any cause for you to be modest on my account."

The play opened quietly and with some restraint, the faces of the men remaining impassive, their watchful glances evidencing nothing either of success or failure. Hampton played with extreme caution for some time, his eyes studying keenly the others about the table, seeking some deeper understanding of the nature of his opponents, their strong and weak points, and whether or not there existed any prior arrangement between them. He was there for a purpose, a clearly defined purpose, and he felt no inclination to accept unnecessary chances with the fickle Goddess of Fortune. To one trained in the calm observation of small things, and long accustomed to weigh his adversaries with care, it was not extremely difficult to class the two strangers, and Hampton smiled softly on observing the size of the rolls rather ostentatiously exhibited by them. He felt that his lines had fallen in pleasant places, and looked forward with serene confidence to the enjoyment of a royal game, provided only he exercised sufficient patience and the other gentlemen possessed the requisite nerve. His satisfaction was in noways lessened by the sound of their voices, when incautiously raised in anger over some unfortunate play. He immediately recognized them as the identical individuals who had loudly and vainly protested over his occupancy of the best rooms at the hotel. He chuckled grimly.

But what bothered him particularly was Slavin. The cool gray eyes, glancing with such apparent negligence across the cards in his hands, noted every slight movement of the red-bearded gambler, in expectation of detecting some sign of trickery, or some evidence that he had been selected by this precious trio for the purpose of easy plucking. Knavery was Slavin's style, but apparently he was now playing a straight game, no doubt realizing clearly, behind his impassive mask of a face, the utter futility of seeking to outwit one of Hampton's enviable reputation.

It was, unquestionably, a fairly fought four-handed battle, and at last, thoroughly convinced of this, Hampton settled quietly down, prepared to play out his game. The hours rolled on unnoted, the men tireless, their faces immovable, the cards dealt silently. The stakes grew steadily larger, and curious visitors, hearing vague rumors without, ventured in, to stand behind the chairs of the absorbed players and look on. Now and then a startled exclamation evidenced the depth of their interest and excitement, but at the table no one spoke above a strained whisper, and no eye ventured to wander from the board. Several times drinks were served, but Hampton contented himself with a gulp of water, always gripping an unlighted cigar between his teeth. He was playing now with apparent recklessness, never hesitating over a card, his eye as watchful as that of a hawk, his betting quick, confident, audacious. The contagion of his spirit seemed to affect the others, to force them into desperate wagers, and thrill the lookers-on. The perspiration was beading Slavin's forehead, and now and then an oath burst unrestrained from his hairy lips. Hawes and Willis sat white-faced, bent forward anxiously over the table, their fingers shaking as they handled the fateful cards, but Hampton played without perceptible tremor, his utterances few and monosyllabic, his calm face betraying not the faintest emotion.

And he was steadily winning. Occasionally some other hand drew in the growing stock of gold and bank notes, but not often enough to offset those continued gains that began to heap up in such an alluring pile upon his portion of the table. The watchers began to observe this, and gathered more closely about his chair, fascinated by the luck with which the cards came floating into his hands, the cool judgment of his critical plays, the reckless abandon with which he forced success. The little room was foul with tobacco smoke and electric with ill-repressed excitement, yet he played on imperturbably, apparently hearing nothing, seeing nothing, his entire personality concentrated on his play. Suddenly he forced the fight to a finish. The opportunity came in a jack-pot which Hawes had opened. The betting began with a cool thousand. Then Hampton's turn came. Without drawing, his cards yet lying face downward before him on the board, his calm features as immovable as the Sphinx, he quietly pushed his whole accumulated pile to the centre, named the sum, and leaned back in his chair, his eyes cold, impassive. Hawes threw down his hand, wiping his streaming face with his handkerchief; Willis counted his remaining roll, hesitated, looked again at the faces of his cards, flung aside two, drawing to fill, and called loudly for a show-down, his eyes protruding. Slavin, cursing fiercely under his red beard, having drawn one card, his perplexed face instantly brightening as he glanced at it, went back into his hip pocket for every cent he had, and added his profane demand for a chance at the money.

A fortune rested on the table, a fortune the ownership of which was to be decided in a single moment, and by the movement of a hand. The crowd swayed eagerly forward, their heads craned over to see more clearly, their breathing hushed. Willis was gasping, his whole body quivering; Slavin was watching Hampton's hands as a cat does a mouse, his thick lips parted, his fingers twitching nervously. The latter smiled grimly, his motions deliberate, his eyes never wavering. Slowly, one by one, he turned up his cards, never even deigning to glance downward, his entire manner that of unstudied indifference. One—two—three. Willis uttered a snarl like a stricken wild beast, and sank back in his chair, his eyes closed, his cheeks ghastly. Four. Slavin brought down his great clenched fist with a crash on the table, a string of oaths bursting unrestrained from his lips. Five. Hampton, never stirring a muscle, sat there like a statue, watching. His right hand kept hidden beneath the table, with his left he quietly drew in the stack of bills and coin, pushing the stuff heedlessly into the side pocket of his coat, his gaze never once wandering from those stricken faces fronting him. Then he softly pushed back his chair and stood erect. Willis never moved, but Slavin rose unsteadily to his feet, gripping the table fiercely with both hands.

"Gentlemen," said Hampton, gravely, his clear voice sounding like the sudden peal of a bell, "I can only thank you for your courtesy in this matter, and bid you all good-night. However, before I go it may be of some interest for me to say that I have played my last game."

Somebody laughed sarcastically, a harsh, hateful laugh. The speaker whirled, took one step forward; there was the flash of an extended arm, a dull crunch, and Red Slavin went crashing backward against the wall. As he gazed up, dazed and bewildered, from the floor, the lights glimmered along a blue-steel barrel.

"Not a move, you red brute," and Hampton spurned him contemptuously with his heel. "This is no variety show, and your laughter was in poor taste. However, if you feel particularly hilarious to-night I'll give you another chance. I said this was my last game; I'll repeat it—*this was my last game*! Now, damn you! if you feel like it, laugh!"

He swept the circle of excited faces, his eyes glowing like two diamonds, his thin lips compressed into a single straight line.

"Mr. Slavin appears to have lost his previous sense of humor," he remarked, calmly. "I will now make my statement for the third time—*this was my last game*. Perhaps some of you gentlemen also may discover this to be amusing."

The heavy, strained breathing of the motionless crowd was his only answer, and a half smile of bitter contempt curled Hampton's lips, as he swept over them a last defiant glance.

"Not quite so humorous as it seemed to be at first, I reckon," he commented, dryly. "Slavin," and he prodded the red giant once more with his foot, "I'm going out; if you make any attempt to leave this room within the next five minutes I'll kill you in your tracks, as I would a mad dog. You stacked cards twice to-night, but the last time I beat you fairly at your own game."

He held aside the heavy curtains with his left hand and backed slowly out facing them, the deadly revolver shining ominously in the other. Not a man moved: Slavin glowered at him from the floor, an impotent curse upon his lips. Then the red drapery fell.

While the shadows of the long night still hung over the valley, Naida, tossing restlessly upon her strange bed within the humble yellow house at the fork of the trails, was aroused to wakefulness by the pounding of a horse's hoofs on the plank bridge spanning the creek. She drew aside the curtain and looked out, shading her eyes to see clearer through the poor glass. All she perceived was a somewhat deeper smudge when the rider swept rapidly past, horse and man a shapeless shadow. Three hours later she awoke again, this time to the full glare of day, and to the remembrance that she was now facing a new life. As she lay there thinking, her eyes troubled but tearless, far away on the sun-kissed uplands Hampton was spurring forward his horse, already beginning to exhibit signs of weariness. Bent slightly over the saddle pommel, his eyes upon these snow-capped peaks still showing blurred and distant, he rode steadily on, the only moving object amid all that wide, desolate landscape.

PART II

WHAT OCCURRED IN GLENCAID

CHAPTER I

THE ARRIVAL OF MISS SPENCER

There was a considerable period when events of importance in Glencaid's history were viewed against the background of the opening of its first school. This was not entirely on account of the deep interest manifested in the cause of higher education by the residents, but owing rather to the personality of the pioneer school-teacher, and the deep, abiding impress which she made upon the community.

Miss Phoebe Spencer came direct to Glencaid from the far East, her starting-point some little junction place back in Vermont, although she proudly named Boston as her home, having once visited in that metropolis for three delicious weeks. She was of an ardent, impressionable nature. Her mind was nurtured upon Eastern conceptions of our common country, her imagination aglow with weird tales of the frontier, and her bright eyes perceived the vivid coloring of romance in each prosaic object west of the tawny Missouri. All appeared so different from that established life to which she had grown accustomed,—the people, the country, the picturesque language,—while her brain so teemed with lurid pictures of border experiences and heroes as to reveal romantic possibilities everywhere. The vast, mysterious West, with its seemingly boundless prairies, grand, solemn mountains, and frankly spoken men peculiarly attired and everywhere bearing the inevitable "gun," was to her a newly discovered world. She could scarcely comprehend its reality. As the apparently illimitable plains, barren, desolate, awe-inspiring, rolled away behind, mile after mile, like a vast sea, and left a measureless expanse of grim desert between her and the old life, her unfettered imagination seemed to expand with the fathomless blue of the Western sky. As her eager eyes traced the serrated peaks of a snow-clad mountain range, her heart throbbed with anticipation of wonders yet to come. Homesickness was a thing undreamed of; her active brain responded to each new impression.

She sat comfortably ensconced in the back seat of the old, battered red coach, surrounded by cushions for protection from continual jouncing, as the Jehu in charge urged his restive mules down the desolate valley of the Bear Water. Her cheeks were flushed, her wide-open eyes filled with questioning, her pale fluffy hair frolicking with the breeze, as pretty a picture of young womanhood as any one could wish to see. Nor was she unaware of this fact. During the final stage other long journey she had found two congenial souls, sufficiently picturesque to harmonize with her ideas of wild Western romance.

These two men were lolling in the less comfortable seat opposite, secretly longing for a quiet smoke outside, yet neither willing to desert this Eastern divinity to his rival. The big fellow, his arm run carelessly through the leather sling, his bare head projecting half out of the open window, was Jack Moffat, half-owner of the "Golden Rule," and enjoying a well-earned reputation as the most ornate and artistic liar in the Territory. For two hours he had been exercising his talent to the full, and merely paused now in search of some fresh inspiration, holding in supreme and silent contempt the rather feeble imitations of his less-gifted companion. It is also just to add that Mr. Moffat personally formed an ideal accompaniment to his vivid narrations of adventure, and he was fully aware of the fact that Miss Spencer's appreciative eyes wandered frequently in his direction, noting his tanned cheeks, his long silky mustache, the somewhat melancholy gleam of his dark eyes—hiding beyond doubt some mystery of the past, the nature of which was yet to be revealed. Mr. Moffat, always strong along this line of feminine sympathy, felt newly inspired by these evidences of interest in his tales, and by something in Miss Spencer's face which bespoke admiration.

The fly in the ointment of this long day's ride, the third party, whose undesirable presence and personal knowledge of Mr. Moffat's past career rather seriously interfered with the latter's flights of imagination, was William McNeil, foreman of the "Bar V" ranch over on Sinsiniwa Creek. McNeil was not much of a talker, having an impediment in his speech, and being a trifle bashful in the presence of a lady. But he caught the eye,—a slenderly built, reckless fellow, smoothly shaven, with a strong chin and bright laughing eyes,—and as he lolled carelessly back in his bearskin "chaps" and wide-brimmed sombrero, occasionally throwing in some cool, insinuating comment regarding Moffat's recitals, the latter experienced a strong inclination to heave him overboard. The slight hardening of McNeil's eyes at such moments had thus far served, however, as sufficient restraint, while the unobservant Miss Spencer, unaware of the silent duel thus being conducted in her very presence, divided her undis-guised admiration, playing havoc with the susceptible heart of each, and all unconsciously laying the foundations for future trouble.

"Why, how truly remarkable!" she exclaimed, her cheeks glowing. "It's all so different from the East; heroism seems to be in the very air of this country, and your adventure was so very unusual. Don't you think so, Mr. McNeil?"

The silent foreman hitched himself suddenly upright, his face unusually solemn. "Why—eh—yes, miss—you might—eh—say that. He," with a flip of his hand toward the other, "eh—reminds me—of—eh—an old friend."

"Indeed? How extremely interesting!" eagerly scenting a new story. "Please tell me who it was, Mr. McNeil."

"Oh—eh—knew him when I was a boy—eh—Munchausen."

Mr. Moffat drew in his head violently, with an exclamation nearly profane, yet before he could speak Miss Spencer intervened.

"Munchausen! Why, Mr. McNeil, you surely do not intend to question the truth of Mr. Moffat's narrative?"

The foreman's eyes twinkled humorously, but the lines of his face remained calmly impassive. "My—eh—reference," he explained, gravely, "was—eh—entirely to the—eh—local color, the—eh—expert touches."

"Oh!"

"Yes, miss. It's—eh—bad taste out here to—eh—doubt anybody's word—eh—publicly."

Moffat stirred uneasily, his hand flung behind him, but McNeil was gazing into the lady's fair face, apparently unconscious of any other presence.

"But all this time you have not favored me with any of your own adventures, Mr. McNeil. I am very sure you must have had hundreds out on these wide plains."

The somewhat embarrassed foreman shook his head discouragingly.

"Oh, but I just know you have, only you are so modest about recounting them. Now, that scar just under your hair—really it is not at all unbecoming—surely that reveals a story. Was it caused by an Indian arrow?"

McNeil crossed his legs, and wiped his damp forehead with the back of his hand. "Hoof of a damn pack-mule," he explained, forgetting himself. "The—eh—cuss lifted me ten feet."

Moffat laughed hoarsely, but as the foreman straightened up quickly, the amazed girl joined happily in, and his own face instantly exhibited the contagion.

"Ain't much—eh—ever happens out on a ranch," he said, doubtfully, "except dodgin' steers, and—eh—bustin' broncoes."

"Your blame mule story," broke in Moffat, who had at last discovered his inspiration, "reminds me of a curious little incident occurring last year just across the divide. I don't recall ever telling it before, but it may interest you, Miss Spencer, as illustrative of one phase of life in this country. A party of us were out after bear, and one night when I chanced to be left all alone in camp, I didn't dare fall asleep and leave everything unguarded, as the Indians were all around as thick as leaves on a tree. So I decided to sit up in front of the tent on watch. Along about midnight, I suppose, I dropped off into a doze, for the first thing I heard was the hee-haw of a mule right in my ear. It sounded like a clap of thunder, and I jumped up, coming slap-bang against the brute's nose so blamed hard it knocked me flat; and then, when I fairly got my eyes open, I saw five Sioux Indians creeping along through the moonlight, heading right toward our pony herd. I tell you things looked mighty skittish for me just then, but what do you suppose I did with 'em?"

"Eh—eat 'em, likely," suggested McNeil, thoughtfully, "fried with plenty of—eh—salt; heard they were—eh—good that way."

Mr. Moffat half rose to his feet.

"You damn—"

"O Mr. McNeil, how perfectly ridiculous!" chimed in Miss Spencer. "Please do go on, Mr. Moffat; it is so exceedingly interesting."

The incensed narrator sank reluctantly back into his seat, his eyes yet glowing angrily. "Well, I crept carefully along a little gully until I got where them Indians were just exactly opposite me in a direct line. I had an awful heavy gun, carrying a slug of lead near as big as your fist. Had it fixed up specially fer grizzlies. The fellow creepin' along next me was a tremendous big buck; he looked like a plum giant in that moonlight, and I'd just succeeded in drawin' a bead on him when a draught of air from up the gully strikin' across the back of my neck made me sneeze, and that buck turned round and saw me. You wouldn't hardly believe what happened."

"Whole—eh—bunch drop dead from fright?" asked McNeil, solicitously.

Moffat glared at him savagely, his lips moving, but emitting no sound.

"Oh, please don't mind," urged his fair listener, her flushed cheeks betraying her interest. "He is so full of his fun. What did follow?"

The story-teller swallowed something in his throat, his gaze still on his persecutor. "No, sir," he continued, hoarsely, "them bucks jumped to their feet with the most awful yells I ever heard, and made a rush toward where I was standing. They was exactly in a line, and I let drive at that first buck, and blame me if that slug didn't go plum through three of 'em, and knock down the fourth. You can roast me alive if that ain't a fact! The fifth one got away, but I roped the wounded fellow, and was a-sittin' on him when the rest of the party got back to camp. Jim Healy was along, and he'll tell you the same story."

There was a breathless silence, during which McNeil spat meditatively out of the window.

"Save any—eh—locks of their hair?" he questioned, anxiously.

"Oh, please don't tell me anything about that!" interrupted Miss Spencer, nervously. "The whites don't scalp, do they?"

"Not generally, miss, but I—eh—didn't just know what Mr. Moffat's—eh—custom was."

The latter gentleman had his head craned out of the window once more, in an apparent determination to ignore all such frivolous remarks. Suddenly he pointed directly ahead.

"There's Glencaid now, Miss Spencer," he said, cheerfully, glad enough of an opportunity to change the topic of conversation. "That's the spire of the new Presbyterian church sticking up above the ridge."

"Oh, indeed! How glad I am to be here safe at last!"

"How—eh—did you happen to—eh—recognize the church?" asked McNeil with evident admiration. "You—eh —can't see it from the saloon."

Moffat disdained reply, and the lurching stage rolled rapidly down the valley, the mules now lashed into a wild gallop to the noisy accompaniment of the driver's whip.

The hoofs clattered across the narrow bridge, and, with a sudden swing, all came to a sharp stand, amid a cloud of dust before a naked yellow house.

"Here's where you get out, miss," announced the Jehu, leaning down from his seat to peer within. "This yere is the Herndon shebang."

The gentlemen inside assisted Miss Spencer to descend in safety to the weed-bordered walk, where she stood shaking her ruffled plumage into shape, and giving directions regarding her luggage. Then the two gentlemen emerged, Moffat bearing a grip-case, a bandbox, and a basket, while McNeil supported a shawl-strap and a small trunk. Thus decorated they meekly followed her lead up the narrow path toward the front door. The latter opened suddenly, and Mrs. Herndon bounced forth with vociferous welcome.

"Why, Phoebe Spencer, and have you really come! I didn't expect you'd get along before next week. Oh, this seems too nice to see you again; almost as good as going home to Vermont. You must be completely tired out."

"Dear Aunt Lydia; of course I'm glad to be here. But I'm not in the least tired. I've had such a delightful trip." She glanced around smilingly upon her perspiring cavaliers. "Oh, put those things down, gentlemen—anywhere there on the grass; they can be carried in later. It was so kind of you both."

"Hey, there!" sang out the driver, growing impatient, "if you two gents are aimin' to go down town with this outfit, you'd better be pilin' in lively, fer I can't stay here all day."

Moffat glanced furtively aside at McNeil, only to discover that individual quietly seated on the trunk. He promptly dropped his own grip.

"Drive on with your butcher's cart," he called out spitefully. "I reckon it's no special honor to ride to town."

The pleasantly smiling young woman glanced from one to the other, her eyes fairly dancing, as the lumbering coach disappeared through the red dust.

"How very nice of you to remain," she exclaimed. "Aunt Lydia, I am so anxious for you to meet my friends, Mr. Moffat and Mr. McNeil. They have been so thoughtful and entertaining all the way up the Bear Water, and they explained so many things that I did not understand."

She swept impulsively down toward them, both hands extended, the bright glances of her eyes bestowed impartially.

"I cannot invite you to come into the house now," she exclaimed, sweetly, "for I am almost like a stranger here myself, but I do hope you will both of you call. I shall be so very lonely at first, and you are my earliest acquaintances. You will promise, won't you?"

McNeil bowed, painfully clearing his throat, but Moffat succeeded in expressing his pleasure with a well-rounded sentence.

"I felt sure you would. But now I must really say good-bye for this time, and go in with Aunt Lydia. I know I must be getting horribly burned out here in this hot sun. I shall always be so grateful to you both."

The two radiant knights walked together toward the road, neither uttering a word. McNeil whistled carelessly, and Moffat gazed intently at the distant hills. Just beyond the gate, and without so much as glancing toward his companion, the latter turned and strode up one of the numerous diverging trails. McNeil halted and stared after him in surprise.

"Ain't you—eh—goin' on down town?"

"I reckon not. Take a look at my mine first."

McNeil chuckled. "You—eh—better be careful goin' up that—eh—gully," he volunteered, soberly, "the—eh—ghosts of them four—eh—Injuns might—eh—haunt ye!"

Moffat wheeled about as if he had been shot in the back. "You blathering, mutton-headed cowherd!" he yelled, savagely.

But McNeil was already nearly out of hearing.

CHAPTER II

BECOMING ACQUAINTED

Once within the cool shadows of the livingroom, Mrs. Herndon again bethought herself to kiss her niece in a fresh glow of welcome, while the latter sank into a convenient rocker and began enthusiastically expressing her unbounded enjoyment of the West, and of the impressions gathered during her journey. Suddenly the elder woman glanced about and exclaimed, laughingly, "Why, I had completely forgotten. You have not yet met your room-mate. Come out here, Naida; this is my niece, Phoebe Spencer."

The girl thus addressed advanced, a slender, graceful figure dressed in white, and extended her hand shyly. Miss Spencer clasped it warmly, her eyes upon the flushed, winsome face.

"And is this Naida Gillis!" she cried. "I am so delighted that you are still here, and that we are to be together. Aunt Lydia has written so much about you that I feel as If we must have known each other for years. Why, how pretty you are!"

Naida's cheeks were burning, and her eyes fell, but she had never yet succeeded in conquering the blunt independence of her speech. "Nobody else ever says so," she said, uneasily. "Perhaps it's the light."

Miss Spencer turned her about so as to face the window. "Well, you are," she announced, decisively. "I guess I know; you've got magnificent hair, and your eyes are perfectly wonderful. You just don't fix yourself up right; Aunt Lydia never did have any taste in such things, but I'll make a new girl out of you. Let's go upstairs; I'm simply dying to see our room, and get some of my dresses unpacked. They must look perfect frights by this time."

They came down perhaps an hour later, hand in hand, and chattering like old friends. The shades of early evening were already falling across the valley. Herndon had returned home from his day's work, and had brought with him the Rev. Howard Wynkoop for supper. Miss Spencer viewed the young man with approval, and immediately became more than usually vivacious in recounting the incidents of her long journey, together with her early impressions of the Western country. Mr. Wynkoop responded with an interest far from being assumed.

"I have found it all so strange, so unique, Mr. Wynkoop," she explained. "The country is like a new world to me, and the people do not seem at all like those of the East. They lead such a wild, untrammelled life. Everything about seems to exhale the spirit of romance; don't you find it so?"

He smiled at her enthusiasm, his glance of undisguised admiration on her face. "I certainly recall some such earlier conception," he admitted. "Those just arriving from the environment of an older civilization perceive merely the picturesque elements; but my later experiences have been decidedly prosaic."

"Why, Mr. Wynkoop! how could they be? Your work is heroic. I cannot conceive how any minister of the Cross, having within him any of the old apostolic fervor, can consent to spend his days amid the dreary commonplaces of those old, dead Eastern churches. You, nobly battling on the frontier, are the true modern Crusaders, the Knights of the Grail. Here you are ever in the very forefront of the battle against sin, associated with the Argonauts, impressing your faith upon the bold, virile spirits of the age. It is perfectly grand! Why the very men I meet seem to yield me a broader conception of life and duty; they are so brave, so modest, so active. Is—is Mr. Moffat a member of your church?"

The minister cleared his throat, his cheeks reddening. "Mr. Moffat? Ah, no; not exactly. Do you mean the mine-owner, Jack Moffat?"

"Yes, I think so; he told me he owned a mine—the Golden Rule the name was; the very choice in words would seem, to indicate his religious nature. He's such a pleasant, intelligent man. There is a look in his eyes as though he sorrowed over something. I was in hopes you knew what it was, and I am very sure he would welcome your ministrations. You have the only church in Glencaid, I understand, and I wonder greatly he has never joined you. But perhaps he may be prejudiced against your denomination. There is so much narrowness in religion. Now, I am an Episcopalian myself, but I do not mean to permit that to interfere in any way with my church work out here. I wonder if Mr. Moffat can be an Episcopalian. If he is, I am just going to show him that it is clearly his duty to assist in any Christian service. Isn't that the true, liberal, Western spirit, Mr. Wynkoop?"

"It most assuredly should be," said the young pastor.

"I left every prejudice east of the Missouri," she declared, laughingly, "every one, social and religious. I'm going to be a true Westerner, from the top of my head to the toe of my shoe. Is Mr. McNeil in your church?"

The minister hesitated. "I really do not recall the name," he confessed at last, reluctantly. "I scarcely think I can have ever met the gentleman."

"Oh, you ought to; he is so intensely original, and his face is full of character. He reminds me of some old paladin of the Middle Ages. You would be interested in him at once. He is the foreman of the 'Bar V' ranch, somewhere near here."

"Do you mean Billy McNeil, over on Sinsiniwa Creek?" broke in Herndon.

"I think quite likely, uncle; wouldn't he make a splendid addition to Mr. Wynkoop's church?"

Herndon choked, his entire body shaking with ill-suppressed enjoyment. "I should imagine yes," he admitted finally. "Billy McNeil—oh, Lord! There's certainly a fine opening for you to do some missionary work, Phoebe."

"Well, and I'm going to," announced the young lady, firmly. "I guess I can read men's characters, and I know all Mr. McNeil needs is to have some one show an interest in him. Have you a large church, Mr. Wynkoop?"

"Not large if judged from an Eastern standpoint," he confessed, with some regret. "Our present membership is composed of eight women and three men, but the congregational attendance is quite good, and constantly increasing."

"Only eight women and three men!" breathlessly. "And you have been laboring upon this field for five years! How could it be so small?"

Wynkoop pushed back his chair, anxious to redeem himself in the estimation of this fair stranger.

"Miss Spencer," he explained, "it is perhaps hardly strange that you should misapprehend the peculiar conditions under which religious labor is conducted in the West. You will undoubtedly understand all this better presently. My parish comprises this entire mining region, and I am upon horseback among the foothills and up in the ranges for fully a third of my time. The spirit of the mining population, as well as of the cattlemen, while not actually hostile, is one of indifference to religious thought. They care nothing whatever for it in the abstract, and have no use for any minister, unless it may be to marry their children or bury their dead. I am hence obliged to meet with them merely as man to man, and thus slowly win their confidence before I dare even approach a religious topic. For three long years I worked here without even a church organization or a building; and apparently without the faintest encouragement. Now that we have a nucleus gathered, a comfortable building erected and paid for, with an increasing congregation, I begin to feel that those seemingly barren five years were not without spiritual value."

She quickly extended her hands. "Oh, it is so heroic, so self-sacrificing! No doubt I was hasty and wrong. But I have always been accustomed to so much larger churches. I am going to help you, Mr. Wynkoop, in every way I possibly can—I shall certainly speak to both Mr. Moffat and Mr. McNeil the very first opportunity. I feel almost sure that they will join."

The unavoidable exigencies of a choir practice compelled Mr. Wynkoop to retire early, nor was it yet late when the more intimate family circle also dissolved, and the two girls discovered themselves alone. Naida drew down the shades and lit the lamp. Miss Spencer slowly divested herself of her outer dress, replacing it with a light wrapper, encased her feet snugly in comfortable slippers, and proceeded to let down her flossy hair in gleaming waves across her shoulders. Naida's dark eyes bespoke plainly her admiration, and Miss Spencer shook back her hair somewhat coquettishly.

"Do you think I look nice?" she questioned, smilingly.

"You bet I do. Your hair is just beautiful, Miss Spencer."

The other permitted the soft strands to slip slowly between her white fingers. "You should never say 'you bet,' Naida. Such language is not at all lady-like. I am going to call you Naida, and you must call me Phoebe. People use their given names almost entirely out here in the West, don't they?"

"I never have had much training in being a lady," the young girl explained, reddening, "but I can learn. Yes, I reckon they do mostly use the first names out here."

"Please don't say 'I reckon,' either; it has such a vulgar sound. What is his given name?"

"Whose?"

"Why, I was thinking of Mr. Wynkoop."

"Howard; I saw it written in some books he loaned me. But the people here never address him in that way."

"No, I suppose not, only I thought I should like to know what it was."

There was a considerable pause; then the speaker asked, calmly, "Is he married?"

"Mr. Wynkoop? Why, of course not; he doesn't care for women in that way at all."

Miss Spencer bound her hair carefully with a bright ribbon. "Maybe he might, though, some time. All men do."

She sat down in the low rocker, her feet comfortably crossed. "Do you know, Naida dear, it is simply wonderful to me just to remember what you have been through, and it was so beautifully romantic—everybody killed except you and that man, and then he saved your life. It's such a pity he was so miserable a creature."

"He wasn't!" Naida exclaimed, in sudden, indignant passion. "He was perfectly splendid."

"Aunt Lydia didn't think so. She wrote he was a common gambler,—a low, rough man."

"Well, he did gamble; nearly everybody does out here. And sometimes I suppose he had to fight, but he wasn't truly bad."

Miss Spencer's eyes evinced a growing interest.

"Was he real nice-looking?" she asked.

Naida's voice faltered. "Ye—es," she said. "I thought so. He—he looked like he was a man."

"How old are you, Naida?"

"Nearly eighteen."

Miss Spencer leaned impulsively forward, and clasped the other's hands, her whole soul responding to this suggestion of a possible romance, a vision of blighted hearts. "Why, it is perfectly delightful," she exclaimed. "I had no idea it was so serious, and really I don't in the least blame you. You love him, don't you, Naida?"

The girl flashed a shy look into the beaming, inquisitive face. "I don't know," she confessed, soberly. "I have not even seen him for such a long time; but—but, I guess, he is more to me than any one else—"

"Not seen him? Do you mean to say Mr. Hampton is not here in Glencaid? Why, I am so sorry; I was hoping to meet him."

"He went away the same night I came here to live."

"And you never even hear from him?"

Naida hesitated, but the frankly displayed interest of the other won her complete girlish confidence. "Not directly, but Mr. Herndon receives money from him for me. He doesn't let your aunt know anything about it, because she got angry and refused to accept any pay from him. He is somewhere over yonder in the Black Range."

Miss Spencer shook back her hair with a merry laugh, and clasped her hands. "Why, it is just the most delightful situation I ever heard about. He is just certain to come back after you, Naida. I wouldn't miss being here for anything."

They were still sitting there, when the notes of a softly touched guitar stole in through the open window. Both glanced about in surprise, but Miss Spencer was first to recover speech.

"A serenade! Did you ever!" she whispered. "Do you suppose it can be he?" She extinguished the lamp and knelt upon the floor, peering eagerly forth into the brilliant moonlight. "Why, Naida, what do you think? It's Mr. Moffat. How beautifully he plays!"

Randall Parrish

Naida, her face pressed against the other window, gave vent to a single note of half-suppressed laughter. "There's going to be something happening," she exclaimed. "Oh, Miss Spencer, come here quick—some one is going to turn on the hydraulic."

Miss Spencer knelt beside her. Moffat was still plainly visible, his pale face upturned in the moonlight, his long silky mustaches slightly stirred by the soft air, his fingers touching the strings; but back in the shadows of the bushes was seen another figure, apparently engaged upon some task with feverish eagerness. To Miss Spencer all was mystery.

"What is it?" she anxiously questioned.

"The hydraulic," whispered the other. "There's a big lake up in the hills, and they've piped the water down here. It's got a force like a cannon, and that fellow—I don't know whether it is Herndon or not—is screwing on the hose connection. I bet your Mr. Moffat gets a shock!"

"It's a perfect shame, an outrage! I'm going to tell him."

Naida caught her sleeve firmly, her eyes full of laughter. "Oh, please don't, Miss Spencer. It will be such fun. Let's see where it hits him!"

For one single instant the lady yielded, and in it all opportunity for warning fled. There was a sharp sizzling, which caused Moffat to suspend his serenade; then something struck him,—it must have been fairly in the middle, for he shut up like a jack-knife, and went crashing backwards with an agonized howl. There was a gleam of shining water, something black squirming among the weeds, a yell, a volley of half-choked profanity, and a fleeing figure, apparently pursued by a huge snake. Naida shook with laughter, clinging with both hands to the sill, but Miss Spencer was plainly shocked.

"Oh, did you hear what—what he said?" she asked. "Wasn't it awful?"

The younger nodded, unable as yet to command her voice. "I—I don't believe he is an Episcopalian; do you?"

"I don't know. I imagine that might have made even a Methodist swear."

The puckers began to show about the disapproving mouth, under the contagion of the other's merriment. "Wasn't it perfectly ridiculous? But he did play beautifully, and it was so very nice of him to come my first night here. Do you suppose that was Mr. Herndon?"

Naida shook her head doubtfully. "He looked taller, but I couldn't really tell. He's gone now, and the water is turned off."

They lit the lamp once more, discussing the scene just witnessed, while Miss Spencer, standing before the narrow mirror, prepared her hair for the night. Suddenly some object struck the lowered window shade and dropped upon the floor. Naida picked it up.

"A letter," she announced, "for Miss Phoebe Spencer."

"For me? What can it be? Why, Naida, it is poetry! Listen:

Sweetest flower from off the Eastern hills,
So lily-like and fair;
Your very presence stirs and thrills
Our buoyant Western air;

The plains grow lovelier in their span,
The skies above more blue,
While the heart of Nature and of man
Beats quick response for you.

"Oh, isn't that simply beautiful? And it is signed 'Willie'—why, that must be Mr. McNeil."

"I reckon he copied it out of some book," said Naida.

"Oh, I know he didn't. It possesses such a touch of originality. And his eyes, Naida! They have that deep poetical glow!"

The light was finally extinguished; the silvery moonlight streamed across the foot of the bed, and the regular breathing of the girls evidenced slumber.

CHAPTER III

UNDER ORDERS

Many an unexpected event has resulted from the formal, concise orders issued by the War Department. Cupid in the disguise of Mars has thus frequently toyed with the fate of men, sending many a gallant soldier forward, all unsuspecting, into a battle of the heart.

It was no pleasant assignment to duty which greeted First Lieutenant Donald Brant, commanding Troop N, Seventh Cavalry, when that regiment came once more within the environs of civilization, from its summer exercises in the field. Bethune had developed into a somewhat important post, socially as well as from a strictly military standpoint, and numerous indeed were the attractions offered there to any young officer whose duty called him to serve the colors on those bleak Dakota prairies. Brant frowned at the innocent words, reading them over again with gloomy eyes and an exclamation of unmitigated disgust, yet there was no escaping their plain meaning. Trouble was undoubtedly brewing among the Sioux, trouble in which the Cheyennes, and probably others also, were becoming involved. Every soldier patrolling that long northern border recognized the approach of some dire development, some early coup of savagery. Restlessness pervaded the Indian country;

recalcitrant bands roamed the "badlands"; dissatisfied young warriors disappeared from the reservation limits and failed to return; while friendly scouts told strange tales of weird dances amid the brown Dakota hills. Uneasiness, the spirit of suspected peril, hung like a pall over the plains; yet none could safely predict where the blow might first descend.

Brant was not blind to all this, nor to the necessity of having in readiness selected bodies of seasoned troops, yet it was not in soldier nature to refrain from grumbling when the earliest detail chanced to fall to him. But orders were orders in that country, and although he crushed the innocent paper passionately beneath his heel, five hours later he was in saddle, riding steadily westward, his depleted troop of horsemen clattering at his heels. Up the valley of the Bear Water, slightly above Glencaid,—far enough beyond the saloon radius to protect his men from possible corruption, yet within easy reach of the military telegraph,—they made camp in the early morning upon a wooded terrace overlooking the stage road, and settled quietly down as one of those numerous posts with which the army chiefs sought to hem in the dissatisfied redmen, and learn early the extent of their hostile plans.

Brant was now in a humor considerably happier than when he first rode forth from Bethune. A natural soldier, sincerely ambitious in his profession, anything approximating to active service instantly aroused his interest, while his mind was ever inclined to respond with enthusiasm to the fascination of the plains and the hills across which their march had extended. Somewhere along that journey he had dropped his earlier burden of regret, and the spirit of the service had left him cheerfully hopeful of some stern soldierly work. He watched the men of his troop while with quip and song they made comfortable camp; he spoke a few brief words of instruction to the grave-faced first sergeant, and then strolled slowly up the valley, his own affairs soon completely forgotten in the beauty of near-by hills beneath the golden glory of the morning sun. Once he paused and looked back upon ugly Glencaid, dingy and forlorn even at that distance; then he crossed the narrow stream by means of a convenient log, and clambered up the somewhat steep bank. A heavy fringe of low bushes clung close along the edge of the summit, but a plainly defined path led among their intricacies. He pressed his way through, coming into a glade where sunshine flickered through the overarching branches of great trees, and the grass was green and short, like that of a well-kept lawn.

As Brant emerged from the underbrush he suddenly beheld a fair vision of young womanhood resting on the grassy bank just before him. She was partially reclining, as if startled by his unannounced approach, her face turned toward him, one hand grasping an open book, the other shading her eyes from the glare of the sun. Something in the graceful poise, the piquant, uplifted face, the dark gloss of heavy hair, and the unfrightened gaze held him speechless until the picture had been impressed forever upon his memory. He beheld a girl on the verge of womanhood, fair of skin, the red glow of health flushing her cheeks, the lips parted in surprise, the sleeve fallen back from one white, rounded arm, the eyes honest, sincere, mysterious. She recognized him with a glance, and her lips closed as she remembered how and when they had met before. But there was no answering recollection within his eyes, only admiration—nothing clung about this Naiad to remind him of a neglected waif of the garrison. She read all this in his face, and the lines about her mouth changed quickly into a slightly quizzical smile, her eyes brightening.

"You should at least have knocked, sir," she ventured, sitting up on the grassy bank, the better to confront him, "before intruding thus uninvited."

He lifted his somewhat dingy scouting hat and bowed humbly.

"I perceived no door giving warning that I approached such presence, and the first shock of surprise was perhaps as great to me as to you. Yet, now that I have blundered thus far, I beseech that I be permitted to venture upon yet another step."

She sat looking at him, a trim, soldierly figure, his face young and pleasant to gaze upon, and her dark eyes sensibly softened.

"What step?"

"To tarry for a moment beside the divinity of this wilderness."

She laughed with open frankness, her white teeth sparkling behind the red, parted lips.

"Perhaps you may, if you will first consent to be sensible," she said, with returning gravity; "and I reserve the right to turn you away whenever you begin to talk or act foolish. If you accept these conditions, you may sit down."

He seated himself upon the soft grass ledge, retaining the hat in his hands. "You must be an odd sort of a girl," he commented, soberly, "not to welcome an honest expression of admiration."

"Oh, was that it? Then I duly bow my acknowledgment. I took your words for one of those silly compliments by which men believe they honor women."

He glanced curiously aside at her half-averted face. "At first sight I had supposed you scarcely more than a mere girl, but now you speak like a woman wearied of the world, utterly condemning all complimentary phrases."

"Indeed, no; not if they be sincerely expressed as between man and man."

"How is it as between man and woman?"

"Men generally address women as you started to address me, as if there existed no common ground of serious thought between them. They condescend, they flatter, they indulge in fulsome compliment, they whisper soft nonsense which they would be sincerely ashamed to utter in the presence of their own sex, they act as if they were amusing babies, rather than conversing with intelligent human beings. Their own notion seems to be to shake the rattle-box, and awaken a laugh. I am not a baby, nor am I seeking amusement."

He glanced curiously at her book. "And yet you condescend to read love stories," he said, smiling. "I expected to discover a treatise on philosophy."

"I read whatever I chance to get my hands on, here in Glencaid," she retorted, "just as I converse with whoever comes along. I am hopeful of some day discovering a rare gem hidden in the midst of the trash. I am yet young."

"You are indeed young," he said, quietly, "and with some of life's lessons still to learn. One is that frankness is not necessarily flippancy, nor honesty harshness. Beyond doubt much of what you said regarding ordinary social conversation is true, yet the man is no more to be blamed than the woman. Both seek to be entertaining, and are to be praised for the effort rather than censured. A stranger cannot instinctively know the likes and dislikes of one he has just met; he can feel his way only by commonplaces. However, if you will offer me a topic worthy the occasion, in either philosophy, science, or literature, I will endeavor to feed your mind."

She uplifted her innocent eyes demurely to his face. "You are so kind. I am deeply interested just now In the Japanese conception of the transmigration of souls."

"How extremely fortunate! It chances to be my favorite theme, but my mental processes are peculiar, and you must permit me to work up toward it somewhat gradually. For instance, as a question leading that way, how, in the incarnation of this world, do you manage to exist in such a hole of a place?—that is, provided you really reside here."

"Why, I consider this a most delightful nook."

"My reference was to Glencaid."

"Oh! Why, I live from within, not without. Mind and heart, not environment, make life, and my time is occupied most congenially. I am being faithfully nurtured on the Presbyterian catechism, and also trained in the graces of earthly society. These alternate, thus preparing me for whatever may happen in this world or the next."

His face pictured bewilderment, but also a determination to persevere. "An interesting combination, I admit. But from your appearance this cannot always have been your home?"

"Oh, thank you. I believe not always; but I wonder at your being able to discern my superiority to these surroundings. And do you know your questioning is becoming quite personal? Does that yield me an equal privilege?"

He bowed, perhaps relieved at thus permitting her to assume the initiative, and rested lazily back upon the grass, his eyes intently studying her face.

"I suppose from your clothes you must be a soldier. What is that figure 7 on your hat for?"

"The number of my regiment, the Seventh Cavalry."

Her glance was a bit disdainful as she coolly surveyed him from head to foot, "I should imagine that a strong, capable-appearing fellow like you might do much better than that. There is so much work in the world worth doing, and so much better pay."

"What do you mean? Isn't a soldier's life a worthy one?"

"Oh, yes, of course, in a way. We have to have soldiers, I suppose; but if I were a man I'd hate to waste all my life tramping around at sixteen dollars a month."

He smothered what sounded like a rough ejaculation, gazing into her demure eyes as if she strongly suspected a joke hid in their depths. "Do—do you mistake me for an enlisted man?"

"Oh, I didn't know; you said you were a soldier, and that's what I always heard they got. I am so glad if they give you more. I was only going to say that I believed I could get you a good place in McCarthy's store if you wanted it. He pays sixty-five dollars, and his clerk has just left."

Brant stared at her with open mooch, totally unable for the moment to decide whether or not that innocent, sympathetic face masked mischief. Before he succeeded in regaining confidence and speech, she had risen to her feet, holding back her skirt with one hand.

"Really, I must go," she announced calmly, drawing back toward the slight opening between the rushes. "No doubt YOU have done fully as well as you could considering your position in life; but this has proved another disappointment. You have fallen, far, very far, below my ideal. Good-bye."

He sprang instantly erect, his cheeks flushed. "Please don't go without a farther word. We seem predestined to mis-understand. I am even willing to confess myself a fool in the hope of some time being able to convince you otherwise. You have not even told me that you live here; nor do I know your name."

She shook her head positively, repressed merriment darke-ning her eyes and wrinkling the corners of her mouth. "It would be highly improper to introduce myself to a stranger —we Presbyterians never do that."

"But do you feel no curiosity as to who I may be?"

"Why, not in the least; the thought is ridiculous. How very conceited you must be to imagine such a thing!"

He was not a man easily daunted, nor did he recall any previous embarrassment in the presence of a young woman. But now he confronted something utterly unique; those quiet eyes seemed to look straight through him. His voice faltered sadly, yet succeeded in asking: "Are we, then, never to meet again? Am I to understand this to be your wish?"

She laughed. "Really, sir, I am not aware that I have the slightest desire in the matter. I have given it no thought, but I presume the possibility of our meeting again depends largely upon yourself, and the sort of society you keep. Surely you cannot expect that I would seek such an opportunity?"

He bowed humbly. "You mistake my purpose. I merely meant to ask if there was not some possibility of our again coming together socially the presence of mutual friends."

"Oh, I scarcely think so; I do not remember ever having met any soldiers at the social functions here—excepting officers. We are extremely exclusive in Glencaid," she dropped him a mocking courtesy, "and I have always moved in the most exclusive set."

Piqued by her tantalizing manner, he asked, "What particular social functions are about to occur that may possibly open a passage into your guarded presence?"

She seemed immersed in thought, her face turned partially aside. "Unfortunately, I have not my list of engagements here," and she glanced about at him shyly. "I can recall only one at present, and I am not even certain—that is, I do not promise—to attend that. However, I may do so. The Miners' Bachelor Club gives a reception and ball to-morrow evening in honor of the new schoolmistress."

"What is her name?" with responsive eagerness.

She hesitated, as if doubtful of the strict propriety of mentioning it to a stranger.

"Miss Phoebe Spencer," she said, her eyes cast demurely down.

"Ah!" he exclaimed, in open triumph; "and have I, then, at last made fair capture of your secret? You are Miss Phoebe Spencer."

She drew back still farther within the recesses of the bushes, at his single victorious step forward.

"I? Why certainly not. I am merely Miss Spencer's 'star' pupil, so you may easily judge something of what her superior attainments must necessarily be. But I am really going now, and I sincerely trust you will be able to secure a ticket for to-morrow night; for if you once meet this Miss Spencer you will never yield another single thought to me, Mr.—Mr.—" her eyes dancing with laughter—"First Lieutenant Donald Brant."

CHAPTER IV

SILENT MURPHY

Brant sprang forward, all doubt regarding this young woman instantly dissipated by those final words of mischievous mockery. She had been playing with him as unconcernedly as if he were a mere toy sent for her amusement, and his pride was stung.

But pursuit proved useless. Like a phantom she had slipped away amid the underbrush, leaving him to flounder blindly in the labyrinth. Once she laughed outright, a clear burst of girlish merriment ringing through the silence, and he leaped desperately forward, hoping to intercept her flight. His incautious foot slipped along the steep edge of the shelving bank, and he went down, half stumbling, half sliding, until he came to a sudden pause on the brink of the little stream. The chase was ended, and he sat up, confused for the moment, and half questioning the evidence of his own eyes.

A small tent, dirty and patched, stood with its back against the slope of earth down which he had plunged. Its flap flung aside revealed within a pile of disarranged blankets, together with some scattered articles of wearing apparel, while just before the opening, his back pressed against the supporting pole, an inverted pipe between his yellow, irregular teeth, sat a hideous looking man. He was a withered, dried-up fellow, whose age was not to be guessed, having a skin as yellow as parchment, drawn in tight to the bones like that of a mummy, his eyes deep sunken like wells, and his head totally devoid of hair, although about his lean throat there was a copious fringe of iron-gray beard, untrimmed and scraggy. Down the entire side of one cheek ran a livid scar, while his nose was turned awry.

He sat staring at the newcomer, unwinking, his facial expression devoid of interest, but his fingers opening and closing in apparent nervousness. Twice his lips opened, but nothing except a peculiar gurgling sound issued from the throat, and Brant, who by this time had attained his feet and his self-possession, ventured to address him.

"Nice quiet spot for a camp," he remarked, pleasantly, "but a bad place for a tumble."

The sunken eyes expressed nothing, but the throat gurgled again painfully, and finally the parted lips dropped a detached word or two. "Blame—pretty girl—that."

The lieutenant wondered how much of their conversation this old mummy had overheard, but he hesitated to question him. One inquiry, however, sprang to his surprised lips. "Do you know her?"

"Damn sight—better—than any one around here—know her—real name."

Brant stared incredulously. "Do you mean to insinuate that that young woman is living in this community under an assumed one? Why, she is scarcely more than a child! What do you mean, man?"

The soldier's hat still rested on the grass where it had fallen, its military insignia hidden.

"I guess—I know—what I—know," the fellow muttered. "What's—your—regiment?"

"Seventh Cavalry."

The man stiffened up as if an electric shock had swept through his limp frame. "The hell!—and—did—she—call you—Brant?"

The young officer's face exhibited his disgust. Beyond doubt that sequestered nook was a favorite lounging spot for the girl, and this disreputable creature had been watching her for some sinister purpose.

"So you have been eavesdropping, have you?" said Brant, gravely. "And now you want to try a turn at defaming a woman? Well, you have come to a poor market for the sale of such goods. I am half inclined to throw you bodily into the creek. I believe you are nothing but a common liar, but I'll give you one chance—you say you know her real name. What is it?"

The eyes of the mummy had become spiteful.

"It's—none of—your damn—business. I'm—not under—your orders."

"Under my orders! Of course not; but what do you mean by that? Who and what are you?"

The fellow stood up, slightly hump-backed but broad of shoulder, his arms long, his legs short and somewhat bowed, his chin protruding impudently, and Brant noticed an oddly shaped black scar, as if burned there by powder, on the back of his right hand.

"Who—am I?" he said, angrily. "I'm—Silent—Murphy."

An expression of bewilderment swept across the lieutenant's face. "Silent Murphy! Do you claim to be Custer's scout?"

The fellow nodded. "Heard—of me—maybe?"

Brant stood staring at him, his mind occupied with vague garrison rumors connected with this odd personality. The name had long been a familiar one, and he had often had the man pictured out before him, just such a wizened face and hunched-up figure, half crazed, at times malicious, yet keen and absolutely devoid of fear; acknowledged as the best scout in all the Indian country, a daring rider, an incomparable trailer, tireless, patient, and as tricky and treacherous as the wily savages he was employed to spy upon. There could remain no reasonable doubt of his identity, but what was he doing there? What purpose underlay his insinuations against that young girl? If this was indeed Silent Murphy, he assuredly had some object in being there, and however hastily he may have spoken, it was not altogether probable that he deliberately lied. All this flashed across his mind in that single instant of hesitation.

"Yes, I've heard of you,"—and his crisp tone instinctively became that of terse military command,—"although we have never met, for I have been upon detached service ever since my assignment to the regiment. I have a troop in camp below," he pointed down the stream, "and am in command here."

The scout nodded carelessly.

"Why did you not come down there, and report your presence in this neighborhood to me?"

Murphy grinned unpleasantly. "Rather be—alone—no report —been over—Black Range—telegraphed—wait orders."

"Do you mean you are in direct communication with headquarters, with Custer?"

The man answered, with a wide sweep of his long arm toward the northwest. "Goin' to—be hell—out there—damn soon."

"How? Are things developing into a truly serious affair—a real campaign?"

"Every buck—in the—Sioux nation—is makin'—fer the— bad lands," and he laughed noiselessly, his nervous fingers gesticulating. "I—guess that—means—business."

Brant hesitated. Should he attempt to learn more about the young girl? Instinctively he appreciated the futility of endeavoring to extract information from Murphy, and he experienced a degree of shame at thus seeking to penetrate her secret. Besides, it was none of his affair, and if ever it should chance to become so, surely there were more respectable means by which he could obtain information. He glanced about, seeking some way of recrossing the stream.

"If you require any new equipment," he said tersely, "we can probably supply you at the camp. How do you manage to get across here?"

Murphy, walking stiffly, led the way down the steep slope, and silently pointed out a log bridging the narrow stream. He stood watching while the officer picked his steps across, but made no responsive motion when the other waved his hand from the opposite shore, his sallow face looking grim and unpleasant.

"Damn—the luck!" he grumbled, shambling back up the bank. "It don't—look—right. Three of 'em—all here—at once—in this—cussed hole. Seems if—this yere world—ought ter be—big 'nough—ter keep 'em apart;—but hell—it ain't. Might make—some trouble—if them—people—ever git—their heads—tergether talkin'. Hell of a note—if the boy—falls in love with—her. Likely to do it—too. Curse such—fool luck. Maybe I—better talk—it over again—with Red—he's in it—damn near—as deep as—I am." And he sank down again in his old position before the tent, continuing to mutter, his chin sunk into his chest, his whole appearance that of deep dejection, perhaps of dread.

The young officer marched down the road, his heedless feet kicking up the red dust in clouds, his mind busied with the peculiar happenings of the morning, and that prospect for early active service hinted at in the brief utterances of the old scout. Brant was a thorough soldier, born into the service and deeply enamored of its dangers; yet beyond this he remained a man, a young man, swayed by those emotions which when at full tide sweep aside all else appertaining to life.

Just now the vision of that tantalizing girl continued to haunt his memory, and would not down even to the glorious hope of a coming campaign. The mystery surrounding her, her reticence, the muttered insinuation dropping from the unguarded lips of Murphy, merely served to render her the more attractive, while her own naive witchery of manner, and her seemingly unconscious coquetry, had wound about him a magic spell, the full power of which as yet remained but dimly appreciated. His mind lingered longingly upon the marvel of the dark eyes, while the cheery sound of that last rippling outburst of laughter reechoed in his ears like music.

His had been a lonely life since leaving West Point and joining his regiment—a life passed largely among rough men and upon the desolate plains. For months at a time he had known nothing of refinement, nor enjoyed social intercourse with the opposite sex; life had thus grown as barren and bleak as those desert wastes across which he rode at the command of his superiors. For years the routine of his military duties had held him prisoner, crushing out the dreams of youth. Yet, beneath his mask of impassibility, the heart continued to beat with fierce desire, biding the time when it should enjoy its own sweet way. Perhaps that hour had already dawned; certainly something new, something inspiring, had now come to awaken an interest unfelt before, and leave him idly dreaming of shadowed eyes and flushed, rounded cheeks.

He was in this mood when he overtook the Rev. Howard Wynkoop and marked the thoughtful look upon his pale face.

"I called at your camp," explained Wynkoop, after the first words of greeting had been exchanged, "as soon as I learned you were here in command, but only to discover your absence. The sergeant, however, was very courteous, and assured me there would be no difficulty in arranging a religious service for the men, unless sudden orders should arrive. No doubt I may rely on your cooeperation."

"Most certainly," was the cordial response, "and I shall also permit those desiring to attend your regular Sunday services so long as we are stationed here. How is your work prospering?"

"There is much to encourage me, but spiritual progress is slow, and there are times when my faith falters and I feel unworthy of the service in which I am engaged. Doubtless this is true of all labor, yet the minister is particularly susceptible to these influences surrounding him."

"A mining camp is so intensely material seven days of the week that it must present a difficult field for the awakening of any religious sentiment," confessed Brant sympathetically, feeling not a little interested in the clear-cut, intellectual countenance of the other. "I have often wondered how you consented to bury your talents in such a place."

The other smiled, but with a trace of sadness in his eyes. "I firmly believe that every minister should devote a portion of his life to the doing of such a work as this. It is both a religious and a patriotic duty, and there is a rare joy connected with it."

"Yet it was surely not joy I saw pictured within your face when we met; you were certainly troubled over some problem."

Wynkoop glanced up quickly, a slight flush rising in his pale cheeks. "Perplexing questions which must be decided off-hand are constantly arising. I have no one near to whom I can turn for advice in unusual situations, and just now I scarcely know what action to take regarding certain appli-cations for church membership."

Brant laughed. "I hardly consider myself a competent adviser in matters of church polity," he admitted, "yet I have always been informed that all so desiring are to be made welcome in religious fellowship."

"Theoretically, yes." And the minister stopped still in the road, facing his companion. "But this special case presents certain peculiarities. The applicants, as I learn from others, are not leading lives above reproach. So far as I know, they have never even attended church service until last Sunday, and I have some reason to suspect an ulterior motive. I am anxious to put nothing in the way of any honestly seeking soul, yet I confess that in these cases I hesitate."

"But your elders? Do not they share the responsibility of passing upon such applications?"

The flush on Mr. Wynkoop's cheeks deepened, and his eyes fell. "Ordinarily, yes; but in this case I fear they may prove unduly harsh. I—I feel—that these applications came through the special intercession of a certain young lady, and I am anxious not to hurt her feelings in any way, or to discourage her enthusiasm."

"Oh, I see! Would you mind telling me the names of the two gentlemen?"

"Mr. John Moffat and Mr. William McNeil. Unfortunately, I know neither personally."

"And the young lady?"

"A Miss Phoebe Spencer; she has but lately arrived from the East to take charge of our new school—a most interesting and charming young woman, and she is proving of great assistance to me in church work."

The lieutenant cleared his throat, and emitted a sigh of suddenly awakened memory. "I fear I can offer you no advice, for if, as I begin to suspect,—though she sought most bravely to avoid the issue and despatch me upon a false trail,—she prove to be that same fascinating young person I met this morning, my entire sympathies are with the gentlemen concerned. I might even be strongly tempted to do likewise at her solicitation."

"You? Why, you arrived only this morning, and do you mean to say you have met already?"

"I at least suspect as much, for there can scarcely exist two in this town who will fill the description. My memory holds the vision of a fair young face, vivacious, ever changing in its expression, yet constantly both piquant and innocent; a perfect wealth of hair, a pair of serious eyes hiding mysteries within their depths, and lips which seem made to kiss. Tell me, is not this a fairly drawn portrait of your Miss Spencer?"

The minister gripped his hands nervously together. "Your description is not unjust; indeed, it is quite accurate from a mere outer point of view; yet beneath her vivacious manner I have found her thoughtful, and possessed of deep spiritual yearnings. In the East she was a communicant of the Episcopal Church."

Brant did not answer him at once. He was studying the minister's downcast face; but when the latter finally turned to depart, he inquired, "Do you expect to attend the reception to-morrow evening?"

Wynkoop stammered slightly. "I—I could hardly refuse under the circumstances; the committee sent me an especially urgent invitation, and I understand there is to be no dancing until late. One cannot be too straight-laced out here."

"Oh, never mind apologizing. I see no reason why you need hesitate to attend. I merely wondered if you could procure me an invitation."

"Did she tell you about it?"

"Well, she delicately hinted at it, and, you know, things are pretty slow here in a social way. She merely suggested that I might possibly meet her again there."

"Of course; it is given in her honor."

"So I understood, although she sought to deceive me into the belief that she was not the lady. We met purely by accident, you understand, and I am desirous of a more formal presentation."

The minister drew in his breath sharply, but the clasp of his extended hand was not devoid of warmth. "I will have a card of invitation sent you at the camp. The committee will be very glad of your presence; only I warn you frankly regarding the lady, that competition will be strong."

"Oh, so far as that is concerned I have not yet entered the running," laughed Brant, in affected carelessness, "although I must confess my sporting proclivities are somewhat aroused."

He watched the minister walking rapidly away, a short, erect figure, appearing slender in his severely cut black cloth. "Poor little chap," he muttered, regretfully. "He's hard hit. Still, they say all's fair in love and war."

CHAPTER V

IN HONOR OF MISS SPENCER

Mr. Jack Moffat, president of the Bachelor Miners' Pleasure Club, had embraced the idea of a reception for Miss Spencer with unbounded enthusiasm. Indeed, the earliest conception of such an event found birth within his fertile brain, and from the first he determined upon making it the most notable social function ever known in that portion of the Territory.

Heretofore the pastime of the Bachelors' Club had been largely bibulous, and the members thereof had exhibited small inclination to seek the ordinary methods of social relaxation as practised in Glencaid. Pink teas, or indeed teas of any conceivable color, had never proved sufficiently attractive to wean the members from the chaste precincts of the Occidental or the Miners' Retreat, while the mysterious pleasure of "Hunt the Slipper" and "Spat in and Spat out" had likewise utterly failed to inveigle them from retirement. But Mr. Moffat's example wrought an immediate miracle, so that, long before the fateful hour arrived, every registered bachelor was laboring industriously to make good the proud boast of their enthusiastic president, that this was going to be "the swellest affair ever pulled off west of the Missouri."

The large space above the Occidental was secured for the

occasion, the obstructing subdivisions knocked away, an entrance constructed with an outside stairway leading up from a vacant lot, and the passage connecting the saloon boarded up. Incidentally, Mr. Moffat took occasion to announce that if "any snoozer got drunk and came up them stairs" he would be thrown bodily out of a window. Mr. McNeil, who was observing the preliminary proceedings with deep interest from a pile of lumber opposite, sarcastically intimated that under such circumstances the attendance of club members would be necessarily limited. Mr. Moffat's reply it is manifestly impossible to quote literally. Mrs. Guffy was employed to provide the requisite refreshments in the palatial dining-hall of the hotel, while Buck Mason, the vigilant town marshal, popularly supposed to know intimately the face of every "rounder" in the Territory, agreed to collect the cards of invitation at the door, and bar out obnoxious visitors.

These preliminaries having been duly attended to, Mr. Moffat and his indefatigable committee of arrangements proceeded to master the details of decoration and entertainment, drawing heavily upon the limited resources of the local merchants, and even invading private homes in search after beautifying material. Jim Lane drove his buckboard one hundred and sixty miles to Cheyenne to gather up certain needed articles of adornment, the selection of which could not be safely confided to the inartistic taste of the stage-driver. Upon his rapid return journey loaded down with spoils, Peg Brace, a cow-puncher in the "Bar O" gang, rode recklessly alongside his speeding wheels for the greater portion of the distance, apparently in most jovial humor, and so unusually inquisitive as to make Mr. Lane, as he later expressed it, "plum tired." The persistent rider finally deserted him, however, at the ford over the Sinsiniwa, shouting derisively back from a safe distance that the Miners' Club was a lot of chumps, and promising them a severe "jolt" in the near future.

Indeed, it was becoming more and more apparent that a decided feeling of hostility was fast developing between the respective partisans of Moffat and McNeil. Thus far the feud merely smouldered, finding occasional expression in sarcastic speech, and the severance of former friendly relations, but it boded more serious trouble for the near future. To a loyal henchman, Moffat merely condescended to remark, glancing disdainfully at a knot of hard riders disconsolately sitting their ponies in front of the saloon door, "We've got them fellers roped and tied, gents, and they simply won't be ace-high with the ladies of this camp after our fandango is over with. We're a holdin' the hand this game, an' it simply sweeps the board clean. That duffer McNeil's the sickest looking duck I've seen in a year, an' the whole blame bunch of cow-punchers is corralled so tight there can't a steer among 'em get a nose over the pickets."

He glanced over the waiting scene of festivities with intense satisfaction. From bare squalor the spacious apartment had been converted into a scene of almost gorgeous splendor. The waxed floor was a perfect marvel of smoothness; the numerous windows had been heavily draped in red, white, and blue hangings; festoons of the same rich hues hung gracefully suspended from the ceiling, trembling to the least current of air; oil lamps, upheld by almost invisible wires, dangled in profusion; while within the far corner, occupying a slightly raised platform later to be utilized by the orchestra, was an imposing pulpit chair lent by the Presbyterian Church, resting upon a rug of skins, and destined as the seat of honor for the fair guest of the evening. Moffat surveyed all this thoughtfully, and proceeded proudly to the hotel to don a "boiled" shirt, and in other ways prepare himself to do honor to his exalted office. Much to the surprise of McNeil, lounging with some cronies on the shaded porch, he nodded to him genially, adding a hearty, "Hello there, Bill," as he passed carelessly by.

The invited guests arrived from the sparsely settled regions round about, not a few riding for a hundred miles over the hard trails. The majority came early, arrayed in whatsoever apparel their limited wardrobes could supply, but ready for any wild frolic. The men outnumbered the gentler sex five to one, but every feminine representative within a radius of about fifty miles, whose respectability could possibly pass muster before the investigations of a not too critical invitation committee, was present amid the throng, attired in all the finery procurable, and supremely and serenely happy in the assured consciousness that she would not lack partners whenever the enticing music began.

The gratified president of the Pleasure Club had occasion to expand his chest with just pride. Jauntily twirling his silky mustaches, he pushed his way through the jostling, good-natured crowd already surging toward the entrance of the hall, and stepped briskly forth along the moonlit road toward the Herndon home, where the fair queen of the revels awaited his promised escort. It was his hour of supreme triumph, and his head swam with the delicious intoxication of well-earned success, the plaudits of his admirers, and the fond anticipation of Miss Spencer's undoubted surprise and gratitude. His, therefore, was the step and bearing of a conqueror, of one whose cup was already filled to the brim, and running over with the joy of life.

The delay incident to the completion of an elaborate toilet, together with the seductive charms of a stroll through the moon-haunted night beneath the spell of bright eyes and whispered words, resulted in a later arrival at the scene of festivities than had been intended. The great majority of the expected guests had already assembled, and were becoming somewhat restless. No favored courtier ever escorted beloved queen with greater pride or ceremony than that with which Mr. Moffat led his blushing charge through the throng toward her chair of state. The murmuring voices, the admiring eyes, the hush of expectancy, all contributed to warm the cockles of his heart and to color his face with the glow of victory. Glancing at his companion, he saw her cheeks flushed, her head held proudly poised, her countenance evidencing the enjoyment of the moment, and he felt amply rewarded for the work which had produced so glorious a result. A moment he bent above her chair, whispering one last word of compliment into the little ear which reddened at his bold speech, and feasting his ardent eyes upon the flushed and animated countenance. The impatient crowd wondered at the nature of the coming ceremony, and Mr. Moffat strove to recall the opening words of his introductory address.

Suddenly his gaze settled upon one face amid the throng. A moment of hesitation followed; then a quick whisper of excuse to the waiting divinity in the chair, and the perturbed president pressed his way toward the door. Buck Mason stood there on guard, carelessly leaning against the post, his star of office gleaming beneath the light.

"Buck," exclaimed Moffat, "how did that feller McNeil, and those other cow-punchers, get in here? You had your orders."

Mason turned his quid deliberately and spat at the open door. "You bet I did, Jack," he responded cheerfully, yet with a trifle of exasperation evident in his eyes. "And what's more, I reckon they was obeyed. There ain't nobody got in yere ternight without they had a cyard."

"Well, there has"; and Moffat forgot his natural caution in a sudden excess of anger. "No invitations was sent them fellers. Do you mean to say they come in through the roof?"

Mason straightened up, his face darkening, his clinched fist thrashing the air just in front of Moffat's nose.

"I say they come in yere, right through this door! An' every mother's son of 'em, hed a cyard. I know what I'm a-talkin' about, you miserable third-class idiot, an' if you give me any more of your lip I'll paste you good an' proper. Go back thar whar you belong, an' tind to your part of this fandango; I'm a runnin' mine."

Moffat hesitated, his brow black as a thunder cloud, but the crowd was manifestly growing restless over the delay, calling "Time!" and "Play ball!" and stamping their feet. Besides, Buck was never known to be averse to a quarrel, and Moffat's bump of caution was well developed. He went back, nursing his wrath and cursing silently. The crowd greeted his reappearance with prolonged applause, and some of the former consciousness of victory returned. He glanced down into the questioning eyes of Miss Spencer, cleared his throat, then grasped her hand, and, as they stood there together, all his confidence came surging back.

"Ladies and Gentlemen of Glencaid," he began gracefully, "as president of the Bachelor Miners' Pleasure Club, it affords me extreme gratification to welcome you to this the most important social event ever pulled off in this Territory. It's going to be a swell affair from the crack of the starter's pistol to the last post, and you can bet on getting your money's worth every time. That's the sort of hairpins we are—all wool and a yard wide. Now, ladies and gents, while it is not designed that the pleasure of this evening be marred by any special formalities, any such unnatural restrictions as disfigure such functions in the effete East [applause], and while I am only too anxious to exclaim with the poet, 'On with the dance, let joy be unconfined' [great applause], yet it must be remembered that this high-toned outfit has been got up for a special, definite purpose, as a fit welcome to one who has come among us with the high and holy object of instructing our offspring and elevating the educational ideals of this community. We, of this Bachelors' Club, may possess no offspring to instruct, but we sympathize with them others who have, and desire to show our interest in the work. We have here with us to-night one of the loveliest of her sex, a flower of refinement and culture plucked from the Eastern hills, who, at the stern call of duty, has left her home and friends to devote her talents to this labor of love. In her honor we meet, in her honor this room has been decorated with the colors of our beloved country, and to her honor we now dedicate the fleeting hours of this festal night. It is impossible for her to greet you all personally, much as she wishes to do so, but as president of the Bachelor Miners' Pleasure Club, and also," with a deep bow to his blushing and embarrassed companion, "I may venture to add, as an intimate friend of our fair guest, I now introduce to you Glencaid's new schoolmistress—Miss Phoebe Spencer. Hip! Hip! *Hurrah*!"

Swinging his hand high above his head, the enthusiastic orator led the noisy cheers which instantly burst forth in unrestrained volume; and before which Miss Spencer shrank back into her chair, trembling, yet strangely happy. Good humor swayed that crowd, laughter rippled from parted lips, while voices here and there began a spontaneous demand for a speech. Miss Spencer shook her flossy head helplessly, feeling too deeply agitated to utter a word; and Moffat, now oblivious to everything but the important part he was playing in the brilliant spectacle, stepped before her, waving the clamorous assembly into temporary and expectant silence.

"Our charming guest," he announced, in tones vibrant with authority, "is so deeply affected by this spontaneous outpouring of your good-will as to be unable to respond in words. Let us respect her natural embarrassment; let us now exhibit that proud Western chivalry which will cause her to feel perfectly at home in our midst. The orchestra will strike up, and amid the mazy whirling of the dance we will at once sink all formality, as becomes citizens of this free and boundless West, this land of gold, of sterling manhood, and womanly beauty. To slightly change the poet's lines, written of a similar occasion:

> "There was a sound of revelry by night,
> And proud Glencaid had gathered then
> Her beauty and her chivalry, and bright
> The lamps shone o'er fair women and brave men.

"So, scatter out, gents, and pick up your partners for the first whirl. This is our turn to treat, and our motto is 'Darn the expense.'"

He bent over, purposing to lead the lady of his heart forth to the earliest strains of the violins, his genial smile evidencing his satisfaction.

"Say,—eh—just hold on—eh—a minute!"

Moffat wheeled about, a look of amazement replacing his previous jovial smile. His eyes hardened dangerously as they encountered the face of McNeil. The latter was white about the lips, but primed for action, and not inclined to waste time in preliminaries.

"Look here, this ain't your time to butt in—" began Moffat, angrily, but the other waved his hand.

"Say, gents,—eh—that feller had his spiel all right—eh—ain't he? He wants to be—eh—the whole hog, but—eh,—I reckon this is a—eh—free country, ain't it? Don't I have—eh—no show?"

"Go on, Bill!"

"Of course you do."

"Make Jack Moffat shut up!"

The justly indignant president of the Bachelors' Club remained motionless, his mouth still open, struggling to restrain those caustic and profane remarks which, in that presence, he dare not utter. He instinctively flung one hand back to his hip, only to remember that all guns had been left at the door. McNeil eyed him calmly, as he might eye a chained bear, his lips parted in a genial smile.

"I—eh—ain't no great shakes of an—eh—orator," he began, apologetically, waving one hand toward his gasping rival, "like Mr.—eh—Moffat. I can't sling words round—eh—reckless, like the—eh—gent what just had the floor, ner—eh—spout poetry, but I reckon—eh—I kin git out—eh—'bout what I got to say. Mr. Moffat has—eh—told you what the—eh—Bachelor Miners' Club—eh—has been a-doin'. He—eh—spread it on pretty blame thick, but—eh—I reckon they ain't—eh—all of 'em miners round this yere—eh—camp. As the—eh—president of the—eh—Cattlemen's Shakespearian—eh—Reading Circle, I am asked to present to—eh—Miss Spencer a slight token—eh—of our esteem, and—eh—to express our pleasure at—eh—being permitted," he bowed to the choking Mr. Moffat, "eh—to participate in this—eh—most glorious occasion."

He stepped forward, and dropped into Miss Spencer's lap a

small plush-covered box. Her fingers pressed the spring, and, as the lid flew open, the brilliant flash of a diamond dazzled her eyes. She sat staring at it, unable for the moment to find speech. Then the assemblage burst into an unrestrained murmur of admiration, and the sound served to arouse her.

"Oh, how beautiful it all is!" she exclaimed, rapturously. "I hardly know what to say, or whom to thank. I never heard of anything so perfectly splendid before. It makes me cry just to remember that it is all done for me. Oh, Mr. Moffat, I want to thank, through you, the gentlemen of the Bachelors' Club for this magnificent reception. I know I do not deserve it, but it makes me so proud to realize the interest you all take in my work. And, Mr. McNeil, I beg you to return my gratitude to the gentlemen of the—the (oh, thank you)—the Cattlemen's Shakespearian Reading Circle (how very nice of you to have such an organization for the study of higher literature!) for this superb gift. I shall never forget this night, or what it has brought me, and I simply cannot express my real feelings at all; I—I don't know what to say, or—or what to do."

She paused, burying her face in her hands, her body shaken with sobs. Moffat, scarcely knowing whether to swear or smile, hastily signalled for the waiting musicians to begin. As they swung merrily into waltz measure he stepped forward, fully confident of his first claim for that opening dance, and vaguely conscious that, once upon the floor with her, he might thus regain his old leadership. Miss Spencer glanced up at him through her tears.

"I—I really feel scarcely equal to the attempt," she murmured nervously, yet rising to her feet. Then a new thought seemed suddenly to occur to her. "Oh, Mr. Moffat, I have been so highly favored, and I am so extremely anxious to do everything I can to show my gratitude. I know it is requesting so much of you to ask your relinquishment of this first dance with me to-night. As president of the Bachelors' Club it is your right, of course, but don't you truly think I ought to give it to Mr. McNeil? We were together all the way from the house, you know, and we had such a delightful walk. You wouldn't truly mind yielding up your claim for just this once, would you?"

Moffat did not reply, simply because he could not; he was struck dumb, gasping for breath, the room whirling around before him, while he stared at her with dazed, unseeing eyes. His very helplessness to respond she naturally interpreted as acquiescence.

"It is so good of you, Mr. Moffat, for I realize how you were counting upon this first dance, weren't you? But Mr. McNeil being here as the guest of your club, I think it is perfectly beautiful of you to waive your own rights as president, so as to acknowledge his unexpected contribution to the joy of our evening." She touched him playfully with her hand, the other resting lightly upon McNeil's sleeve, her innocent, happy face upturned to his dazed eyes. "But remember, the next turn is to be yours, and I shall never forget this act of chivalry."

It is doubtful if he saw her depart, for the entire room was merely an indistinct blur. He was too desperately angry even to swear. In this emergency, Mr. Wynkoop, dimly realizing that something unpleasant had occurred, sought to attract the attention of his new parishioner along happier lines.

"How exceedingly strange it is, Mr. Moffat," he ventured, "that beings otherwise rational, and possessing souls destined for eternity, can actually appear to extract pleasure from such senseless exercises? I do not in the least blame Miss Spencer, for she is yet young, and probably thoughtless about such matters, as the youthful are wont to be, but I am, indeed, rejoiced to note that you do not dance."

Moffat wheeled upon him, his teeth grinding savagely together. "Shut up!" he snapped, fiercely, and shaking off the pastor's gently restraining fingers, shouldered his passage through the crowd toward the door.

CHAPTER VI

THE LIEUTENANT MEETS MISS SPENCER

Lieutenant Brant was somewhat delayed in reaching the scene of Miss Spencer's social triumph. Certain military requirements were largely responsible for this delay, and he had patiently wrestled with an unsatisfactory toilet, mentally excoriating a service which would not permit the transportation of dress uniforms while on scouting detail. Nevertheless, when he finally stepped forth into the brilliant moonlight, he presented an interesting, soldierly figure, his face still retaining a bit of the boy about it, his blue eyes bright with expectancy. That afternoon he had half decided not to go at all, the glamour of such events having long before grown dim, but the peculiar attraction of this night proved too strong; not thus easily could he erase from memory the haunting witchery of a face. Beyond doubt, when again viewed amid the conventionalities, much of its imagined charm would vanish; yet he would see her once more, although no longer looking forward to drawing a prize.

The dance was already in full swing, the exciting preliminaries having been largely forgotten in the exuberance of motion, when he finally pushed his way through the idle loungers gathered about the door, and gained entrance to the hall. Many glanced curiously at him, attracted by the glitter of his uniform, but he recognized none among them, and therefore passed steadily toward the musicians' stand, where there appeared to be a few unoccupied chairs.

The scene was one of color and action. The rapid, pulsating music, the swiftly whirling figures, the quivering drapery overhead, the bright youthful faces, the glow of numerous lamps, together with the ceaseless voices and merry shuffling of feet, all combined to create a scene sufficiently picturesque. It was altogether different from what he had anticipated. He watched the speeding figures, striving in vain to distinguish the particular one whose charms had lured him thither. He looked upon fair faces in plenty, flushed cheeks and glowing eyes skurried past him, with swirling skirts and flashes of neatly turned ankles, as these enthusiastic maids and matrons from hill and prairie strove to make amends for long abstinence. But among them all he was unable to distinguish the wood-nymph whose girlish frankness and grace had left so deep an impression on his memory. Yet surely she must be present, for, to his understanding, this whole gay festival was in her honor. Directly across the room he caught sight of the Reverend Mr. Wynkoop conversing with a lady of somewhat rounded charms, and picked his way in their direction.

The missionary, who had yet scarcely recovered from the shock of Moffat's impulsive speech, and who, in truth, had been hiding an agonized heart behind a smiling face, was only too delighted at any excuse which would enable him to approach Miss Spencer, and press aside those cavaliers who were monopolizing her attention. The handicap of not being able to dance he felt to be heavy, and he greeted the lieutenant with unusual heartiness of manner.

"Why, most assuredly, my dear sir, most assuredly," he said. "Mrs. Herndon, permit me to make you acquainted with

Lieutenant Brant, of the Seventh Cavalry."

The two, thus introduced, bowed, and exchanged a few words, while Mr. Wynkoop busied himself in peering about the room, making a great pretence at searching out the lady guest, who, in very truth, had scarcely been absent from his sight during the entire evening.

"Ah!" he ejaculated, "at last I locate her, and, fortunately, at this moment she is not upon the floor, although positively hidden by the men clustering about her chair. You will excuse us, Mrs. Herndon, but I have promised Lieutenant Brant a presentation to your niece."

They slipped past the musicians' stand, and the missionary pressed in through the ring of admirers.

"Why, Mr. Wynkoop!" and she extended both hands impulsively. "And only to think, you have never once been near me all this evening; you have not congratulated me on my good fortune, nor exhibited the slightest interest! You don't know how much I have missed you. I was just saying to Mr. Moffat—or it might have been Mr. McNeil—that I was completely tired out and wished you were here to sit out this dance with me."

Wynkoop blushed and forgot the errand which had brought him there, but she remained sufficiently cool and observant. She touched him gently with her hand.

"Who is that fine-looking young officer?" she questioned softly, yet without venturing to remove her glance from his face.

Mr. Wynkoop started. "Oh, exactly; I had forgotten my mission. He has requested an introduction." He drew the lieutenant forward. "Lieutenant Brant, Miss Spencer."

The officer bowed, a slight shadow of disappointment in his eyes. The lady was unquestionably attractive, her face animated, her reception most cordial, yet she was not the maiden of the dark, fathomless eyes and the wealth of auburn hair.

"Such a pleasure to meet you," exclaimed Miss Spencer, her eyes uplifted shyly, only to become at once modestly shaded behind their long lashes. "Do you know, Lieutenant, that actually I have never before had the privilege of meeting an officer of the army. Why, we in the East scarcely realize that we possess such a body of brave men. But I have read much regarding the border, and all the dreams of my girlhood seem on the point of realization since I came here and began mingling in its free, wild life. Your appearance supplies the one touch of color that was lacking to make the picture complete. Mr. Moffat has done so much to make me realize the breadth of Western experience, and now, I do so hope, you will some time find opportunity to recount to me some of your army exploits."

The lieutenant smiled. "Most gladly; yet just now, I confess, the music invites me, and I am sufficiently bold to request your company upon the floor."

Miss Spencer sighed regretfully, her eyes sweeping across those numerous manly faces surrounding them. "Why, really, Lieutenant Brant, I scarcely see how I possibly can. I have already refused so many this evening, and even now I almost believe I must be under direct obligation to some one of those gentlemen. Still," hesitatingly, "your being a total stranger here must be taken into consideration. Mr. Moffat, Mr. McNeil, Mr. Mason, surely you will grant me release this once?"

There was no verbal response to the appeal, only an uneasy movement; but her period of waiting was extremely brief.

"Oh, I knew you would; you have all been so kind and considerate." She arose, resting her daintily gloved hand upon Brant's blue sleeve, her pleased eyes smiling up confidingly into his. Then with a charming smile, "Oh, Mr. Wynkoop, I have decided to claim your escort to supper. You do not care?"

Wynkoop bowed, his face like a poppy.

"I thought you would not mind obliging me in this. Come, Lieutenant."

Miss Spencer, when she desired to be, was a most vivacious companion, and always an excellent dancer. Brant easily succumbed to her sway, and became, for the time being, a victim to her charms. They circled the long room twice, weaving their way skilfully among the numerous couples, forgetful of everything but the subtile intoxication of that swinging cadence to which their feet kept such perfect time, occasionally exchanging brief sentences in which compliment played no insignificant part. To Brant, as he marked the heightened color flushing her fair cheeks, the experience brought back fond memories of his last cadet ball at the Point, and he hesitated to break the mystic spell with abrupt questioning. Curiosity, however, finally mastered his reticence.

"Miss Spencer," he asked, "may I inquire if you possess such a phenomenon as a 'star' pupil?"

The lady laughed merrily, but her expression became somewhat puzzled. "Really, what a very strange question! Why, not unless it might be little Sammy Worrell; he can certainly use the longest words I ever heard of outside a dictionary. Why, may I ask? Are you especially interested in prodigies?"

"Oh, not in the least; certainly not in little Sammy Worrell. The person I had reference to chances to be a young woman, having dark eyes, and a wealth of auburn hair. We met quite by accident, and the sole clew I now possess to her identity is a claim she advanced to being your 'star' pupil."

Miss Spencer sighed somewhat regretfully, and her eyes fell. "I fear it must have been Naida, from your description. But she is scarcely more than a child. Surely, Lieutenant, it cannot be possible that you have become interested in her?"

He smiled pleasantly. "At least eighteen, is she not? I was somewhat impressed with her evident originality, and hoped to renew our slight acquaintanceship here in more formal manner. She is your 'star' pupil, then?"

"Why, she is not really in my school at all, but I outline the studies she pursues at home, and lend her such books as I consider best adapted for her reading. She is such a strange girl!"

"Indeed? She appeared to me to be extremely unconventional, with a decided tendency for mischief. Is that your meaning?"

"Partially. She manages to do everything in a different way from other people. Her mind seems peculiarly independent, and she is so unreservedly Western in her ways and language. But I was referring rather to her taste in books— she devours everything."

"You mean as a student?"

"Well, yes, I suppose so; at least she appears to possess the faculty of absorbing every bit of information, like a sponge. Sometimes she actually startles me with her odd questions; they are so unexpected and abstruse, falling from the lips of so young a girl. Then her ideas are so crude and uncommon, and she is so frankly outspoken, that I become actually nervous when I am with her. I really believe Mr. Wynkoop seeks to avoid meeting her, she has shocked him so frequently in religious matters."

"Does she make light of his faith?"

"Oh, no, not that exactly, at least it is not her intention. But she wants to know everything—why we believe this and why we believe that, doctrines which no one else ever dreams of questioning, and he cannot seem to make them clear to her mind. Some of her questions are so irreverent as to be positively shocking to a spiritually minded person."

They lapsed into silence, swinging easily to the guidance of the music. His face was grave and thoughtful. This picture just drawn of the perverse Naida had not greatly lowered her in his estimation, although he felt instinctively that Miss Spencer was not altogether pleased with his evident interest in another. It was hardly in her nature patiently to brook a rival, but she dissembled with all the art of a clever woman, smiling happily up into his face as their eyes again met.

"It is very interesting to know that you two met in so unconventional a way," she ventured, softly, "and so sly of her not even to mention it to me. We are room-mates, you know, and consequently quite intimate, although she possesses many peculiar characteristics which I cannot in the least approve. But after all, Naida is really a good-hearted girl enough, and she will probably outgrow her present irregular ways, for, indeed, she is scarcely more than a child.

I shall certainly do my best to guide her aright. Would you mind giving me some details of your meeting?"

For a moment he hesitated, feeling that if the girl had not seen fit to confide her adventure to this particular friend, it was hardly his place to do so. Then, remembering that he had already said enough to arouse curiosity, which might easily be developed into suspicion, he determined his course. In a few words the brief story was frankly told, and apparently proved quite amusing to Miss Spencer.

"Oh, that was Naida, beyond a doubt," she exclaimed, with a laugh of satisfaction. "It is all so characteristic of her. I only wonder how she chanced to guess your name; but really the girl appears to possess some peculiar gift in thus discerning facts hidden from others. Her instincts seem so finely developed that at times she reminds me of a wild animal."

This caustic inference did not please him, but he said nothing, and the music coming to a pause, they slowly traversed the room.

"I presume, then, she is not present?" he said, quietly.

Miss Spencer glanced into his face, the grave tone making her apprehensive that she might have gone too far.

"She was here earlier in the evening, but now that you remind me of it, I do not recall having noticed her of late. But, really, Lieutenant, it is no part of my duty to chaperon the young girl. Mrs. Herndon could probably inform you of her present whereabouts."

Miss Spencer was conscious of the sting of failure, and her face flushed with vexation. "It is extremely close in here, don't you think?" she complained. "And I was so careless as to mislay my fan. I feel almost suffocated."

"Did you leave it at home?" he questioned. "Possibly I might discover a substitute somewhere in the room."

"Oh, no; I would never think of troubling you to such an extent. No doubt this feeling of lassitude will pass away shortly. It was very foolish of me, but I left the fan with my wraps at the hotel. It can be recovered when we go across to supper."

In spite of Miss Spencer's quiet words of renunciation, there was a look of pleading in her shyly uplifted eyes impossible to resist. Brant promptly surrendered before this masked battery.

"It will be no more than a pleasure to recover it for you," he protested, gallantly.

The stairs leading down from the hall entrance were shrouded in darkness, the street below nearly deserted of loiterers, although lights streamed forth resplendently from the undraped windows of the Occidental and the hotel opposite. Assisted in his search by Mrs. Guffy, the officer succeeded in recovering the lost fan, and started to return. Just without the hotel door, under the confusing shadows of the wide porch, he came suddenly face to face with a young woman, the unexpected encounter a mutual and embarrassing surprise.

CHAPTER VII

AN UNUSUAL GIRL

The girl was without wraps, her dress of some light, fleecy material fitting her slender figure exquisitely, her head uncovered; within her eyes Brant imagined he could detect the glint of tears. She spoke first, her voice faltering slightly.

"Will you kindly permit me to pass?"

He stepped instantly to one side, bowing as he did so.

"I beg your pardon for such seeming rudeness," he said, gravely. "I have been seeking you all the evening, yet this unexpected meeting caught me quite unawares."

"You have been seeking me? That is strange. For what reason, pray?"

"To achieve what you were once kind enough to suggest as possible—the formality of an introduction. It would seem, however, that fate makes our meetings informal."

"That is your fault, not mine."

"I gladly assume all responsibility, if you will only waive the formality and accept my friendship."

Her face seemed to lighten, while her lips twitched as if suppressing a smile. "You are very forgetful. Did I not tell you that we Presbyterians are never guilty of such indiscretions?"

"I believe you did, but I doubt your complete surrender to the creed."

"Doubt! Only our second time of meeting, and you already venture to doubt! This can scarcely be construed into a compliment, I fear."

"Yet to my mind it may prove the very highest type of compliment," he returned, reassured by her manner. "For a certain degree of independence in both thought and action is highly commendable. Indeed, I am going to be bold enough to add that it was these very attributes that awakened my interest in you."

"Oh, indeed; you cause me to blush already. My frankness, I fear, bids fair to cost me all my friends, and I may even go beyond your pardon, if the perverse spirit of my nature so move me."

"The risk of such a catastrophe is mine, and I would gladly dare that much to get away from conventional commonplace. One advantage of such meetings as ours is an immediate insight into each other's deeper nature. For one I shall sincerely rejoice if you will permit the good fortune of our chance meeting to be alone sponsor for our future friendship. Will you not say yes?"

She looked at him with greater earnestness, her young face sobered by the words spoken. Whatever else she may have seen revealed there, the countenance bending slightly toward her was a serious, manly one, inspiring respect, awakening confidence.

"And I do agree," she said, extending her hand in a girlish impulse. "It will, at least, be a new experience and therefore worth the trial. I will even endeavor to restrain my rebellious spirit, so that you will not be unduly shocked."

He laughed, now placed entirely at his ease. "Your need of mercy is appreciated, fair lady. Is it your desire to return to the hall?"

She shook her head positively. "A cheap, gaudy show, all bluster and vulgarity. Even the dancing is a mere parody. I early tired of it."

"Then let us choose the better part, and sit here on the bench, the night our own."

He conducted her across the porch to the darkest corner, where only rifts of light stole trembling in between the shadowing vines, and there found convenient seats. A moment they remained in silence, and he could hear her breathing.

"Have you truly been at the hall," she questioned, "or were you merely fibbing to awaken my interest?"

"I truly have been," he answered, "and actually have danced a measure with the fair guest of the evening."

"With Phoebe Spencer! And yet you dare pretend now to retain an interest in me? Lieutenant Brant, you must be a most talented deceiver, or else the strangest person I ever met. Such a miracle has never occurred before!"

"Well, it has certainly occurred now; nor am I in this any vain deceiver. I truly met Miss Spencer. I was the recipient of her most entrancing smiles; I listened to her modulated voice; I bore her off, a willing captive, from a throng of despairing admirers; I danced with her, gazing down into her eyes, with her fluffy hair brushing my cheek, yet resisted all her charms and came forth thinking only of you."

"Indeed? Your proof?"

He drew the white satin fan forth from his pocket, and held it out toward her with mock humility. "This, unbelieving princess. Despatched by the fair lady in question to fetch this bauble from the dressing-room, I forgot my urgent errand in the sudden delight of finding you."

"The case seems fully proved," she confessed, laughingly, "and it is surely not my duty to punish the culprit. What did you talk about? But, pshaw, I know well enough without asking—she told you how greatly she admired the romance of the West, and begged you to call upon her with a recital of your own exploits. Have I not guessed aright?"

"Partially, at least; some such expressions were used."

"Of course, they always are. I do not know whether they form merely a part of her stock in trade, or are spoken earnestly. You would laugh to hear the tales of wild and thrilling adventure which she picks up, and actually believes. That Jack Moffat possesses the most marvellous imagination for such things, and if I make fun of his impossible stories she becomes angry in an instant."

"I am afraid you do not greatly admire this Miss Spencer?"

"Oh, but I do; truly I do. You must not think me ungrateful.

No one has ever helped me more, and beneath this mask of artificiality she is really a noble-hearted woman. I do not understand the necessity for people to lead false lives. Is it this way in all society—Eastern society, I mean? Do men and women there continually scheme and flirt, smile and stab, forever assuming parts like so many play-actors?"

"It is far too common," he admitted, touched by her naive questioning. "What is known as fashionable social life has become an almost pitiful sham, and you can scarcely conceive the relief it is to meet with one utterly uncontaminated by its miserable deceits, its shallow make-believes. It is no wonder you shock the nerves of such people; the deed is easily accomplished."

"But I do not mean to." And she looked at him gravely, striving to make him comprehend. "I try so hard to be—be commonplace, and—and satisfied. Only there is so much that seems silly, useless, pitifully contemptible that I lose all patience. Perhaps I need proper training in what Miss Spencer calls refinement; but why should I pretend to like what I don't like, and to believe what I don't believe? Cannot one act a lie as well as speak one? And is it no longer right to search after the truth?"

"I have always felt it was our duty to discover the truth wherever possible," he said, thoughtfully; "yet, I confess, the search is not fashionable, nor the earnest seeker popular."

A little trill of laughter flowed from between her parted lips, but the sound was not altogether merry.

"Most certainly I am not. They all scold me, and repeat with manifest horror the terrible things I say, being unconscious that they are evil. Why should I suspect thoughts that come to me naturally? I want to know, to understand. I grope about in the dark. It seems to me sometimes that this whole world is a mystery. I go to Mr. Wynkoop with my questions, and they only seem to shock him. Why should they? God must have put all these doubts and wonderings into my mind, and there must be an answer for them somewhere. Mr. Wynkoop is a good man, I truly respect him. I want to please him, and I admire his intellectual attainments; but how can he accept so much on faith, and be content? Do you really suppose he is content? Don't you think he ever questions as I do? or has he actually succeeded in smothering every doubt? He cannot answer what I ask him; he cannot make things clear. He just pulls up a few, cheap, homely weeds,—useless common things,—when I beg for flowers; he hands them to me, and bids me seek greater faith through prayer. I know I am a perfect heathen,—Miss Spencer says I am,—but do you think it is so awful for me to want to know these things?"

He permitted his hand to drop upon hers, and she made no motion of displeasure.

"You merely express clearly what thousands feel without the moral courage to utter it. The saddest part of it all is, the deeper we delve the less we are satisfied in our intellectual natures. We merely succeed in learning that we are the veriest pygmies. Men like Mr. Wynkoop are simply driven back upon faith as a last resort, absolutely baffled by an inpenetrable wall, against which they batter mentally in vain. They have striven with mystery, only to meet with ignominious defeat. Faith alone remains, and I dare not deny that such faith is above all knowledge. The pity of it is, there are some minds to whom this refuge is impossible. They are forever doomed to be hungry and remain unfed; thirsty, yet unable to quench their thirst."

"Are you a church member?"

"Yes."

"Do you believe those things you do not understand?"

He drew a deep breath, scarcely knowing at that moment how best to answer, yet sincerely anxious to lead this girl toward the light.

"The majority of men do not talk much about such matters. They hold them sacred. Yet I will speak frankly with you. I could not state in words my faith so that it would be clearly apprehended by the mind of another. I am in the church because I believe its efforts are toward righteousness, because I believe the teachings of Christ are perfect. His life the highest possible type of living, and because through Him we receive all the information regarding a future existence which we possess. That my mind rests satisfied I do not say; I simply accept what is given, preferring a little light to total darkness."

"But here they refuse to accept any one like that. They say I am not yet in a fit state of mind."

"Such a judgment would seem to me narrow. I was fortunate in coming under the influence of a broad-minded religious teacher. To my statement of doubts he simply said: 'Believe what you can; live the very best you can, and keep your mind open toward the light.' It seems to me now this is all that anyone can do whose nature will not permit of blind, unquestioning faith. To require more of ordinary human beings is unreasonable, for God gave us mind and ability to think."

There was a pause, so breathless they could hear the rustle of the leaves in the almost motionless air, while the strains of gay music floating from the open windows sounded loud and strident.

"I am so glad you have spoken in that way," she confessed. "I shall never feel quite so much alone in the world again, and I shall see these matters from a different viewpoint. Is it wrong—unwomanly, I mean—for me to question spiritual things?"

"I am unable to conceive why it should be. Surely woman ought to be as deeply concerned in things spiritual as man."

"How very strange it is that we should thus drift into such an intimate talk at our second meeting!" she exclaimed. "But it seems so easy, so natural, to converse frankly with some people—they appear to draw out all that is best in one's heart. Then there are others who seem to parch and wither up every germ of spiritual life."

"There are those in the world who truly belong together," he urged, daringly. "They belong to each other by some divine law. They may never be privileged to meet; but if they do, the commingling of their minds and souls is natural. This talk of ours to-night has, perhaps, done me as much good as you."

"Oh, I am so glad if it has! I—I do not believe you and Miss Spencer conversed in this way?"

"Heaven forbid! And yet it might puzzle you to guess what was the main topic of our conversation."

"Did it interest you?"

"Deeply."

"Well, then, it could not be dress, or men, or Western

romance, or society in Boston, or the beautiful weather. I guess it was books."

"Wrong; they were never mentioned."

"Then I shall have to give up, for I do not remember any other subjects she talks about."

"Yet it was the most natural topic imaginable—yourself."

"You were discussing me? Why, how did that happen?"

"Very simply, and I was wholly to blame. To be perfectly honest, Miss Naida, I attended the dance to-night for no other object than to meet you again. But I had argued myself into the belief that you were Miss Spencer. The discovery of my mistake merely intensified my determination to learn who you really were. With this purpose, I interviewed Miss Spencer, and during the course of our conversation the facts of my first meeting with you became known."

"You told her how very foolish I acted?"

"I told her how deeply interested I had become in your outspoken manner."

"Oh! And she exclaimed, 'How romantic!'"

"Possibly; she likewise took occasion to suggest that you were merely a child, and seemed astonished that I should have given you a second thought."

"Why, I am eighteen."

"I told her I believed you to be of that age, and she ignored my remark. But what truly surprised both of us was, how you happened to know my name."

The girl did not attempt to answer, and she was thankful enough that there was not sufficient light to betray the reddening of her cheeks.

"And you do not mean, even now, to make clear the mystery?" he asked.

"Not—now," she answered, almost timidly. "It is nothing much, only I would rather not now."

The sudden sound of voices and laughter in the street beneath brought them both to their feet.

"Why, they are coming across to supper," she exclaimed, in surprise. "How long we have been here, and it has seemed scarcely a moment! I shall certainly be in for a scolding, Lieutenant Brant; and I fear your only means of saving me from being promptly sent home in disgrace will be to escort me in to supper."

"A delightful punishment!" He drew her hand through his arm, and said: "And then you will pledge me the first dance following?"

"Oh, you mustn't ask me. Really, I have not been on the floor to-night; I am not in the mood."

"Do you yield to moods?"

"Why, of course I do. Is it not a woman's privilege? If you know me long it will be to find me all moods."

"If they only prove as attractive as the particular one swaying you to-night, I shall certainly have no cause for complaint.

Come, Miss Naida, please cultivate the mood to say yes, before those others arrive."

She glanced up at him, shaking her dark hair, her lips smiling. "My present mood is certainly a good-natured one," she confessed, softly, "and consequently it is impossible to say no."

His hand pressed hers, as the thronging couples came merrily up the steps.

"Why, Naida, is this you, child? Where have you been all this time?" It was Miss Spencer, clinging to Mr. Wynkoop's arm.

"Merely sitting out a dance," was the seemingly indifferent answer; then she added sweetly, "Have you ever met my friend, Lieutenant Brant, of the Seventh Cavalry, Phoebe? We were just going in to supper."

Miss Spencer's glance swept over the silent young officer. "I believe I have had the honor. It was my privilege to be introduced to the gentleman by a mutual friend."

The inward rush of hungry guests swept them all forward in laughing, jostling confusion; but Naida's cheeks burned with indignation.

CHAPTER VIII

THE REAPPEARANCE OF AN OLD FRIEND

After supper the Lieutenant and Naida danced twice together, the young girl's mood having apparently changed to one of buoyant, careless happiness, her dark eyes smiling, her lips uttering freely whatever thought came uppermost. Outwardly she pictured the gay and merry spirit of the night, yet to Brant, already observing her with the jealousy of a lover, she appeared distrait and restless, her affectation of abandon a mere mask to her true feelings. There was a peculiar watchfulness in her glances about the crowded room, while her flushed cheeks, and the distinctly false note in her laughter, began to trouble him not a little. Perhaps these things might have passed unnoted but for their contrast with the late confidential chat.

He could not reconcile this sudden change with what he believed of her. It was not carried out with the practised art of one accustomed to deceit. There must be something real influencing her action. These misgivings burdened his mind even as he swung lightly with her to the music, and they talked together in little snatches.

He had forgotten Miss Spencer, forgotten everything else about him, permitting himself to become enthralled by this strange girl whose name even he did not know. In every way she had appealed to his imagination, awakening his interest, his curiosity, his respect, and even now, when some secret seemed to sway her conduct, it merely served to strengthen his resolve to advance still farther in her regard. There are natures which welcome strife; they require opposition, difficulty, to develop their real strength. Brant was of this breed. The very conception that some person, even some inanimate thing, might stand between him and the heart of this fair woman acted upon him like a stimulant.

The last of the two waltzes ended, they walked slowly through the scattering throng, he striving vainly to arouse her to the former independence and intimacy of speech. While endeavoring bravely to exhibit interest, her mind too clearly wandered, and there was borne in slowly upon him the distasteful idea that she would prefer being left alone. Brant had been secretly hoping it might become his privilege to escort her home, but now he durst not breathe the words of such a request. Something indefinable had arisen between them which held the man dumb and nerveless. Suddenly they came face to face with Mrs. Herndon, and Brant felt the girl's arm twitch.

"I have been looking everywhere for you, Naida," Mrs. Herndon said, a slight complaint in her voice. "We were going home."

Naida's cheeks reddened painfully.

"I am so sorry if I have kept you waiting," her words spoken with a rush, "but—but, Lieutenant Brant was intending to accompany me. We were just starting for the cloak-room."

"Oh, indeed!" Mrs. Herndon's expression was noncommittal, while her eyes surveyed the lieutenant.

"With your permission, of course," he said.

"I hardly think I have any need to interfere."

They separated, the younger people walking slowly, silently toward the door. He held her arm, assisting her to descend the stairway, his lips murmuring a few commonplaces, to which she scarcely returned even monosyllabic replies, although she frequently flashed shy glances at his grave face. Both realized that some explanation was forthcoming, yet neither was quite prepared to force the issue.

"I have no wraps at the hotel," she said, as he attempted to turn that way. "That was a lie also; let us walk directly down the road."

He indulged in no comment, his eyes perceiving a pathetic pleading in her upturned face. Suddenly there came to him a belief that the girl was crying; he could feel the slight tremor of her form against his own. He glanced furtively at her, only to catch the glitter of a falling tear. To her evident distress, his heart made instant and sympathetic response. With all respect influencing the action, his hand closed warmly over the smaller one on his sleeve.

"Little girl," he said, forgetting the shortness of their acquaintance in the deep feeling of the moment, "tell me what the trouble is."

"I suppose you think me an awful creature for saying that," she blurted out, without looking up. "It wasn't ladylike or nice, but—but I simply couldn't help it, Lieutenant Brant."

"You mean your sudden determination to carry me home with you?" he asked, relieved to think this might prove the entire difficulty. "Don't let that worry you. Why, I am simply rejoiced at being permitted to go. Do you know, I wanted to request the privilege all the time we were dancing together. But you acted so differently from when we were beneath the vines that I actually lost my nerve."

She looked up, and he caught a fleeting glimpse into her unveiled eyes.

"I did not wish you to ask me."

"What?" He stopped suddenly. "Why then did you make such an announcement to Mrs. Herndon?"

"Oh, that was different," she explained, uneasily. "I had to do that; I had to trust you to help me out, but—but I really wanted to go home alone."

He swept his unbelieving eyes around over the deserted night scene, not knowing what answer to return to so strange an avowal. "Was that what caused you to appear so distant to me in the hall, so vastly different from what you had been before?"

She nodded, but with her gaze still upon the ground.

"Miss Naida," he said, "it would be cowardly for me to attempt to dodge this issue between us. Is it because you do not like me?"

She looked up quickly, the moonlight revealing her flushed face.

"Oh, no, no! you must never think that. I told you I was a girl of moods; under those vines I had one mood, in the hall another. Cannot you understand?"

"Very little," he admitted, "for I am more inclined to believe you are the possessor of a strong will than that you are swayed by moods. Listen. If I thought that a mere senseless mood had caused your peculiar treatment of me to-night, I should feel justified in yielding to a mood also. But I will not lower you to that extent in my estimation; I prefer to believe that you are the true-hearted, frankly spoken girl of the vine shadow. It is this abiding conviction as to your true nature which holds me loyal to a test. Miss Naida, is it now your desire that I leave you?"

He stepped aside, relinquishing her arm, his hat in hand, but she did not move from where he left her.

"It—it hurts me," she faltered, "for I truly desire you to think in that way of me, and I—I don't know what is best to do. If I tell you why I wished to come alone, you might misunderstand; and if I refuse, then you will suspect wrong, and go away despising me."

"I sincerely wish you might repose sufficient confidence in me as a gentleman to believe I never betray a trust, never pry into a lady's secret."

"Oh, I do, Lieutenant Brant. It is not doubt of you at all; but I am not sure, even within my own heart, that I am doing just what is right. Besides, it will be so difficult to make you, almost a stranger, comprehend the peculiar conditions which influence my action. Even now you suspect that I am deceitful—a masked sham like those others we discussed to-night; but I have never played a part before, never skulked in the dark. To-night I simply had to do it."

Her voice was low and pleading, her eyes an appeal; and Brant could not resist the impulse to comfort.

"Then attempt no explanation," he said, gently, "and believe me, I shall continue to trust you. To-night, whatever your wish may be, I will abide by it. Shall I go, or stay? In either case you have nothing to fear."

She drew a deep breath, these open words of faith touching her more strongly than would any selfish fault-finding.

"Trust begets trust," she replied, with new firmness, and now gazing frankly into his face. "You can walk with me a portion of the way if you wish, but I am going to tell you the truth,—I have an appointment with a man."

"I naturally regret to learn this," he said, with assumed calmness. "But the way is so lonely I prefer walking with you until you have some other protector."

She accepted his proffered arm, feeling the constraint in his tone, the formality in his manner, most keenly. An older woman might have resented it, but it only served to sadden and embarrass her. He began speaking of the quiet beauty of the night, but she had no thought of what he was saying.

"Lieutenant Brant," she said, at last, "you do not ask me who the man is."

"Certainly not, Miss Naida; it is none of my business."

"I think, perhaps, it might be; the knowledge might help you to understand. It is Bob Hampton."

He stared at her. "The gambler? No wonder, then, your meeting is clandestine."

She replied indignantly, her lips trembling. "He is not a gambler; he is a miner, over in the Black Range. He has not touched a card in two years."

"Oh, reformed has he? And are you the instrument that has worked such a miracle?"

Her eyes fell. "I don't know, but I hope so." Then she glanced up again, wondering at his continued silence. "Don't you understand yet?"

"Only that you are secretly meeting a man of the worst reputation, one known the length and breadth of this border as a gambler and fighter."

"Yes; but—but don't you know who I am?"

He smiled grimly, wondering what possible difference that could make. "Certainly; you are Miss Naida Herndon."

"I? You have not known? Lieutenant Brant, I am Naida Gillis."

He stopped still, again facing her. "Naida Gillis? Do you mean old Gillis's girl? Is it possible you are the same we rescued on the prairie two years ago?"

She bowed her head. "Yes; do you understand now why I trust this Bob Hampton?"

"I perhaps might comprehend why you should feel grateful to him, but not why you should thus consent to meet with him clandestinely."

He could not see the deep flush upon her cheeks, but he was not deaf to the pitiful falter in her voice.

"Because he has been good and true to me," she explained,

frankly, "better than anybody else in all the world. I don't care what you say, you and those others who do not know him, but I believe in him; I think he is a man. They won't let me see him, the Herndons, nor permit him to come to the house. He has not been in Glencaid for two years, until yesterday. The Indian rising has driven all the miners out from the Black Range, and he came down here for no other purpose than to get a glimpse of me, and learn how I was getting on. I—I saw him over at the hotel just for a moment—Mrs. Guffy handed me a note—and I—I had only just left him when I encountered you at the door. I wanted to see him again, to talk with him longer, but I couldn't manage to get away from you, and I didn't know what to do. There, I've told it all; do you really think I am so very bad, because—because I like Bob Hampton?"

He stood a moment completely nonplussed, yet compelled to answer.

"I certainly have no right to question your motives," he said, at last, "and I believe your purposes to be above reproach. I wish I might give the same credit to this man Hampton. But, Miss Naida, the world does not often consent to judge us by our own estimation of right and wrong; it prefers to place its own interpretation on acts, and thus often condemns the innocent. Others might not see this as I do, nor have such unquestioning faith in you."

"I know," she admitted, stubbornly, "but I wanted to see him; I have been so lonely for him, and this was the only possible way."

Brant felt a wave of uncontrollable sympathy sweep across him, even while he was beginning to hate this man, who, he felt, had stolen a passage into the innocent heart of a girl not half his age, one knowing little of the ways of the world. He saw again that bare desert, with those two half-dead figures clasped in each other's arms, and felt that he understood the whole miserable story of a girl's trust, a man's perfidy.

"May I walk beside you until you meet him?" he asked.

"You will not quarrel?"

"No; at least not through any fault of mine."

A few steps in the moonlight and she again took his arm, although they scarcely spoke. At the bridge she withdrew her hand and uttered a peculiar call, and Hampton stepped forth from the concealing bushes, his head bare, his hat in his hand.

"I scarcely thought it could be you," he said, seemingly not altogether satisfied, "as you were accompanied by another."

The younger man took a single step forward, his uniform showing in the moonlight. "Miss Gillis will inform you later why I am here," he said, striving to speak civilly. "You and I, however, have met before—I am Lieutenant Brant, of the Seventh Cavalry."

Hampton bowed, his manner somewhat stiff and formal, his face inpenetrable.

"I should have left Miss Gillis previous to her meeting with you," Brant continued, "but I desired to request the privilege of calling upon you to-morrow for a brief interview."

"With pleasure."

"Shall it be at ten?"

"The hour is perfectly satisfactory. You will find me at the hotel."

"You place me under obligations," said Brant, and turned toward the wondering girl. "I will now say good-night, Miss Gillis, and I promise to remember only the pleasant events of this evening."

Their hands met for an instant of warm pressure, and then the two left behind stood motionless and watched him striding along the moonlit road.

CHAPTER IX

THE VERGE OF A QUARREL

Brant's mind was a chaos of conflicting emotions, but a single abiding conviction never once left him—he retained implicit faith in her, and he purposed to fight this matter out with Hampton. Even in that crucial hour, had any one ventured to suggest that he was in love with Naida, he would merely have laughed, serenely confident that nothing more than gentlemanly interest swayed his conduct. It was true, he greatly admired the girl, recalled to memory her every movement, her slightest glance, her most insignificant word, while her marvellous eyes constantly haunted him, yet the dawn of love was not even faintly acknowledged.

Nevertheless, he manifested an unreasonable dislike for Hampton. He had never before felt thus toward this person; indeed, he had possessed a strong man's natural admiration for the other's physical power and cool, determined courage. He now sincerely feared Hampton's power over the innocent mind of the girl, imagining his influence to be much stronger than it really was, and he sought after some suitable means for overcoming it. He had no faith in this man's professed reform, no abiding confidence in his word of honor; and it seemed to him then that the entire future of the young woman's life rested upon his deliverance of her from the toils of the gambler. He alone, among those who might be considered as her true friends, knew the secret of her infatuation, and upon him alone, therefore, rested the burden of her release. It was his heart that drove him into such a decision, although he conceived it then to be the reasoning of the brain.

And so she was Naida Gillis, poor old Gillis's little girl! He stopped suddenly in the road, striving to realize the thought. He had never once dreamed of such a consummation, and it staggered him. His thought drifted back to that pale-faced, red-haired, poorly dressed slip of a girl whom he had occasionally viewed with disapproval about the post-trader's store at Bethune, and it seemed simply an impossibility. He recalled the unconscious, dust-covered, nameless waif he had once held on his lap beside the Bear Water. What was there in common between that outcast, and this well-groomed, frankly spoken young woman? Yet, whoever she was or had been, the remembrance of her could not be conjured out of his brain. He might look back with repugnance upon those others, those misty phantoms of the past, but the vision of his mind, his ever-changeable divinity of the vine shadows, would not become obscured, nor grow less fascinating. Let her be whom she might, no other could ever win that place she occupied in his heart. His mind dwelt upon her flushed cheeks, her earnest face, her wealth of glossy hair, her dark eyes filled with mingled roguery and thoughtfulness,—in utter unconsciousness that he was already her humble slave. Suddenly there occurred to him a recollection of Silent Murphy, and his strange, unguarded remark. What could the fellow have meant? Was there, indeed, some secret in the life history of this young girl?—some story of shame, perhaps? If so, did Hampton know about it?

Already daylight rested white and solemn over the silent valley, and only a short distance away lay the spot where the crippled scout had made his solitary camp. Almost without volition the young officer turned that way, crossed the stream by means of the log, and clambered up the bank. But it was clear at a glance that Murphy had deserted the spot. Convinced of this, Brant retraced his steps toward the camp of his own troop, now already astir with the duties of early morning. Just in front of his tent he encountered his first sergeant.

"Watson," he questioned, as the latter saluted and stood at attention, "do you know a man called Silent Murphy?"

"The scout? Yes, sir; knew him as long ago as when he was corporal in your father's troop. He was reduced to the ranks for striking an officer."

Brant wheeled in astonishment. "Was he ever a soldier in the Seventh?"

"He was that, for two enlistments, and a mighty tough one; but he was always quick enough for a fight in field or garrison."

"Has he shown himself here at the camp?"

"No, sir; didn't know he was anywhere around. He and I were never very good friends, sir."

The lieutenant remained silent for several moments, endeavoring to perfect some feasible plan.

"Despatch an orderly to the telegraph-office," he finally commanded, "to inquire if this man Murphy receives any messages there, and if they know where he is stopping. Send an intelligent man, and have him discover all the facts he can. When he returns bring him in to me."

He had enjoyed a bath and a shave, and was yet lingering over his coffee, when the two soldiers entered with their report. The sergeant stepped aside, and the orderly, a tall, boyish-looking fellow with a pugnacious chin, saluted stiffly.

"Well, Bane," and the officer eyed his trim appearance with manifest approval, "what did you succeed in learning?"

"The operator said this yere Murphy hed never bin thar himself, sir, but there wus several messages come fer him. One got here this mornin'."

"What becomes of them?"

"They're called fer by another feller, sir."

"Oh, they are! Who?"

"Red Slavin wus the name he give me of thet other buck."

When the two had disappeared, Brant sat back thinking rapidly. There was a mystery here, and such actions must have a cause. Something either in or about Glencaid was compelling Murphy to keep out of sight—but what? Who? Brant was unable to get it out of his head that all this secrecy centred around Naida. With those incautiously spoken words as a clew, he suspected that Murphy knew something about her, and that knowledge was the cause for his present erratic actions. Perhaps Hampton knew; at least he might possess some additional scrap of information which would help to solve the problem. He looked at his watch, and ordered his horse to be saddled.

It did not seem quite so simple now, this projected interview with Hampton, as it had appeared the night before. In the clear light of day, he began to realize the weakness of his position, the fact that he possessed not the smallest right to speak on behalf of Naida Gillis. He held no relationship whatsoever to her, and should he venture to assume any, it was highly probable the older man would laugh contemptuously in his face. Brant knew better than to believe Hampton would ever let go unless he was obliged to do so; he comprehended the impotence of threats on such a character, as well as his probable indifference to moral obligations. Nevertheless, the die was cast, and perhaps, provided an open quarrel could be avoided, the meeting might result in good to all concerned.

Hampton welcomed him with distant but marked courtesy, having evidently thought out his own immediate plan of action, and schooled himself accordingly. Standing there, the bright light streaming over them from the open windows, they presented two widely contrasting personalities, yet each exhibiting in figure and face the evidences of hard training and iron discipline. Hampton was clothed in black, standing straight as an arrow, his shoulders squared, his head held proudly erect, while his cool gray eyes studied the face of the other as he had been accustomed to survey his opponents at the card-table. Brant looked the picture of a soldier on duty, trim, well built, erect, his resolute blue eyes never flinching from the steady gaze bent upon ham, his bronzed young face grave from the seriousness of his mission. Neither was a man to temporize, to mince words, or to withhold blows; yet each instinctively felt that this was an occasion rather for self-restraint. In both minds the same thought lingered—the vague wonder how much the other knew. The elder man, however, retained the better self-control, and was first to break the silence.

"Miss Gillis informed me of your kindness to her last evening," he said, quietly, "and in her behalf I sincerely thank you. Permit me to offer you a chair."

Brant accepted it, and sat down, feeling the calm tone of proprietorship in the words of the other as if they had been a blow. His face flushed, yet he spoke firmly. "Possibly I misconstrue your meaning," he said, with some bluntness, determined to reach the gist of the matter at once. "Did Miss Gillis authorize you to thank me for these courtesies?"

Hampton smiled with provoking calmness, holding an unlighted cigar between his fingers. "Why, really, as to that I do not remember. I merely mentioned it as expressing the natural gratitude of us both."

"You speak as if you possessed full authority to express her mind as well as your own."

The other bowed gravely, his face impassive. "My words would quite naturally bear some such construction."

The officer hesitated, feeling more doubtful than ever regarding his own position. Chagrined, disarmed, he felt like a prisoner standing bound before his mocking captor. "Then I fear my mission here is useless."

"Entirely so, if you come for the purpose I suspect," said Hampton, sitting erect in his chair, and speaking with more rapid utterance. "To lecture me on morality, and demand my yielding up all influence over this girl,—such a mission is assured of failure. I have listened with some degree of calmness in this room already to one such address, and surrendered to its reasoning. But permit me to say quite plainly, Lieutenant Brant, that you are not the person from whom I will quietly listen to another."

"I had very little expectation that you would."

"You should have had still less, and remained away entirely.

However, now that you are here, and the subject broached, it becomes my turn to say something, and to say it clearly. It seems to me you would exhibit far better taste and discrimination if from now on you would cease forcing your attentions upon Miss Gillis."

Brant leaped to his feet, but the other never deigned to alter his position.

"Forcing my attentions!" exclaimed the officer. "God's mercy, man! do you realize what you are saying? I have forced no attentions upon Miss Gillis."

"My reference was rather to future possibilities. Young blood is proverbially hot, and I thought it wise to warn you in time."

Brant stared into that imperturbable face, and somehow the very sight of its calm, inflexible resolve served to clear his own brain. He felt that this cool, self-controlled man was speaking with authority.

"Wait just a moment," he said, at last. "I wish this made perfectly clear, and for all time. I met Miss Gillis first through pure accident. She impressed me strongly then, and I confess I have since grown more deeply interested in her personality. I have reasons to suppose my presence not altogether distasteful to her, and she has certainly shown that she reposed confidence in me. Not until late last night did I even suspect she was the same girl whom we picked up with you out on the desert. It came to me from her own lips and was a total surprise. She revealed her identity in order to justify her proposed clandestine meeting with you."

"And hence you requested this pleasant conference," broke in Hampton, coolly, "to inform me, from your calm eminence of respectability, that I was no fit companion for such a young and innocent person, and to warn me that you were prepared to act as her protector."

Brant slightly inclined his head.

"I may have had something of that nature in my mind."

"Well, Lieutenant Brant," and the older man rose to his feet, his eyes still smiling, "some might be impolite enough to say that it was the conception of a cad, but whatever it was, the tables have unexpectedly turned. Without further reference to my own personal interests in the young lady, which are, however, considerable, there remain other weighty reasons, that I am not at liberty to discuss, which make it simply impossible for you to sustain any relationship to Miss Gillis other than that of ordinary social friendship."

"You—you claim the right—"

"I distinctly claim the right, for the reason that I possess the right, and no one has ever yet known me to relinquish a hold once fairly gained. Lieutenant Brant, if I am any judge of faces you are a fighting man by nature as well as profession, but there is no opportunity for your doing any fighting here. This matter is irrevocably settled—Naida Gillis is not for you."

Brant was breathing hard. "Do you mean to insinuate that there is an understanding, an engagement between you?" he faltered, scarcely knowing how best to resent such utterance.

"You may place your own construction upon what I have said," was the quiet answer. "The special relations existing between Miss Gillis and myself chance to be no business of yours. However, I will consent to say this—I do enjoy a relationship to her that gives me complete authority to say what I have said to you. I regret having been obliged by your persistency to speak with such plainness, but this knowledge should prove sufficient to control the actions of a gentleman."

For a moment the soldier did not answer, his emotions far too strong to permit of calm utterance, his lips tightly shut. He felt utterly defeated. "Your language is sufficiently explicit," he acknowledged, at last. "I ask pardon for my unwarranted intrusion."

At the door he paused and glanced back toward that motionless figure yet standing with one hand grasping the back of the chair.

"Before I go, permit me to ask a single question," he said, frankly. "I was a friend of old Ben Gillis, and he was a friend to my father before me. Have you any reason to suspect that he was not Naida Gillis's father?"

Hampton took one hasty step forward. "What do you mean?" he exclaimed, fiercely, his eyes two coals of fire.

Brant felt that the other's display of irritation gave him an unexpected advantage.

"Nothing that need awaken anger, I am sure. Something caused me to harbor the suspicion, and I naturally supposed you would know about it. Indeed, I wondered if some such knowledge might not account for your very deep interest in keeping her so entirely to yourself."

Hampton's fingers twitched in a nervousness altogether unusual to the man, yet when he spoke his voice was like steel. "Your suspicions are highly interesting, and your cowardly insinuations base. However, if, as I suppose, your purpose is to provoke a quarrel, you will find me quite ready to accommodate you."

An instant they stood thus, eye to eye. Suddenly Brant's memory veered to the girl whose name would be smirched by any blow struck between them, and he forced back the hasty retort burning upon his lips.

"You may be, Mr. Hampton," he said, standing like a statue, his back to the door, "but I am not. As you say, fighting is my trade, yet I have never sought a personal quarrel. Nor is there any cause here, as my only purpose in asking the question was to forewarn you, and her through you, that such a suggestion had been openly made in my hearing. I presume it was a lie, and wished to be able to brand it so."

"By whom?"

"A fellow known as Silent Murphy, a government scout."

"I have heard of him. Where is he?"

"He claimed to be here waiting orders from Custer. He had camp up the Creek two days ago, but is keeping well out of sight for some reason. Telegrams have been received for him at the office but another man has called for them."

"Who?"

"Red Slavin."

"The cur!" said Hampton. "I reckon there is a bad half-hour waiting for those two fellows. What was it that Murphy said?"

"That he knew the girl's real name."

"Was that all?"

"Yes; I tried to discover his meaning, but the fellow became suspicious and shut up like a clam. Is there anything in it?"

Hampton ignored the question. "Lieutenant Brant," he said, "I am glad we have had this talk together, and exceedingly sorry that my duty has compelled me to say what I have said. Some time, however, you will sincerely thank me for it, and rejoice that you escaped so easily. I knew your father once, and I should like now to part on friendly relations with his son."

He held out his hand, and, scarcely knowing why he did so, Brant placed his own within its grasp, and as the eyes of the two men met, there was a consciousness of sympathy between them.

CHAPTER X

A SLIGHT INTERRUPTION

The young officer passed slowly down the dark staircase, his mind still bewildered by the result of the interview. His feelings toward Hampton had been materially changed. He found it impossible to nurse a dislike which seemingly had no real cause for existence. He began besides to comprehend something of the secret of his influence over Naida; even to experience himself the power of that dominating spirit. Out of controversy a feeling of respect had been born.

Yet Brant was far from being satisfied. Little by little he realized that he had gained nothing, learned nothing. Hampton had not even advanced a direct claim; he had dodged the real issue, leaving the soldier in the dark regarding his relationship to Naida, and erecting a barrier between the other two. It was a masterpiece of defence, puzzling, irritating, seemingly impassable. From the consideration of it all, Brant emerged with but one thought clearly defined—whoever she might prove to be, whatever was her present connection with Hampton, he loved this dark-eyed, auburn-haired waif. He knew it now, and never again could he doubt it. The very coming of this man into the field of contest, and his calm assumption of proprietorship and authority, had combined to awaken the slumbering heart of

Randall Parrish

the young officer. From that instant Naida Gillis became to him the one and only woman in all this world. Ay, and he would fight to win her; never confessing defeat until final decision came from her own lips. He paused, half inclined to retrace his steps and have the matter out. He turned just in time to face a dazzling vision of fluffy lace and flossy hair beside him in the dimly lighted hall.

"Oh, Lieutenant Brant!" and the vision clung to his arm tenderly. "It is such a relief to find that you are unhurt. Did—did you kill him?"

Brant stared. "I—I fear I scarcely comprehend, Miss Spencer. I have certainly taken no one's life. What can you mean?"

"Oh, I am so glad; and Naida will be, too. I must go right back and tell the poor girl, for she is nearly distracted. Oh, Lieutenant, isn't it the most romantic situation that ever was? And he is such a mysterious character!"

"To whom do you refer? Really, I am quite in the dark."

"Why, Mr. Hampton, of course. Oh, I know all about it. Naida felt so badly over your meeting this morning that I just compelled her to confide her whole story to me. And didn't you fight at all?"

"Most assuredly not," and Brant's eyes began to exhibit amusement; "indeed, we parted quite friendly."

"I told Naida I thought you would. People don't take such things so seriously nowadays, do they? But Naida is such a child and so full of romantic notions, that she worried terribly about it. Isn't it perfectly delightful what he is going to do for her?"

"I am sure I do not know."

"Why, hadn't you heard? He wants to send her East to a boarding-school and give her a fine education. Do you know, Lieutenant, I am simply dying to see him; he is such a perfectly splendid Western character."

"It would afford me pleasure to present you," and the soldier's downcast face brightened with anticipation.

"Do—do you really think it would be proper? But they do things so differently out here, don't they? Oh, I wish you would."

Feeling somewhat doubtful as to what might be the result, Brant knocked upon the door he had just closed, and, in response to the voice within, opened it. Hampton sat upon the chair by the window, but as his eyes caught a glimpse of the returned soldier with a woman standing beside him, he instantly rose to his feet.

"Mr. Hampton," said Brant, "I trust I may be pardoned for again troubling you, but this is Miss Spencer, a great admirer of Western life, who is desirous of making your acquaintance."

Miss Spencer swept gracefully forward, her cheeks flushed, her hand extended. "Oh, Mr. Hampton, I have so wished to meet with you ever since I first read your name in Aunt Lydia's letters—Mrs. Herndon is my aunt, you know,—and all about that awful time you had with those Indians. You see, I am Naida Gillis's most particular friend, and she tells me so much about you. She is such a dear, sweet girl! She felt so badly this morning over your meeting with Lieutenant Brant, fearing you might quarrel! It was such a relief to find him unhurt, but I felt that I must see you also, so as to relieve

Naida's mind entirely. I have two special friends, Mr. Moffat and Mr. McNeil,—perhaps you know them?—who have told me so much about these things. But I do think the story of your acquaintance with Naida is the most romantic I ever heard of,—exactly like a play on the stage, and I could never forgive myself if I failed to meet the leading actor. I do not wonder Naida fairly worships you."

"I most certainly appreciate your frankly expressed interest, Miss Spencer," he said, standing with her hand still retained in his, "and am exceedingly glad there is one residing in this community to whom my peculiar merits are apparent. So many are misjudged in this world, that it is quite a relief to realize that even one is appreciative, and the blessing becomes doubled when that one chances to be so very charming a young woman."

Miss Spencer sparkled instantly, her cheeks rosy. "Oh, how very gracefully you said that! I do wish you would some time tell me about your exploits. Why, Mr. Hampton, perhaps if you were to call upon me, you might see Naida, too. I wish you knew Mr. Moffat, but as you don't, perhaps you might come with Lieutenant Brant."

Hampton bowed. "I would hardly venture thus to place myself under the protection of Lieutenant Brant, although I must confess the former attractions of the Herndon home are now greatly increased. From my slight knowledge of Mr. Moffat's capabilities, I fear I should be found a rather indifferent entertainer; yet I sincerely hope we shall meet again at a time when I can 'a tale unfold.'"

"How nice that will be, and I am so grateful to you for the promise. By-the-bye, only this very morning a man stopped me on the street, actually mistaking me for Naida."

"What sort of a looking man, Miss Spencer?"

"Large, and heavily set, with a red beard. He was exceedingly polite when informed of his mistake, and said he merely had a message to deliver to Miss Gillis. But he refused to tell it to me."

The glances of the two men met, but Brant was unable to decipher the meaning hidden within the gray eyes. Neither spoke, and Miss Spencer, never realizing what her chatter meant, rattled merrily on.

"You see there are so many who speak to me now, because of my public position here. So I thought nothing strange at first, until I discovered his mistake, and then it seemed so absurd that I nearly laughed outright. Isn't it odd what such a man could possibly want with her? But really, gentlemen, I must return with my news; Naida will be so anxious. I am so glad to have met you both."

Hampton bowed politely, and Brant conducted her silently down the stairway. "I greatly regret not being able to accompany you home," he explained, "but I came down on horseback, and my duty requires that I return at once to the camp."

"Oh, indeed! how very unfortunate for me!" Even as she said so, some unexpected vision beyond flushed her cheeks prettily. "Why, Mr. Wynkoop," she exclaimed, "I am so glad you happened along, and going my way too, I am sure. Good morning, Lieutenant; I shall feel perfectly safe with Mr. Wynkoop."

CHAPTER XI

THE DOOR OPENS, AND CLOSES AGAIN

In one sense Hampton had greatly enjoyed Miss Spencer's call. Her bright, fresh face, her impulsive speech, her unquestioned beauty, had had their effect upon him, changing for the time being the gloomy trend of his thoughts. She was like a draught of pure Spring air, and he had gratefully breathed it in, and even longed for more.

But gradually the slight smile of amusement faded from his eyes. Something, which he had supposed lay securely hidden behind years and distance, had all at once come back to haunt him,—the unhappy ghost of an expiated crime, to do evil to this girl Naida. Two men, at least, knew sufficient of the past to cause serious trouble. This effort by Slavin to hold personal communication with the girl was evidently made for some definite purpose. Hampton was unable to decide what that purpose could be. He entertained no doubt regarding the enmity of the big gambler, or his desire to "get even" for all past injuries; but how much did he know? What special benefit did he hope to gain from conferring with Naida Gillis? Hampton decided to have a face-to-face interview with the man himself; he was accustomed to fight his battles in the open, and to a finish. A faint hope, which had been growing dimmer and dimmer with every passing year, began to flicker once again within his heart. He desired to see this man Murphy, and to learn exactly what he knew.

He had planned his work, and was perfectly prepared to meet its dangers. He entered the almost deserted saloon opposite the hotel, across the threshold of which he had not stepped for two years, and the man behind the bar glanced up apprehensively.

"Red Slavin?" he said. "Well, now see here, Hampton, we don't want no trouble in this shebang."

"I'm not here seeking a fight, Jim," returned the inquirer, genially. "I merely wish to ask 'Red' an unimportant question or two."

"He's there in the back room, I reckon, but he's damn liable to take a pot shot at you when you go in."

Hampton's genial smile only broadened, as he carelessly rolled an unlighted cigar between his lips.

"It seems to me you are becoming rather nervous for this line of business, Jim. You should take a good walk in the fresh air every morning, and let up on the liquor. I assure you, Mr. Slavin is one of my most devoted friends, and is of that tender disposition he would not willingly injure a fly."

He walked to the door, flung it swiftly and silently open, and stepping within, closed it behind him with his left hand. In the other glittered the steel-blue barrel of a drawn revolver.

"Slavin, sit down!"

The terse, imperative words seemed fairly to cut the air, and the red-bearded gambler, who had half risen to his feet, an oath upon his lips, sank back into his seat, staring at the apparition confronting him as if fascinated. Hampton jerked a chair up to the opposite side of the small table, and planted himself on it, his eyes never once deserting the big gambler's face.

"Put your hands on the table, and keep them there!" he said. "Now, my dear friend, I have come here in peace, not war, and take these slight precautions merely because I have heard a rumor that you have indulged in a threat or two since we last parted, and I know something of your impetuous disposition. No doubt this was exaggerated, but I am a careful man, and prefer to have the'drop,' and so I sincerely hope you will pardon my keeping you covered during what is really intended as a friendly call. I regret the necessity, but trust you are resting comfortably."

"Oh, go to hell!"

"We will consider that proposition somewhat later." Hampton laid his hat with calm deliberation on the table. "No doubt, Mr. Slavin,—if you move that hand again I'll fill your system with lead,—you experience some very natural curiosity regarding the object of my unanticipated, yet I hope no less welcome, visit."

Slavin's only reply was a curse, his bloodshot eyes roaming the room furtively.

"I suspected as much," Hampton went on, coolly. "Indeed, I should have felt hurt had you been indifferent upon such an occasion. It does credit to your heart, Slavin. Come now, keep your eyes on me! I was about to gratify your curiosity, and, in the first place, I came to inquire solicitously regarding the state of your health during my absence, and incidentally to ask why you are exhibiting so great an interest in Miss Naida Gillis."

Slavin straightened up, his great hands clinching nervously, drops of perspiration appearing on his red forehead. "I don't understand your damned fun."

Hampton's lips smiled unpleasantly. "Slavin, you greatly discourage me. The last time I was here you exhibited so fine a sense of humor that I was really quite proud of you. Yet, truly, I think you do understand this joke. Your memory can scarcely be failing at your age.—Make another motion like that and you die right there! You know me.—However, as you seem to shy over my first question, I'll honor you with a second,—Where's Silent Murphy?"

Slavin's great square jaws set, a froth oozing from between his thick lips, and for an instant the other man believed that in his paroxysm of rage he would hurl himself across the table. Then suddenly the ungainly brute went limp, his face grown haggard.

"You devil!" he roared, "what do you mean?"

Surprised as Hampton was by this complete breaking down, he knew his man far too well to yield him the slightest opportunity for treachery. With revolver hand resting on the table, the muzzle pointing at the giant's heart, he leaned forward, utterly remorseless now, and keen as an Indian on the trail.

"Do you know who I am?"

The horror in Slavin's eyes had changed to sullenness, but he nodded silently.

"How do you know?"

There was no reply, although the thick lips appeared to move.

"Answer me, you red sneak! Do you think I am here to be played with? Answer!"

Slavin gulped down something which seemed threatening to choke him, but he durst not lift a hand to wipe the sweat from his face. "If—if I didn't have this beard on you might guess. I thought you knew me all the time."

Hampton stared at him, still puzzled. "I have certainly seen you somewhere. I thought that from the first. Where was it?"

"I was in D Troop, Seventh Cavalry."

"D Troop? Brant's troop?"

The big gambler nodded. "That's how I knew you, Captain," he said, speaking with greater ease, "but I never had no reason to say anything about it round here. You was allers decent 'nough ter me."

"Possibly,"—and it was plainly evident from his quiet tone Hampton had steadied from his first surprise,—"the boot was on the other leg, and you had some good reason not to say anything."

Slavin did not answer, but he wet his lips with his tongue, his eyes on the window.

"Who is this fellow Murphy?"

"He was corporal in that same troop, sir." The ex-cavalryman dropped insensibly into his old form of speech. "He knew you too, and we talked it over, and decided to keep still, because it was none of our affair anyhow."

"Where is he now?"

"He left last night with army despatches for Cheyenne."

Hampton's eyes hardened perceptibly, and his fingers closed more tightly about the butt of his revolver. "You lie, Slavin! The last message did not reach here until this morning. That fellow is hiding somewhere in this camp, and the two of you have been trying to get at the girl. Now, damn you, what is your little game?"

The big gambler was thinking harder then, perhaps, than he had ever thought in his life before. He was no coward, although there was a yellow, wolfish streak of treachery in him, and he read clearly enough in the watchful eyes glowing behind that blue steel barrel a merciless determination which left him nerveless. He knew Hampton would kill him if he needed to do so, but he likewise realized that he was not likely to fire until he had gained the information he was seeking. Cunning pointed the only safe way out from this difficulty. Lies had served his turn well before, and he hoped much from them now. If he only knew how much information the other possessed, it would be easy enough. As he did not, he must wield his weapon blindly.

"You're makin' a devil of a fuss over little or nuthin'," he growled, simulating a tone of disgust. "I never ain't hed no quarrel with ye, exceptin' fer the way ye managed ter skin me at the table bout two years ago. I don't give two screeches in hell for who you are; an' besides, I reckon you ain't the only ex-convict a-ranging Dakota either fer the matter o' that. No more does Murphy. We ain't no bloomin' detectives, an' we ain't buckin' in on no business o' yourn; ye kin just bet your sweet life on thet."

"Where is Murphy, then? I wish to see the fellow."

"I told you he'd gone. Maybe he didn't git away till this mornin', but he's gone now all right. What in thunder do ye want o' him? I reckon I kin tell ye all thet Murphy knows."

For a breathless moment neither spoke, Hampton fingering his gun nervously, his eyes lingering on that brutal face.

"Slavin," he said at last, his voice hard, metallic, "I've figured it out, and I do know you now, you lying brute. You are the fellow who swore you saw me throw away the gun that did the shooting, and that afterwards you picked it up."

There was the spirit of murder in his eyes, and the gambler cowered back before them, trembling like a child.

"I—I only swore to the last part, Captain," he muttered, his voice scarcely audible. "I—I never said I saw you throw—"

"And I swore," went on Hampton, "that I would kill you on sight. You lying whelp, are you ready to die?"

Slavin's face was drawn and gray, the perspiration standing in beads upon his forehead, but he could neither speak nor think, fascinated by those remorseless eyes, which seemed to burn their way down into his very soul.

"No? Well, then, I will give you, to-day, just one chance to live—one, you dog—one. Don't move an eyelash! Tell me honestly why you have been trying to get word with the girl, and you shall go out from here living. Lie to me about it, and I am going to kill you where you sit, as I would a mad dog. You know me, Slavin—now speak!"

So intensely still was it, Hampton could distinguish the faint ticking of the watch in his pocket, the hiss of the breath between the giant's clinched teeth. Twice the fellow tried to utter something, his lips shaking as with the palsy, his ashen face the picture of terror. No wretch dragged shrieking to the scaffold could have formed a more pitiful sight, but there was no mercy in the eyes of the man watching him.

"Speak, you cringing hound!"

Slavin gripped his great hands together convulsively, his throat swelling beneath its red beard. He knew there was no way of escape. "I—I had to do it! My God, Captain, I had to do it!"

"Why?"

"I had to, I tell you. Oh, you devil, you fiend! I'm not the one you're after—it's Murphy!"

For a single moment Hampton stared at the cringing figure. Then suddenly he rose to his feet in decision. "Stand up! Lift your hands first, you fool. Now unbuckle your gun-belt with your left hand—your left, I said! Drop it on the floor."

There was an unusual sound behind, such as a rat might have made, and Hampton glanced aside apprehensively. In that single second Slavin was upon him, grasping his pistol-arm at the wrist, and striving with hairy hand to get a death-grip about his throat. Twice Hampton's left drove straight out into that red, gloating face, and then the giant's crushing weight bore him backward. He fought savagely, silently, his slender figure like steel, but Slavin got his grip at last, and with giant strength began to crunch his victim within his vise-like arms. There was a moment of superhuman strain, their breathing mere sobs of exhaustion. Then Slavin slipped, and Hampton succeeded in wriggling partially free from his death-grip. It was for scarcely an instant, yet it served; for as he bent aside, swinging his burly opponent with him, some one struck a vicious blow at his back; but the descending knife, missing its mark, sunk instead deep into Slavin's breast.

Hampton saw the flash of a blade, a hand, a portion of an arm, and then the clutching fingers of Slavin swept him down. He reached out blindly as he fell, his hand closing about the deserted knife-hilt. The two crashed down together upon the floor, the force of the fall driving the blade home to the gambler's heart.

CHAPTER XII

THE COHORTS OF JUDGE LYNCH

Hampton staggered blindly to his feet, looking down on the motionless body. He was yet dazed from the sudden cessation of struggle, dazed still more by something he had seen in the instant that deadly knife flashed past him. For a moment the room appeared to swim before his eyes, and he clutched at the overturned table for support, Then, as his senses returned, he perceived the figures of a number of men jamming the narrow doorway, and became aware of their loud, excited voices. Back to his benumbed brain there came with a rush the whole scene, the desperation of his present situation. He had been found alone with the dead man. Those men, when they came surging in attracted by the noise of strife, had found him lying on Slavin, his hand clutching the knife-hilt. He ran his eyes over their horrified faces, and knew instantly they held him the murderer.

The shock of this discovery steadied him. He realized the meaning, the dread, terrible meaning, for he knew the West, its fierce, implacable spirit of vengeance, its merciless code of lynch-law. The vigilantes of the mining camps were to him an old story; more than once he had witnessed their work, been cognizant of their power. This was no time to parley or to hesitate. He had seen and heard in that room that which left him eager to live, to be free, to open a long-closed door hiding the mystery of years. The key, at last, had fallen almost within reach of his fingers, and he would never consent to be robbed of it by the wild rage of a mob. He grabbed the loaded revolver lying upon the floor, and swung Slavin's discarded belt across his shoulder. If it was to be a fight, he would be found there to the death, and God have mercy on the man who stopped him!

"Stand aside, gentlemen," he commanded. "Step back, and let me pass!"

They obeyed. He swept them with watchful eyes, stepped past, and slammed the door behind him. In his heart he held them as curs, but curs could snap, and enough of them might dare to pull him down. Men were already beginning to pour into the saloon, uncertain yet of the facts, and shouting questions to each other. Totally ignoring these, Hampton thrust himself recklessly through the crowd. Half-way down the broad steps Buck Mason faced him, in shirt sleeves, his head uncovered, an ugly "45" in his up-lifted hand. Just an instant the eyes of the two men met, and neither doubted the grim purpose of the other.

"You've got ter do it, Bob," announced the marshal, shortly, "dead er alive."

Hampton never hesitated. "I'm sorry I met you. I don't want to get anybody else mixed up in this fuss. If you'll promise me a chance for my life, Buck, I'll throw up my hands. But I prefer a bullet to a mob."

The little marshal was sandy-haired, freckle-faced, and all nerve. He cast one quick glance to left and right. The crowd jammed within the Occidental had already turned and were surging toward the door; the hotel opposite was beginning to swarm; down the street a throng of men was pouring forth from the Miners' Retreat, yelling fiercely, while hurrying figures could be distinguished here and there among the scattered buildings, all headed in their direction. Hampton knew from long experience what this meant; these were the quickly inflamed cohorts of Judge Lynch—they would act first, and reflect later. His square jaws set like a trap.

"All right, Bob," said the marshal. "You're my prisoner, and there'll be one hell of a fight afore them lads git ye. There's a chance left—leg it after me."

Just as the mob surged out of the Occidental, cursing and struggling, the two sprang forward and dashed into the narrow space between the livery-stable and the hotel. Moffat chanced to be in the passage-way, and pausing to ask no questions, Mason promptly landed that gentleman on the back of his head in a pile of discarded tin cans, and kicked viciously at a yellow dog which ventured to snap at them as they swept past. Behind arose a volley of curses, the thud of feet, an occasional voice roaring out orders, and a sharp spat of revolver shots. One ball plugged into the siding of the hotel, and a second threw a spit of sand into their lowered faces, but neither man glanced back. They were running for their lives now, racing for a fair chance to turn at bay and fight, their sole hope the steep, rugged hill in their front. Hampton began to understand the purpose of his companion, the quick, unerring instinct which had led him to select the one suitable spot where the successful waging of battle against such odds was possible—the deserted dump of the old Shasta mine.

With every nerve strained to the uttermost, the two men raced side by side down the steep slope, ploughed through the tangled underbrush, and toiled up the sharp ascent beyond. Already their pursuers were crowding the more open spaces below, incited by that fierce craze for swift vengeance which at times sweeps even the law-abiding off their feet. Little better than brutes they came howling on, caring only in this moment to strike and slay. The whole affair had been like a flash of fire, neither pursuers nor pursued realizing the half of the story in those first rapid seconds of breathless action. But back yonder lay a dead man, and every instinct of the border demanded a victim in return.

At the summit of the ore dump the two men flung themselves panting down, for the first time able now to realize what it all meant. They could perceive the figures of their pursuers among the shadows of the bushes below, but these were not venturing out into the open—the first mad, heedless rush had evidently ended. There were some cool heads among the mob leaders, and it was highly probable that negotiations would be tried before that crowd hurled itself against two desperate men, armed and entrenched. Both fugitives realized this, and lay there coolly watchful, their breath growing more regular, their eyes softening.

"Whut is all this fuss about, anyhow?" questioned the marshal, evidently somewhat aggrieved. "I wus just eatin' dinner when a feller stuck his head in an' yelled ye'd killed somebody over at the Occidental."

Hampton turned his face gravely toward him. "Buck, I don't know whether you'll believe me or not, but I guess you never heard me tell a lie, or knew of my trying to dodge out of a bad scrape. Besides, I haven't anything to gain now, for I reckon you're planning to stay with me, guilty or not guilty, but I did not kill that fellow. I don't exactly see how I can prove it, the way it all happened, but I give you my word as a man, I did not kill him."

Mason looked him squarely in the eyes, his teeth showing

behind his stiff, closely clipped mustache. Then he deliberately extended his hand, and gripped Hampton's. "Of course
I believe ye. Not that you're any too blame good, Bob, but
you ain't the kind what pleads the baby act. Who was the
feller?"

"Red Slavin."

"No!" and the hand grip perceptibly tightened. "Holy Moses,
what ingratitude! Why, the camp ought to get together and
give ye a vote of thanks, and instead, here they are trying
their level best to hang you. Cussedest sorter thing a mob is,
anyhow; goes like a flock o' sheep after a leader, an' I bet I
could name the fellers who are a-runnin' that crowd. How did
the thing happen?"

Both men were intently observing the ingathering of their
scattered pursuers, but Hampton answered gravely, telling
his brief story with careful detail, appreciating the importance of reposing full confidence in this quiet, resourceful
companion. The little marshal was all grit, nerve, faithfulness
to duty, from his head to his heels.

"All I really saw of the fellow," he concluded, "was a hand
and arm as they drove in the knife. You can see there where
it ripped me, and the unexpected blow of the man's body
knocked me forward, and of course I fell on Slavin. It may
be I drove the point farther in when I came down, but that
was an accident. The fact is, Buck, I had every reason to
wish Slavin to live. I was just getting out of him some
information I needed."

Mason nodded, his eyes wandering from Hampton's
expressive face to the crowd beginning to collect beneath the
shade of a huge oak a hundred yards below.

"Never carry a knife, do ye?"

"No."

"Thought not; always heard you fought with a gun. Caught no sight of the feller after ye got up?"

"All I saw then was the crowd blocking the door-way. I knew they had caught me lying on Slavin, with my hand grasping the knife-hilt, and, someway, I couldn't think of anything just then but how to get out of there into the open. I've seen vigilantes turn loose before, and knew what was likely to happen!"

"Sure. Recognize anybody in that first bunch?"

"Big Jim, the bartender, was the only one I knew; he had a bung-starter in his hand."

Mason nodded thoughtfully, his mouth puckered. "It's him, and half a dozen other fellers of the same stripe, who are kickin' up all this fracas. The most of 'em are yonder now, an' if it wusn't fer leavin' a prisoner unprotected, darn me if I wudn't like to mosey right down thar an' pound a little hoss sense into thet bunch o' cattle. Thet's 'bout the only thing ye kin do fer a plum fool, so long as the law won't let ye kill him."

They lapsed into contemplative silence, each man busied with his own thought, and neither perceiving clearly any probable way out of the difficulty. Hampton spoke first.

"I'm really sorry that you got mixed up in this, Buck, for it looks to me about nine chances out of ten against either of us getting away from here unhurt."

"Oh, I don't know. It's bin my experience thet there's allers chances if you only keep yer eyes skinned. Of course them fellers has got the bulge; they kin starve us out, maybe they kin smoke us out, and they kin sure make things onpleasant whenever they git their long-range guns to throwin' lead permiscous. Thet's their side of the fun. Then, on the other hand, if we kin only manage to hold 'em back till after dark we maybe might creep away through the bush to take a hand in this little game. Anyhow, it's up to us to play it out to the limit. Bless my eyes, if those lads ain't a-comin' up right now!"

A half-dozen men were starting to climb the hillside, following a dim trail through the tangled underbrush. Looking down upon them, it was impossible to distinguish their faces, but two among them, at least, carried firearms. Mason stepped up on to the ore-dump where he could see better, and watched their movements closely.

"Hi, there!" he called, his voice harsh and strident. "You fellers are not invited to this picnic, an' there'll be somethin' doin' if you push along any higher."

The little bunch halted instantly just without the edge of the heavy timber, turning their faces up toward the speaker. Evidently they expected to be hailed, but not quite so soon.

"Now, see here, Buck," answered one, taking a single step ahead of the others, and hollowing his hand as a trumpet to speak through, "it don't look to us fellers as if this affair was any of your funeral, nohow, and we've come 'long ahead of the others just on purpose to give you a fair show to pull out of it afore the real trouble begins. *Sabe*?"

"Is thet so?"

The little marshal was too far away for them to perceive how his teeth set beneath the bristly mustache.

"You bet! The boys don't consider thet it's hardly the square deal your takin' up agin 'em in this way. They 'lected you marshal of this yere camp, but it warn't expected you'd ever take no sides 'long with murderers. Thet's too stiff fer us to abide by. So come on down, Buck, an' leave us to attend to the cuss."

"If you mean Hampton, he's my prisoner. Will you promise to let me take him down to Cheyenne fer trial?"

"Wal, I reckon not, old man. We kin give him a trial well 'nough right here in Glencaid," roared another voice from out the group, which was apparently growing restless over the delay. "But we ain't inclined to do you no harm onless ye ram in too far. So come on down, Buck, throw up yer cards; we've got all the aces, an' ye can't bluff this whole darn camp."

Mason spat into the dump contemptuously, his hands thrust into his pockets. "You're a fine-lookin' lot o' law-abidin' citizens, you are! Blamed if you ain't. Why, I wouldn't give a snap of my fingers fer the whole kit and caboodle of ye, you low-down, sneakin' parcel o' thieves. Ye say it wus yer votes whut made me marshal o' this camp. Well, I reckon they did, an' I reckon likewise I know 'bout whut my duty under the law is, an' I'm a-goin' to do it. If you fellers thought ye 'lected a chump, this is the time you git left. This yere man, Bob Hampton, is my prisoner, an' I'll take him to Cheyenne, if I have ter brain every tough in Glencaid to do it. Thet's me, gents."

"Oh, come off; you can't run your notions agin the whole blame moral sentiment of this camp."

"Moral sentiment! I'm backin' up the law, not moral sentiment, ye cross-eyed beer-slinger, an' if ye try edgin' up ther another step I'll plug you with this '45.'"

There was a minute of hesitancy while the men below conferred, the marshal looking contemptuously down upon them, his revolver gleaming ominously in the light. Evidently the group hated to go back without the prisoner.

"Oh, come on, Buck, show a little hoss sense," the leader sang out. "We've got every feller in camp along with us, an' there ain't no show fer the two o' ye to hold out against that sort of an outfit."

Mason smiled and patted the barrel of his Colt.

"Oh, go to blazes! When I want any advice, Jimmie, I'll send fer ye."

Some one fired, the ball digging up the soft earth at the marshal's feet, and flinging it in a blinding cloud into Hampton's eyes. Mason's answer was a sudden fusilade, which sent the crowd flying helter-skelter into the underbrush. One among them staggered and half fell, yet succeeded in dragging himself out of sight.

"Great Scott, if I don't believe I winged James!" the shooter remarked cheerfully, reaching back into his pocket for more cartridges. "Maybe them boys will be a bit more keerful if they once onderstand they're up agin the real thing. Well, perhaps I better skin down, fer I reckon it's liable ter be rifles next."

It was rifles next, and the "winging" of Big Jim, however it may have inspired caution, also developed fresh animosity in the hearts of his followers, and brought forth evidences of discipline in their approach. Peering across the sheltering dump pile, the besieged were able to perceive the dark figures cautiously advancing through the protecting brush; they spread out widely until their two flanks were close in against the wall of rock, and then the deadly rifles began to spit spitefully, the balls casting up the soft dirt in clouds or flattening against the stones. The two men crouched lower, hugging their pile of slag, unable to perceive even a stray assailant within range of their ready revolvers. Hampton remained cool, alert, and motionless, striving in vain to discover some means of escape, but the little marshal kept grimly cheerful, creeping constantly from point to point in the endeavor to get a return shot at his tormentors.

"This whole blame country is full of discharged sojers," he growled, "an' they know their biz all right. I reckon them fellers is pretty sure to git one of us yit; anyhow, they've got us cooped. Say, Bob, thet lad crawling yonder ought to be in reach, an' it's our bounden duty not to let the boys git too gay."

Hampton tried the shot suggested, elevating considerable to overcome distance. There was a yell, and a swift skurrying backward which caused Mason to laugh, although neither knew whether this result arose from fright or wound.

"'Bliged ter teach 'em manners onct in a while, or they'll imbibe a fool notion they kin come right 'long up yere without no invite. 'T ain't fer long, no how, 'less all them guys are ijuts."

Hampton turned his head and looked soberly into the freckled face, impressed by the speaker's grave tone.

"Why?"

"Fire, my boy, fire. The wind's dead right fer it; thet brush will burn like so much tinder, an' with this big wall o' rock back of us, it will be hell here, all right. Some of 'em are bound to think of it pretty blame soon, an' then, Bob, I reckon you an' I will hev' to take to the open on the jump."

Hampton's eyes hardened. God, how he desired to live just then, to uncover that fleeing Murphy and wring from him the whole truth which had been eluding him all these years! Surely it was not justice that all should be lost now. The smoke puffs rose from the encircling rifles, and the hunted men cowered still lower, the whistling of the bullets in their ears.

CHAPTER XIII

"SHE LOVES ME; SHE LOVES ME NOT"

Unkind as the Fates had proved to Brant earlier in the day, they relented somewhat as the sun rose higher, and consented to lead him to far happier scenes. There is a rare fortune which seems to pilot lovers aright, even when they are most blind to the road, and the young soldier was now most truly a lover groping through the mists of doubt and despair.

It was no claim of military duty which compelled him to relinquish Miss Spencer so promptly at the hotel door, but rather a desire to escape her ceaseless chatter and gain retirement where he could reflect in quiet over the revelations of Hampton. In this quest he rode slowly up the valley of the Bear Water, through the bright sunshine, the rare beauty of the scene scarcely leaving the slightest impress on his mind, so busy was it, and so preoccupied. He no longer had any doubt that Hampton had utilized his advantageous position, as well as his remarkable powers of pleasing, to ensnare the susceptible heart of this young, confiding girl. While the man had advanced no direct claim, he had said enough to make perfectly clear the close intimacy of their relation and the existence of a definite understanding between them. With this recognized as a fact, was he justified in endeavoring to win Naida Gillis for himself? That the girl would find continued happiness with such a man as Hampton he did not for a moment believe possible; that she had been deliberately deceived regarding his true character he felt no doubt. The fellow had impressed her by means of his picturesque personality, his cool, dominating manner, his veneer of refinement; he had presumed on her natural gratitude, her girlish susceptibility, her slight knowledge of the world, to worm his way into her confidence, perhaps even to inspire love. These probabilities, as Brant understood them, only served to render him more ardent in his quest, more eager to test his strength in the contest for a prize so well worth the winning. He acknowledged no right that such a man as Hampton could justly hold over so innocent and trustful a heart. The girl was morally so far above him as to make his very touch a profanation, and at the unbidden thought of it, the soldier vowed to oppose such an unholy consummation. Nor did he, even then, utterly despair of winning, for he recalled afresh the intimacy of their few past meetings, his face brightening in memory of this and that brief word or shy glance. There is a voiceless language of love which a lover alone can interpret, and Brant rode on slowly, deciphering its messages, and attaining new courage with every step of his horse.

All the world loves a lover, and all the fairies guide him. As the officer's eyes, already smiling in anticipated victory, glanced up from the dusty road, he perceived just ahead the same steep bank down which he had plunged in his effort at capturing his fleeing tormentor. With the sight there came upon him a desire to loiter again in the little glen where they had first met, and dream once more of her who had given to the shaded nook both life and beauty. Amid the sunshine and the shadow he could picture afresh that happy, piquant face, the dark coils of hair, those tantalizing eyes. He swung himself from the saddle, tied a loose rein to a scrub oak, and clambered up the bank.

With the noiseless step of a plainsman he pushed in through the labyrinths of bush, only to halt petrified upon the very edge of that inner barrier. No figment of imagination, but the glowing reality of flesh and blood, awaited him. She had neither seen nor heard his approach, and he stopped in perplexity. He had framed a dozen speeches for her ears, yet now he could do no more than stand and gaze, his heart in his eyes. And it was a vision to enchain, to hold lips speechless. She was seated with unstudied grace on the edge of the bank, her hands clasped about one knee, her sweet face sobered by thought, her eyes downcast, the long lashes plainly outlined against the clear cheeks. He marked the graceful sweep of her dark, close-fitting dress, the white fringe of dainty underskirt, the small foot, neatly booted, peeping from beneath, and the glimpse of round, white throat, rendered even fairer by the creamy lace encircling it. Against the darker background of green shrubs she resembled a picture entitled "Dreaming," which he dimly recalled lingering before in some famous Eastern gallery, and his heart beat faster in wonderment at what the mystic dream might be. To draw back unobserved was impossible, even had he possessed strength of will sufficient to make the attempt, nor would words of easy greeting come to his relief. He could merely worship silently as before a sacred shrine. It was thus she glanced up and saw him with startled eyes, her hands unclasping, her cheeks rose-colored.

"Lieutenant Brant, you here?" she exclaimed, speaking as if his presence seemed unreal. "What strange miracles an idle thought can work!"

"Thoughts, I have heard," he replied, coming toward her with head uncovered, "will sometimes awaken answers through vast distances of time and space. As my thought was with you I may be altogether to blame for thus arousing your own. From the expression of your face I supposed you dreaming."

She smiled, her eyes uplifted for a single instant to his own. "It was rather thought just merging into dream, and there are few things in life more sweet. I know not whether it is the common gift of all minds, but my day-dreams are almost more to me than my realities."

"First it was moods, and now dreams." He seated himself comfortably at her feet. "You would cause me to believe you a most impractical person, Miss Naida."

She laughed frankly, that rippling peal of unaffected merriment which sounded so like music to his ears. "If that were only true, I am sure I should be most happy, for it has been my fortune so far to conjure up only pleasure through day-dreaming—the things I like and long for become my very own then. But if you mean, as I suspect, that I do not enjoy the dirt and drudgery of life, then my plea will have to be guilty. I, of course, grant their necessity, yet apparently there are plenty who find them well worth while, and there should be other work for those who aspire. Back of what you term practical some one has said there is always a dream, a first conception. In that sense I choose to be a dreamer."

"And not so unwise a choice, if your dreams only tend toward results." He sat looking into her animated face, deeply puzzled by both words and actions. "I cannot help noticing that you avoid all reference to my meeting with Mr. Hampton. Is this another sign of your impractical mind?"

"I should say rather the opposite, for I had not even supposed it concerned me."

"Indeed! That presents a vastly different view from the one given us an hour since. The distinct impression was then conveyed to both our minds that you were greatly distressed regarding the matter. Is it possible you can have been acting again?"

"I? Certainly not!" and she made no attempt to hide her indignation. "What can you mean?"

He hesitated an instant in his reply, feeling that possibly he was treading upon thin ice. But her eyes commanded a direct answer, and he yielded to them.

"We were informed that you experienced great anxiety for fear we might quarrel,—so great, indeed, that you had confided your troubles to another."

"To whom?"

"Miss Spencer. She came to us ostensibly in your name, and as a peacemaker."

A moment she sat gazing directly at him, then she laughed softly.

"Why, how supremely ridiculous; I can hardly believe it true, only your face tells me you certainly are not in play. Lieutenant Brant, I have never even dreamed of such a thing. You had informed me that your mission was one of peace, and he pledged me his word not to permit any quarrel. I had the utmost confidence in you both."

"How, then, did she even know of our meeting?"

"I am entirely in the dark, as mystified as you," she acknowledged, frankly, "for it has certainly never been a habit with me to betray the confidence of my friends, and I learned long since not to confide secrets to Miss Spencer."

Apparently neither cared to discuss the problem longer, yet he remained silent considering whether to venture the asking of those questions which might decide his fate. He was uncertain of the ground he occupied, while Miss Naida, with all her frankness, was not one to approach thoughtlessly, nor was the sword of her tongue without sharp point.

"You speak of your confidence in us both," he said, slowly. "To me the complete trust you repose in Mr. Hampton is scarcely comprehensible. Do you truly believe in his reform?"

"Certainly. Don't you?"

The direct return question served to nettle and confuse him. "It is, perhaps, not my place to say, as my future happiness does not directly depend on the permanence of his reformation. But if his word can be depended upon, your happiness to a very large extent does."

She bowed. "I have no doubt you can safely repose confidence in whatever he may have told you regarding me."

"You indorse, then, the claims he advances?"

"You are very insistent; yet I know of no good reason why I should not answer. Without at all knowing the nature of those claims to which you refer, I have no hesitancy in saying that I possess such complete confidence in Bob Hampton as to reply unreservedly yes. But really, Lieutenant Brant, I should prefer talking upon some other topic. It is evident that you two gentlemen are not friendly, yet there is no reason why any misunderstanding between you should interfere with our friendship, is there?"

She asked this question with such perfect innocence that Brant believed she failed to comprehend Hampton's claims.

"I have been informed that it must," he explained. "I have been told that I was no longer to force my attentions upon Miss Gillis."

"By Bob Hampton?"

"Yes. Those were, I believe, his exact words. Can you wonder that I hardly know how I stand in your sight?"

"I do not at all understand," she faltered. "Truly, Lieutenant Brant, I do not. I feel that Mr. Hampton would not say that without a good and sufficient reason. He is not a man to be swayed by prejudice; yet, whatever the reason may be, I know nothing about it."

"But you do not answer my last query."

"Perhaps I did not hear it."

"It was, How do I stand in your sight? That is of far more importance to me now than any unauthorized command from Mr. Hampton."

She glanced up into his serious face shyly, with a little dimple of returning laughter. "Indeed; but perhaps he might not care to have me say. However, as I once informed you that you were very far from being my ideal, possibly it may now be my duty to qualify that harsh statement somewhat."

"By confessing that I am your ideal?"

"Oh, indeed, no! We never realize our ideals, you know, or else they would entirely cease to be ideals. My confession is limited to a mere admission that I now consider you a very pleasant young man."

"You offer me a stone when I cry unto you for bread," he exclaimed. "The world is filled with pleasant young men. They are a drug on the market. I beg some special distinction, some different classification in your eyes."

"You are becoming quite hard to please," her face turned partially away, her look meditative, "and—and dictatorial; but I will try. You are intelligent, a splendid dancer, fairly good-looking, rather bright at times, and, no doubt, would prove venturesome if not held strictly to your proper place. Take it all in all, you are even interesting, and—I admit—I am inclined to like you."

The tantalizing tone and manner nerved him; he grasped the white hand resting invitingly on the grass, and held it firmly within his own. "You only make sport as you did once before. I must have the whole truth."

"Oh, no; to make sport at such a time would be sheerest mockery, and I would never dare to be so free. Why, remember we are scarcely more than strangers. How rude you are! only our third time of meeting, and you will not release my hand."

"Not unless I must, Naida," and the deep ringing soberness of his voice startled the girl into suddenly uplifting her eyes to his face. What she read there instantly changed her mood from playfulness to earnest gravity.

"Oh, please do not—do not say what you are tempted to," her voice almost pleading. "I cannot listen; truly I cannot; I must not. It would make us both very unhappy, and you would be sure to regret such hasty words."

"Regret!" and he yet clung to the hand which she scarcely endeavored to release, bending forward, hoping to read in her hidden eyes the secret her lips guarded. "Am I, then, not old enough to know my own mind?"

"Yes—yes; I hope so, yes; but it is not for me; it can never be for me—I am no more than a child, a homeless waif, a nobody. You forget that I do not even know who I am, or the name I ought rightfully to bear. I will not have it so."

"Naida, sweetheart!" and he burst impetuously through all bonds of restraint, her flushed cheeks the inspiration to his daring. "I will speak, for I care nothing for all this. It is you I love—love forever. Do you understand me, darling? I love you! I love you!"

For an instant,—one glad, weak, helpless, forgetful instant,—she did not see him, did not even know herself; the very world was lost. Then she awoke as if from a dream, his strong arms clasped about her, his lips upon hers.

"You must not," she sobbed. "I tell you no! I will not consent; I will not be false to myself. You have no right; I gave you no right."

He permitted her to draw away, and they stood facing each other, he eager, mystified, thrilling with passion almost beyond mastery, she trembling and unstrung, her cheeks crimson, her eyes filled with mute appeal.

"I read it in your face," he insisted. "It told of love."

"Then my face must have lied," she answered, her soft voice

tremulous, "or else you read the message wrongly. It is from my lips you must take the answer."

"And they kissed me."

"If so, I knew it not. It was by no volition of mine. Lieutenant Brant, I have trusted you so completely; that was not right."

"My heart exonerates me."

"I cannot accept that guidance."

"Then you do not love me."

She paused, afraid of the impulse that swept her on. "Perhaps," the low voice scarcely audible, "I may love you too well."

"You mean there is something—some person, perhaps—standing between?"

She looked frankly at him. "I do mean just that. I am not heartless, and I sincerely wish we had never met; but this must be the end."

"The end? And with no explanation?"

"There is no other way." He could perceive tears in her eyes, although she spoke bravely. "Nor can I explain, for all is not clear even to me. But this I know, there is a barrier between us insurmountable; not even the power of love can overcome it; and I appeal to you to ask me no more."

It was impossible for him to doubt her sober earnestness, or the depth of her feelings; the full truth in her words was pictured upon her face, and in the pathetic appeal of her eyes. She extended both hands.

"You will forgive me? Truly, this barrier has not been raised by me."

He bowed low, until his lips pressed the white fingers, but before he could master himself to utter a word in reply, a distant voice called his name, and both glanced hastily around.

"That cry came from the valley," he said. "I left my horse tied there. I will go and learn what it means."

She followed him part of the way through the labyrinth of underbrush, hardly knowing why she did so. He stood alone upon the summit of the high bluff whence he could look across the stream. Miss Spencer stood below waving her parasol frantically, and even as he gazed at her, his ears caught the sound of heavy firing down the valley.

CHAPTER XIV

PLUCKED FROM THE BURNING

That Miss Spencer was deeply agitated was evident at a glance, while the nervous manner in which she glanced in the direction of those distant gun shots, led Brant to jump to the conclusion that they were in some way connected with her appearance.

"Oh, Lieutenant Brant," she cried, excitedly, "they are going to kill him down there, and he never did it at all. I know he didn't, and so does Mr. Wynkoop. Oh, please hurry! Nobody knew where you were, until I saw your horse tied here, and Mr. Wynkoop has been hunting for you everywhere. He is nearly frantic, poor man, and I cannot learn where either Mr. Moffat or Mr. McNeil is, and I just know those dreadful creatures will kill him before we can get help."

"Kill whom?" burst in Brant, springing down the bank fully awakened to the realization of some unknown emergency. "My dear Miss Spencer, tell me your story quickly if you wish me to act. Who is in danger, and from what?"

The girl burst into tears, but struggled bravely through with her message.

"It's those awful men, the roughs and rowdies down in Glencaid. They say he murdered Red Slavin, that big gambler who spoke to me this morning, but he didn't, for I saw the man who did, and so did Mr. Wynkoop. He jumped out of the saloon window, his hand all bloody, and ran away. But they've got him and the town marshal up behind the Shasta dump, and swear they're going to hang him if they can only take him alive. Oh, just hear those awful guns!"

"Yes, but who is it?"

"Bob Hampton, and—and he never did it at all."

Before Brant could either move or speak, Naida swept past him, down the steep bank, and her voice rang out clear, insistent. "Bob Hampton attacked by a mob? Is that true, Phoebe? They are fighting at the Shasta dump, you say? Lieutenant Brant, you must act—you must act now, for my sake!"

She sprang toward the horse, nerved by Brant's apparent slowness to respond, and loosened the rein from the scrub oak. "Then I will myself go to him, even if they kill me also, the cowards!"

But Brant had got his head now. Grasping her arm and the rein of the plunging horse, "You will go home," he commanded, with the tone of military authority. "Go home with Miss Spencer. All that can possibly be done to aid Hampton I shall do—will you go?"

She looked helplessly into his face. "You—you don't like him," she faltered; "I know you don't. But—but you will help him, won't you, for my sake?"

He crushed back an oath. "Like him or not like him, I will

save him if it be in the power of man. Now will you go?"

"Yes," she answered, and suddenly extended her arms. "Kiss me first."

With the magical pressure of her lips upon his, he swung into the saddle and spurred down the road. It was a principle of his military training never to temporize with a mob—he would strike hard, but he must have sufficient force behind him. He reined up before the seemingly deserted camp, his horse flung back upon its haunches, white foam necking its quivering flanks.

"Sergeant!" The sharp snap of his voice brought that officer forward on the run. "Where are the men?"

"Playin' ball, most of 'em, sir, just beyond the ridge."

"Are the horses out in herd?"

"Yes, sir."

"Sound the recall; arm and mount every man; bring them into Glencaid on the gallop. Do you know the old Shasta mine?"

"No, sir."

"Half-way up the hill back of the hotel. You'll find me somewhere in front of it. This is a matter of life or death, so jump lively now!"

He drove in his spurs, and was off like the wind. A number of men were in the street, all hurrying forward in the same direction, but he dashed past them. These were miners mostly, eager to have a hand in the man-hunt. Here and there a rider skurried along and joined in the chase. Just beyond the hotel, half-way up the hill, rifles were speaking irregularly, the white puffs of smoke blown quickly away by the stiff breeze. Near the centre of this line of skirmishers a denser cloud was beginning to rise in spirals. Brant, perceiving the largest group of men gathered just before him, rode straight toward them. The crowd scattered slightly at his rapid approach, but promptly closed in again as he drew up his horse with taut rein. He looked down into rough, bearded faces. Clearly enough these men were in no fit spirit for peace-making.

"You damn fool!" roared one, hoarsely, his gun poised as if in threat, "what do you mean by riding us down like that? Do you own this country?"

Brant flung himself from the saddle and strode in front of the fellow. "I mean business. You see this uniform? Strike that, my man, and you strike the United States. Who is leading this outfit?"

"I don't know as it's your affair," the man returned, sullenly. "We ain't takin' no army orders at present, mister. We're freeborn American citizens, an' ye better let us alone."

"That is not what I asked you," and Brant squared his shoulders, his hands clinched. "My question was, Who is at the head of this outfit? and I want an answer."

The spokesman looked around upon the others near him with a grin of derision. "Oh, ye do, hey? Well, I reckon we are, if you must know. Since Big Jim Larson got it in the shoulder this outfit right yere hes bin doin' most of the brain work. So, if ye've got anythin' ter say, mister officer man, I reckon ye better spit it out yere ter me, an' sorter relieve yer mind."

"Who are you?"

The fellow expectorated vigorously into the leaves under foot, and drawing one hairy hand across his lips, flushed angrily to the unexpected inquiry.

"Oh, tell him, Ben. What's the blame odds? He can't do ye no hurt."

The man's look became dogged. "I'm Ben Colton, if it'll do ye any good to know."

"I thought I had seen you somewhere before," said Brant, contemptuously, and then swept his glance about the circle. "A nice leader of vigilantes you are, a fine representative of law and order, a lovely specimen of the free-born American citizen! Men, do you happen to know what sort of a cur you are following in this affair?"

"Oh, Ben's all right."

"What ye got against him, young feller?"

"Just this," and Brant squarely fronted the man, his voice ringing like steel. "I've seen mobs before to-day, and I've dealt with them. I'm not afraid of you or your whole outfit, and I've got fighting men to back me up. I never yet saw any mob which wasn't led and incited by some cowardly, revengeful rascal. Honest men get mixed up in such affairs, but they are invariably inflamed by some low-down sneak with an axe to grind. I confess I don't know all about this Colton, but I know enough to say he is an army deserter, a liar, a dive-keeper, a gambler, and, to my certain knowledge, the direct cause of the death of three men, one a soldier of my troop. Now isn't he a sweet specimen to lead in the avenging of a supposed crime?"

Whatever else Colton might have failed in, he was a man of action. Like a flash his gun flew to the level, but was instantly knocked aside by the grizzled old miner standing next him.

"None o' that, Ben," he growled, warningly. "It don't never pay to shoot holes in Uncle Sam."

Brant smiled. He was not there just then to fight, but to secure delay until his own men could arrive, and to turn aside the fierce mob spirit if such a result was found possible. He knew thoroughly the class of men with whom he dealt, and he understood likewise the wholesome power of his uniform.

"I really would enjoy accommodating you, Colton," he said, coolly, feeling much more at ease, "but I never fight personal battles with such fellows as you. And now, you other men, it is about time you woke up to the facts of this matter. A couple of hundred of you chasing after two men, one an officer of the law doing his sworn duty, and the other innocent of any crime. I should imagine you would feel proud of your job."

"Innocent? Hell!"

"That is what I said. You fellows have gone off half-cocked—a mob generally does. Both Miss Spencer and Mr. Wynkoop state positively that they saw the real murderer of Red Slavin, and it was not Bob Hampton."

The men were impressed by his evident earnestness, his unquestioned courage. Colton laughed sneeringly, but Brant gave him no heed beyond a quick, warning glance. Several voices spoke almost at once.

"Is that right?"

"Oh, say, I saw the fellow with his hand on the knife."

"After we git the chap, we'll give them people a chance to tell what they know."

Brant's keenly attentive ears heard the far-off chug of numerous horses' feet.

"I rather think you will," he said, confidently, his voice ringing out with sudden authority.

He stepped back, lifted a silver whistle to his lips, and sounded one sharp, clear note. There was a growing thunder of hoofs, a quick, manly cheer, a crashing through the underbrush, and a squad of eager troopers, half-dressed but with faces glowing in anticipation of trouble, came galloping up the slope, swinging out into line as they advanced, their carbines gleaming in the sunlight. It was prettily, sharply performed, and their officer's face brightened.

"Very nicely done, Watson," he said to the expectant sergeant. "Deploy your men to left and right, and clear out those shooters. Make a good job of it, but no firing unless you have to."

The troopers went at it as if they enjoyed the task, forcing their restive horses through the thickets, and roughly handling more than one who ventured to question their authority. Yet the work was over in less time than it takes to tell, the discomfited regulators driven pell-mell down the hill and back into the town, the eager cavalrymen halting only at the command of the bugle. Brant, confident of his first sergeant in such emergency, merely paused long enough to watch the men deploy, and then pressed straight up the hill, alone and on foot. That danger to the besieged was yet imminent was very evident. The black spiral of smoke had become an enveloping cloud, spreading rapidly in both directions from its original starting-point, and already he could distinguish the red glare of angry flames leaping beneath, fanned by the wind into great sheets of fire, and sweeping forward with incredible swiftness. These might not succeed in reaching the imprisoned men, but the stifling vapor, the suffocating smoke held captive by that over-hanging rock, would prove a most serious menace.

He encountered a number of men running down as he toiled anxiously forward, but they avoided him, no doubt already aware of the trouble below and warned by his uniform. He arrived finally where the ground was charred black and covered with wood ashes, still hot under foot and smoking, but he pressed upward, sheltering his eyes with uplifted arm, and seeking passage where the scarcity of underbrush rendered the zone of fire less impassable. On both sides trees were already wrapped in flame, yet he discovered a lane along which he stumbled until a fringe of burning bushes extended completely across it. The heat was almost intole-rable, the crackling of the ignited wood was like the reports of pistols, the dense pall of smoke was suffocating. He could see scarcely three yards in advance, but to the rear the narrow lane of retreat remained open. Standing there, as though in the mouth of a furnace, the red flames scorching his face, Brant hollowed his hands for a call.

"Hampton!" The word rang out over the infernal crackling and roaring like the note of a trumpet.

"Ay! What is it?" The returning voice was plainly not Hampton's, yet it came from directly in front, and not faraway.

"Who are you? Is that you, Marshal?"

"Thet's the ticket," answered the voice, gruffly, "an' just as full o' fight es ever."

Brant lifted his jacket to protect his face from the scorching heat. There was certainly no time to lose in any exchange of compliments. Already, the flames were closing in; in five minutes more they would seal every avenue of escape.

"I'm Brant, Lieutenant Seventh Cavalry," he cried, choking with the thickening smoke. "My troop has scattered those fellows who were hunting you. I'll protect you and your prisoner, but you'll have to get out of there at once. Can you locate me and make a dash for it? Wrap your coats around your heads, and leave your guns behind."

An instant he waited for the answer, fairly writhing in the intense heat, then Mason shouted, "Hampton's been shot, and I'm winged a little; I can't carry him."

It was a desperately hard thing to do, but Brant had given his promise, and in that moment of supreme trial, he had no other thought than fulfilling it. He ripped off his jacket, wrapped it about his face, jammed a handkerchief into his mouth, and, with a prayer in his heart, leaped forward into the seemingly narrow fringe of fire in his front. Head down, he ran blindly, stumbling forward as he struck the ore-dump, and beating out with his hands the sparks that scorched his clothing. The smoke appeared to roll higher from the ground here, and the coughing soldier crept up beneath it, breathing the hot air, and feeling as though his entire body were afire. Mason, his countenance black and unrecognizable, his shirt soaked with blood, peered into his face.

"Hell, ain't it!" he sputtered, "but you're a dandy, all right."

"Is Hampton dead?"

"I reckon not. Got hit bad, though, and clear out of his head."

Brant cast one glance into the white, unconscious face of his rival, and acted with the promptness of military training.

"Whip off your shirt, Mason, and tie it around your face," he commanded, "Lively now!"

He bound his silk neckerchief across Hampton's mouth, and lifted the limp form partially from the ground. "Help me to get him up. There, that will do. Now keep as close as you can so as to steady him if I trip. Straight ahead—run for it!"

They sprang directly into the lurid flames, bending low, Brant's hands grasping the inert form lying across his shoulder. They dashed stumbling through the black, smouldering lane beyond. Half-way down this, the ground yet hot beneath their feet, the vapor stifling, but with clearer breaths of air blowing in their faces, Brant tripped and fell. Mason beat out the smouldering sparks in his clothing, and assisted him to stagger to his feet once more. Then together they bore him, now unconscious, slowly down below the first fire-line.

CHAPTER XV

THE DOOR CLOSES

Totally exhausted, the two men dropped their heavy burden on the earth. Mason swore as the blood began dripping again from his wound, which had been torn open afresh in his efforts to bear Hampton to safety. Just below them a mounted trooper caught sight of them and came forward. He failed to recognize his officer in the begrimed person before him, until called to attention by the voice of command.

"Sims, if there is any water in your canteen hand it over. Good; here, Marshal, use this. Now, Sims, note what I say carefully, and don't waste a minute. Tell the first sergeant to send a file of men up here with some sort of litter, on the run. Then you ride to the Herndon house—the yellow house where the roads fork, you remember,—and tell Miss Naida Gillis (don't forget the name) that Mr. Hampton has been seriously wounded, and we are taking him to the hotel. Can you remember that?"

"Yes, sir."

"Then off with you, and don't spare the horse."

He was gone instantly, and Brant began bathing the pallid,

upturned face.

"You'd better lie down, Marshal," he commanded. "You're pretty weak from loss of blood, and I can do all there is to be done until those fellows get here."

In fifteen minutes they appeared, and five minutes later they were toiling slowly down to the valley, Brant walking beside his still unconscious rival. Squads of troopers were scattered along the base of the hill, and grouped in front of the hotel. Here and there down the street, but especially about the steps of the Occidental, were gathered the discomfited vigilantes, busily discussing the affair, and cursing the watchful, silent guard. As these caught sight of the little party approaching, there were shouts of derision, which swelled into triumph when they perceived Hampton's apparently lifeless form, and Mason leaning in weakness on the arm of a trooper. The sight and sound angered Brant.

"Carry Hampton to his room and summon medical attendance at once," he ordered. "I have a word to say to those fellows."

Seeing Mr. Wynkoop on the hotel porch, Brant said to him: "Miss Spencer informed me that you saw a man leap from the back window of the Occidental. Is that true?"

The missionary nodded.

"Good; then come along with me. I intend breaking the back of this lynching business right here and now."

He strode directly across the street to the steps of the Occidental, his clothing scarcely more than smouldering rags. The crowd stared at him sullenly; then suddenly a reaction came, and the American spirit of fair play, the frontier appreciation of bulldog courage, burst forth into a confused murmur, that became half a cheer. Brant did not mince his words.

"Now, look here, men! If you want any more trouble we're here to accommodate you. Fighting is our trade, and we don't mind working at it. But I wish to tell you right now, and straight off the handle, that you are simply making a parcel of fools of yourselves. Slavin has been killed, and nine out of ten among you are secretly glad of it. He was a curse to this camp, but because some of his friends and cronies—thugs, gamblers, and dive-keepers—accuse Bob Hampton of having killed him, you start in blindly to lynch Hampton, never even waiting to find out whether the charge is the truth or a lie. You act like sheep, not American citizens. Now that we have pounded a little sense into some of you, perhaps you'll listen to the facts, and if you must hang some one put your rope on the right man. Bob Hampton did not kill Red Slavin. The fellow who did kill him climbed out of the back window of the Occidental here, and got away, while you were chasing the wrong man. Mr. Wynkoop saw him, and so did your schoolteacher, Miss Spencer."

Then Wynkoop stepped gamely to the front. "All that is true, men. I have been trying ever since to tell you, but no one would listen. Miss Spencer and I both saw the man jump from the window; there was blood on his right arm and hand. He was a misshapen creature whom neither of us ever saw before, and he disappeared on a run up that ravine. I have no doubt he was Slavin's murderer."

No one spoke, the crowd apparently ashamed of their actions. But Brant did not wait for any outward expression.

"Now, you fellows, think that over," he said. "I intend to post a guard until I find out whether you are going to prove yourselves fools or men, but if we sail in again those of you who start the trouble can expect to get hurt, and pay the piper. That's all."

In front of the hotel porch he met his first sergeant coming out.

"What does the doctor say about Hampton?"

"A very bad wound, sir, but not necessarily fatal; he has regained consciousness."

"Has Miss Gillis arrived?"

"I don't know, sir; there's a young woman cryin' in the parlor."

The lieutenant leaped up the steps and entered the house. But it was Miss Spencer, not Naida, who sprang to her feet.

"Oh, Lieutenant Brant; can this be truly you! How perfectly awful you look! Do you know if Mr. Hampton is really going to die? I came here just to find out about him, and tell Naida. She is almost frantic, poor thing."

Though Brant doubted Miss Spencer's honesty of statement, his reply was direct and unhesitating. "I am informed that he has a good chance to live, and I have already despatched word to Miss Gillis regarding his condition. I expect her at any moment."

"How very nice that was of you! Oh, I trembled so when you first went to face those angry men! I don't see how you ever dared to do it. I did wish that either Mr. Moffat or Mr. McNeil could have been here to go with you. Mr. Moffat especially is so daring; he is always risking his life for some one else—and no one seems able to tell me anything about either of them." The lady paused, blushing violently, as she realized what she had been saying. "Really you must not suppose me unmaidenly, Lieutenant," she explained, her eyes shyly lifting, "but you know those gentlemen were my very earliest acquaintances here, and they have been so kind. I was so shocked when Naida kissed you, Lieutenant; but the poor girl was so grateful to you for going to the help of Bob Hampton that she completely forgot herself. It is simply wonderful how infatuated the poor child is with that man. He seems almost to exercise some power of magic over her, don't you think?"

"Why frankly, Miss Spencer, I scarcely feel like discussing that topic just now. There are so many duties pressing me—" and Brant took a hasty step toward the open door, his attentive ear catching the sound of a light footstep in the hallway. He met Naida just without, pale and tearless. Both her hands were extended to him unreservedly.

"Tell me, will he live?"

"The doctor thinks yes."

"Thank God! Oh, thank God!" She pressed one hand against her heart to control its throbbing. "You cannot know what this means to me." Her eyes seemed now for the first time to mark his own deplorable condition. "And you? You have not been hurt, Lieutenant Brant?"

He smiled back into her anxious eyes. "Nothing that soap and water and a few days' retirement will not wholly remedy. My wounds are entirely upon the surface. Shall I conduct you to him?"

She bowed, apparently forgetful that one of her hands yet

remained imprisoned in his grasp. "If I may go, yes. I told Mrs. Herndon I should remain here if I could be of the slightest assistance."

They passed up the staircase side by side, exchanging no further speech. Once she glanced furtively at his face, but its very calmness kept the words upon her lips unuttered. At the door they encountered Mrs. Guffy, her honest eyes red from weeping.

"This is Miss Gillis, Mrs. Guffy," explained Brant. "She wishes to see Mr. Hampton if it is possible."

"Sure an' she can thet. He's been askin' after her, an' thet pretty face would kape any man in gud spirits, I'm thinkin'. Step roight in, miss."

She held the door ajar, but Naida paused, glancing back at her motionless companion, a glint of unshed tears showing for the first time in her eyes. "Are you not coming also?"

"No, Miss Naida. It is best for me to remain without, but my heart goes with you."

Then the door closed between them.

CHAPTER XVI

THE RESCUE OF MISS SPENCER

While Hampton lingered between life and death, assiduously waited upon by both Naida and Mrs. Guffy, Brant nursed his burns, far more serious than he had at first supposed, within the sanctity of his tent, longing for an order to take him elsewhere, and dreading the possibility of again having to encounter this girl, who remained to him so perplexing an enigma. Glencaid meanwhile recovered from its mania of lynch-law, and even began exhibiting some faint evidences of shame over what was so plainly a mistake. And the populace were also beginning to exhibit no small degree of interest in the weighty matters which concerned the fast-culminating love affairs of Miss Spencer.

Almost from her earliest arrival the extensive cattle and mining interests of the neighborhood became aggressively arrayed against each other; and now, as the fierce personal rivalry between Messrs. Moffat and McNeil grew more intense, the breach perceptibly widened. While the infatuation of the Reverend Mr. Wynkoop for this same fascinating young lady was plainly to be seen, his chances in the race were not seriously regarded by the more active partisans upon either side. As the stage driver explained to an inquisitive party of tourists, "He's a mighty fine little feller, gents, but he ain't got the git up an' git necessary ter take the boundin' fancy of a high-strung heifer like her. It needs a plum good man ter' rope an' tie any female critter in this Territory, let me tell ye."

With this conception of the situation in mind, the citizens generally settled themselves down to enjoy the truly Homeric struggle, freely wagering their gold-dust upon the outcome. The regular patrons of the Miners' Retreat were backing Mr. Moffat to a man, while those claiming head-quarters at the Occidental were equally ardent in their support of the prospects of Mr. McNeil. It must be confessed that Miss Spencer flirted outrageously, and enjoyed life as she never had done in the effete East.

In simple truth, it was not in Miss Spencer's sympathetic disposition to be cruel to any man, and in this puzzling situation she exhibited all the impartiality possible. The Reverend Mr. Wynkoop always felt serenely confident of an uninterrupted welcome upon Sunday evenings after service, while the other nights of the week were evenly apportioned between the two more ardent aspirants. The delvers after mineral wealth amid the hills, and the herders on the surrounding ranches, felt that this was a personal matter between them, and acted accordingly. Three-finger Boone, who was caught red-handed timing the exact hour of Mr. Moffat's exit from his lady-love's presence, was indignantly ducked in the watering-trough before the Miners' Retreat, and given ten minutes in which to mount his cayuse and get safely across the camp boundaries. He required only five. Bad-eye Connelly, who was suspected of having cut Mr. McNeil's lariat while that gentleman tarried at the Occidental for some slight refreshments while on his way home, was very promptly rendered a fit hospital subject by an inqui-sitive cowman who happened upon the scene.

On Monday, Wednesday, and Friday evenings the Miners' Retreat was a scene of wild hilarity, for it was then that Mr. Moffat, gorgeously arrayed in all the bright hues of his imported Mexican outfit, his long silky mustaches properly curled, his melancholy eyes vast wells of mysterious sorrow, was known to be comfortably seated in the Herndon parlor, relating gruesome tales of wild mountain adventure which paled the cheeks of his fair and entranced listener. Then on Tuesday, Thursday, and Saturday nights, when Mr. McNeil rode gallantly in on his yellow bronco, bedecked in all the picturesque paraphernalia of the boundless plains, revolver swinging at thigh, his wide sombrero shadowing his dare-devil eyes, the front of the gay Occidental blazed with lights, and became crowded to the doors with enthusiastic herders drinking deep to the success of their representative.

It is no more than simple justice to the fair Phoebe to state that she was, as her aunt expressed it, "in a dreadful state of mind." Between these two picturesque and typical knights of plain and mountain she vibrated, unable to make deliberate choice. That she was ardently loved by each she realized with recurring thrills of pleasure; that she loved in return she felt no doubt—but alas! which? How perfectly delightful it would be could she only fall into some desperate plight, from which the really daring knight might rescue her! That would cut the Gordian knot. While laboring in this state of indecision she must have voiced her ambition in some effective manner to the parties concerned, for late one Wednesday night Moffat tramped heavily into the Miners' Retreat and called Long Pete Lumley over into a deserted corner of the bar-room.

"Well, Jack," the latter began expectantly, "hev ye railly got the cinch on that cowboy at last, hey?"

"Dern it all, Pete, I'm blamed if I know; leastwise, I ain't got no sure prove-up. I tell ye thet girl's just about the toughest piece o' rock I ever had any special call to assay. I think first I got her good an' proper, an' then she drops out all of a sudden, an' I lose the lead. It's mighty aggravating let me tell ye. Ye see it's this way. She's got some durn down East-notion that she's got ter be rescued, an' borne away in the arms of her hero (thet's 'bout the way she puts it), like they do in them pesky novels the Kid's allers reading and so I reckon I've got ter rescue her!"

"Rescue her from whut, Jack? Thar' ain't nuthin' 'round yere just now as I know of, less it's rats."

The lover glanced about to make sure they were alone. "Well, ye see, Pete, maybe I'm partly to blame. I've sorter been entertainin' her nights with some stories regardin' road-agents an' things o' thet sort, while, so fur as I kin larn, thet blame chump of a McNeil hes been fillin' her up scandalous with Injuns, until she's plum got 'em on the brain. Ye know a feller jist hes ter gas along 'bout somethin' like thet, fer it's no fool job ter entertain a female thet's es frisky es a young colt. And now, I reckon as how it's got ter be Injuns."

"Whut's got ter be Injuns?"

"Why thet outfit whut runs off with her, of course. I reckon you fellers will stand in all right ter help pull me out o' this hole?"

Long Pete nodded.

"Well, Pete, this is 'bout whut's got ter be done, es near es I kin figger it out. You pick out maybe half a dozen good fellers, who kin keep their mouths shet, an' make Injuns out of 'em. 'Tain't likely she'll ever twig any of the boys fixed up proper in thet sorter outfit—anyhow, she'd be too durned skeered. Then you lay fer her, say 'bout next Wednesday, out in them Carter woods, when she's comin' home from school. I'll kinder naturally happen 'long by accident 'bout the head o' the gulch, an' jump in an' rescue her. *Sabe*?"

Lumley gazed at his companion with eyes expressive of admiration. "By thunder, if you haven't got a cocoanut on ye, Jack! Lord, but thet ought to get her a flyin'! Any shootin'?"

"Sure!" Moffat's face exhibited a faint smile at these words of praise. "It wouldn't be no great shucks of a rescue without, an' this hes got ter be the real thing. Only, I reckon, ye better shoot high, so thar' won't be no hurt done."

When the two gentlemen parted, a few moments later, the conspiracy was fully hatched, all preliminaries perfected, and the gallant rescue of Miss Spencer assured. Indeed, there is some reason now to believe that this desirable result was rendered doubly certain, for as Moffat moved slowly past the Occidental on his way home, a person attired in chaps and sombrero, and greatly resembling McNeil, was in the back room, breathing some final instructions to a few bosom friends.

"Now don't—eh—any o' you fellers—eh—go an' forget the place. Jump in—eh—lively. Just afore she—eh—gits ter thet thick bunch—eh—underbrush, whar' the trail sorter—eh—drops down inter the ravine. An' you chumps wanter—eh—git—yerselves up so she can't pipe any of ye off—eh—in this yere—eh—road-agent act. I tell ye, after what thet—eh—Moffat's bin a-pumpin' inter her, she's just got ter be—eh—rescued, an' in blame good style, er—eh—it ain't no go."

"Oh, you rest easy 'bout all thet, Bill," chimed in Sandy Winn, his black eyes dancing in anticipation of coming fun. "We'll git up the ornariest outfit whut ever hit the pike."

The long shadows of the late afternoon were already falling across the gloomy Carter woods, while the red sun sank lower behind old Bull Mountain. The Reverend Howard Wynkoop, who for more than an hour past had been vainly dangling a fishing-line above the dancing waters of Clear Creek, now reclined dreamily on the soft turf of the high bank, his eyes fixed upon the distant sky-line. His thoughts were on the flossy hair and animated face of the fair Miss Spencer, who he momentarily expected would round the edge of the hill, and so deeply did he become sank in blissful reflection as to be totally oblivious to everything but her approach.

Just above his secret resting-place, where the great woods deepen, and the gloomy shadows lie darkly all through the long afternoons, a small party of hideously painted savages skulked silently in ambush. Suddenly to their strained ears was borne the sound of horses' hoofs; and then, all at once, a woman's voice rang out in a single shrill, startled cry.

"Whut is up?" questioned the leading savage, hoarsely. "Is he a-doin' this little job all by hisself?"

"Dunno," answered the fellow next him, flipping his quirt uneasily; "but I reckon as how it's her as squealed, an' we'd better be gitting in ter hev our share o' the fun."

The "chief," with an oath of disgust, dashed forward, and his band surged after. Just below them, and scarcely fifty feet away, a half-score of roughly clad, heavily bearded men were clustered in the centre of the trail, two of their number lifting the unconscious form of a fainting woman upon a horse.

"Cervera's gang, by gosh!" panted the leading savage. "How did they git yere?"

"You bet! She's up agin the real thing," ejaculated a voice beside him. "Let's ride 'em off the earth! Whoop!"

With wild yells to awaken fresh courage, the whole band plunged headlong down the sharp decline, striking the surprised "road-agents" with a force and suddenness which sent half of them sprawling. Revolvers flashed, oaths and shouts rang out fiercely, men clinched each other, striking savage blows. Lumley grasped the leader of the other party by the hair, and endeavored to beat him over the head with his revolver butt. Even as he uplifted his hand to strike, the man's beard fell off, and the two fierce combatants paused as though thunderstruck.

"Hold on yere, boy!" yelled Lumley. "This yere is some blame joke. These fellers is Bill McNeil's gang."

"By thunder! if it ain't Pete Lumley," ejaculated the other. "Whut did ye hit me fer, ye long-legged minin' jackass?"

The explanation was never uttered. Out from the surrounding gloom of underbrush a hatless, dishevelled individual on foot suddenly dashed into the centre of that hesitating ring of horsemen. With skilful twist of his foot he sent a dismounted road-agent spinning over backward, and managed to wrench a revolver from his hand. There was a blaze of red flame, a cloud of smoke, six sharp reports, and a wild stampede of frantic horsemen.

Then the Reverend Howard Wynkoop flung the empty gun disdainfully down into the dirt, stepped directly across the motionless outstretched body, and knelt humbly beside a slender, white-robed figure lying close against the fringe of bushes. Tenderly he lifted the fair head to his throbbing bosom, and gazed directly down into the white, unconscious face. Even as he looked her eyes unclosed, her body trembling within his arms.

"Have no fear," he implored, reading terror in the expression of her face. "Miss Spencer—Phoebe—it is only I, Mr. Wynkoop."

"You! Have those awful creatures gone?"

"Yes, yes; be calm, I beg you. There is no longer the slightest danger. I am here to protect you with my life if need be."

"Oh, Howard—Mr. Wynkoop—it is all so strange, so bewildering; my nerves are so shattered! But it has taught me a great, great lesson. How could I have ever been so blind? I thought Mr. Moffat and Mr. McNeil were such heroes, and yet now in this hour of desperate peril it was you who flew gallantly to my rescue! It is you who are the true Western knight!"

And Mr. Wynkoop gazed down into those grateful eyes, and modestly confessed it true.

CHAPTER XVII

THE PARTING HOUR

To Lieutenant Brant these proved days of bitterness. His sole comfort was the feeling that he had performed his duty; his sustaining hope, that the increasing rumors of Indian atrocity might soon lead to his despatch upon active service. He had called twice upon Hampton, both times finding the wounded man propped up in bed, very affable, properly grateful for services rendered, yet avoiding all reference to the one disturbing element between them.

Once he had accidentally met Naida, but their brief conversation left him more deeply mystified then ever, and later she seemed to avoid him altogether. The barrier between them no longer appeared as a figment of her misguided imagination, but rather as a real thing neither patience nor courage might hope to surmount. If he could have flattered himself that Naida was depressed also in spirit, the fact might have proved both comfort and inspiration, but to his view her attitude was one of almost total indifference. One day he deemed her but an idle coquette; the next, a warm-hearted woman, doing her duty bravely. Yet through it all her power over him never slackened. Twice he walked with Miss Spencer as far as the Herndon house, hopeful that that vivacious young lady might chance to let fall some unguarded hint of guidance. But Miss Spencer was then too deeply immersed in her own affairs of the heart to waste either time or thought upon others.

The end to this nervous strain came in the form of an urgent despatch recalling N Troop to Fort Abraham Lincoln by forced marches. The commander felt no doubt as to the full meaning of this message, and the soldier in him made prompt and joyful response. Little Glencaid was almost out of the world so far as recent news was concerned. The military telegraph, however, formed a connecting link with the War Department, so that Brant knew something of the terrible condition of the Northwest. He had thus learned of the consolidation of the hostile savages, incited by Sitting Bull, into the fastness of the Big Horn Range; he was aware that General Crook was already advancing northward from the Nebraska line; and he knew it was part of the plan of operation for Custer and the Seventh Cavalry to strike directly westward across the Dakota hills. Now he realized that he was to be a part of this chosen fighting force, and his heart responded to the summons as to a bugle-call in battle.

Instantly the little camp was astir, the men feeling the enthusiasm of their officers. With preparations well in hand, Brant's thoughts veered once again toward Naida—he could not leave her, perhaps ride forth to death, without another effort to learn what was this impassable object between them. He rode down to the Herndon house with grave face and sober thought. If he could only understand this girl; if he could only once look into her heart, and know the meaning of her ever-changing actions, her puzzling words! He felt convinced he had surprised the reflection of love within her eyes; but soon the reflection vanished. The end was ever the same—he only knew he loved her.

He recalled long the plainly furnished room into which Mrs.

Herndon ushered him to await the girl's appearance—the formal look of the old-fashioned hair-cloth furniture, the prim striped paper on the walls, the green shades at the windows, the clean rag carpet on the floor. The very stiffness chilled him, left him ill at ease. To calm his spirit he walked to a window, and stood staring out into the warm sunlight. Then he heard the rustle of Naida's skirt and turned to meet her. She was pale from her weeks of nursing, and agitated for fear of what this unexpected call might portend. Yet to his thought she appeared calm, her manner restrained. Nor could anything be kinder than her first greeting, the frankly extended hand, the words expressive of welcome.

"Mr. Wynkoop informed me a few minutes ago that you had at last received your orders for the north," she said, her lips slightly trembling. "I wondered if you would leave without a word of farewell."

He bowed low. "I do not understand how you could doubt, for I have shown my deep interest in you even from the first. If I have lately seemed to avoid you, it has only been because I believed you wished it so."

A slight flush tinged the pallor of her cheeks, while the long lashes drooped over the eyes, concealing their secrets.

"Life is not always as easy to live aright as it appears upon the surface," she confessed. "I am learning that I cannot always do just as I should like, but must content myself with the performance of duty. Shall we not be seated?"

There was an embarrassing pause, as though neither knew how to get through the interview.

"No doubt you are rejoiced to be sent on active service again," she said, at last.

"Yes, both as a soldier and as a man, Miss Naida. I am glad to get into the field again with my regiment, to do my duty under the flag, and I am equally rejoiced to have something occur which will tend to divert my thoughts. I had not intended to say anything of this kind, but now that I am with you I simply cannot restrain the words. This past month has been, I believe, the hardest I have ever been compelled to live through. You simply mystify me, so that I alternately hope and despair. Your methods are cruel."

"Mine?" and she gazed at him with parted lips. "Lieutenant Brant, what can you mean? What is it I have done?"

"It may have been only play to you, and so easily forgotten," he went on, bitterly. "But that is a dangerous game, very certain to hurt some one. Miss Naida, your face, your eyes, even your lips almost continually tell me one thing; your words another. I know not which to trust. I never meet you except to go away baffled and bewildered."

"You wish to know the truth?"

"Ay, and for ail time! Are you false, or true? Coquette, or woman? Do you simply play with hearts for idle amusement, or is there some true purpose ruling your actions?"

She looked directly at him, her hands clasped, her breath almost sobbing between the parted lips. At first she could not speak. "Oh, you hurt me so," she faltered at last. "I did not suppose you could ever think that. I—I did not mean it; oh, truly I did not mean it! You forget how young I am; how very little I know of the world and its ways. Perhaps I have not even realized how deeply in earnest you were, have deceived myself into believing you were merely amusing yourself with me. Why, indeed, should I think otherwise? How could I venture to believe you would ever really care in that way for such a waif as I? You have seen other women in that great Eastern world of which I have only read—refined, cultured, princesses, belonging to your own social circle,—how should I suppose you could forget them, and give your heart to a little outcast, a girl without a name or a home? Rather should it be I who might remain perplexed and bewildered."

"I love you," he said, with simple honesty. "I seek you for my wife."

She started at these frankly spoken words, her hands partially concealing her face, her form trembling. "Oh, I wish you hadn't said that! It is not because I doubt you any longer; not that I fail to appreciate all you offer me. But it is so hard to appear ungrateful, to give nothing in return for so vast a gift."

"Then it is true that you do not love me?"

The blood flamed suddenly up into her face, but there was no lowering of the eyes, no shrinking back. She was too honest to play the coward before him.

"I shall not attempt to deceive you," she said, with a slow impressiveness instantly carrying conviction. "This has already progressed so far that I now owe you complete frankness. Donald Brant, now and always, living or dead, married or single, wherever life may take us, I shall love you."

Their eyes were meeting, but she held up her hand to restrain him from the one step forward.

"No, no; I have confessed the truth; I have opened freely to you the great secret of my heart. With it you must be content to leave me. There is nothing more that I can give you, absolutely nothing. I can never be your wife; I hope, for your sake and mine, that we never meet again."

She did not break down, or hesitate in the utterance of these words, although there was a piteous tremble on her lips, a pathetic appeal in her eyes. Brant stood like a statue, his face grown white. He did not in the least doubt her full meaning of renunciation.

"You will, at least, tell me why?" It was all that would come to his dry lips.

She sank back upon the sofa, as though the strength had suddenly deserted her body, her eyes shaded by an uplifted hand.

"I cannot tell you. I have no words, no courage. You will learn some day from others, and be thankful that I loved you well enough to resist temptation. But the reason cannot come to you from my lips."

He leaned forward, half kneeling at her feet, and she permitted him to clasp her hand within both his own. "Tell me, at least, this—is it some one else? Is it Hampton?"

She smiled at him through a mist of tears, a smile the sad sweetness of which he would never forget. "In the sense you mean, no. No living man stands between us, not even Bob Hampton."

"Does he know why this cannot be?"

"He does know, but I doubt if he will ever reveal his knowledge; certainly not to you. He has not told me all, even in the hour when he thought himself dying. I am convinced of that. It is not because he dislikes you, Lieutenant Brant, but because he knew his partial revealment of the truth was a duty he owed us both."

There was a long, painful pause between them, during which neither ventured to look directly at the other.

"You leave me so completely in the dark," he said, finally; "is there no possibility that this mysterious obstacle can ever be removed?"

"None. It is beyond earthly power—there lies between us the shadow of a dead man."

He stared at her as if doubting her sanity.

"A dead man! Not Gillis?"

"No, it is not Gillis. I have told you this much so that you might comprehend how impossible it is for us to change our fate. It is irrevocably fixed. Please do not question me any more; cannot you see how I am suffering? I beseech your pity; I beg you not to prolong this useless interview. I cannot bear it!"

Brant rose to his feet, and stood looking down upon her bowed head, her slender figure shaken by sobs. Whatever it might prove to be, this mysterious shadow of a dead man, there could be no doubting what it now meant to her. His eyes were filled with a love unutterable.

"Naida, as you have asked it, I will go; but I go better, stronger, because I have heard your lips say you love me. I am going now, my sweetheart, but if I live, I shall come again. I know nothing of what you mean about a dead man being between us, but I shall know when I come back, for, dead or alive, no man shall remain between me and the girl I love."

"This—this is different," she sobbed, "different; it is beyond your power."

"I shall never believe so until I have faced it for myself, nor will I even say good-bye, for, under God, I am coming back to you."

He turned slowly, and walked away. As his hand touched the latch of the door he paused and looked longingly back.

"Naida."

She glanced up at him.

"You kissed me once; will you again?"

She rose silently and crossed over to him, her hands held out, her eyes uplifted to his own. Neither spoke as he drew her gently to him, and their lips met.

"Say it once more, sweetheart?"

"Donald, I love you."

A moment they stood thus face to face, reading the great lesson of eternity within the depths of each other's eyes. Then slowly, gently, she released herself from the clasp of his strong arms.

"You believe in me now? You do not go away blaming me?" she questioned, with quivering lips.

"There is no blame, for you are doing what you think right.

But I am coming back, Naida, little woman; coming back to love and you."

An hour later N Troop trotted across the rude bridge, and circled the bluff, on its way toward the wide plains. Brant, riding ahead of his men, caught a glimpse of something white fluttering from an open window of the yellow house fronting the road. Instantly he whipped off his campaign hat, and bowing to the saddle pommel, rode bareheaded out of sight. And from behind the curtain Naida watched the last horseman round the bluff angle, riding cheerfully away to hardship, danger, and death, her eyes dry and despairing, her heart scarcely beating. Then she crept across the narrow room, and buried her face in the coverlet of the bed.

PART III

ON THE LITTLE BIG HORN

CHAPTER I

MR. HAMPTON RESOLVES

Mr. Bob Hampton stood in the bright sunshine on the steps of the hotel, his appreciative gaze wandering up the long, dusty, unoccupied street, and finally rising to the sweet face of the young girl who occupied the step above. As their eyes met both smiled as if they understood each other. Except for being somewhat pale, the result of long, inactive weeks passed indoors, Mr. Hampton's appearance was that of perfect health, while the expression of his face evidenced the joy of living.

"There is nothing quite equal to feeling well, little girl," he said, genially, patting her hand where it rested on the railing, "and I really believe I am in as fine fettle now as I ever have been. Do you know, I believe I'm perfectly fit to undertake that little detective operation casually mentioned to you a few days ago. It's got to be done, and the sooner I get at it the easier I'll feel. Fact is, I put in a large portion of the night thinking out my plans."

"I wish you would give it up all together, Bob," she said, anxiously. "I shall be so dull and lonely here while you are gone."

"I reckon you will, for a fact, as it's my private impression that lovely Miss Spencer doesn't exert herself over much to be entertaining unless there happens to be a man in sight. Great guns! how she did fling language the last time she blew in to see me! But, Naida, it isn't likely this little affair will require very long, and things are lots happier between us since my late shooting scrape. For one thing, you and I understand each other better; then Mrs. Herndon has been quite decently civil. When Fall comes I mean to take you East and put you in some good finishing school. Don't care quite as much about it as you did, do you?"

"Yes, I think I do, Bob." She strove bravely to express enthusiasm. "The trouble is, I am so worried over your going off alone hunting after that man."

He laughed, his eyes searching her face for the truth. "Well, little girl, he won't exactly be the first I've had call to go after. Besides, this is a particular case, and appeals to me in a sort of personal way. It you only knew it, you're about as deeply concerned in the result as I am, and as for me, I can never rest easy again until the matter is over with."

"It's that awful Murphy, isn't it?"

"He's the one I'm starting after first, and one sight at his right hand will decide whether he is to be the last as well."

"I never supposed you would seek revenge, like a savage," she remarked, quietly. "You never used to be that way."

"Good Lord, Naida, do you think I'm low down enough to go out hunting that poor cuss merely to get even with him for trying to stick me with a knife? Why, there are twenty others who have done as much, and we have been the best of friends afterwards. Oh, no, lassie, it means more than that, and harks back many a long year. I told you I saw a mark on his hand I would never forget—but I saw that mark first fifteen years ago. I'm not taking my life in my hand to revenge the killing of Slavin, or in any memory of that little misunderstanding between the citizens of Glencaid and myself. I should say not. I have been slashed at and shot at somewhat promiscuously during the last five years, but I never permitted such little affairs to interfere with either business, pleasure, or friendship. If this fellow Murphy, or whoever the man I am after may prove to be, had contented himself with endeavoring playfully to carve me, the account would be considered closed. But this is a duty I owe a friend, a dead friend, to run to earth this murderer. Do you understand now? The fellow who did that shooting up at Bethune fifteen years ago had the same sort of a mark on his right hand as this one who killed Slavin. That's why I'm after him, and when I catch up he'll either squeal or die. He won't be very likely to look on the matter as a joke."

"But how do you know?"

"I never told you the whole story, and I don't mean to now until I come back, and can make everything perfectly clear. It wouldn't do you any good the way things stand now, and would only make you uneasy. But if you do any praying over it, my girl, pray good and hard that I may discover some means for making that fellow squeal."

She made no response. He had told her so little, that it left her blindly groping, yet fearful to ask for more. She stood gazing thoughtfully past him.

"Have you heard anything lately, Bob, about the Seventh?" she asked, finally. "Since—since N Troop left here?"

He answered with well-simulated carelessness. "No; but it is most likely they are well into the game by this time. It's bound to prove a hard campaign, to judge from all visible indications, and the trouble has been hatching long enough to get all the hostiles into a bunch. I know most of them, and they are a bad lot of savages. Crook's column, I have just heard, was overwhelmingly attacked on the Rosebud, and forced to fall back. That leaves the Seventh to take the brunt of it, and there is going to be hell up north presently, or I've forgotten all I ever knew about Indians. Sitting Bull is the arch-devil for a plot, and he has found able assistants to lead the fighting. I only wish it were my luck to be in it. But come, little girl, as I said, I'm quite likely to be off before night, provided I am fortunate enough to strike a fresh trail. Under such conditions you won't mind my kissing you out here, will you?"

She held up her lips and he touched them softly with his own. Her eyes were tear-dimmed. "Oh, Bob, I hate so to let you go," she sobbed, clinging to him. "No one could have been more to me than you have been, and you are all I have left in the world. Everything I care for goes away from me. Life is so hard, so hard!"

"Yes, little girl, I know," and the man stroked her hair tenderly, his own voice faltering. "It's all hard; I learned that sad lesson long ago, but I've tried to make it a little bit easier for you since we first came together. Still, I don't see how I can possibly help this. I've been hunting after that fellow a long while now, a matter of fifteen years over a mighty dim trail, and it would be a mortal sin to permit him to get away scot-free. Besides, if this affair only manages to turn out right, I can promise to make you the happiest girl in America. But, Naida, dear, don't cling to me so; it is not at all like you to break down in this fashion," and he gently unclasped her hands, holding her away from him, while he continued to gaze hungrily into her troubled face. "It only

Randall Parrish

weakens me at a time when I require all my strength of will."

"Sometimes I feel just like a coward, Bob. It's the woman of it; yet truly I wish to do whatever you believe to be best. But, Bob, I need you so much, and you will come back, won't you? I shall be so lonely here, for—for you are truly all I have in the world."

With one quick, impulsive motion he pressed her to him, passionately kissing the tears from her lowered lashes, unable longer to conceal the tremor that shook his own voice. "Never, never doubt it, lassie. It will not take me long, and if I live I come straight back."

He watched her slender, white-robed figure as it passed slowly down the deserted street. Once only she paused, and waved back to him, and he returned instant response, although scarcely realizing the act.

"Poor little lonely girl! perhaps I ought to have told her the whole infernal story, but I simply haven't got the nerve, the way it reads now. If I can only get it straightened out, it'll be different."

Mechanically he thrust an unlighted cigar between his teeth, and descended the steps, to all outward appearance the same reckless, audacious Hampton as of old. Mrs. Guffy smiled happily from an open window as she observed the square set of his shoulders, the easy, devil-may-care smile upon his lips.

The military telegraph occupied one-half of the small tent next the Miners' Retreat, and the youthful operator instantly recognized his debonair visitor.

"Well, Billy," was Hampton's friendly greeting, "are they

keeping you fairly busy with 'wars and rumors of wars' these days?"

"Nuthin' doin', just now," was the cheerful reply. "Everything goin' ter Cheyenne. The Injuns are gittin' themselves bottled up in the Big Horn country."

"Oh, that's it? Then maybe you might manage to rush a message through for me to Fort A. Lincoln, without discommoding Uncle Sam?" and Hampton placed a coin upon the rough table.

"Sure; write it out."

"Here it is; now get it off early, my lad, and bring the answer to me over at the hotel. There'll be another yellow boy waiting when you come."

The reply arrived some two hours later.

"FORT A. LINCOLN, June 17, 1876.

"HAMPTON, Glencaid:

"Seventh gone west, probably Yellowstone. Brant with them. Murphy, government scout, at Cheyenne waiting orders.

"BITTON, Commanding."

He crushed the paper in his hand, thinking—thinking of the past, the present, the future. He had borne much in these last years, much misrepresentation, much loneliness of soul. He had borne these patiently, smiling into the mocking eyes of Fate. Through it all—the loss of friends, of profession, of ambition, of love, of home—he had never wholly lost hold of a sustaining hope, and now it would seem that this long-abiding faith was at last to be rewarded. Yet he realized, as he fronted the facts, how very little he really had to build upon,—the fragmentary declaration of Slavin, wrung from him in a moment of terror; an idle boast made to Brant by the surprised scout; a second's glimpse at a scarred hand,—little enough, indeed, yet by far the most clearly marked trail he had ever struck in all his vain endeavor to pierce the mystery which had so utterly ruined his life. To run this Murphy to cover remained his final hope for retrieving those dead, dark years. Ay, and there was Naida! Her future, scarcely less than his own, hung trembling in the balance.

The sudden flashing of that name into his brain was like an electric shock. He cursed his inactivity. Great God! had he become a child again, to tremble before imagined evil, a mere hobgoblin of the mind? He had already wasted time enough; now he must wring from the lips of that misshapen savage the last vestige of his secret.

The animal within him sprang to fierce life. God! he would prove as wary, as cunning, as relentless as ever was Indian on the trail. Murphy would never suspect at this late day that he was being tracked. That was well. Tireless, fearless, half savage as the scout undoubtedly was, one fully his equal was now at his heels, actuated by grim, relentless purpose. Hampton moved rapidly in preparation. He dressed for the road, for hard, exacting service, buckling his loaded cartridge-belt outside his rough coat, and testing his revolvers with unusual care. He spoke a few parting words of instruction to Mrs. Guffy, and went quietly out. Ten minutes later he was in the saddle, galloping down the dusty stage road toward Cheyenne.

CHAPTER II

THE TRAIL OF SILENT MURPHY

The young infantryman who had been detailed for the important service of telegraph operator, sat in the Cheyenne office, his feet on the rude table his face buried behind a newspaper. He had passed through two eventful weeks of unremitting service, being on duty both night and day, and now, the final despatches forwarded, he felt entitled to enjoy a period of well-earned repose.

"Could you inform me where I might find Silent Murphy, a government scout?"

The voice had the unmistakable ring of military authority, and the soldier operator instinctively dropped his feet to the floor.

"Well, my lad, you are not dumb, are you?"

The telegrapher's momentary hesitation vanished; his ambition to become a martyr to the strict laws of service secrecy was not sufficiently strong to cause him to take the doubtful chances of a lie. "He was here, but has gone."

"Where?"

"The devil knows. He rode north, carrying despatches for Custer."

"When?"

"Oh, three or four hours ago."

Hampton swore softly but fervently, behind his clinched teeth.

"Where is Custer?"

"Don't know exactly. Supposed to be with Terry and Gibbons, somewhere near the mouth of the Powder, although he may have left there by this time, moving down the Yellowstone. That was the plan mapped out. Murphy's orders were to intercept his column somewhere between the Rosebud and the Big Horn, and I figure there is about one chance out of a hundred that the Indians let him get that far alive. No other scout along this border would take such a detail. I know, for there were two here who failed to make good when the job was thrown at them—just naturally faded away," and the soldier's eyes sparkled. "But that old devil of a Murphy just enjoys such a trip. He started off as happy as ever I see him."

"How far will he have to ride?"

"Oh, 'bout three hundred miles as the crow flies, a little west of north, and the better part of the distance, they tell me, it's almighty rough country for night work. But then Murphy, he knows the way all right."

Hampton turned toward the door, feeling fairly sick from disappointment. The operator stood regarding him curiously, a question on his lips.

"Sorry you didn't come along a little earlier," he said, genially. "Do you know Murphy?"

"I'm not quite certain. Did you happen to notice a peculiar black scar on the back of his right hand?"

"Sure; looks like the half of a pear. He said it was powder under the skin."

A new look of reviving determination swept into Hampton's gloomy eyes—beyond doubt this must be his man.

"How many horses did he have?"

"Two."

"Did you overhear him say anything definite about his plans for the trip?"

"What, him? He never talks, that fellow. He can't do nothing but sputter if he tries. But I wrote out his orders, and they give him to the twenty-fifth to make the Big Horn. That's maybe something like fifty miles a day, and he's most likely to keep his horses fresh just as long as possible, so as to be good for the last spurt through the hostile country. That's how I figure it, and I know something about scouting. You wasn't planning to strike out after him, was you?"

"I might risk it if I only thought I could overtake him within two days; my business is of some importance."

"Well, stranger, I should reckon you might do that with a dog-gone good outfit. Murphy's sure to take things pretty easy to-day, and he's almost certain to follow the old mining trail as far as the ford over the Belle Fourche, and that's plain enough to travel. Beyond that point the devil only knows where he will go, for then is when his hard ridin' begins."

The moment the operator mentioned that odd scar on Murphy's hand, every vestige of hesitation vanished. Beyond any possibility of doubt he was on the right scent this time. Murphy was riding north upon a mission as desperate as ever man was called upon to perform. The chance of his coming forth alive from that Indian-haunted land was, as the operator truthfully said, barely one out of a hundred. Hampton thought of this. He durst not venture all he was so earnestly striving after—love, reputation, honor—to the chance of a stray Sioux bullet. No! and he remembered Naida again, her dark, pleading eyes searching his face. To the end, to the death if need were, he would follow!

The memory of his old plains craft would not permit any neglect of the few necessaries for the trip. He bought without haggling over prices, but insisted on the best. So it was four in the afternoon when he finally struck into the trail leading northward. This proved at first a broad, plainly marked path, across the alkali plain. He rode a mettlesome, half-broken bronco, a wicked-eyed brute, which required to be conquered twice within the first hour of travel; a second and more quiet animal trailed behind at the end of a lariat, bearing the necessary equipment. Hampton forced the two into a rapid lope, striving to make the most possible out of the narrow margin of daylight remaining.

He had, by persistent questioning, acquired considerable information, during that busy hour spent in Cheyenne, regarding the untracked regions lying before him, as well as the character and disposition of the man he pursued. Both by instinct and training he was able to comprehend those brief hints that must prove of vast benefit in the pathless wilderness. But the time had not yet arrived for him to dwell on such matters. His thoughts were concentrated on Murphy.

He knew that the fellow was a stubborn, silent, sullen savage, devoid of physical fear, yet cunning, wary, malignant, and treacherous. That was what they said of him back in Cheyenne. What, then, would ever induce such a man to open his mouth in confession of a long-hidden crime? To be sure, he might easily kill the fellow, but he would probably die, like a wild beast, without uttering a word.

There was one chance, a faint hope, that behind his gruff, uncouth exterior this Murphy possessed a conscience not altogether dead. Over some natures, and not infrequently to those which seem outwardly the coarsest, superstition wields a power the normal mind can scarcely comprehend. Murphy might be spiritually as cringing a coward as he was physically a fearless desperado. Hampton had known such cases before; he had seen men laugh scornfully before the muzzle of a levelled gun, and yet tremble when pointed at by the finger of accusation. He had lived sufficiently long on the frontier to know that men may become inured to that special form of danger to which they have grown accustomed through repetition, and yet fail to front the unknown and mysterious. Perhaps here might be discovered Murphy's weak point. Without doubt the man was guilty of crime; that its memory continued to haunt him was rendered evident by his hiding in Glencaid, and by his desperate attempt to kill Hampton. That knife-thrust must have been given with the hope of thus stopping further investigation; it alone was sufficient proof that Murphy's soul was haunted by fear.

"Conscience doth make cowards of us all." These familiar words floated in Hampton's memory, seeming to attune themselves to the steady gallop of his horse. They appealed to him as a direct message of guidance. The night was already dark, but stars were gleaming brilliantly overhead, and the trail remained easily traceable. It became terribly lonely on that wilderness stretching away for unknown leagues in every direction, yet Hampton scarcely noted this, so watchful was he lest he miss the trail. To his judgment, Murphy would not be likely to ride during the night until after he had crossed the Fourche. There was no reason to suspect that there were any hostile Indians south of that stream, and probably therefore the old scout would endeavor to conserve his own strength and that of his horses, for the more perilous travel beyond. Hampton hastened on, his eyes peering anxiously ahead into the steadily increasing gloom.

About midnight, the trail becoming obscure, the rider made camp, confident he must have already gained heavily on the man he pursued. He lariated his horses, and flinging himself down on some soft turf, almost immediately dropped asleep. He was up again before daylight, and, after a hasty meal, pressed on. The nature of the country had changed considerably, becoming more broken, the view circumscribed by towering cliffs and deep ravines. Hampton swung forward his field-glasses, and, from the summit of every eminence, studied the topography of the country lying beyond. He must see before being seen, and he believed he could not now be many miles in the rear of Murphy.

Late in the afternoon he reined up his horse and gazed forward into a broad valley, bounded with precipitous bluffs. The trail, now scarcely perceptible, led directly down, winding about like some huge snake, across the lower level, toward where a considerable stream of water shone silvery in the sun, half concealed behind a fringe of willows. Beyond doubt this was the Belle Fourche. And yonder, close in against those distant willows, some black dots were moving. Hampton glued his anxious eyes to the glass. The levelled tubes clearly revealed a man on horseback, leading another horse. The animals were walking. There could be little doubt that this was Silent Murphy.

Hampton lariated his tired horses behind the bluff, and returned to the summit, lying flat upon the ground, with the field-glass at his eyes. The distant figures passed slowly forward into the midst of the willows, and for half an hour the patient watcher scanned the surface of the stream beyond, but there was no sign of attempted passage. The sun sank lower, and finally disappeared behind those desolate ridges to the westward. Hampton's knowledge of plains craft rendered Murphy's actions sufficiently clear. This was the Fourche; beyond those waters lay the terrible peril of Indian raiders. Further advance must be made by swift, secret night riding, and never-ceasing vigilance. This was what Murphy had been saving himself and his horses for. Beyond conjecture, he was resting now within the shadows of those willows, studying the opposite shore and making ready for the dash northward. Hampton believed he would linger thus for some time after dark, to see if Indian fires would afford any guidance. Confident of this, he passed back to his horses, rubbed them down with grass, and then ate his lonely supper, not venturing to light a fire, certain that Murphy's eyes were scanning every inch of sky-line.

Darkness came rapidly, while Hampton sat planning again the details of his night's work. The man's spirits became depressed by the gloom and the silence. Evil fancies haunted his brain. His mind dwelt upon the past, upon that wrong which had wrecked his life, upon the young girl he had left praying for his safe return, upon that miserable creature skulking yonder in the black night. Hampton could not remember when he had ever performed such an act before, nor could he have explained why he did so then, yet he prayed—prayed for the far-off Naida, and for personal guidance in the stern work lying before him. And when he rose to his feet and groped his way to the horses, there remained no spirit of vengeance in his heart, no hatred, merely a cool resolve to succeed in his strange quest. So, the two animals trailing cautiously behind, he felt his slow way on foot down the steep bluff, into the denser blackness of the valley.

CHAPTER III

THE HAUNTING OF A CRIME

Murphy rested on his back in the midst of a thicket of willows, wide awake, yet not quite ready to ford the Fourche and plunge into the dense shadows shrouding the northern shore. Crouched behind a log, he had so far yielded unto temptation as to light his pipe.

Murphy had been amid just such unpleasant environments many times before, and the experience had grown somewhat prosaic. He realized fully the imminent peril haunting the next two hundred miles, but such danger was not wholly unwelcome to his peculiar temperament; rather it was an incentive to him, and, without a doubt, he would manage to pull through somehow, as he had done a hundred times before. Even Indian-scouting degenerates into a commonplace at last. So Murphy puffed contentedly at his old pipe. Whatever may have been his thoughts, they did not burst through his taciturnity, and he reclined there motionless, no sound breaking the silence, save the rippling waters of the Fourche, and the occasional stamping of his horses as they cropped the succulent valley grass.

But suddenly there was the faint crackle of a branch to his left, and one hand instantly closed over his pipe bowl, the other grasping the heavy revolver at his hip. Crouching like a startled tiger, with not a muscle moving, he peered anxiously into the darkness, his arm half extended, scarcely venturing to breathe. There came a plain, undisguised rustling in the grass,—some prowling coyote, probably; then his tense muscles immediately relaxed, and he cursed himself for being so startled, yet he continued to grasp the "45" in his right hand, his eyes alert.

"Murphy!"

That single word, hurled thus unexpectedly out of the black night, startled him more than would a volley of rifles. He sprang half erect, then as swiftly crouched behind a willow, utterly unable to articulate. In God's name, what human could be out there to call? He would have sworn that there was not another white man within a radius of a hundred miles. For the instant his very blood ran cold; he appeared to shrivel up.

"Oh, come, Murphy; speak up, man; I know you're in here."

That terror of the unknown instantly vanished. This was the familiar language of the world, and, however the fellow came to be there, it was assuredly a man who spoke. With a gurgling oath at his own folly, Murphy's anger flared violently forth into disjointed speech, the deadly gun yet clasped ready for instant action.

"Who—the hell—are ye?" he blurted out.

The visitor laughed, the bushes rustling as he pushed toward the sound of the voice. "It's all right, old boy. Gave ye quite a scare, I reckon."

Murphy could now dimly perceive the other advancing

through the intervening willows, and his Colt shot up to the level. "Stop!—ye take another—step an' I'll—let drive. Ye tell me—first—who ye be."

The invader paused, but he realized the nervous finger pressing the trigger and made haste to answer. "It's all right, I tell ye. I'm one o' Terry's scouts."

"Ye are? Jist the same—I've heard—yer voice—afore."

"Likely 'nough. I saw service in the Seventh."

Murphy was still a trifle suspicious. "How'd ye git yere? How'd ye come ter know—whar I wus?"

The man laughed again. "Sorter hurts yer perfessional feelins, don't it, old feller, to be dropped in on in this unceremonious way? But it was dead easy, old man. Ye see I happened thro' Cheyenne only a couple o' hours behind ye, with a bunch o' papers fer the Yellowstone. The trail's plain enough out this far, and I loped 'long at a pretty fair hickory, so thet I was up on the bluff yonder, and saw ye go into camp yere just afore dark. You wus a-keepin' yer eyes skinned across the Fourche, and naturally didn't expect no callers from them hills behind. The rest wus nuthin', an' here I am. It's a darn sight pleasanter ter hev company travellin', ter my notion. Now kin I cum on?"

Murphy reluctantly lowered his Colt, every movement betraying annoyance. "I reckon. But I'd—a damn sight—rather risk it—alone."

The stranger came forward without further hesitation. The night was far too dark to reveal features, but to Murphy's strained vision the newcomer appeared somewhat slender in build, and of good height.

"Whar'd—ye say ye—wus bound?"

"Mouth o' the Powder. We kin ride tergether fer a night or two."

"Ye kin—do as ye—please, but—I ain't a huntin'—no company,—an' I'm a'—goin' 'cross now."

He advanced a few strides toward his horses. Then suddenly he gave vent to a smothered cry, so startling as to cause the stranger to spring hastily after him.

"Oh! My God! Oh! Look there!"

"What is it, man?"

"There! there! The picture! Don't you see?"

"Naw; I don't see nuthin'. Ye ain't gone cracked, hev ye? Whose picture?"

"It's there!—O Lord!—it's there! My God! can't ye see?— An' it's his face—all a-gleamin' with green flames—Holy Mary—an' I ain't seen it—afore in—fifteen year!"

He seemed suddenly to collapse, and the stranger permitted him to drop limp to the earth.

"Darn if I kin see anythin', old man, but I'll scout 'round thar a bit, jest ter ease yer mind, an' see what I kin skeer up."

He had hardly taken a half-dozen steps before Murphy called after him: "Don't—don't go an' leave me—it's not there now—thet's queer!"

The other returned and stood gazing down upon his huddled

figure. "You're a fine scout! afeard o' spooks. Do ye take these yere turns often? Fer if ye do, I reckon as how I'd sooner be ridin' alone."

Murphy struggled to his feet and gripped the other's arm. "Never hed nuthin' like it—afore. But—but it was thar—all creepy—an' green—ain't seen thet face—in fifteen year."

"What face?"

"A—a fellow I knew—once. He—he's dead."

The other grunted, disdainfully. "Bad luck ter see them sort," he volunteered, solemnly. "Blame glad it warn't me es see it, an' I don't know as I keer much right now 'bout keepin' company with ye fer very long. However, I reckon if either of us calculates on doin' much ridin' ternight, we better stop foolin' with ghosts, an' go ter saddlin' up."

They made rapid work of it, the newcomer proving somewhat loquacious, yet holding his voice to a judicious whisper, while Murphy relapsed into his customary sullen silence, but continued peering about nervously. It was he who led the way down the bank, the four horses slowly splashing through the shallow water to the northern shore. Before them stretched a broad plain, the surface rocky and uneven, the northern stars obscured by ridges of higher land. Murphy promptly gave his horse the spur, never once glancing behind, while the other imitated his example, holding his animal well in check, being apparently the better mounted.

They rode silently. The unshod hoofs made little noise, but a loosened canteen tinkled on Murphy's led horse, and he halted to fix it, uttering a curse. The way became more broken and rough as they advanced, causing them to exercise greater caution. Murphy clung to the hollows, apparently guided by some primitive instinct to choose the right path, or else able, like a cat, to see the way through the gloom, his beacon a huge rock to the northward. Silently hour after hour, galloping, trotting, walking, according to the ground underfoot, the two pressed grimly forward, with the unerring skill of the border, into the untracked wilderness. Flying clouds obscured the stars, yet through the rifts they caught fleeting glimpses sufficient to hold them to their course. And the encroaching hills swept in closer upon either hand, leaving them groping their way between as in a pocket, yet ever advancing north.

Finally they attained to the steep bank of a considerable stream, found the water of sufficient depth to compel swimming, and crept up the opposite shore dripping and miserable, yet with ammunition dry. Murphy stood swearing disjointedly, wiping the blood from a wound in his forehead where the jagged edge of a rock had broken the skin, but suddenly stopped with a quick intake of breath that left him panting. The other man crept toward him, leading his horse.

"What is it now?" he asked, gruffly. "Hev' ye got 'em agin?"

The dazed old scout stared, pointing directly across the other's shoulder, his arm shaking desperately.

"It's thar!—an' it's his face! Oh, God!—I know it—fifteen year."

The man glanced backward into the pitch darkness, but without moving his body.

"There's nuthin' out there, 'less it's a firefly," he insisted, in a tone of contempt. "You're plum crazy, Murphy; the night's got on yer nerves. What is it ye think ye see?"

"His face, I tell ye! Don't I know? It's all green and ghastly, with snaky flames playin' about it! But I know; fifteen years, an' I ain't fergot."

He sank down feebly—sank until he was on his knees, his head craned forward. The man watching touched the miserable, hunched-up figure compassionately, and it shook beneath his hand, endeavoring to shrink away.

"My God! was thet you? I thought it was him a-reachin' fer me. Here, let me take yer hand. Oh, Lord! An' can't ye see? It's just there beyond them horses—all green, crawlin', devilish—but it's him."

"Who?"

"Brant! Brant—fifteen year!"

"Brant? Fifteen years? Do you mean Major Brant, the one Nolan killed over at Bethune?"

"He—he didn't—"

The old man heaved forward, his head rocking from side to side; then suddenly he toppled over on his face, gasping for breath. His companion caught him, and ripped open the heavy flannel shirt. Then he strode savagely across in front of his shrinking horse, tore down the flaring picture, and hastily thrust it into his pocket, the light of the phosphorus with which it had been drawn being reflected for a moment on his features.

"A dirty, miserable, low-down trick," he muttered. "Poor old devil! Yet I've got to do it, for the little girl."

He stumbled back through the darkness, his hat filled with

water, and dashed it into Murphy's face. "Come on, Murphy! There's one good thing 'bout spooks; they don't hang 'round fer long at a time. Likely es not this 'un is gone by now. Brace up, man, for you an' I have got ter get out o' here afore mornin'."

Then Murphy grasped his arm, and drew himself slowly to his feet.

"Don't see nuthin' now, do ye?"

"No. Where's my—horse?"

The other silently reached him the loose rein, marking as he did so the quick, nervous peering this way and that, the starting at the slightest sound.

"Did ye say, Murphy, as how it wasn't Nolan after all who plugged the Major?"

"I'm damned—if I did. Who—else was it?"

"Why, I dunno. Sorter blamed odd though, thet ghost should be a-hauntin' ye. Darn if it ain't creepy 'nough ter make a feller believe most anythin'."

Murphy drew himself up heavily into his saddle. Then all at once he shoved the muzzle of a "45" into the other's face. "Ye say nuther word—'bout thet, an' I'll make—a ghost outer ye—blame lively. Now, ye shet up—if ye ride with me."

They moved forward at a walk and reached a higher level, across which the night wind swept, bearing a touch of cold in its breath as though coming from the snow-capped moun-tains to the west. There was renewed life in this invigorating air, and Murphy spurred forward, his companion pressing steadily after. They were but two flitting shadows amid that vast desolation of plain and mountain, their horses' hoofs barely audible. What imaginings of evil, what visions of the past, may have filled the half-crazed brain of the leading horseman is unknowable. He rode steadily against the black night wall, as though unconscious of his actions, yet forgetting no trick, no skill of the plains. But the equally silent man behind clung to him like a shadow of doom, watching his slightest motion—a Nemesis that would never let go.

When the first signs of returning day appeared in the east, the two left their horses in a narrow canyon, and crept to the summit of a ridge. Below lay the broad valley of the Powder. Slowly the misty light strengthened into gray, and became faintly tinged with crimson, while the green and brown tints deepened beneath the advancing light, which ever revealed new clefts in the distant hills. Amid those more northern bluffs a thin spiral of blue smoke was ascending. Undoubtedly it was some distant Indian signal, and the wary old plainsman watched it as if fascinated. But the younger man lay quietly regarding him, a drawn revolver in his hand. Then Murphy turned his head, and looked back into the other's face.

CHAPTER IV

THE VERGE OF CONFESSION

Murphy uttered one sputtering cry of surprise, flinging his hand instinctively to his hip, but attempted no more. Hampton's ready weapon was thrusting its muzzle into the astounded face, and the gray eyes gleaming along the polished barrel held the fellow motionless.

"Hands up! Not a move, Murphy! I have the drop!" The voice was low, but stern, and the old frontiersman obeyed mechanically, although his seamed face was fairly distorted with rage.

"You! Damn you!—I thought I knew—the voice."

"Yes, I am here all right. Rather odd place for us to meet, isn't it? But, you see, you've had the advantage all these years; you knew whom you were running away from, while I was compelled to plod along in the dark. But I've caught up just the same, if it has been a long race."

"What do ye—want me fer?" The look in the face was cunning.

"Hold your hands quiet—higher, you fool! That's it. Now,

don't play with me. I honestly didn 't know for certain I did want you, Murphy, when I first started out on this trip. I merely suspected that I might, from some things I had been told. When somebody took the liberty of slashing at my back in a poker-room at Glencaid, and drove the knife into Slavin by mistake, I chanced to catch a glimpse of the hand on the hilt, and there was a scar on it. About fifteen years before, I was acting as officer of the guard one night at Bethune. It was a bright starlit night, you remember, and just as I turned the corner of the old powder-house there came a sudden flash, a report, a sharp cry. I sprang forward only to fall headlong over a dead body; but in that flash I had seen the hand grasping the revolver, and there was a scar on the back of it, a very peculiar scar. It chanced I had the evening previous slightly quarrelled with the officer who was killed; I was the only person known to be near at the time he was shot; certain other circumstantial evidence was dug up, while Slavin and one other—no, it was not you—gave some damaging, manufactured testimony against me. As a result I was held guilty of murder in the second degree, dismissed the army in disgrace, and sentenced to ten years' imprisonment. So, you see, it was not exactly you I have been hunting, Murphy,—it was a scar."

Murphy's face was distorted into a hideous grin. "I notice you bear exactly that kind of a scar, my man, and you spoke last night as if you had some recollection of the case."

The mocking grin expanded; into the husky voice crept a snarl of defiance, for now Murphy's courage had come back —he was fronting flesh and blood. "Oh, stop preachin'—an' shoot—an' be damned ter ye!"

"You do me a grave injustice, Murphy. In the first place, I do not possess the nature of an Indian, and am not out for revenge. Your slashing at me down in Glencaid hasn't left so much as a sting behind. It's completely blotted out, forgotten. I haven't the slightest desire to kill you, man; but I do want to clear my name of the stain of that crime. I want you to tell the whole truth about that night's work at Bethune; and when you have done so, you can go. I'll never lay a finger on you; you can go where you please."

"Bah!—ye ain't got no proof—agin me—'sides, the case is closed—it can't be opened agin—by law."

"You devil! I'd be perfectly justified in killing you," exclaimed Hampton, savagely.

Murphy stared at him stupidly, the cunning of incipient insanity in his eyes. "En' whar—do ye expect—me ter say— all this, pervidin', of course—I wus fule 'nough—ter do it?"

"Up yonder before Custer and the officers of the Seventh, when we get in."

"They'd nab me—likely."

"Now, see here, you say it is impossible for them to touch you, because the case is closed legally. Now, you do not care very much for the opinion of others, while from every other standpoint you feel perfectly safe. But I've had to suffer for your crime, Murphy, suffer for fifteen years, ten of them behind stone walls; and there are others who have suffered with me. It has cost me love, home, all that a man holds dear. I've borne this punishment for you, paid the penalty of your act to the full satisfaction of the law. The very least you can do in ordinary decency is to speak the truth now. It will not hurt you, but it will lift me out of hell."

Murphy's eyes were cunning, treacherously shifting under the thatch of his heavy brows; he was like an old rat seeking for any hole of refuge. "Well—maybe I might. Anyhow, I'll go on—with ye. Kin I sit up? I'm dog tired—lyin' yere."

"Unbuckle your belt, and throw that over first."

"I'm damned—if I will. Not—in no Injun—country."

"I know it's tough," retorted Hampton, with exasperating coolness, his revolver's muzzle held steady; "but, just the same, it's got to be done. I know you far too well to take chances on your gun. So unlimber."

"Oh, I—guess not," and Murphy spat contemptuously. "Do ye think—I'm afeard o' yer—shootin'? Ye don't dare—fer I'm no good ter ye—dead."

"You are perfectly right. You are quite a philosopher in your way. You would be no good to me dead, Murphy, but you might prove fully as valuable maimed. Now I'm playing this game to the limit, and that limit is just about reached. You unlimber before I count ten, you murderer, or I'll spoil both your hands!"

The mocking, sardonic grin deserted Murphy's features. It was sullen obstinacy, not doubt of the other's purpose, that paralyzed him.

"Unlimber! It's the last call."

With a snarl the scout unclasped his army belt, dropped it to the ground, and sullenly kicked it over toward Hampton. "Now—now—you, you gray-eyed—devil, kin I—sit up?"

The other nodded. He had drawn the fangs of the wolf, and now that he no longer feared, a sudden, unexplainable feeling of sympathy took possession of him. Yet he drew farther away before slipping his own gun into its sheath. For a time neither spoke, their eyes peering across the ridge. Murphy sputtered and swore, but his victorious companion neither spoke nor moved. There were several distant smokes out to the northward now, evidently the answering signals of different bands of savages, while far away, beneath the shadow of the low bluffs bordering the stream, numerous black, moving dots began to show against the light brown background. Hampton, noticing that Murphy had stopped swearing to gaze, swung forward his field-glasses for a better view.

"They are Indians, right enough," he said, at last. "Here, take a look, Murphy. I could count about twenty in that bunch, and they are travelling north."

The older man adjusted the tubes to his eyes, and looked long and steadily at the party. Then he slowly swung the glasses toward the northwest, apparently studying the country inch by inch, his jaws working spasmodically, his unoccupied hand clutching nervously at the grass.

"They seem—to be a-closin' in," he declared, finally, staring around into the other's face, all bravado gone. "There's anuther lot—bucks, all o' 'em—out west yonder—an' over east a smudge is—just startin'. Looks like—we wus in a pocket—an' thar' might be some—har-raisin' fore long."

"Well, Murphy, you are the older hand at this business. What do you advise doing?"

"Me? Why, push right 'long—while we kin keep under cover. Then—after dark—trust ter bull luck an' make— 'nuther dash. It's mostly luck, anyhow. Thet canyon just ahead—looks like it leads a long way—toward the Powder. Its middling deep down, an' if there ain't Injuns in it—them fellers out yonder—never cud git no sight at us. Thet's my notion—thet ivery mile helps in this—business."

"You mean we should start now?"

"Better—let the cattle rest—first. An'—if ye ever feed prisoners—I'd like ter eat a bite—mesilf."

They rested there for over two hours, the tired horses contentedly munching the succulent grass of the *coulee*, their two masters scarcely exchanging a word. Murphy, after satisfying his appetite, rested flat upon his back, one arm flung over his eyes to protect them from the sun. For a considerable time Hampton supposed him asleep, until he accidentally caught the stealthy glance which followed his slightest movement, and instantly realized that the old weasel was alert. Murphy had been beaten, yet evidently remained unconquered, biding his chance with savage stoicism, and the other watched him warily even while seeming to occupy himself with the field-glass.

At last they saddled up, and, at first leading their horses, passed down the *coulee* into the more precipitous depths of the narrow canyon. This proved hardly more than a gash cut through the rolling prairie, rock strewn, holding an insignificant stream of brackish water, yet was an ideal hiding-place, having ample room for easy passage between the rock walls. The men mounted, and Hampton, with a wave of his hand, bade the old scout assume the lead.

Their early advance was slow and cautious, as they never felt certain what hidden enemies might lurk behind the sharp corners of the winding defile, and they kept vigilant eyes upon the serrated sky-line. The savages were moving north, and so were they. It would be remarkably good fortune if they escaped running into some wandering band, or if some stray scout did not stumble upon their trail. So they continued to plod on.

It was fully three o'clock when they attained to the bank of the Powder, and crouched among the rocks to wait for the shades of night to shroud their further advance. Murphy climbed the bluff for a wider view, bearing Hampton's field-glasses slung across his shoulder, for the latter would not leave him alone with the horses. He returned finally to grunt out that there was nothing special in sight, except a shifting of those smoke signals to points farther north. Then they lay down again, Hampton smoking, Murphy either sleeping or pretending to sleep. And slowly the shadows of another black night swept down and shut them in.

It must have been two hours later when they ventured forth. Silence and loneliness brooded everywhere, not so much as a breath of air stirring the leaves. The unspeakable, unsolvable mystery of it all rested like a weight on the spirits of both men. It, was a disquieting thought that bands of savages, eager to discover and slay, were stealing among the shadows of those trackless plains, and that they must literally feel their uncertain way through the cordon, every sound an alarm, every advancing step a fresh peril. They crossed the swift, deep stream, and emerged dripping, chilled to the marrow by the icy water. Then they swung stiffly into the wet saddles, and plunged, with almost reckless abandon, through the darkness. Murphy continued to lead, the light tread of his horse barely audible, Hampton pressing closely behind, revolver in hand, the two pack-horses trailing in the rear. Hampton had no confidence in his sullen, treacherous companion; he looked for early trouble, yet he had little fear regarding any attempt at escape now. Murphy was a plains-man, and would realize the horror of being alone, unarmed, and without food on those demon-haunted prairies. Besides, the silent man behind was astride the better animal.

Midnight, and they pulled up amid the deeper gloom of a great, overhanging bluff, having numerous trees near its summit. There was the glow of a distant fire upon their left, which reddened the sky, and reflected oddly on the edges of a vast cloud-mass rolling up threateningly from the west. Neither knew definitely where they were, although Murphy guessed the narrow stream they had just forded might be the upper waters of the Tongue. Their horses stood with heads hanging wearily down, their sides rising and falling; and Hampton, rolling stiffly from the saddle, hastily loosened his girth.

"They'll drop under us if we don't give them an hour or two," he said, quietly. "They're both dead beat."

Murphy muttered something, incoherent and garnished with oaths, and the moment he succeeded in releasing the buckle, sank down limp at the very feet of his horse, rolling up into a queer ball. The other stared, and took a step nearer.

"What's the matter? Are you sick, Murphy?"

"No—tired—don't want ter see—thet thing agin."

"What thing?"

"Thet green, devilish,—crawlin' face—if ye must know!" And he twisted his long, ape-like arms across his eyes, lying curled up as a dog might.

For a moment Hampton stood gazing down upon him, listening to his incoherent mutterings, his own face grave and sympathetic. Then he moved back and sat down. Suddenly the full conception of what this meant came to his mind—*the man had gone mad*. The strained cords of that diseased brain had snapped in the presence of imagined terrors, and now all was chaos. The horror of it overwhelmed Hampton; not only did this unexpected denouement leave him utterly hopeless, but what was he to do with the fellow? How could he bring him forth from there alive? If this stream was indeed the Tongue, then many a mile of rough country, ragged with low mountains and criss-crossed by deep ravines, yet stretched between where they now were and the Little Big Horn, where they expected to find Custer's men. They were in the very heart of the Indian country,—the country of the savage Sioux. He stared at the curled-up man, now silent and breathing heavily as if asleep. The silence was profound, the night so black and lonely that Hampton involuntarily closed his heavy eyes to shut it out. If he only might light a pipe, or boil himself a cup of black coffee! Murphy never stirred; the horses were seemingly too weary to browse. Then Hampton nodded, and sank into an uneasy doze.

CHAPTER V

ALONE WITH THE INSANE

Beneath the shade of uplifted arms Murphy's eyes remained unclosed. Whatever terrors may have dominated that diseased brain, the one purpose of revenge and escape never deserted it. With patient cunning he could plan and wait, scheme and execute. He was all animal now, dreaming only of how to tear and kill.

And he waited long in order to be perfectly sure, unrolling inch by inch, and like a venomous snake, never venturing to withdraw his baleful eyes from his unconscious victim. He was many minutes thoroughly satisfying himself that Hampton actually slept. His every movement was slow, crafty, cowardly, the savage in his perverted nature becoming more and more manifest. It was more beast than man that finally crept forward on all-fours, the eyes gleaming cruel as a cat's in the night. It was not far he was compelled to go, his movements squirming and noiseless. Within a yard of the peacefully slumbering man he rose up, crouching on his toes and bending stealthily forward to gloat over his victim. Hampton stirred uneasily, possibly feeling the close proximity of that horrible presence. Then the maniac took one more stealthy, slouching step nearer, and flung himself at the exposed throat, uttering a fierce snarl as his fingers clutched the soft flesh. Hampton awoke, gasping and choking, to find those mad eyes glaring into his own, those murderous hands throttling him with the strength of madness.

At first the stupefied, half-awakened man struggled as if in delirium, scarcely realizing the danger. He was aware of suffering, of horror, of suffocation. Then the brain flashed into life, and he grappled fiercely with his dread antagonist. Murphy snapped like a mad dog, his lips snarling curses; but Hampton fought silently, desperately, his brain clearing as he succeeded in wrenching those claws from his lacerated throat, and forced his way up on to one knee. He felt no hatred toward this crazed man striving to kill him; he understood what had loosed such a raging devil. But this was no time to exhibit mercy; Murphy bit and clawed, and Hampton could only dash in upon him in the effort to force him back. He worked his way, inch by inch, to his feet, his slender figure rigid as steel, and closed in upon the other; but Murphy writhed out of his grasp, as a snake might. The younger man realized now to the full his peril, and his hand slipped down to the gun upon his hip. There was a sudden glint in the faint starlight as he struck, and the stunned maniac went down quivering, and lay motionless on the hard ground. For a moment the other remained standing over him, the heavy revolver poised, but the prostrate figure lay still, and the conqueror slipped his weapon back into its leather sheath with a sigh of relief.

The noise of their struggle must have carried far through that solemn stillness, and no one could guess how near at hand might be bands of prowling savages. Yet no sound came to his strained ears except the soft soughing of the night wind through the trees, and the rustling of grass beneath the tread of the horses. With the quick decision of one long accustomed to meet emergencies, Hampton unbuckled the lariat from one of the led animals, and bound Murphy's hands and limbs securely.

As he worked he thought rapidly. He comprehended the extreme desperation of their present situation. While the revolver blow might possibly restore Murphy to a degree of sanity, it was far more probable that he would awaken violent. Yet he could not deliberately leave this man to meet a fate of horror in the wilderness. Which way should they turn? Enough food, if used sparingly, might remain to permit of a hasty retreat to Cheyenne, and there would be comparatively little danger in that direction. All visible signs indicated that the scattered Indian bands were rapidly consolidating to the northward, closing in on those troops scouting the Yellowstone, with determination to give early battle. Granting that the stream they were now on should prove to be the Tongue, then the direct route toward where Custer was supposed to be would be northwest, leading ever deeper into the lonely wilderness, and toward more imminent peril. Then, at the end of that uncertain journey, they might easily miss Custer's column. That which would have been quickly decided had he been alone became a most serious problem when considered in connection with the insane, helpless scout. But then, there were the despatches! They must be of vital importance to have required the sending of Murphy forth on so dangerous a ride; other lives, ay, the result of the entire campaign, might depend upon their early delivery. Hampton had been a soldier, the spirit of the service was still with him, and that thought brought him to final decision. Unless they were halted by Sioux bullets, they would push on toward the Big Horn, and Custer should have the papers.

He knelt down beside Murphy, unbuckled the leather despatch-bag, and rebuckled it across his own shoulder. Then he set to work to revive the prostrate man. The eyes, when opened, stared up at him, wild and glaring; the ugly face bore the expression of abject fear. The man was no longer violent; he had become a child, frightened at the dark. His ceaseless babbling, his incessant cries of terror, only rendered more precarious any attempt at pressing forward through a region overrun with hostiles. But Hampton had resolved.

Securely strapping Murphy to his saddle, and packing all their remaining store of provisions upon one horse, leaving the other to follow or remain behind as it pleased, he advanced directly into the hills, steering by aid of the stars, his left hand ever on Murphy's bridle rein, his low voice of expostulation seeking to calm the other's wild fancies and to curb his violent speech. It was a weird, wild ride through the black night, unknown ground under foot, unseen dangers upon every hand. Murphy's aberrations changed from shrieking terror to a wild, uncontrollable hilarity, with occasional outbursts of violent anger, when it required all Hampton's iron will and muscle to conquer him.

At dawn they were in a narrow gorge among the hills, a dark and gloomy hole, yet a peculiarly safe spot in which to hide, having steep, rocky ledges on either side, with sufficient grass for the horses. Leaving Murphy bound, Hampton clambered up the front of the rock to where he was able to look out. All was silent, and his heart sank as he surveyed the brown sterile hills stretching to the horizon, having merely narrow gulches of rock and sand between, the sheer nakedness of the picture unrelieved by green shrub or any living thing. Then, almost despairing, he slid back, stretched himself out amid the soft grass, and sank into the slumber of exhaustion, his last conscious memory the incoherent babbling of his insane companion.

He awoke shortly after noon, feeling refreshed and renewed

in both body and mind. Murphy was sleeping when he first turned to look at him, but he awoke in season to be fed, and accepted the proffered food with all the apparent delight of a child. While he rested, their remaining pack-animal had strayed, and Hampton was compelled to go on with only the two horses, strapping the depleted store of provisions behind his own saddle. Then he carefully hoisted Murphy into place and bound his feet beneath the animal's belly, the poor fellow gibbering at him, in appearance an utter imbecile, although exhibiting periodic flashes of malignant passion. Then he resumed the journey down one of those sand-strewn depressions pointing toward the Rosebud, pressing the refreshed ponies into a canter, confident now that their greatest measure of safety lay in audacity.

Apparently his faith in the total desertion of these "bad lands" by the Indians was fully justified, for they continued steadily mile after mile, meeting with no evidence of life anywhere. Still the travelling was good, with here and there little streams of icy water trickling over the rocks. They made most excellent progress, Hampton ever grasping the bit of Murphy's horse, his anxious thought more upon his helpless companion in misery than upon the possible perils of the route.

It was already becoming dusk when they swept down into a little nest of green trees and grass. It appeared so suddenly, and was such an unexpected oasis amid that surrounding wilderness, that Hampton gave vent to a sudden exclamation of delight. But that was all. Instantly he perceived numerous dark forms leaping from out the shrubbery, and he wheeled his horses to the left, lashing them into a rapid run. It was all over in a moment—a sputtering of rifles, a wild medley of cries, a glimpse of savage figures, and the two were tearing down the rocks, the din of pursuit dying away behind them. The band were evidently all on foot, yet Hampton continued to press his mount at a swift pace, taking turn after turn about the sharp hills, confident that the hard earth would leave no trace of their passage.

Then suddenly the horse he rode sank like a log, but his tight grip upon the rein of the other landed him on his feet. Murphy laughed, in fiendish merriment; but Hampton looked down on the dead horse, noting the stream of blood oozing out from behind the shoulder. A stray Sioux bullet had found its mark, but the gallant animal had struggled on until it dropped lifeless; and the brave man it had borne so long and so well bent down and stroked tenderly the unconscious head. Then he shifted the provisions to the back of the other horse, grasped the loose rein once more in his left hand, and started forward on foot.

CHAPTER VI

ON THE LITTLE BIG HORN

N Troop, guarding, much to their emphatically expressed disgust, the more slowly moving pack-train, were following Custer's advancing column of horsemen down the right bank of the Little Big Horn. The troopers, carbines at knee, sitting erect in their saddles, their faces browned by the hot winds of the plains, were riding steadily northward. Beside them, mounted upon a rangy chestnut, Brant kept his watchful eyes on those scattered flankers dotting the summit of the near-by bluff. Suddenly one of these waved his hand eagerly, and the lieutenant went dashing up the sharp ascent.

"What is it, now, Lane?"

"Somethin' movin' jist out yonder, sir," and the trooper pointed into the southeast. "They're down in a *coulee* now, I reckon; but will be up on a ridge agin in a minute. I got sight of 'em twice afore I waved."

The officer gazed earnestly in the direction indicated, and was almost immediately rewarded by the glimpse of some indistinct, dark figures dimly showing against the lighter background of sky. He brought his field-glasses to a focus.

"White men," he announced, shortly. "Come with me."

At a brisk trot they rode out, the trooper lagging a pace to the rear, the watchful eyes of both men sweeping suspiciously across the prairie. The two parties met suddenly upon the summit of a sharp ridge, and Brant drew in his horse with an exclamation of astonishment. It was a pathetic spectacle he stared at,—a horse scarcely able to stagger forward, his flanks quivering from exhaustion, his head hanging limply down; on his back, with feet strapped securely beneath and hands bound to the high pommel, the lips grinning ferociously, perched a misshapen creature clothed as a man. Beside these, hatless, his shoes barely holding together, a man of slender figure and sunburnt face held the bridle-rein. An instant they gazed at each other, the young officer's eyes filled with sympathetic horror, the other staring apathetically at his rescuer.

"My God! Can this be you, Hampton?" and the startled lieutenant flung himself from his horse. "What does it mean? Why are you here?"

Hampton, leaning against the trembling horse to keep erect, slowly lifted his hand in a semblance of military salute. "Despatches from Cheyenne. This is Murphy—went crazy out yonder. For God's sake—water, food!"

"Your canteen, Lane!" exclaimed Brant. "Now hold this cup," and he dashed into it a liberal supply of brandy from a pocket-flask. "Drink that all down, Hampton."

The man did mechanically as he was ordered, his hand never relaxing its grasp of the rein. Then a gleam of reawakened intelligence appeared in his eyes; he glanced up into the leering countenance of Murphy, and then back at those others. "Give me another for him."

Brant handed to him the filled cup, noting as he did so the strange steadiness of the hand which accepted it. Hampton lifted the tin to the figure in the saddle, his own gaze directed straight into the eyes as he might seek to control a wild animal.

"Drink it," he commanded, curtly, "every drop!"

For an instant the maniac glared back at him sullenly; then he appeared to shrink in terror, and drank swiftly.

"We can make the rest of the way now," Hampton announced, quietly. "Lord, but this has been a trip!"

Lane dismounted at Brant's order, and assisted Hampton to climb into the vacated saddle. Then the trooper grasped the rein of Murphy's horse, and the little party started toward where the pack-train was hidden in the valley. The young officer rode silent and at a walk, his eyes occasionally studying the face of the other and noting its drawn, gray look. The very sight of Hampton had been a shock. Why was he here and with Murphy? Could this strange journey have anything to do with Naida? Could it concern his own future, as well as hers? He felt no lingering jealousy of this man, for her truthful words had forever settled that matter. Yet who was he? What peculiar power did he wield over her life?

"Is Custer here?" said Hampton.

"No; that is, not with my party. We are guarding the pack-train. The others are ahead, and Custer, with five troops, has moved to the right. He is somewhere among those ridges back of the bluff."

The man turned and looked where the officer pointed, shading his eyes with his hand. Before him lay only the brown, undulating waves of upland, a vast desert of burnt grass, shimmering under the hot sun.

"Can you give me a fresh horse, a bite to eat, and a cup of coffee, down there?" he asked, anxiously. "You see I've got to go on."

"Go on? Good God! man, do you realize what you are saying? Why, you can hardly sit the saddle! You carry despatches, you say? Well, there are plenty of good men in my troop who will volunteer to take them on. You need rest."

"Not much," said Hampton. "I'm fit enough, or shall be as soon as I get food. Good Lord, boy, I am not done up yet, by a long way! It's the cursed loneliness out yonder," he swept his hand toward the horizon, "and the having to care for him, that has broken my heart. He went that way clear back on the Powder, and it's been a fight between us ever since. I'll be all right now if you lads will only look after him. This is going to reach Custer, and I'll take it!" He flung back his ragged coat, his hand on the despatch-bag. "I've earned the right."

Brant reached forth his hand cordially. "That's true; you have. What's more, if you're able to make the trip, there is no one here who will attempt to stop you. But now tell me how this thing happened. I want to know the story before we get in."

For a moment Hampton remained silent, his thoughtful gaze on the near-by videttes, his hands leaning heavily upon the saddle pommel. Perhaps he did not remember clearly; possibly he could not instantly decide just how much of that story to tell. Brant suspected this last to be his difficulty, and he spoke impulsively.

"Hampton, there has been trouble and misunderstanding between us, but that's all past and gone now. I sincerely believe in your purpose of right, and I ask you to trust me. Either of us would give his life if need were, to be of real service to a little girl back yonder in the hills. I don't know what you are to her; I don't ask. I know she has every confidence in you, and that is enough. Now, I want to do what is right with both of you, and if you have a word to say to me regarding this matter, I'll treat it confidentially. This trip with Murphy has some bearing upon Naida Gillis, has it not?"

"Yes."

"Will you tell me the story?"

The thoughtful gray eyes looked at him long and searchingly. "Brant, do you love that girl?"

Just as unwaveringly the blue eyes returned the look. "I do. I have asked her to become my wife."

"And her answer?"

"She said no; that a dead man was between us."

"Is that all you know?"

The younger man bent his head, his face grave and perplexed. "Practically all."

Hampton wet his dry lips with his tongue, his breath quickening.

"And in that she was right," he said at last, his eyes lowered to the ground. "I will tell you why. It was the father of Naida

Gillis who was convicted of the murder of Major Brant."

"Oh, my father? Is she Captain Nolan's daughter? But you say 'convicted.' Was there ever any doubt? Do you question his being guilty?"

Hampton pointed in silence to the hideous creature behind them. "That man could tell, but he has gone mad."

Brant endeavored to speak, but the words would not come; his brain seemed paralyzed. Hampton held himself under better control.

"I have confidence, Lieutenant Brant, in your honesty," he began, gravely, "and I believe you will strive to do whatever is best for her, if anything should happen to me out yonder. But for the possibility of my being knocked out, I wouldn't talk about this, not even to you. The affair is a long way from being straightened out so as to make a pleasant story, but I'll give you all you actually require to know in order to make it clear to her, provided I shouldn't come back. You see, she doesn't know very much more than you do—only what I was obliged to tell to keep her from getting too deeply entangled with you. Maybe I ought to have given her the full story before I started on this trip. I've since wished I had, but you see, I never dreamed it was going to end here, on the Big Horn; besides, I didn't have the nerve."

He swept his heavy eyes across the brown and desolate prairie, and back to the troubled face of the younger man. "You see, Brant, I feel that I simply have to carry these despatches through. I have a pride in giving them to Custer myself, because of the trouble I've had in getting them here. But perhaps I may not come back, and in that case there wouldn't be any one living to tell her the truth. That thought has bothered me ever since I pulled out of Cheyenne. It seems to me that there is going to be a big fight somewhere in these hills before long. I've seen a lot of Indians riding north within the last four days, and they were all bucks, rigged out in war toggery, Sioux and Cheyennes. Ever since we crossed the Fourche those fellows have been in evidence, and it's my notion that Custer has a heavier job on his hands, right at this minute, than he has any conception of. So I want to leave these private papers with you until I come back. It will relieve my mind to know they are safe; if I don't come, then I want you to open them and do whatever you decide is best for the little girl. You will do that, won't you?"

He handed over a long manila envelope securely sealed, and the younger man accepted it, noticing that it was unaddressed before depositing it safely in an inner pocket of his fatigue jacket.

"Certainly, Hampton," he said. "Is that all?"

"All except what I am going to tell you now regarding Murphy. There is no use my attempting to explain exactly how I chanced to find out all these things, for they came to me little by little during several years. I knew Nolan, and I knew your father, and I had reason to doubt the guilt of the Captain, in spite of the verdict of the jury that condemned him. In fact, I knew at the time, although it was not in my power to prove it, that the two principal witnesses against Nolan lied. I thought I could guess why, but we drifted apart, and finally I lost all track of every one connected with the affair. Then I happened to pick up that girl down in the canyon beyond the Bear Water, and pulled her out alive just because she chanced to be of that sex, and I couldn't stand to see her fall into Indian clutches. I didn't feel any special interest in her at the time, supposing she belonged to Old Gillis, but she somehow grew on me—she's that kind, you know; and when I discovered, purely by accident, that she was Captain Nolan's girl, but that it all had been kept from her, I just naturally made up my mind I'd dig out the truth if I possibly could, for her sake. The fact is, I began to think a lot about her—not the way you do, you understand; I'm getting too old for that, and have known too much about women,—but maybe somewhat as a father might feel. Anyhow, I wanted to give her a chance, a square deal, so that she wouldn't be ashamed of her own name if ever she found out what it was."

He paused, his eyes filled with memories, and passed his hand through his uncovered hair.

"About that time I fell foul of Murphy and Slavin there in Glencaid," he went on quickly, as if anxious to conclude. "I never got my eyes on Murphy, you know, and Slavin was so changed by that big red beard that I failed to recognize him. But their actions aroused my suspicions, and I went after them good and hard. I wanted to find out what they knew, and why those lies were told on Nolan at the trial. I had an idea they could tell me. So, for a starter, I tackled Slavin, supposing we were alone, and I was pumping the facts out of him successfully by holding a gun under his nose, and occasionally jogging his memory, when this fellow Murphy got excited, and *chasseed* into the game, but happened to nip his partner instead of me. In the course of our little scuffle I chanced to catch a glimpse of the fellow's right hand, and it had a scar on the back of it that looked mighty familiar. I had seen it before, and I wanted to see it again. So, when I got out of that scrape, and the doctor had dug a stray bullet out of my anatomy, there didn't seem to be any one left for me to chase excepting Murphy, for Slavin was dead. I wasn't exactly sure he was the owner of that scar, but I had my suspicions and wanted to verify them. Having struck his trail, I reached Cheyenne just about four hours after he left there with these despatches for the Big Horn. I caught up with the fellow on the south bank of the Belle Fourche, and being well aware that no threats or gun play would ever force him to confess the truth, I undertook to frighten him by trickery. I brought along some drawing-paper and drew your father's picture in phosphorus, and gave him the benefit in the dark. That caught Murphy all right, and everything was coming my way. He threw up his hands, and even agreed to come in here with me, and tell the whole story, but the poor fellow's brain couldn't stand the strain of the scare I had given him. He went raving mad on the Powder; he jumped on me while I was asleep, and since then every mile has been a little hell. That's the whole of it to date."

They were up with the pack-train by now, and the cavalrymen gazed with interest at the new arrivals. Several among them seemed to recognize Murphy, and crowded about his horse with rough expressions of sympathy. Brant scarcely glanced at them, his grave eyes on Hampton's stern face.

"And what is it you wish me to do?"

"Take care of Murphy. Don't let him remain alone for a minute. If he has any return of reason, compel him to talk. He knows you, and will be as greatly frightened at your presence and knowledge as at mine. Besides, you have fully as much at stake as any one, for in no other way can the existing barrier between Naida and yourself be broken down."

Insisting that now he felt perfectly fit for any service, the impatient Hampton was quickly supplied with the necessary food and clothing, while Murphy, grown violently abusive, was strapped on a litter between two mules, a guard on either side. Brant rode with the civilian on a sharp trot as far as the head of the pack-train, endeavoring to the very last to persuade the wearied man to relinquish this work to another.

"Foster," he said to the sergeant in command of the advance, "did you chance to notice just what *coulee* Custer turned into when his column swung to the right?"

"I think it must have been the second yonder, sir; where you see that bunch of trees. We was a long ways back, but I could see the boys plain enough as they come out on the bluff up there. Some of 'em waved their hats back at us. Is this man goin' after them, sir?"

"Yes, he has despatches from Cheyenne."

"Well, he ought ter have no trouble findin' the trail. It ought ter be 'bout as plain as a road back in God's country, sir, fer there were more than two hundred horses, and they'd leave a good mark even on hard ground."

Brant held out his hand. "I'll certainly do all in my power, Hampton, to bring this out right. You can rely on that, and I will be faithful to the little girl. Now, just a word to guide you regarding our situation here. We have every reason for believing that the Sioux are in considerable force in our front somewhere, and not far down this stream. Nobody knows just how strong they are, but it looks to me as if we were pretty badly split up for a very heavy engagement. Not that I question Custer's plan, you understand, only he may be mistaken about what the Indians will do. Benteen's battalion is out there to the west; Reno is just ahead of us up the valley; while Custer has taken five troops on a detour to the right across the bluffs, hoping to come down on the rear of the Sioux. The idea is to crush them between the three columns. No one of these detachments has more than two hundred men, yet it may come out all right if they only succeed in striking together. Still it's risky in such rough country, not knowing exactly where the enemy is. Well, good luck to you, and take care of yourself."

The two men clasped hands, their eyes filled with mutual confidence. Then Hampton touched spurs to his horse, and galloped swiftly forward.

CHAPTER VII

THE FIGHT IN THE VALLEY

Far below, in the heart of the sunny depression bordering the left bank of the Little Big Horn, the stalwart troopers under Reno's command gazed up the steep bluff to wave farewell to their comrades disappearing to the right. Last of all, Custer halted his horse an instant, silhouetted against the blue sky, and swung his hat before spurring out of sight.

The plan of battle was most simple and direct. It involved a nearly simultaneous attack upon the vast Indian village from below and above, success depending altogether upon the prompt cooeeration of the separate detachments. This was understood by every trooper in the ranks. Scarcely had Custer's slender column of horsemen vanished across the summit before Reno's command advanced, trotting down the valley, the Arikara scouts in the lead. They had been chosen to strike the first blow, to force their way into the lower village, and thus to draw the defending warriors to their front, while Custer's men were to charge upon the rear. It was an old trick of the Seventh, and not a man in saddle ever dreamed the plan could fail.

A half-mile, a mile, Reno's troops rode, with no sound breaking the silence but the pounding of hoofs, the tinkle of accoutrements. Then, rounding a sharp projection of earth and rock, the scattered lodges of the Indian village already partially revealed to those in advance, the riders were brought to sudden halt by a fierce crackling of rifles from rock and ravine, an outburst of fire in their faces, the wild, resounding screech of war-cries, and the scurrying across their front of dense bodies of mounted warriors, hideous in paint and feathers. Men fell cursing, and the frightened horses swerved, their riders struggling madly with their mounts, the column thrown into momentary confusion. But the surprised cavalrymen, quailing beneath the hot fire poured into them, rallied to the shouts of their officers, and swung into a slender battle-front, stretching out their thin line from the bank of the river to the sharp uplift of the western bluffs. Riderless horses crashed through them, neighing with pain; the wounded begged for help; while, with cries of terror, the cowardly Arikara scouts lashed their ponies in wild efforts to escape. Scarcely one hundred and fifty white troopers waited to stem as best they might that fierce onrush of twelve hundred battle-crazed braves.

For an almost breathless space those mingled hordes of Sioux and Cheyennes hesitated to drive straight home their death-blow. They knew those silent men in the blue shirts, knew they died hard. Upon that slight pause pivoted the fate of the day; upon it hung the lives of those other men riding boldly and trustfully across the sunlit ridges above. "Audacity, always audacity," that is the accepted motto for a cavalryman. And be the cause what it may, it was here that Major Reno failed. In that supreme instant he was guilty of hesitancy, doubt, delay. He chose defence in preference to attack, dallied where he should have acted. Instead of hurling like a thunderbolt that handful of eager fighting men straight at the exposed heart of the foe, making dash and momentum, discipline and daring, an offset to lack of numbers, he lingered in indecision, until the observing savages, gathering courage from his apparent weakness, burst forth in resistless torrent against the slender, unsupported line, turned his flank by one fierce charge, and hurled the struggling troopers back with a rush into the narrow strip of timber bordering the river.

Driven thus to bay, the stream at their back rendering farther retreat impossible, for a few moments the light carbines of the soldiers met the Indian rifles, giving back lead for lead. But already every chance for successful attack had vanished; the whole narrow valley seemed to swarm with braves; they poured forth from sheltering *coulees* and shadowed ravines; they dashed down in countless numbers from the distant village. Custer, now far away behind the bluffs, and almost beyond sound of the firing, was utterly ignored. Every savage chief knew exactly where that column was, but it could await its turn; Gall, Crazy Horse, and Crow King mustered their red warriors for one determined effort to crush Reno, to grind him into dust beneath their ponies' hoofs. Ay, and they nearly did it!

In leaderless effort to break away from that swift-gathering cordon, before the red, remorseless folds should close tighter and crush them to death, the troopers, half of them already dismounted, burst from cover in an endeavor to attain the shelter of the bluffs. The deadly Indian rifles flamed in their faces, and they were hurled back, a mere fleeing mob, searching for nothing in that moment of terror but a possible passageway across the stream. Through some rare providence of God, they chanced to strike the banks at a spot where the river proved fordable. They plunged headlong in, officers and men commingled, the Indian bullets churning up the water on every side; they struggled madly through, and spurred their horses up the steep ridge beyond. A few cool-headed veterans halted at the edge of the bank to defend the passage; but the majority, crazed by panic and forgetful of all discipline, raced frantically for the summit. Dr. De Wolf stood at the very water's edge firing until shot down; McIntosh, striving vainly to rally his demoralized men, sank with a bullet in his brain; Hodgson, his leg broken by a ball, clung to a sergeant's stirrup until a second shot stretched him dead upon the bank. The loss in that wild retreat (which Reno later called a "charge") was heavy, the effect demoralizing; but those who escaped found a spot well suited for defence. Even as they swung down from off their wounded, panting horses, and flung themselves flat upon their faces to sweep with hastily levelled carbines the river banks below, Benteen came trotting gallantly down the valley to their aid, his troopers fresh and eager to be thrown forward on the firing-line. The worst was over, and like maddened lions, the rallied soldiers of the Seventh, cursing their folly, turned to strike and slay.

The valley was obscured with clouds of dust and smoke, the day frightfully hot and suffocating. The various troop commanders, gaining control over their men, were prompt to act. A line of skirmishers was hastily thrown forward along the edge of the bluff, while volunteers, urged by the agonized cries of the wounded, endeavored vainly to procure a supply of water from the river. Again and again they made the effort, only to be driven back by the deadly Indian rifle fire. This came mostly from braves concealed behind rocks or protected by the timber along the stream, but large numbers of hostiles were plainly visible, not only in the valley, but also upon the ridges. The firing upon their position continued incessantly, the warriors continually changing their point of attack. By three o'clock, although the majority of the savages had departed down the river, enough remained to keep up a galling fire, and hold Reno strictly on the defensive. These reds skulked in ravines, or lined the banks of the river, their long-range rifles rendering the lighter carbines of the cavalrymen almost valueless. A few

Randall Parrish

crouched along the edge of higher eminences, their shots crashing in among the unprotected troops.

As the men lay exposed to this continuous sniping fire, above the surrounding din were borne to their ears the reports of distant guns. It came distinctly from the northward, growing heavier and more continuous. None among them doubted its ominous meaning. Custer was already engaged in hot action at the right of the Indian village. Why were they kept lying there in idleness? Why were they not pushed forward to do their part? They looked into each other's faces. God! They were three hundred now; they could sweep aside like chaff that fringe of red skirmishers if only they got the word! With hearts throbbing, every nerve tense, they waited, each trooper crouched for the spring. Officer after officer, unable to restrain his impatience, strode back across the bluff summit, amid whistling bullets, and personally begged the Major to speak the one word which should hurl them to the rescue. They cried like women, they swore through clinched teeth, they openly exhibited their contempt for such a commander, yet the discipline of army service made active disobedience impossible. They went reluctantly back, as helpless as children.

It was four o'clock, the shadows of the western bluffs already darkening the river bank. Suddenly a faint cheer ran along the lines, and the men lifted themselves to gaze up the river. Urging the tired animals to a trot, the strong hand of a trooper grasping every halter-strap, Brant was swinging his long pack-train up the smoke-wreathed valley. The outriding flankers exchanged constant shots with the skulking savages hiding in every ravine and coulee. Pausing only to protect their wounded, fighting their way step by step, N Troop ran the gantlet and came charging into the cheering lines with every pound of their treasure safe. Weir of D, whose dismounted troopers held that portion of the line, strode a pace forward to greet the leader, and as the extended hands of the officers met, there echoed down to them from the north the reports of two heavy volleys, fired in rapid succession. The sounds were clear, distinctly audible even above the uproar of the valley. The heavy eyes of the two soldiers met, their dust-streaked faces flushed.

"That was a signal, Custer's signal for help!" the younger man cried, impulsively, his voice full of agony. "For God's sake, Weir, what are you fellows waiting here for?"

The other uttered a groan, his hand flung in contempt back toward the bluff summit. "The cowardly fool won't move; he's whipped to death now."

Brant's jaw set like that of a fighting bulldog.

"Reno, you mean? Whipped? You haven't lost twenty men. Is this the Seventh—the Seventh?—skulking here under cover while Custer begs help? Doesn't the man know? Doesn't he understand? By heaven, I'll face him myself! I'll make him act, even if I have to damn him to his face."

He swung his horse with a jerk to the left, but even as the spurs touched, Weir grasped the taut rein firmly.

"It's no use, Brant. It's been done; we've all been at him. He's simply lost his head. Know? Of course he knows. Martini struck us just below here, as we were coming in, with a message from Custer. It would have stirred the blood of any one but him—Oh, God! it's terrible."

"A message? What was it?"

"Cook wrote it, and addressed it to Benteen. It read: 'Come on. Big village. Be quick. Bring packs.' And then, 'P.

S.—Bring packs.' That means they want ammunition badly; they're fighting to the death out yonder, and they need powder. Oh, the coward!"

Brant's eyes ran down the waiting line of his own men, sitting their saddles beside the halted pack-animals. He leaned over and dropped one hand heavily on Weir's shoulder. "The rest of you can do as you please, but N Troop is going to take those ammunition packs over to Custer if there's any possible way to get through, orders or no orders." He straightened up in the saddle, and his voice sounded down the wearied line like the blast of a trumpet.

"Attention! N Troop! Right face; dress. Number four bring forward the ammunition packs. No, leave the others where they are; move lively, men!"

He watched them swing like magic into formation, their dust-begrimed faces lighting up with animation. They knew their officer, and this meant business.

"Unsling carbines—load!"

Weir, the veteran soldier, glanced down that steady line of ready troopers, and then back to Brant's face. "Do you mean it? Are you going up those bluffs? Good Heavens, man, it will mean a court-martial."

"Custer commands the Seventh. I command the pack-train," said Brant. "His orders are to bring up the packs. Perhaps I can't get through alone, but I'll try. Better a court-martial than to fail those men out there. Going? Of course I'm going. Into line—take intervals—forward!"

"Attention, D Troop!" It was Weir's voice, eager and determined now. Like an undammed current his orders rang out above the uproar, and in a moment the gallant troopers of N and D, some on foot, some in saddle, were rushing up the face of the bluff, their officers leading, the precious ammunition packs at the centre, all alike scrambling for the summit, in spite of the crackling of Indian rifles from every side. Foot by foot they fought their way forward, sliding and stumbling, until the little blue wave burst out against the sky-line and sent an exultant cheer back to those below. Panting, breathless from the hard climb, their carbines spitting fire while the rapidly massing savages began circling their exposed position, the little band fought their way forward a hundred yards. Then they halted, blocked by the numbers barring their path, glancing back anxiously in hope that their effort would encourage others to join them. They could do it; they could do it if only the rest of the boys would come. They poured in their volleys and waited. But Reno made no move. Weir and Brant, determined to hold every inch thus gained, threw the dismounted men on their faces behind every projection of earth, and encircled the ridge with flame. If they could not advance, they would not be driven back. They were high up now, where they could overlook the numerous ridges and valleys far around; and yonder, perhaps two miles away, they could perceive vast bodies of mounted Indians, while the distant sound of heavy firing was borne faintly to their ears. It was vengeful savages shooting into the bodies of the dead, but that they did not know. Messenger after messenger, taking life in hand, was sent skurrying down the bluff, to beg reinforcements to push on for the rescue, swearing it was possible. But it was after five o'clock before Reno moved. Then cautiously he advanced his column toward where N and D Troops yet held desperately to the exposed ridge. He came too late. That distant firing had ceased, and all need for further advance had ended. Already vast forces of Indians, flushed with victory and waving bloody scalps, were sweeping back across the ridges to attack in force. Scarcely had reinforcements attained the summit before the torrent of savagery burst screeching on their front.

From point to point the grim struggle raged, till nightfall wrought partial cessation. The wearied troopers stretched out their lines so as to protect the packs and the field hospital, threw themselves on the ground, digging rifle-pits with knives and tin pans. Not until nine o'clock did the Indian fire slacken, and then the village became a scene of savage revel, the wild yelling plainly audible to the soldiers above. Through the black night Brant stepped carefully across the recumbent forms of his men, and made his way to the field hospital. In the glare of the single fire the red sear of a bullet showed clearly across his forehead, but he wiped away the slowly trickling blood, and bent over a form extended on a blanket.

"Has he roused up?" he questioned of the trooper on guard.

"Not to know nuthin', sir. He's bin swearin' an' gurglin' most o' ther time, but he's asleep now, I reckon."

The young officer stood silent, his face pale, his gaze upon the distant Indian fires. Out yonder were defeat, torture, death, and to-morrow meant a renewal of the struggle. His heart was heavy with foreboding, his memory far away with one to whom all this misfortune might come almost as a death-blow. It was Naida's questioning face that haunted him; she was waiting for she knew not what.

CHAPTER VIII

THE OLD REGIMENT

By the time Hampton swung up the *coulee*, he had dismissed from his attention everything but the business that had brought him there. No lingering thought of Naida, or of the miserable Murphy, was permitted to interfere with the serious work before him. To be once again with the old Seventh was itself inspiration; to ride with them into battle was the chief desire of his heart. It was a dream of years, which he had never supposed possible of fulfilment, and he rode rapidly forward, his lips smiling, the sunshine of noonday lighting up his face.

He experienced no fear, no premonition of coming disaster, yet the reawakened plainsman in him kept him sufficiently wary and cautious. The faint note of discontent apparent in Brant's concluding words—doubtless merely an echo of that ambitious officer's dislike at being put on guard over the pack-train at such a moment—awoke no response in his mind. He possessed a soldier's proud confidence in his regiment—the supposition that the old fighting Seventh could be defeated was impossible; the Indians did not ride those uplands who could do the deed! Then there came to him a nameless dread, that instinctive shrinking which a proud, sensitive man must ever feel at having to face his old companions with the shadow of a crime between. In his memory he saw once more a low-ceiled room, having a table extending down the centre, with grave-faced men, dressed in the full uniform of the service, looking at him amid a silence like unto death; and at the head sat a man with long fair hair and mustache, his proud eyes never to be forgotten. Now, after silent years, he was going to look into those accusing eyes again. He pressed his hand against his forehead, his body trembled; then he braced himself for the interview, and the shuddering coward in him shrank back.

He had become wearied of the endless vista of desert, rock, and plain. Yet now it strangely appealed to him in its beauty. About him were those uneven, rolling hills, like a vast storm-lashed sea, the brown crests devoid of life, yet with depressions between sufficient to conceal multitudes. Once he looked down through a wide cleft in the face of the bluff, and could perceive the head of the slowly advancing pack-train far below. Away to the left something was moving, a dim, shapeless dash of color. It might be Benteen, but of Reno's columns he could perceive nothing, nor anything of Custer's excepting that broad track across the prairies marked by his horses' hoofs. This track Hampton followed, pressing his fresh mount to increased speed, confident that no Indian spies would be loitering so closely in the rear of that body of cavalry, and becoming fearful lest the attack should occur before he could arrive.

He dipped over a sharp ridge and came suddenly upon the rear-guard. They were a little squad of dusty, brown-faced troopers, who instantly wheeled into line at sound of approaching hoofs, the barrels of their lowered carbines glistening in the sun. With a swing of the hand, and a hoarse shout of "Despatches!" he was beyond them, bending low over his saddle pommel, his eyes on the dust cloud of the moving column. The extended line of horsemen, riding in column of fours, came to a sudden halt, and he raced swiftly on. A little squad of officers, several of their number dismounted, were out in front, standing grouped just below the summit of a slight elevation, apparently looking off into the valley through some cleft In the bluff beyond. Standing among these, Hampton perceived the long fair hair, and the erect figure clad in the well-known frontier costume, of the man he sought,—the proud, dashing leader of light cavalry, that beau ideal of the *sabreur*, the one he dreaded most, the one he loved best,—Custer. The commander stood, field-glasses in hand, pointing down into the valley, and the despatch bearer, reining in his horse, his lips white but resolute, trotted straight up the slope toward him. Custer wheeled, annoyed at the interruption, and Hampton swung down from the saddle, his rein flung across his arm, took a single step forward, lifting his hand in salute, and held forth the sealed packet.

"Despatches, sir," he said, simply, standing motionless as a statue.

The commander, barely glancing toward him, instantly tore open the long official envelope and ran his eyes over the despatch amid a hush in the conversation.

"Gentlemen," he commented to the little group gathered about him, yet without glancing up from the paper in his hand, "Crook was defeated over on the Rosebud the seventeenth, and forced to retire. That will account for the unexpected number of hostiles fronting us up here, Cook; but the greater the task, the greater the glory. Ah, I thought as much. I am advised by the Department to keep in close touch with Terry and Gibbons, and to hold off from making a direct attack until infantry can arrive in support. Rather late in the day, I take it, when we are already within easy rifle-shot. I see nothing in these orders to interfere with our present plans, nor any military necessity for playing hide and seek all Summer in these hills. That looks like a big village down yonder, but I have led the dandy Seventh into others just as large."

He stopped speaking, and glanced up inquiringly into the face of the silent messenger, apparently mistaking him for one of his own men.

"Where did you get this?"

"Cheyenne, sir."

"What! Do you mean to say you brought it through from there?"

"Silent Murphy carried it as far as the Powder River. He went crazy there, and I was compelled to strap him. I brought it the rest of the way."

"Where is Murphy?"

"Back with the pack-train, sir. I got him through alive, but entirely gone in the head."

"Run across many hostiles in that region?"

"They were thick this side the Rosebud; all bucks, and travelling north."

"Sioux?"

"Mostly, sir, but I saw one band wearing Cheyenne war-bonnets."

A puzzled look slowly crept into the strong face of the abrupt questioner, his stern, commanding eyes studying the man standing motionless before him, with freshly awakened interest. The gaze of the other faltered, then came back courageously.

"I recognize you now," Custer said, quietly. "Am I to understand you are again in the service?"

"My presence here is purely accidental, General Custer. The opportunity came to me to do this work, and I very gladly accepted the privilege."

The commander hesitated, scarcely knowing what he might be justified in saying to this man.

"It was a brave deed, well performed," he said at last, with soldierly cordiality, "although I can hardly offer you a fitting reward."

The other stood bareheaded, his face showing pale under its sunburn, his hand trembling violently where it rested against his horse's mane.

"There is little I desire," he replied, slowly, unable to altogether disguise the quiver in his voice, "and that is to be permitted to ride once more into action in the ranks of the Seventh."

The true-hearted, impulsive, manly soldier fronting him reddened to the roots of his fair hair, his proud eyes instantly softening. For a second Hampton even imagined he would extend his hand, but the other paused with one step forward, discipline proving stronger than impulse.

"Spoken like a true soldier," he exclaimed, a new warmth in his voice. "You shall have your wish. Take position in

Calhoun's troop yonder."

Hampton turned quietly away, leading his horse, yet had scarcely advanced three yards before Custer halted him.

"I shall be pleased to talk with you again after the fight," he said, briefly, as though half doubting the propriety of such words.

The other bowed, his face instantly brightening. "I thank you sincerely."

The perplexed commander stood motionless, gazing after the receding figure, his face grown grave and thoughtful. Then he turned to the wondering adjutant beside him.

"You never knew him, did you, Cook?"

"I think not, sir; who is he?"

"Captain Nolan—you have heard the story."

The younger officer wheeled about, staring, but the despatch bearer had already become indistinguishable among the troopers.

"Is that so?" he exclaimed, in evident surprise. "He has a manly face."

"Ay, and he was as fine a soldier as ever fought under the flag," declared Custer, frankly. "Poor devil! The hardest service I was ever called upon to perform was the day we broke him. I wonder if Calhoun will recognize the face; they were good friends once."

He stopped speaking, and for a time his field-glasses were

fastened upon a small section of Indian village nestled in the green valley. Its full extent was concealed by the hills, yet from what the watchers saw they realized that this would prove no small encampment.

"I doubt if many warriors are there," he commented, at last. "They may have gone up the river to intercept Reno's advance, and if so, this should be our time to strike. But we are not far enough around, and this ground is too rough for cavalry. There looks to be considerable level land out yonder, and that *coulee* ought to lead us into it without peril of observation from below. Return to your commands, gentlemen, and with the order of march see personally that your men move quietly. We must strike quick and hard, driving the wedge home with a single blow."

His inquiring gaze swept thoughtfully over the expectant faces of his troop commanders. "That will be all at present, gentlemen; you will require no further instructions until we deploy. Captain Calhoun, just a word, please."

The officer thus directly addressed, a handsome, stalwart man of middle age, reined in his mettlesome horse and waited.

"Captain, the messenger who has just brought us despatches from Cheyenne is a civilian, but has requested permission to have a share in this coming fight. I have assigned him to your troop."

Calhoun bowed.

"I thought it best to spare you any possible embarrassment by saying that the man is not entirely unknown to you."

"May I ask his name?"

"Robert Nolan."

The strong, lion-like face flushed under its tan, then quickly lit up with a smile. "I thank you. Captain Nolan will not suffer at my hands."

He rode straight toward his troop, his eyes searching the ranks until they rested upon the averted face of Hampton. He pressed forward, and leaned from the saddle, extending a gauntleted hand. "Nolan, old man, welcome back to the Seventh!"

For an instant their eyes met, those of the officer filled with manly sympathy, the other's moistened and dim, his face like marble. Then the two hands clasped and clung, in a grip more eloquent than words. The lips of the disgraced soldier quivered, and he uttered not a word. It was Calhoun who spoke.

"I mean it all, Nolan. From that day to this I have believed in you,—have held you friend."

For a moment the man reeled; then, as though inspired by a new-born hope, he sat firmly erect, and lifted his hand in salute. "Those are words I have longed to hear spoken for fifteen years. They are more to me than life. May God help me to be worthy of them. Oh, Calhoun, Calhoun!"

For a brief space the two remained still and silent, their faces reflecting repressed feeling. Then the voice of command sounded out in front; Calhoun gently withdrew his hand from the other's grasp, and with bowed head rode slowly to the front of his troop.

In column of fours, silent, with not a canteen rattling, with scabbards thrust under their stirrup leathers, each man sitting his saddle like a statue, ready carbine flung forward across the pommel, those sunburnt troopers moved steadily down the broad *coulee*. There was no pomp, no sparkle of gay uniforms. No military band rode forth to play their famous battle tune of "Garryowen"; no flags waved above to inspire them, yet never before or since to a field of strife and death rode nobler hearts or truer. Troop following troop, their faded, patched uniforms brown with dust, their campaign hats pulled low to shade them from the glare, those dauntless cavalrymen of the Seventh swept across the low intervening ridge toward the fateful plain below. The troopers riding at either side of Hampton, wondering still at their captain's peculiar words and action, glanced curiously at their new comrade, marvelling at his tightly pressed lips, his moistened eyes. Yet in all the glorious column, no heart lighter than his, or happier, pressed forward to meet a warrior's death.

CHAPTER IX

THE LAST STAND

However daring the pen, it cannot but falter when attempting to picture the events of those hours of victorious defeat. Out from the scene of carnage there crept forth no white survivor to recount the heroic deeds of the Seventh Cavalry. No voice can ever repeat the story in its fulness, no eye penetrate into the heart of its mystery. Only in motionless lines of dead, officers and men lying as they fell while facing the foe; in emptied carbines strewing the prairie; in scattered, mutilated bodies; in that unbroken ring of dauntless souls whose lifeless forms lay clustered about the figure of their stricken chief on that slight eminence marking the final struggle— only in such tokens can we trace the broken outlines of the historic picture. The actors in the great tragedy have passed beyond either the praise or the blame of earth. With moistened eyes and swelling hearts, we vainly strive to imagine the whole scene. This, at least, we know: no bolder, nobler deed of arms was ever done.

It was shortly after two o'clock in the afternoon when that compact column of cavalrymen moved silently forward down the concealing *coulee* toward the more open ground beyond. Custer's plan was surprise, the sudden smiting of that village in the valley from the rear by the quick charge of his horsemen. From man to man the whispered purpose travelled down the ranks, the eager troopers greeting the welcome message with kindling eyes. It was the old way of the Seventh, and they knew it well. The very horses seemed to feel the electric shock. Worn with hard marches, bronzed by long weeks of exposure on alkali plains, they advanced now with the precision of men on parade, under the observant eyes of the officers. Not a canteen tinkled, not a sabre rattled within its scabbard, as at a swift, noiseless walk those tried warriors of the Seventh pressed forward to strike once more their old-time foes.

Above them a few stray, fleecy clouds flecked the blue of the arching sky, serving only to reveal its depth of color. On every side extended the rough irregularity of a region neither mountain nor plain, a land of ridges and bluffs, depressions and ravines. Over all rested the golden sunlight of late June; and in all the broad expanse there was no sign of human presence.

With Custer riding at the head of the column, and only a little to the rear of the advance scouts, his adjutant Cook, together with a volunteer aide, beside him, the five depleted troops filed resolutely forward, dreaming not of possible defeat. Suddenly distant shots were heard far off to their left and rear, and deepening into a rumble, evidencing a warm engagement. The interested troopers lifted their heads, listening intently, while eager whispers ran from man to man along the closed files.

"Reno is going in, boys; it will be our turn next."

"Close up! Quiet there, lads, quiet," officer after officer passed the word of command.

Yet there were those among them who felt a strange

dread—that firing sounded so far up the stream from where Reno should have been by that time. Still it might be that those overhanging bluffs would muffle and deflect the reports. Those fighting men of the Seventh rode steadily on, unquestioningly pressing forward at the word of their beloved leader. All about them hovered death in dreadful guise. None among them saw those cruel, spying eyes watching from distant ridges, peering at them from concealed ravines; none marked the rapidly massing hordes, hideous in war-paint, crowded into near-by *coulees* and behind protecting hills.

It burst upon them with wild yells. The gloomy ridges blazed into their startled faces, the dark ravines hurled at them skurrying horsemen, while, wherever their eyes turned, they beheld savage forms leaping forth from hill and *coulee*, gulch and rock shadow. Horses fell, or ran about neighing; men flung up their hands and died in that first awful minute of consternation, and the little column seemed to shrivel away as if consumed by the flame which struck it, front and flank and rear. It was as if those men had ridden into the mouth of hell. God only knows the horror of that first moment of shrinking suspense—the screams of agony from wounded men and horses, the dies of fear, the thunder of charging hoofs, the deafening roar of rifles.

Yet it was for scarcely more than a minute. Men trained, strong, clear of brain, were in those stricken lines—men who had seen Indian battle before. The recoil came, swift as had been the surprise. Voice after voice rang out in old familiar orders, steadying instantly the startled nerves; discipline conquered disorder, and the shattered column rolled out, as if by magic, into the semblance of a battle line. On foot and on horseback, the troopers of the Seventh turned desperately at bay.

It was magnificently done. Custer and his troop-commanders brought their sorely smitten men into a position of defence, even hurled them cheering forward in short, swift charges, so as to clear the front and gain room in which to deploy. Out of confusion emerged discipline, confidence, *esprit de corps*. The savages skurried away on their quirt-lashed ponies, beyond range of those flaming carbines, while the cavalry-men, pausing from vain pursuit, gathered up their wounded, and re-formed their disordered ranks.

"Wait till Reno rides into their village," cried encouraged voices through parched lips. "Then we'll give them hell!"

Safe beyond range of the troopers' light carbines, the Indians, with their heavier rifles, kept hurling a constant storm of lead, hugging the gullies, and spreading out until there was no rear toward which the harassed cavalrymen could turn for safety. One by one, continually under a heavy fire, the scattered troops were formed into something more nearly resembling a battle line—Calhoun on the left, then Keogh, Smith, and Yates, with Tom Custer holding the extreme right. The position taken was far from being an ideal one, yet the best possible under the circumstances, and the exhausted men flung themselves down behind low ridges, seeking protection from the Sioux bullets, those assigned to the right enjoying the advantage of a somewhat higher elevation. Thus they waited grimly for the next assault.

Nor was it long delayed. Scarcely had the troopers recovered, refilled their depleted cartridge belts from those of their dead comrades, when the onslaught came. Lashing their ponies into mad gallop, now sitting erect, the next moment lying hidden behind the plunging animals, cons-tantly screaming their shrill war-cries, their guns brandished in air, they swept onward, seeking to crush that thin line in one terrible onset. But they reckoned wrong. The soldiers waited their coming. The short, brown-barrelled carbines gleamed at the level in the sunlight, and then belched forth their message of flame into the very faces of those reckless horsemen. It was not in flesh and blood to bear such a blow. With screams of rage, the red braves swerved to left and right, leaving many a dark, war-bedecked figure lying dead behind them, and many a riderless pony skurrying over the prairie. Yet their wild ride had not been altogether in vain; like a whirlwind they had struck against Calhoun on the flank, forcing his troopers to yield sullen ground, thus contracting the little semicircle of defenders, pressing it back against that central hill. It was a step nearer the end, yet those who fought scarcely realized its significance. Exultant over their seemingly successful repulse, the men flung themselves again upon the earth, their cheers ringing out above the thud of retreating hoofs.

"We can hold them here, boys, until Reno comes," they shouted to each other.

The skulking red riflemen crept ever closer behind the ridges, driving their deadly missiles into those ranks exposed in the open. Twice squads dashed forth to dislodge these bands, but were in turn driven back, the line of fire continually creeping nearer, clouds of smoke concealing the cautious marksmen lying prone in the grass. Custer walked up and down the irregular line, cool, apparently unmoved, speaking words of approval to officers and men. To the command of the bugle they discharged two roaring volleys from their carbines, hopeful that the combined sound might reach the ears of the lagging Reno. They were hopeful yet, although one troop had only a sergeant left in command, and the dead bodies of their comrades strewed the plain.

Twice those fierce red horsemen tore down upon them, forcing the thin, struggling line back by sheer strength of overwhelming numbers, yet no madly galloping warrior succeeded in bursting through. The hot brown barrels belched forth their lightnings into those painted faces, and the swarms of savagery melted away. The living sheltered themselves behind the bodies of their dead, fighting now in desperation, their horses stampeded, their ammunition all gone excepting the few cartridges remaining in the waist-belts. From lip to lip passed the one vital question: "In God's name, where is Reno? What has become of the rest of the boys?"

It was four o'clock. For two long hours they had been engaged in ceaseless struggle; and now barely a hundred men, smoke-begrimed, thirsty, bleeding, half their carbines empty, they still formed an impenetrable ring around their chief. The struggle was over, and they realized the fact. When that wave of savage horsemen swept forth again it would be to ride them down, to crush them under their horses' pounding hoofs. They turned their loyal eyes toward him they loved and followed for the last time, and when he uttered one final word of undaunted courage, they cheered him faintly, with parched and fevered lips.

Like a whirlwind those red demons came,—howling wolves now certain of their prey. From rock and hill, ridge, ravine, and *coulee*, lashing their half-crazed ponies, yelling their fierce war-cries, swinging aloft their rifles, they poured resistlessly forth, sweeping down on that doomed remnant. On both flanks of the short slender line struck Gall and Crazy Horse, while like a thunderbolt Crow-King and Rain-in-the-Face attacked the centre. These three storms converged at the foot of the little hill, crushing the little band of troopers. With ammunition gone, the helpless victims could meet that mighty on-rushing torrent only with clubbed guns, for one instant of desperate struggle. Shoulder to shoulder, in ever-contracting circle, officers and men stood shielding their commander to the last. Foot by foot, they were forced back, treading on their wounded, stumbling over their dead; they were choked in the stifling smoke, scorched by the flaming guns, clutched at by red hands, beaten down by horses' hoofs. Twenty or thirty made a despairing dash, in a vain endeavor to burst through the red enveloping lines, only to be tomahawked or shot; but the most remained, a thin struggling ring, with Custer in its centre. Then came the inevitable end. The red waves surged completely across the crest, no white man left alive upon the field. They had fought a good fight; they had kept the faith.

Two days later, having relieved Reno from his unpleasant predicament in the valley, Terry's and Gibbons's infantry tramped up the ravine, and emerged upon the stricken field. In lines of motionless dead they read the fearful story; and there they found that man we know. Lying upon a bed of emptied cartridge-shells, his body riddled with shot and mutilated with knives, his clothing torn to rags, his hands grasping a smashed and twisted carbine, his lips smiling even in death, was that soldier whom the Seventh had disowned and cast out, but who had come back to defend its chief and to die for its honor,—Robert Hampton Nolan.

CHAPTER X

THE CURTAIN FALLS

Bronzed by months of scouting on those northern plains, a graver, older look upon his face, and the bars of a captain gracing the shoulders of his new cavalry jacket, Donald Brant trotted down the stage road bordering the Bear Water, his heart alternating between hope and dread. He was coming back as he had promised; yet, ardently as he longed to look into the eyes of his beloved, he shrank from the duty laid upon him by the dead.

The familiar yellow house at the cross-roads appeared so unattractive as to suggest the thought that Naida must have been inexpressibly lonely during those months of waiting. He knocked at the sun-warped door. Without delay it was flung open, and a vision of flushed face and snowy drapery confronted him.

"Why, Lieutenant Brant! I was never more surprised in my life. Do, pray, come right in. Yes, Naida is here, and I will have her sent for at once. Oh, Howard, this is Lieutenant Brant, just back from his awful Indian fighting. How very nice that he should happen to arrive just at this time, isn't it?"

The young officer, as yet unable to discover an opportunity for speech, silently accepted Mr. Wynkoop's extended hand, and found a convenient chair, as Miss Spencer hastened from the room to announce his arrival.

"Why 'just at this time'?" he questioned.

Mr. Wynkoop cleared his throat. "Why—why, you see, we are to be married this evening—Miss Spencer and myself. We—we shall be so delighted to have you witness the ceremony. It is to take place at the church, and my people insist upon making quite an affair out of the occasion— Phoebe is so popular, you know."

The lady again bustled in, her eyes glowing with enthusiasm. "Why, I think it is perfectly delightful. Don't you, Howard? Now Lieutenant Brant and Naida can stand up with us. You will, won't you, Lieutenant?"

"That must be left entirely with Miss Naida for decision," he replied, soberly. "However, with my memory of your popularity I should suppose you would have no lack of men seeking such honor. For instance, one of your old-time 'friends' Mr. William McNeil."

The lady laughed noisily, regardless of Mr. Wynkoop's look of annoyance. "Oh, it is so perfectly ridiculous! And didn't you know? haven't you heard?"

"Nothing, I assure you."

"Why he—he actually married the Widow Guffy. She's twice his age, and has a grown-up son. And to think that I supposed he was so nice! He did write beautiful verses. Isn't it a perfect shame for such a man to throw himself away like that?"

"It would seem so. But there was another whose name I recall—Jack Moffat. Why not have him?"

Miss Spencer glanced uneasily at her chosen companion, her cheeks reddening. But that gentleman remained provokingly silent, and she was compelled to reply.

"We—we never mention him any more. He was a very bad man."

"Indeed?"

"Yes; it seems he had a wife and four children he had run away from, back in Iowa. Perhaps that was why his eyes always looked so sad. She actually advertised for him in one of the Omaha papers. It was a terrible shock to all of us. I was so grateful to Howard that he succeeded in opening my eyes in time."

Mr. Wynkoop placed his hand gently upon her shoulder. "Never mind, dearie," he said, cheerfully. "The West was all so strange to you, and it seemed very wonderful at first. But that is all safely over with now, and, as my wife, you will forget the unpleasant memories."

And Miss Spencer, totally oblivious to Brant's presence, turned impulsively and kissed him.

There was a rustle at the inner door, and Naida stood there. Their eyes met, and the color mounted swiftly to the girl's cheeks. Then he stepped resolutely forward, forgetful of all other presence, and clasped her hand in both his own. Neither spoke a word, yet each understood something of what was in the heart of the other.

"Will you walk outside with me?" he asked, at last. "I have

much to say which I am sure you would rather hear alone."

She bent her head, and with a brief word of explanation to the others, the young officer conducted her forth into the bright July sunshine. They walked in silence side by side along the bank of the little stream. Brant glanced furtively toward the sweet, girlish face. There was a pallor on her countenance, a shadow in her eyes, yet she walked with the same easy grace, her head firmly poised above her white throat. The very sadness marking her features seemed to him an added beauty.

He realized where they were going now, where memory had brought them without conscious volition. As he led her across the rivulet she glanced up into his face with a smile, as though a happy recollection had burst upon her. Yet not a word was spoken until the barrier of underbrush had been completely penetrated, and they stood face to face under the trees. Then Brant spoke.

"Naida," he said, gravely, "I have come back, as I said I would, and surely I read welcome in your eyes?"

"Yes."

"And I have come to say that there is no longer any shadow of the dead between us."

She looked up quickly, her hands clasped, her cheeks flushing. "Are you sure? Perhaps you misunderstand; perhaps you mistake my meaning."

"I know it all," he answered, soberly, "from the lips of Hampton."

"You have seen him? Oh, Lieutenant Brant, please tell me

the whole truth. I have missed him so much, and since the day he rode away to Cheyenne not one word to explain his absence has come back to me. You cannot understand what this means, how much he has become to me through years of kindness."

"You have heard nothing?"

"Not a word."

Brant drew a long, deep breath. He had supposed she knew this. At last he said gravely:

"Naida, the truth will prove the kindest message, I think. He died in that unbroken ring of defenders clustered about General Custer on the bluffs of the Little Big Horn."

Her slight figure trembled so violently that he held her close within his arms.

"There was a smile upon his face when we found him. He performed his full duty, Naida, and died as became a soldier and a gentleman."

"But—but, this cannot be! I saw the published list; his name was not among them."

"The man who fell was Robert Nolan."

Gently he drew her down to a seat upon the soft turf of the bank. She looked up at him helplessly, her mind seemingly dazed, her eyes yet filled with doubt.

"Robert Nolan? My father?"

He bent over toward her, pressing his lips to her hair and

stroking it tenderly with his hand.

"Yes, Naida, darling; it was truly Robert Hampton Nolan who died in battle, in the ranks of his old regiment,—died as he would have chosen to die, and died, thank God! completely cleared of every stain upon his honor. Sit up, little girl, and listen while I tell you. There is in the story no word which does not reflect nobility upon the soldier's daughter."

She uplifted her white face. "Tell me," she said, simply, "all you know."

He recounted to her slowly, carefully, the details of that desperate journey northward, of their providential meeting on the Little Big Horn, of the papers left in his charge, of Hampton's riding forward with despatches, and of his death at Custer's side. While he spoke, the girl scarcely moved; her breath came in sobs and her hands clasped his.

"These are the papers, Naida. I opened the envelope as directed, and found deeds to certain properties, including the mine in the Black Range; a will, duly signed and attested, naming you as his sole heir, together with a carefully prepared letter, addressed to you, giving a full account of the crime of which he was convicted, as well as some other matters of a personal nature. That letter you must read alone as his last message, but the truth of all he says has since been proved."

She glanced up at him quickly. "By Murphy?"

"Yes, by Murphy, who is now lying in the hospital at Bethune, slowly recovering. His sworn deposition has been forwarded to the Department at Washington, and will undoubtedly result in the honorable replacing of your father's name on the Army List. I will tell you briefly the man's confession, together with the few additional facts necessary to make it clear.

"Your father and mine were for many years friends and army comrades. They saw service together during the great war, and afterward upon the plains in Indian campaigning. Unfortunately a slight misunderstanding arose between them. This, while not serious in itself, was made bitter by the interference of others, and the unaccountable jealousies of garrison life. One night they openly quarrelled when heated by wine, and exchanged blows. The following evening, your father chancing to be officer of the guard and on duty, my father, whose wife had then been dead a year, was thoughtless enough to accompany Mrs. Nolan home at a late hour from the post ball. It was merely an act of ordinary courtesy; but gossips magnified the tale, and bore it to Nolan. Still smarting from the former quarrel, in which I fear my father was in the wrong, he left the guard-house with the openly avowed intention of seeking immediate satisfaction. In the meanwhile Slavin, Murphy, and a trooper named Flynn, who had been to town without passes, and were half-drunk, stole through the guard lines, and decided to make a midnight raid on the colonel's private office. Dodging along behind the powder-house, they ran suddenly upon my father, then on the way to his own quarters. Whether they were recognized by him, or whether drink made them reckless of consequences, is unknown, but one of the men instantly fired. Then they ran, and succeeded in gaining the barracks unsuspected."

She sat as if fascinated by his recital.

"Your father heard the shot, and sprang toward the sound, only to fall headlong across my father's lifeless body. As he came down heavily, his revolver was jarred out of its holster and dropped unnoticed in the grass. An instant later the guard came running up, and by morning Captain Nolan was under arrest, charged with murder. The circumstantial evidence was strong—his quarrel with the murdered man, his heated language a few moments previous, the revolver lying beside the body, having two chambers discharged, and his being found there alone with the man he had gone forth to seek. Slavin and Flynn both strengthened the case by positive testimony. As a result, a court martial dismissed the prisoner in disgrace from the army, and a civil court sentenced him to ten years' imprisonment."

"And my mother?" The question was a trembling whisper from quivering lips.

"Your mother," he said, regretfully, "was an exceedingly proud woman, belonging to a family of social prominence in the East. She felt deeply the causeless gossip connecting her name with the case, as well as the open disgrace of her husband's conviction. She refused to receive her former friends, and even failed in loyalty to your father in his time of trial. It is impossible now to fix the fault clearly, or to account for her actions. Captain Nolan turned over all his property to her, and the moment she could do so, she disappeared from the fort, taking you with her. From that hour none of her old acquaintances could learn anything regarding her whereabouts. She did not return to her family in the East, nor correspond with any one in the army. Probably, utterly broken-hearted, she sought seclusion in some city. How Gillis obtained possession of you remains a mystery."

"Is that all?"

"Everything."

They kept silence for a long while, the slow tears dropping

from her eyes, her hands clasped in her lap. His heart, heavy with sympathy, would not permit him to break in upon her deep sorrow with words of comfort.

"Naida," he whispered, at last, "this may not be the time for me to speak such words, but you are all alone now. Will you go back to Bethune with me—back to the old regiment as my wife?"

A moment she bowed her head before him; then lifted it and held out her hands. "I will."

"Say to me again what you once said."

"Donald, I love you."

Gently he drew her down to him, and their lips met.

The red sun was sinking behind the fringe of trees, and the shadowed nook in which they sat was darkening fast. He had been watching her in silence, unable to escape feeling a little hurt because of her grave face, and those tears yet clinging to her lashes.

"I wish you to be very happy, Naida dear," he whispered, drawing her head tenderly down until it found rest upon his shoulder.

"Yes, I feel you do, and I am; but it cannot come all at once, Donald, for I have lost so much—so much. I—I hope he knows."

Choose from Thousands of 1stWorldLibrary Classics By

A. M. Barnard
Ada Leverson
Adolphus William Ward
Aesop
Agatha Christie
Alexander Aaronsohn
Alexander Kielland
Alexandre Dumas
Alfred Gatty
Alfred Ollivant
Alice Duer Miller
Alice Turner Curtis
Alice Dunbar
Allen Chapman
Alleyne Ireland
Ambrose Bierce
Amelia E. Barr
Amory H. Bradford
Andrew Lang
Andrew McFarland Davis
Andy Adams
Angela Brazil
Anna Alice Chapin
Anna Sewell
Annie Besant
Annie Hamilton Donnell
Annie Payson Call
Annie Roe Carr
Annonaymous
Anton Chekhov
Archibald Lee Fletcher
Arnold Bennett
Arthur C. Benson
Arthur Conan Doyle
Arthur M. Winfield
Arthur Ransome
Arthur Schnitzler
Arthur Train
Atticus
B.H. Baden-Powell
B. M. Bower
B. C. Chatterjee
Baroness Emmuska Orczy
Baroness Orczy
Basil King
Bayard Taylor
Ben Macomber
Bertha Muzzy Bower
Bjornstjerne Bjornson

Booth Tarkington
Boyd Cable
Bram Stoker
C. Collodi
C. E. Orr
C. M. Ingleby
Carolyn Wells
Catherine Parr Traill
Charles A. Eastman
Charles Amory Beach
Charles Dickens
Charles Dudley Warner
Charles Farrar Browne
Charles Ives
Charles Kingsley
Charles Klein
Charles Hanson Towne
Charles Lathrop Pack
Charles Romyn Dake
Charles Whibley
Charles Willing Beale
Charlotte M. Braeme
Charlotte M. Yonge
Charlotte Perkins Stetson
Clair W. Hayes
Clarence Day Jr.
Clarence E. Mulford
Clemence Housman
Confucius
Coningsby Dawson
Cornelis DeWitt Wilcox
Cyril Burleigh
D. H. Lawrence
Daniel Defoe
David Garnett
Dinah Craik
Don Carlos Janes
Donald Keyhoe
Dorothy Kilner
Dougan Clark
Douglas Fairbanks
E. Nesbit
E. P. Roe
E. Phillips Oppenheim
E. S. Brooks
Earl Barnes
Edgar Rice Burroughs
Edith Van Dyne
Edith Wharton

Edward Everett Hale
Edward J. O'Biren
Edward S. Ellis
Edwin L. Arnold
Eleanor Atkins
Eleanor Hallowell Abbott
Eliot Gregory
Elizabeth Gaskell
Elizabeth McCracken
Elizabeth Von Arnim
Ellem Key
Emerson Hough
Emilie F. Carlen
Emily Bronte
Emily Dickinson
Enid Bagnold
Enilor Macartney Lane
Erasmus W. Jones
Ernie Howard Pie
Ethel May Dell
Ethel Turner
Ethel Watts Mumford
Eugene Sue
Eugenie Foa
Eugene Wood
Eustace Hale Ball
Evelyn Everett-green
Everard Cotes
F. H. Cheley
F. J. Cross
F. Marion Crawford
Fannie E. Newberry
Federick Austin Ogg
Ferdinand Ossendowski
Fergus Hume
Florence A. Kilpatrick
Fremont B. Deering
Francis Bacon
Francis Darwin
Frances Hodgson Burnett
Frances Parkinson Keyes
Frank Gee Patchin
Frank Harris
Frank Jewett Mather
Frank L. Packard
Frank V. Webster
Frederic Stewart Isham
Frederick Trevor Hill
Frederick Winslow Taylor

Friedrich Kerst
Friedrich Nietzsche
Fyodor Dostoyevsky
G.A. Henty
G.K. Chesterton
Gabrielle E. Jackson·
Garrett P. Serviss
Gaston Leroux
George A. Warren
George Ade
Geroge Bernard Shaw
George Cary Eggleston
George Durston
George Ebers
George Eliot
George Gissing
George MacDonald
George Meredith
George Orwell
George Sylvester Viereck
George Tucker
George W. Cable
George Wharton James
Gertrude Atherton
Gordon Casserly
Grace E. King
Grace Gallatin
Grace Greenwood
Grant Allen
Guillermo A. Sherwell
Gulielma Zollinger
Gustav Flaubert
H. A. Cody
H. B. Irving
H.C. Bailey
H. G. Wells
H. H. Munro
H. Irving Hancock
H. R. Naylor
H. Rider Haggard
H. W. C. Davis
Haldeman Julius
Hall Caine
Hamilton Wright Mabie
Hans Christian Andersen
Harold Avery
Harold McGrath
Harriet Beecher Stowe
Harry Castlemon
Harry Coghill
Harry Houidini

Hayden Carruth
Helent Hunt Jackson
Helen Nicolay
Hendrik Conscience
Hendy David Thoreau
Henri Barbusse
Henrik Ibsen
Henry Adams
Henry Ford
Henry Frost
Henry James
Henry Jones Ford
Henry Seton Merriman
Henry W Longfellow
Herbert A. Giles
Herbert Carter
Herbert N. Casson
Herman Hesse
Hildegard G. Frey
Homer
Honore De Balzac
Horace B. Day
Horace Walpole
Horatio Alger Jr.
Howard Pyle
Howard R. Garis
Hugh Lofting
Hugh Walpole
Humphry Ward
Ian Maclaren
Inez Haynes Gillmore
Irving Bacheller
Isabel Cecilia Williams
Isabel Hornibrook
Israel Abrahams
Ivan Turgenev
J.G.Austin
J. Henri Fabre
J. M. Barrie
J. M. Walsh
J. Macdonald Oxley
J. R. Miller
J. S. Fletcher
J. S. Knowles
J. Storer Clouston
J. W. Duffield
Jack London
Jacob Abbott
James Allen
James Andrews
James Baldwin

James Branch Cabell
James DeMille
James Joyce
James Lane Allen
James Lane Allen
James Oliver Curwood
James Oppenheim
James Otis
James R. Driscoll
Jane Abbott
Jane Austen
Jane L. Stewart
Janet Aldridge
Jens Peter Jacobsen
Jerome K. Jerome
Jessie Graham Flower
John Buchan
John Burroughs
John Cournos
John F. Kennedy
John Gay
John Glasworthy
John Habberton
John Joy Bell
John Kendrick Bangs
John Milton
John Philip Sousa
John Taintor Foote
Jonas Lauritz Idemil Lie
Jonathan Swift
Joseph A. Altsheler
Joseph Carey
Joseph Conrad
Joseph E. Badger Jr
Joseph Hergesheimer
Joseph Jacobs
Jules Vernes
Julian Hawthrone
Julie A Lippmann
Justin Huntly McCarthy
Kakuzo Okakura
Karle Wilson Baker
Kate Chopin
Kenneth Grahame
Kenneth McGaffey
Kate Langley Bosher
Kate Langley Bosher
Katherine Cecil Thurston
Katherine Stokes
L. A. Abbot
L. T. Meade

L. Frank Baum
Latta Griswold
Laura Dent Crane
Laura Lee Hope
Laurence Housman
Lawrence Beasley
Leo Tolstoy
Leonid Andreyev
Lewis Carroll
Lewis Sperry Chafer
Lilian Bell
Lloyd Osbourne
Louis Hughes
Louis Joseph Vance
Louis Tracy
Louisa May Alcott
Lucy Fitch Perkins
Lucy Maud Montgomery
Luther Benson
Lydia Miller Middleton
Lyndon Orr
M. Corvus
M. H. Adams
Margaret E. Sangster
Margret Howth
Margaret Vandercook
Margaret W. Hungerford
Margret Penrose
Maria Edgeworth
Maria Thompson Daviess
Mariano Azuela
Marion Polk Angellotti
Mark Overton
Mark Twain
Mary Austin
Mary Catherine Crowley
Mary Cole
Mary Hastings Bradley
Mary Roberts Rinehart
Mary Rowlandson
M. Wollstonecraft Shelley
Maud Lindsay
Max Beerbohm
Myra Kelly
Nathaniel Hawthrone
Nicolo Machiavelli
O. F. Walton
Oscar Wilde

Owen Johnson
P.G. Wodehouse
Paul and Mabel Thorne
Paul G. Tomlinson
Paul Severing
Percy Brebner
Percy Keese Fitzhugh
Peter B. Kyne
Plato
Quincy Allen
R. Derby Holmes
R. L. Stevenson
R. S. Ball
Rabindranath Tagore
Rahul Alvares
Ralph Bonehill
Ralph Henry Barbour
Ralph Victor
Ralph Waldo Emmerson
Rene Descartes
Ray Cummings
Rex Beach
Rex E. Beach
Richard Harding Davis
Richard Jefferies
Richard Le Gallienne
Robert Barr
Robert Frost
Robert Gordon Anderson
Robert L. Drake
Robert Lansing
Robert Lynd
Robert Michael Ballantyne
Robert W. Chambers
Rosa Nouchette Carey
Rudyard Kipling
Saint Augustine
Samuel B. Allison
Samuel Hopkins Adams
Sarah Bernhardt
Sarah C. Hallowell
Selma Lagerlof
Sherwood Anderson
Sigmund Freud
Standish O'Grady
Stanley Weyman
Stella Benson
Stella M. Francis

Stephen Crane
Stewart Edward White
Stijn Streuvels
Swami Abhedananda
Swami Parmananda
T. S. Ackland
T. S. Arthur
The Princess Der Ling
Thomas A. Janvier
Thomas A Kempis
Thomas Anderton
Thomas Bailey Aldrich
Thomas Bulfinch
Thomas De Quincey
Thomas Dixon
Thomas H. Huxley
Thomas Hardy
Thomas More
Thornton W. Burgess
U. S. Grant
Upton Sinclair
Valentine Williams
Various Authors
Vaughan Kester
Victor Appleton
Victor G. Durham
Victoria Cross
Virginia Woolf
Wadsworth Camp
Walter Camp
Walter Scott
Washington Irving
Wilbur Lawton
Wilkie Collins
Willa Cather
Willard F. Baker
William Dean Howells
William le Queux
W. Makepeace Thackeray
William W. Walter
William Shakespeare
Winston Churchill
Yei Theodora Ozaki
Yogi Ramacharaka
Young E. Allison
Zane Grey